THE GIRL FROM NORWAY

ALSO BY EMMA PASS

Before the Dawn

THE GIRL FROM NORWAY

Emma Pass

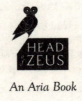

HEAD
ZEUS

An Aria Book

ISBN (PB): 9781801105576
ISBN (E): 9781801105552

Cover design: Becky Glibbery

Typeset by Siliconchips Services Ltd UK

Printed and bound in Great Britain by
CPI Group (UK) Ltd, Croydon CR0 4YY

Head of Zeus
First Floor East
5–8 Hardwick Street
London EC1R 4RG

WWW.HEADOFZEUS.COM

For my parents, Anne and John, who opened the door
to the magic of stories, books and words.

Nothing can crush me, or silence me long,
Though the heart be bowed, yet the soul will rise,
Higher and higher on wings of song,
Till it swims like the lark in a sea of skies...

Ella Wheeler Wilcox
Courage
1916

PART ONE

1942

ONE

HEDDA
Kirkenes, Finnmark County, Norway
August

'Look at this. *Look.*' Anders loomed over me, his shirt crumpled in his fist, pushing it into my face as I shrank away from him against the wall. His breath was still pungent with the fumes of the *Akevitt* he'd been drinking the evening before, his face twisted and purple with fury. 'What will people say?' he growled. Before I could answer him – before I could even draw breath – he went on: 'I'll tell you what they'll say. They'll say, *there goes the man whose wife is too lazy to mend his shirts! She lets him go out on the streets with holes in his clothes so that everyone will laugh at him!*'

He shook the shirt out. 'Look at that!'

I saw a tiny hole near the elbow, no more, really, than a snagged thread I'd somehow failed to notice when I'd washed and pressed the shirt earlier that week.

'I – I'm sorry,' I stammered, finding my voice at last. 'I didn't see it.'

'"*I didn't see it,*"' he mocked me in a whining, sing-song voice. 'You stupid bitch. Can't you do *anything* properly?'

I shrank back again. Despite the fact that he had never hit me, I felt sick and panicky, my heart racing. My husband used words, not his fists, but each one was as brutal as a physical blow and he knew exactly where to land them. Even though I was taller than him, his presence filled any room he walked into; almost fifteen years my senior, he was a manager at the Sydvaranger iron ore company at the western edge of Kirkenes, an important man, and well-respected in the town. People thought him handsome; I had once, too, with his thick, golden hair, his piercing blue eyes the colour of a midsummer sky and his compact, wiry body that didn't have an ounce of spare fat on it. He had a mania for exercise, no matter what the weather, and would tell people, patting his flat stomach proudly, 'I will still be skiing across the mountains at seventy – just you wait and see!'

I, meanwhile, was nothing – nobody. And none of the people who admired Anders for his status and physical prowess saw the man he became behind closed doors – the one who drank and turned more and more spiteful and cruel with every mouthful he took. He even blamed his drinking on me, saying I drove him to it.

I wish I'd never married you, I thought, a familiar litany, as I turned my head away, keeping my body tensed and my eyes trained on the floor, feeling his breath hot against my cheek as he continued to rail at me about all the ways I failed him as a wife. I prayed Eirik would not come in and see us; I knew he would be listening. How naive I'd been, to think marrying Anders might be the start of a new life for me! But when I was sent to Finnmark by my father to hide me away with an elderly aunt, I'd been nineteen, pregnant, cut off from the nursing career I'd dreamed of having for so long, and my aunt made no effort to disguise how little she thought of me. Anders had offered me an escape from her, or so I'd thought.

It wasn't until after my aunt died that I discovered she'd agreed to leave Anders all her money – not an inconsiderable sum – if he took me off her hands and saved my family the shame of having an unwed mother in their midst. I had been nothing more than a transaction.

Anders finally ran out of insults. He flung the shirt down at my feet and stalked out of the kitchen. I slid down against the wall, my arms hugged around my knees, trembling as I listened to him storming around the house that had once been his mother's, and where he had brought me to live after we were married: a narrow, semi-detached dwelling up on the hill called the Haugen, with dark, oppressive rooms and heavy, old-fashioned furniture that took hours to clean and dust.

Only once the front door had slammed behind him did I hear smaller, lighter footsteps coming down the stairs. Quickly, I stood, smoothing my skirt and snatching the shirt off the floor. By the time Eirik came into the kitchen, I was at the sink, running water to wash the dishes as if nothing had happened.

'Mamma?' Eirik said. Although he had turned six two months ago, like so many of the children in Kirkenes these days he was small for his age – there simply wasn't enough for them to eat. Breakfast that morning had been half a piece of bread each with a smear of unsweetened jam, and even Anders' barely concealed rage at this meagre fare could not make our food ration stretch any further.

'Hello, my angel,' I said, stroking Eirik's hair as he leaned against me, wrapping his arms around my waist. Neither of us spoke of Anders; the few precious hours ahead without my husband's brooding presence stretched ahead like a lifeline. 'Are you ready to go next door to *Tante* Ingunn's?'

'I want to come to the shops with you, Mamma,' he said.

'Not today,' I told him. 'There's too much to do. Besides, Marianne will be waiting for you.'

Marianne was Ingunn's granddaughter, and Eirik's best friend. At the mention of her name, his face lit up. With school – such as it was – not starting again until next week, they spent a lot of time together at my neighbour's house. Ingunn was a kindly widow in her seventies, and always glad to see Eirik.

'Fetch my basket,' I said, pointing to where it sat in the corner, by the dresser, 'and then you can go. Don't forget your gas mask!' I called after him as, depositing the basket by my feet, he raced out into the hall.

'I've got it, Mamma!' he called, and I heard the front door open and thump close again.

I let out a breath I didn't realise I'd been holding and quickly finished the dishes. Then I lifted my basket onto the table and, glancing behind me at the door to make sure Eirik had really left, lifted the cloth folded neatly inside. Underneath was a false bottom, and underneath *that* was the small bundle of messages I had collected from Mette Simensen at the telegraph station last night. They were from the families of teachers who were being held at the camp nearby, and it was my job to deliver them.

I wasn't part of the resistance – not officially. I couldn't risk being arrested and taken away from Eirik, leaving him alone with Anders. But neither could I stand by and do nothing, not when these men had invaded our town, turned our world on its head and now walked around like they had a God-given right to the place. There were many in the town who took part in daily acts of civil disobedience, keen to defy the

Germans in any small way we could, and I was among them. Some even wore paperclips on their lapels as a symbol of non-compliance, although I didn't go that far – Anders was no sympathiser, but would have been furious with me for risking unwanted attention from the occupiers. My tiny part in resisting the Germans was a secret I kept close to my chest. The pre-war Hedda would probably have been shocked that I even agreed to get involved, but when it came down to it – when Mette asked if I would take the messages for the first time – I knew I *had* to do it. 'And after all, Hedda,' she said, 'as Doctor Johannessen's assistant, you have a better reason than most to be walking all over town during the day.'

Even then I'd hesitated, still thinking of the danger I could be putting Eirik in if I was caught. '*Please*, Hedda,' Mette begged me. 'You are one of the few people who can help. There is no one else who can do this – the Germans will be suspicious of anyone else. If anything happens to you, I promise I will make sure that Eirik is all right.'

I'd taken a deep breath, and thought about how I wasn't able to stand up to Anders – how helpless and useless it made me feel. Did I really want to feel the same way about the Germans as well? I'd taken a deep breath and said, 'I'll do it,' and Mette had smiled, relieved.

Once the dishes were done, I wrapped a shawl around my shoulders and left the house, walking quickly. I had a lot to do. Before I delivered the messages, I needed to go to the shops and see what I could find there for our dinner that evening; if I went down to the docks with an empty basket someone might see, and question it. And after I delivered the messages, Doctor Johannessen needed me to call in on a few people who were unwell and check how they were getting on.

I didn't have high hopes of getting much at the shops. Since the Germans had come to Norway almost everything was rationed, or 'on the card' as we called it: food, the bitter-smelling tobacco Anders smoked, clothes, even curtains and bed linen. Meanwhile, the Germans swanned around town, never having to worry about getting enough to eat, or whether they'd be able to stay warm when the winter snows arrived, and keep the lamps burning when the sun no longer rose above the horizon. I hated them as much as I hated Anders; perhaps more.

I hurried through the streets, head down. When I'd first arrived here, Kirkenes had been a true melting pot with people settling here not only from other parts of Norway but from Finland, Russia, Sweden and even Germany, drawn by the promise of work at the iron ore company; every time you went into town you'd hear different languages being spoken. It had always been a hard place to live due to its location and the long, dark, harsh winters, but despite the hardships, people thrived. Now the Germans had taken over, there was a palpable atmosphere of anxiety everywhere. From some buildings hung the Nazi flag with its ugly swastika slashed across it; many other buildings were in ruins, bombed by the Soviets who kept up a relentless campaign to chase the Nazi menace away from their borders, with raids occurring almost daily. I often wondered, if this war ever ended, whether there would be anything of the town – or its inhabitants – left.

At the shops, I was lucky: I managed to get a bag of greyish flour, some pieces of salted fish, even a small skein of yarn I could use to make Eirik some socks for the winter. I packed them neatly in my basket, the cloth arranged over the top.

As I was about to leave, I was cornered by Agnes Pedersen,

a woman whose husband worked for Anders at Sydvaranger, and who had twin girls the same age as Eirik. 'Hedda!' she said. 'I am so glad to see you! Reidun and Ruth both came down with terrible sore throats last night and I was hoping you might be able to give me some advice – I can't get medicine anywhere and I've not been able to get hold of Doctor Johannessen either.'

'I'm sorry to hear that,' I said, my outward demeanour calm even though, inside, I was desperate to get to the docks and drop off the messages hidden in the bottom of my basket as soon as I could.

Only a few weeks after I married Anders, I was shopping and witnessed a young girl stray too close to a horse. Startled, the horse reared up, lashing out with its back hooves and striking the girl on the side of the head. There hadn't been time to think; even though I'd only worked in a hospital for a few months after qualifying as a nurse, my medical training kicked in automatically as I rushed over and fell to my knees beside the girl, rapidly assessing the deep wound at her temple and trying to work out what to do. By the time Doctor Johannessen had arrived, summoned by a nearby shopkeeper, I'd managed to stop the bleeding and the girl was beginning to regain consciousness.

That day I went from being a lonely outsider, known only by the townspeople as *Hanna Larsdatter's grand-niece* and then *Anders Dahlström's new wife*, politely acknowledged when I went into town but nothing more, to being accepted as one of their own. Word soon got around about what I'd done, and before I knew it people were stopping me in the street to ask for advice on their headaches, their painful knees, their children's sore throats and colds. Not long after, Doctor

Johannessen mentioned to me that he could use a trained assistant. Kirkenes wasn't a large town – at that time the population was around eight thousand – but the winters were always hard and long and dark, and brought with them many illnesses, especially among the young and the old, meaning that he was often overworked.

At first, Anders had refused to let me, scoffing and saying I would be useless, but Doctor Johannessen was insistent, even coming to the house to speak to my husband personally. He was one of the few people who didn't seem to be scared of Anders; I listened from the kitchen as he argued passionately with him, telling him, 'For God's sake, man, finding a trained nurse up here in the middle of nowhere is like your workers finding a seam of gold in the iron ore mine!'

'You're mad,' Anders retorted. 'She's barely qualified! She'll kill every patient she touches!'

But Doctor Johannessen had persisted, until there wasn't any way Anders could refuse without losing face. Grudgingly, he agreed to let me become Doctor Johannessen's nurse, although I paid for it for weeks afterwards with his hissed, vicious insults and insinuations. *What nonsense! It'll all be well and good until you slip up – then they'll see you for what you really are!* But, scared as I was that he was right, I tried not to let his words get to me. After falling pregnant and having to leave the hospital, I'd thought I would never work as a nurse again; this unexpected opportunity gave my life a new purpose and meaning that – outside of Eirik – I'd assumed was lost forever.

And now, since the invasion, I was needed more than ever: with the supply of good food becoming increasingly scarce, there was more and more sickness, especially among the town's children. However, there was always a small part of me that was scared Anders was right, and that I wasn't as competent as Doctor Johannessen thought me; that one day I'd harm, or even worse, kill someone with my ignorance.

'Are you able to get a little honey from somewhere?' I said now. 'Or brandy?'

Agnes's forehead creased in a frown. 'I don't think so...' she said. Then her expression darkened. 'Unless I ask Solveig, I suppose.'

Solveig, her sister, was seeing a German officer. He had moved in with her last year and they were living as husband and wife, although rumour was he had a family back in Germany. Many people in the town would no longer even speak to Solveig, but Agnes had not been able to bring herself to shun her own flesh and blood completely.

'If you can get it from somewhere,' I said diplomatically, 'mix a little honey with the brandy and some hot water, and give the girls a few spoonfuls three times a day. They'll soon feel better.'

Agnes gave me a sad smile. 'Thank you, Hedda. I'll try. I do not know what this town would do without you!'

'It's nothing,' I murmured.

At last, I was able to escape. I stepped out onto the street again just as a group of German soldiers marched past, their boots tramping in unison against the hard surface of the road, guns held upright against their shoulders. I averted my gaze so I did not have to look at them, anger burning like dull fire in the pit of my stomach. *Swines. How dare you come here.*

I'd never forget that terrible day in April 1940 when we heard on the radio that Norway had fallen, seemingly overnight, or the tension and fear as we waited for the German army to reach Kirkenes. At first, Allied troops had tried to help Norway fight back, and there had been a tremendous battle at Narvik, five hundred miles or so west of here, but they had soon been overwhelmed. At the same time, our King, Haakon VII, and his family had to flee to Britain after refusing the Germans' demands to legitimise Vidkun Quisling's fascist government and install him as Prime Minister.

After that, it felt as if all we could do was wait as the enemy spread like a slow but relentless cancer across our country.

On the street ahead of me, the soldiers had gone. I took a deep breath and pulled my shawl tighter around my shoulders. It was time to deliver the messages.

Two

HEDDA

Although my heart was pounding, I tried to look nonchalant as I strolled towards the docks where a group of prisoners was unloading crates of ammunition from a ship called the *Hallingdal*. The men looked tired, grey-faced and thin; they'd been incarcerated at the camp since April, after being arrested for refusing to sign up to Vidkun Quisling's new teacher's union and teach a Nazi-approved curriculum, and there were more being held at another, larger camp at Elvenes, nine kilometres away. The Germans were using the prisoners for forced labour around the town.

I could see the German guards watching them; none of them were looking at me. But why would they be? I was just one of the local women, returning home after doing her chores. *I'm no threat to anybody*, my body language and neutral expression said. Or at least, I hoped so.

Finally, I reached my destination: a rubbish bin at the side of the road, near to where the men at the back of the line were loading the crates onto lorries. Without breaking my stride, I extracted the bundle from my basket and dropped it into the bin, retrieving the small roll of paper already waiting for me there and sliding it up the sleeve of my jumper in one fluid, well-practised motion. As I walked on, I caught the eye of one of the prisoners briefly, a middle-aged man wearing wire-framed glasses; he gave me a tiny nod.

'*Zurück an die Arbeit!*' one of the guards barked at him, noticing. *Back to work!* He marched over and cracked the man across the shoulder blades with the butt of his rifle. I heard the man cry out, but I didn't look back; I didn't dare. I continued walking along the road, my heart rate climbing another notch. I felt scared, yet strangely exhilarated. I knew if Anders found out what I was doing he'd be angry – apoplectic – but it gave me a thrill to think that I was playing a small part in helping to defy these dreadful Germans.

I had to go home now and put everything away. Then I needed to go back up to the telegraph station and pass the roll of paper – more messages, this time from the prisoners to their families – on to Mette. After that, I'd visit the patients on the list Doctor Johannessen had given me yesterday.

As I walked, I turned my thoughts to the last of the vegetables growing in the little garden behind our house, wondering what might be ready. If I couldn't make a proper meal this evening, Anders would be angry; he worked long hours at Sydvaranger and always came home hungry and tired, his temper on even more of a hair trigger than usual.

Then the air raid sirens began to wail and all thoughts of Anders and the evening meal fled from my mind. Raids were a common enough occurrence in Kirkenes – this close to the Russian border, we'd grown to expect regular attacks by the Soviets. But I didn't have time to run back home; my only option was to head for the underground air raid shelter nearby, and pray Ingunn would keep Eirik safe.

With a lump in my throat, I made for the shelter, hearing the familiar drone of Russian planes approaching the town. Another wave of panic went through me, squeezing my insides. *Please, please let Eirik be all right*, I thought automatically. *He's all I have. If anything happens to him, I don't know if I will be able to carry on.*

The shelter quickly grew crowded as the townspeople continued to pour in down the steps. It had been built right beneath Kirkenes, a low-ceilinged, cave-like hollow carved out of the rock and lit sporadically by flickering lanterns. I knew everyone was thinking the same thing: *What will happen this time? Will our houses still be standing when the planes leave?* I managed to secure a spot near the shelter entrance where it felt marginally less claustrophobic, and leaned against the wall, my basket jammed between my feet. I remembered the messages pushed up my sleeve, and taking advantage of the gloom, bent down to conceal them in the bottom of my basket.

'Mamma!'

I straightened up again and saw Ingunn coming towards me, Eirik and Marianne clinging to her skirt. Relief flooded through me.

'It was such a nice day that we decided to take a walk through the town,' Ingunn told me in slow, lilting Norwegian as Eirik flung himself at me – her ancestors were Sámi, but she had lived in Finnmark all her life, moving to Kirkenes after she married. I picked Eirik up and he buried his face in my shoulder. 'Luckily we were near the shelter when the sirens went off.' Ingunn had her own basket, her meagre food rations for the week neatly packed inside, which she put down on the floor. Then she put an arm around Marianne, drawing her close. Marianne had come to live with her last year after her father, Ingunn's son Stian, was killed and his wife Sofia arrested. I wasn't sure exactly what had happened to them or why – Ingunn never talked about it – but she loved her granddaughter fiercely and rarely let her out of her sight.

With my free hand, I clasped one of hers. 'Thank you. I was so worried.' Then I turned my face, making soothing noises in Eirik's ear. 'Shh, shh. It's all right.'

Ingunn smiled, her face, framed with its cloud of white hair, wrinkling like a winter apple. 'It's no trouble. You know I don't mind looking after him – he's such a good child, and it's so lovely for Marianne to have someone her own age to play with.'

I slid my gaze away from hers, suddenly feeling ashamed. Had she heard Anders shouting at me this morning? I'd tried to hide from Ingunn how bad things were with my marriage at first, like I did with everyone else, but one day, after Anders had spent a long, exhausting night insulting and berating me, I'd broken down in front of her, weeping as I lamented about how useless I was. She had listened, her usually smiling face sombre, before gathering me into her arms and rocking me like a child as she murmured comforting words. Since then, she had been like a mother to me – more of a mother than my own ever had. There was nothing I could do to make Anders love me or treat me with kindness, but knowing I had an ally in Ingunn made the pain of my marriage that little bit easier to bear.

From over our heads came the now-familiar *crump* as the first bomb fell close by, the impact showering dust from the shelter's stone walls. Everyone went silent for a moment before starting to talk again, all at once, speculating where the bombs were falling this time. *Perhaps you will get lucky and one will hit the administration buildings at the Company*, said a treasonous little voice in my head. I silenced it immediately, reminding myself that without Anders and the wage he earned, Eirik and I would have no home at all. Like everyone else here, I had to cross my fingers and hope that when we finally emerged from the shelter, the damage wouldn't be too bad.

Another explosion came. As more dust sifted from the walls and roof, I heard someone mutter, 'That was a close one.' Then a high-pitched wail tore through the air inside the shelter – the keening, animal sound of someone in terrible pain.

Marianne frowned up at Ingunn. 'What's that, Grandmother?'

'Mamma?' Eirik said at the same time, his eyes wide with alarm. I held him close to me, stroking his hair again as I looked around, trying to find the source of the sound. The wail came again and I noticed a commotion nearby, people gathering around someone who appeared to have fallen to the floor.

'Is Doctor Johannessen here?' someone called, their voice raw and desperate. 'It's Anna Larsen – her baby is coming!'

A ripple of alarm ran through the shelter.

'He is out of town!' someone else called back. 'I saw him leave this morning for old Åse Hagen's farm and he hasn't come back yet.'

My heart began to pound.

Ingunn looked at me. 'Hedda…' she said quietly.

'I can't,' I said, holding Eirik tight against me. 'I've never delivered a baby. I don't know what to do! What if I harm her?'

I could hear Anders' voice in my head, the words he spat at me if I was so much as a minute late getting home to cook his dinner, or if I forgot myself and yawned in front of him because I'd had a busy day: *Call yourself a nurse – all you're good for is handing out headache tablets and diagnosing sore throats! I should never have let Doctor Johannessen talk me into letting you help him!*

'But you can reassure her. You may not have worked as a nurse for long when you were in Oslo, but you did get your qualification, and you are so good at what you do here for us in Kirkenes.'

As Anna cried out again, I continued to stare at Ingunn, frozen to the spot by panic. Inside my head, Anders was shouting at me now: *Don't do it! The poor woman and her child will be lucky to survive!*

'Go. I will look after Eirik,' Ingunn said.

Wordlessly, I pushed Eirik gently towards her and made my way to where Anna was lying on the floor, someone's coat already rolled up under her head. She was nine months pregnant, her belly enormous. When the people around her saw me, their strained expressions changed to relief. 'Hedda,' someone said. 'Thank God.'

I knelt down beside Anna, trying to ignore Anders' snarling inside my head and keep my face composed as I noted, with some alarm, the wetness spreading on the ground around her. 'Her waters have broken?' I asked Kari Jensen, who was crouching beside me.

Kari nodded. 'Five minutes ago.'

Anna rolled her eyes towards me, her face white and sheened with sweat. She was only twenty; this was her first child.

Panicking wouldn't help Anna, or me; I knew that. And I could tell from the way she kept grimacing and crying out that her contractions were getting closer and closer together. This baby was going to be born soon, whether I liked it or not. 'Is there any way I can get some hot water?' I asked Kari. She and several others had now formed a protective circle around Anna to protect her from prying eyes.

She frowned, then nodded and said, 'I will see what I can do,' before turning and pushing her way through the huddled bodies towards the shelter entrance.

'And please find out if Doctor Johannessen has come back from the Hagens'!' I called after her, hoping my anxiety didn't show in my voice.

I made Anna as comfortable as I could. 'It'll be OK,' I told her, taking her hand. *Liar*, Anders snarled in my ear as Anna groaned and rolled her eyes wordlessly at me. She was only a year older than I had been when I had Eirik. Again, I tried to remember what we had learned in nursing school about childbirth, and cursed Magnus Tonning: for making me fall in love with him; for pretending I didn't exist when I told him I was pregnant; for being the reason I had to leave home before Eirik was born because my father wanted nothing more to do with me. And I cursed him a thousandfold for my marriage to Anders that, at the time, had felt like the only option available to me; Anders had preyed on me when I was at my lowest, and made me feel as if he was the only way to escape the shame of what I'd done.

The only part of that time I didn't – *couldn't* – regret was Eirik. Anna didn't know how lucky she was that her child would grow up loved and wanted by both its parents. Her husband, Ivar, worked at the Company too and was a fireman in his spare time.

I took a deep breath. *Concentrate, Hedda.* 'All right,' I told Anna. 'Do you feel as if you need to push yet?'

She nodded, and my heartbeat sped up again, my mind

racing too. 'I'll have to take a look at you,' I told her. 'I need to make sure—'

Then the all-clear sounded. As it faded away, someone cried, 'Doctor Johannessen is here!'

Thank God, I murmured silently to myself, and inside my head, Anders barked a bitter laugh. *Thank God indeed.*

Moments later, the doctor was there, a gruff-looking man with a bushy white moustache, clutching his bag in one hand. I stood, stepping back from Anna to give him room. 'Thank you, Hedda,' he said as he knelt beside the girl. 'I'm sorry it took me so long to get here – my car broke down and I was walking back to town when the sirens began. I had to hide in a basement.'

I nodded, mute with relief. Doctor Johannessen was one of the very few inhabitants of Kirkenes who'd owned a car before the war, and when the Germans came he'd insisted on keeping it. He turned to Anna again and began, briskly, to talk to her. By now, people were beginning to leave the shelter. As I made my way back over to where Ingunn was waiting for me with Eirik, I passed one of the women who had been with Anna; she was carrying a bucket full of hot water, towels and a blanket.

'She's in safe hands,' I told Ingunn as Eirik flung himself at me again, wrapping his arms around my legs.

'She was in safe hands with you,' Ingunn said, as Marianne gazed at me, wide-eyed. 'You should give yourself more credit, Hedda.'

I didn't know what to say to that. I shrugged.

When the four of us emerged from the shelter, the sunshine seemed very bright. I had to squint and blink until my eyes adjusted.

'Ingunn, will you take Eirik back with you?' I said. 'I still need to call in on Mette at the telegraph station. I won't be long.'

Ingunn nodded. 'Of course.' She didn't ask me what I was doing; she didn't need to. I had told her what I was doing some months before, and she too had promised to keep Eirik safe for me if I was ever arrested.

'Let us all walk back together,' Ingunn said brightly to Eirik. 'Your mamma will be home before you know it!'

It seemed that this time, Kirkenes had got off lightly. As I made my way through the town I saw that all the buildings not already damaged by bombs were still standing. People were already going about their business again, the raid nothing more than a brief interruption to their day. I wondered when we'd all become so used to what was happening – to the raids, and the troops infesting our town. If I thought about it all for long enough, it seemed crazy to me. But what choice did we have other than to accept it?

At the telegraph station, a small blue-painted building on the hill that overlooked the town, Mette was waiting for me. She was ten years older than me, a small woman full of nervous energy with a wicked sense of humour, and, a dear friend of mine. She wore a paperclip on the lapel of her smart jacket with pride.

'How did it go?' Mette asked as we went inside.

I took the roll of messages from my sleeve and handed them to her. Mette grinned. 'Excellent,' she said, tucking them into an inside pocket. 'Do you have a minute?' When I nodded, she said, 'I'll make us some tea.'

As I followed her into the station's main room, my foot caught a small brown leather suitcase lying on the floor near the wall.

'Be careful!' Mette said.

'Are you going on your holidays?' I asked, puzzled.

Mette shook her head and grinned again. 'It's a radio. Rolf Rasmussen is on his way to pick it up – he should be here any minute.'

'A radio?' I frowned. The Germans had confiscated all our radio sets to stop us listening to BBC broadcasts from Britain; if you were caught with one, you would be arrested. 'Is it for the teachers?'

She shook her head. 'There are some men at a farm nearby. It's for them, so that they can get their messages out.'

I knew straight away that she was referring to men working for *Milorg – Militær Organisasjon*, Norway's main resistance movement. 'I'm sorry,' I said. 'I hope I haven't damaged it.'

Shaking her head, Mette crouched and took a key from her pocket, unlocking the latches on the case. 'It'll be fine. Take a look.'

I peered over her shoulder and gazed at it, fascinated. It looked nothing like the wireless set Anders and I had had in the house before the Germans took everyone's radios away, although I could see something that looked like a speaker grill, and various dials and buttons. There was also a box with the word *SPARES* printed on it in English. 'That's a radio? How does it work?'

'It's a transmitter and receiver set made in Britain,' Mette said. 'Everything has been miniaturised. See this here, on the red and black wire?' She pointed. 'It's a morse code key. These are headphones so that the operator can listen in. And these pieces here are the crystal wireless equipment. They'll mainly use it at night – the signal is stronger then and can travel further; something to do with the atmosphere.'

I shook my head. 'I don't understand any of it, but how marvellous,' I said, trying to imagine people hundreds of miles away listening to the messages transmitted by the people using this radio. Here in isolated Kirkenes, it was easy to feel as if we'd been brutally cut off from the rest of the world by our invaders, but seeing that little set reminded me that we had friends and allies out there who were just as determined to beat the Nazis as we were.

Smiling, Mette snapped the case closed. 'It will certainly come in useful for Rolf and his men. Now, I'll go and make the tea and you can tell me what happened in the shelter. I hear Anna Larsen nearly had her baby while the bombs were still falling!'

Amused too, I sank into a chair. I wasn't surprised Mette knew about Anna already. She was the town's eyes and ears; nothing got past her.

We'd just begun sipping our tea when there was a pounding at the door, loud enough to make us both jump.

'Is that Rolf?' I said.

'It must be,' Mette said, but she was frowning. As the pounding came again, she stood, grabbed the suitcase containing the radio and hid it behind some equipment. Then, smoothing down her skirt, she went to answer the door.

She returned a moment later, pinch-lipped and pale. Before I could ask what was wrong, two German officers came in behind her. For a moment, I thought they were there because of the radio in the case. Then I realised one of them was the guard that had been down at the docks – the one who'd hit the teacher with his gun.

'Is that her?' the other officer said, looking directly at me. My heart gave a painful jolt.

He spoke German, but I understood perfectly. I'd always picked up languages quickly – like many in Norway, I spoke English as a second language, and since the occupation, Mette and I had made it a priority to learn basic German, too. It had been her idea; 'I want to know what these bastards are saying,' she'd told me the day she suggested it, her normally delicate features set in a fierce scowl.

'*Ja,*' the guard said, also in German. 'I caught one of the men taking messages from the rubbish bin after she'd walked past. There was no one else around, and I saw him nod at her. It must have been her who put them there.'

My heart gave another jolt. I glanced at Mette. Her expression was perfectly composed, but a muscle at the corner of her eye was twitching.

'I don't know what you're talking about,' I said in German, my pronunciation halting but clear; for a moment the two men looked surprised to hear me speaking their native tongue, but they quickly recovered themselves.

'Arrest her,' the first officer said.

As the guard from the docks stepped forwards, my mind was racing. Arrest would mean being sent to a prison camp. What would happen to Eirik? Both Mette and Ingunn had said they'd keep him safe if anything happened to me, but Mette had her own family to think about and Ingunn was an old woman. If the Germans came for Eirik too there would be nothing she could do. They would take him away and I might never see him again.

I shot Mette a desperate look. She returned it, but I knew there was nothing she could do either. Rolf was on his way – he would be here any minute.

One of the officers took my arm and pushed me towards

the door. As they marched me to the car waiting outside, I was overtaken by a creeping sense of unreality.

Then the officer slammed the door in my face, and climbed into the front of the car with his colleague. The engine coughed into life, and I realised this was very real indeed.

As we drove away from the telegraph station, I twisted my head and saw Mette in the doorway, her face white and shocked. Moments later we passed a man trudging along the road towards her, a cap pulled down low over his eyes; a man who could only be Rolf. I looked away from him and stared straight ahead, my hands clenched into fists in my lap, my thoughts racing. Perhaps I'd be all right. Perhaps the Germans would just interview me, tell me off and let me go.

But I knew that was unlikely. A sudden memory detonated in the middle of my whirling thoughts like a bomb, something I had tried to wipe from my mind. Two months ago, a woman had been caught hiding a Soviet prisoner who'd escaped from one of the camps in her cellar. The Germans had dragged them both out onto the street and shot them along with the woman's teenage daughter. I hadn't witnessed it myself, thank God, but Mette had told me all about it, her eyes bright with angry tears.

Nausea zigzagged through me; I slumped against the seat. Anders always told me I was useless, and he was right. If I had any sense at all, I'd never have agreed to take those messages to the docks. What had I been thinking? Both Ingunn and Mette had reassured me they would make sure Eirik was all right, but what if the Germans decided to send him away too?

My gaze fell on the door handle. Sitting up a little straighter, I glanced at the officers in the front of the car. They were talking and laughing at some joke one of them had just made, behaving as if they were driving somewhere for a holiday rather than transporting a prisoner. They seemed to have forgotten I was there.

My hand snaked out and gripped the handle. The door would be locked. Of course it would. I would not be that lucky.

But it was not; the handle gave easily.

The car was bumping fast along the uneven road, and when I pushed the door open and leaped out, I hit the ground hard enough to knock all the air from my lungs. There was no time to recover; gasping, I scrambled to my feet and ran. I thought I heard shouts but I didn't look behind me to see if the car had stopped or if the German officers were following. I went as fast as my legs could carry me, ducking between houses and through back gardens like a deer fleeing a pack of wolves, until I reached the Haugen.

I hammered on Ingunn's door. She answered immediately, looking startled as I pushed past her into the house. Gasping for breath, my lungs burning, I explained as rapidly as I could what had happened. 'God, what will I do?' I said, putting my hands up to clutch the sides of my head. 'They are going to arrest me... they will send me away, they will take Eirik—'

'Shh. Shh.' Ingunn held her finger to her lips, giving me a warning glare. I realised Eirik and Marianne were staring at me, their eyes huge. Ingunn removed her shawl from around her shoulders – she always wore it, no matter the weather or time of year – then pulled me into the kitchen, picking up her basket that still contained her shopping: bread, some fish, and some cheese. As she pushed it into my hands, her shawl folded on top, I realised I'd left my own basket behind at the telegraph station.

I stared at her, uncomprehending.

'You must go west,' she continued, pushing me and Eirik towards the back door. 'I have a nephew in Munkelva – I will tell you the address – you must try to get there as soon as you can.'

'But how can he help me?' I said faintly, still not quite knowing what she meant. I felt sick with panic.

'He is part of *Milorg*, the same group Stian was involved with,' Ingunn said. 'He has been helping people escape the Germans. *Gud villig*, if they can get you to Narvik then you may be able to escape over the border into Sweden.'

Sweden. Lately, Anders had been talking about us leaving Norway if things got too bad; of trying to get to Sweden where he had a relative. So far, it had all been talk – when it came down to it, he was unwilling to leave his job and his friends.

Understanding dawned on me, finally, about what had happened to Stian and his wife. 'Ingunn, are you part of the resistance too?' I said.

Ingunn shook her head. 'Me? Not really – I am too old to be of any use to them. But I help where I can.' She pressed her lips together, then added, 'It's a long, long journey, and dangerous. Many do not make it. But if you stay here…' She glanced meaningfully at Eirik as she trailed off.

I gazed at Ingunn, at her kindly, wrinkled face, overwhelmed by her kindness. She told me her nephew's address in Munkelva, then waved her hands at me. 'Go now. *Right now*. They will come and search the houses for you – they could be here at any moment. Leave town by the back way, keep off the roads and do not stop until you get to Munkelva, even if it means walking all night. I'll get a message to my nephew, and in the meantime I will lead the Germans on a merry dance so that you have time to get away.' She turned to Eirik, who was still watching us both in wide-eyed silence, and added, 'Can you be very brave for your mamma, *lille vennen*? Can you walk and walk, even if you feel tired and long to stop?'

Eirik nodded.

'Ingunn—' I began, my voice cracking.

Emotions flickered across Ingunn's face. 'Hedda, you *must* leave now. There is no more time to waste.' But she stepped forwards and enveloped me in a hug.

'I know. Thank you,' I said, pressing my face against her shoulder for a moment. Then I gave Marianne a quick hug too. 'Will you both be all right?'

Ingunn pushed me away again. 'We'll be fine. *Go.*'

I glanced back at them once as we crept out of the back door. Ingunn was watching us with a grim expression, her shoulders set; Marianne simply looked bewildered. Wondering what she'd say to the Germans, I made myself look away again, and instead tried to calculate the best route to slip out of Kirkenes unseen and get all the way to Munkelva, almost forty kilometres away. Just the thought of the long journey ahead of us made fear balloon inside me again, and my legs felt weak. Surely it was impossible? We'd never make it. I could hear Anders inside my head, laughing at me for even thinking such a thing.

But we had to try.

THREE

BILL
Suffolk, England
August

Stepping into the hangar at RAF Mildenhall, I was hit by a wall of pure noise. There had to be a hundred or more people milling around in here, men and women, all in blue uniforms like my own. The huge space echoed with their voices and laughter. There was a stage set up at the front, and folding chairs arranged across the floor, although hardly anyone was sitting down yet.

And I didn't want to be here.

Don't be an idiot, Gauthier, I told myself, shaking my head. *You're tired, is all.*

I was the wireless operator on a seven-man heavy bomber crew based at Chedburgh aerodrome, fifteen miles south-east of here, and a long run of back-to-back missions, sometimes with only seven or eight hours between them, had a way of doing that to a guy. We'd been granted a couple of days' leave since our most recent flight, with one more to go, but I hadn't exactly caught up on sleep yet. Hardly surprising, given what had happened to Des Williams.

I spotted Jonny Grant, our navigator, standing near the hangar doors. He was talking to Amir Singh, our pilot, a wiry

27

twenty-one-year-old Sikh who hailed from the Punjab. With them was our rear gunner Jack Trow, bomb aimer Robert Cauldwell, who was a Canadian like me, and another pilot from our squadron, a Polish fellow called Lukasz Krol. I knew Kenneth Knight, our flight engineer, was here somewhere too, and seeing them made Des's absence hit home all the harder. I could tell from the serious expressions on Amir, Jonny, Jack and Robert's faces that they were feeling it as well. Another two flights, and Des's tour would have been completed. We'd always joked about him being the old man in our crew – he was twenty-seven – due to get married to his childhood sweetheart in August back in their hometown in Wales. Now all that hung in the balance.

Swallowing hard against the sudden tightness in my throat, I gave myself another talking to. *Shit happens, Gauthier. We all knew what we were signing up for. Stop being so goddamned windy and enjoy yourself, eh? Des will pull through – he has to.*

Forcing a cheerful grin onto my face, I walked over to join the little group. 'Hey, why so glum, fellas?' I said. 'Just wait till the concert starts – then you'll *really* have something to be miserable about.'

It did the trick; everyone laughed. We'd all been to concerts put on by ENSA, the Entertainments National Service Association, before, and the other version of their name they were widely known by, *Every Night Something Awful*, was pretty well earned.

'Think it'll be as bad as the last one?' Jack, the youngest member of our crew at eighteen, joked as we began making our way to our seats.

I dropped heavily into one of the hard wooden chairs. 'Bet you four shillings it's worse.'

Robert shook his head. 'It can't be. Remember the opera singer?'

'No one is *ever* going to forget the opera singer,' Amir said seriously. 'I will hear that woman in my nightmares for the rest of my life.' We all laughed again. The question I *really* wanted to ask – *Any news about Des?* – stayed sealed behind my lips. If I hadn't heard anything, it was unlikely any of the others had either, and I didn't want to bring the mood down.

A man in a dark suit, holding a conductor's baton, stepped onto the stage and clapped his hands together. When that didn't work, he coughed into one of the microphones, sending a squeal of feedback through the loudspeakers and making everyone wince.

'My apologies, ladies and gentlemen,' he said with a smile, as the noise in the hangar subsided to a low murmur. 'Thank you for having us here at Mildenhall this evening. I am pleased to present to you Rose Legge and the Reg Brown Orchestra!'

There was a smattering of applause. I quirked an eyebrow at Robert, who was sitting next to me, and we waited as the orchestra, four of them in all, walked onstage, followed by Rose Legge herself.

She caught my eye immediately. She was in her early twenties, about the same age as me. Her dark-blonde hair was arranged in careful waves that just skimmed her shoulders, and she wore a sheer silver dress that left her arms and shoulders bare, and matching silver shoes. She had no makeup on except for her lips, which were bright red. As she smiled out at the audience, complete silence fell. We all applauded again, more enthusiastically this time, and a few men whistled.

Robert and I exchanged another look. I wondered whether now was the time to remind him he was taking one of the Women's Auxiliary Air Force telephone operators at Chedburgh to a dance tomorrow.

The man in the suit turned, gave the orchestra a little bow and raised his baton in the air. When Rose began to sing, I forgot all about Robert; all about Des and that disastrous mission to the Kattegat; all about everything except her voice, soaring up into the vast roof space of the hangar in perfect harmony with the orchestra. I'd never heard anything like it. By the time the concert finished, I felt as if I was in a dream.

Afterwards, Jonny, Robert and I headed to the mess with the others. I spotted the slender figure in the silver dress by the bar straight away.

'Beer, Skipper?' Jonny said. He was a quiet, mild-mannered twenty-one-year-old from Trinidad and had the reputation as one of the best navigators on the base.

'Yeah, sure,' I said absent-mindedly. When he'd gone, I pushed my way through the men waiting to be served to lean against the bar next to Rose.

'You were amazing,' I said as she turned and saw me beside her.

For a moment Rose looked startled. Then she smiled – a wide, genuine smile. 'Thank you,' she said, then shivered, rubbing her bare arms. 'Gosh, it's cold for August, isn't it?'

I took off my jacket and draped it over her shoulders. 'Here.'

'Thank you,' she said again, pulling it around her. 'Er…'

'Flight Sergeant Bill Gauthier.'

'Pleased to meet you, Flight Sergeant Gauthier.'

'Call me Bill, please.'

She held out a hand, smiling again, and I shook it. 'Are you American, Bill?' she asked.

'I'm from Edmonton – Canada. Came over here in 1940.'

'I'm sorry – of course.'

'How about you? Where do you call home?'

'Oh, nowhere exciting, I'm afraid – just little old London.'

'Can I get you a drink?'

'That would be lovely. A scotch and soda, please.'

I had a scotch too, minus the soda, and we took them over to a quieter corner so we could talk. On the way, I saw Robert and Jonny watching us. Robert grinned at me and shook his head. '*Jammy bastard*,' he mouthed, then turned and said something to Jonny, who threw his head back and laughed, indicating the two pints of beer in front of him. I rolled my eyes at them. Not my fault they were too slow off the mark.

'So are you a pilot?' Rose asked after I'd fetched a couple of folding chairs and we'd sat down.

I shook my head, indicating the badge on my jacket sleeve – a clenched fist with lightning bolts radiating from either side. 'Wireless operator.'

She gave a silvery little laugh. 'I'm sorry. You must think me jolly ignorant. I don't know much about these things, I'm afraid, even after my time in ENSA.'

Already I could feel the scotch starting to spread its gentle warmth through my veins; I'd not had much appetite since the Kattegat mission, and it was several hours since I'd last managed to force myself to eat.

'No offence taken,' I reassured her, and shrugged. 'It's not very exciting, I'm afraid. I'm basically a glorified message boy, keeping the plane in touch with our base.'

Of course, there was a hell of a lot more to my job than that. As the crew's Sparks, as wireless operators were nicknamed, I worked in close tandem with Jonny while we were in the air, assisting with the navigation by getting bearings and fixes from transmitters based on the ground; listening for new instructions from base; sending and receiving weather reports, and monitoring the radar warning system. I'd had first aid training and even been prepared to take over from Jonny if there was an emergency. But I didn't tell Rose any of this. I didn't know her from Adam, and we'd had it drummed into us from the first day of training that absolutely anyone could be working for the Germans as a spy.

We spent the next couple of hours chatting about safer subjects, with me getting up every now and then to replenish our glasses, although after her third drink, Rose insisted on soda only. I stuck to scotch; this was the first proper chance I'd had to loosen up since that awful raid two nights ago, and every burning mouthful pushed thoughts of Des – how he'd looked when Jonny and Jack helped me lift him from the plane after we'd landed, his skin icy cold, his eyes half open; the memory of the gore puddled all over the floor in the gun turret, soaking into his seat, more than it seemed possible for one human body to hold – further towards a dark, distant corner of my mind where I could lock it up out of sight forever. It didn't seem to matter how many times I told myself that this happened to other crews all the time, or that it was sheer luck we'd managed to return from mission after mission unscathed; I still felt guilty for not being able to do more. And now Des's life hung by a thread in a London hospital, the doctors waiting to see if he'd wake up.

No. Stop. Stop.

I shook my head and focused on Rose to try and distract myself. She was easy to talk to. I told her about growing up in Edmonton, and about my parents: how, when war was declared, I'd been working as a clerk in one of my father's factories; not a glamorous job, but most of the workers there were women and the Edmonton nightlife was fairly lively, so I'd enjoyed an active social life. I also told her how my parents had tried to convince me to stay and help them run the factories instead of enlisting, something I'd never have forgiven myself for. In turn she told me about her family. She lived in London, the youngest of five, with four brothers who were all in the army. Her father was rather domineering, from the sounds of it, and she'd joined ENSA because she was desperate to do her bit too, but he wouldn't hear of her becoming a land girl.

'Not that I'm actually all that desperate to plough fields and dig potatoes,' she said with another one of those silvery laughs. 'Look at me – can you imagine me in khakis with mud under my nails?'

Smiling, I shook my head.

'I think Mother and Father were rather afraid I might end up marrying a farmer,' she said. She made a self-deprecating face. 'That would be *terribly* beneath me, of course.'

'They'd rather you were engaged to an officer, eh?'

Rose's expression grew distant suddenly, and I got the uncomfortable feeling I'd hit a sore spot. As I was trying to figure out what to say to smooth things out again, she said, 'As it happens, I was seeing a man in the Navy, but he was killed last year.'

'I'm sorry,' I said. I got another flash of Des's face, pale and cold. *Damn*. I took a hasty gulp of scotch and some of it went down the wrong way, making me splutter.

'What about you?' Rose asked when I'd recovered. 'Don't you have someone?'

I laughed. 'Chance'd be a fine thing.' There were women

– there were *always* women – but after a few dances, a few kisses, occasionally more than that, I'd find myself drifting away from them. I couldn't see the point of forming a lasting connection with a girl when I knew that next time I went out on a mission, I might not be coming back. Some of the fellows saw it as a reason to dive straight in and get engaged, but whenever I met anyone there was always this voice in the back of my head that said, *what's the point in getting attached?*

'Drat, I have to go,' Rose said, standing up; across the hangar, I saw the man in the suit – the one who'd conducted the orchestra – waving at us. 'Clive's the orchestra manager as well as our conductor – he gets terribly impatient.'

I stood too, surreptitiously holding onto the back of my chair – I was drunker than I'd realised. Taking my jacket from her shoulders and handing it back to me, Rose smiled, and there was a moment of awkward silence.

Not getting attached doesn't mean you never have to see her again, a little voice in my head said, and I took a deep breath. 'Fancy doing this again sometime?' I asked her. 'I'm not back on duty until the day after tomorrow…'

She smiled again, and her cheeks flushed slightly. 'I'm in Suffolk for the whole week, staying at a hotel in Bury St Edmunds, and I'm free tomorrow afternoon. Have you got a piece of paper and a pencil?'

I did have, in my jacket pocket. I gave them to her and she wrote down a telephone number. 'That's our hotel,' she said. 'Telephone tomorrow, about lunchtime.'

Clive waved again, looking slightly irritated. Rose waved back. 'Coming!' she called.

I watched her cross the hangar with a sudden, unaccountable lightness in my heart.

FOUR

BILL

Someone clapped me on the shoulder, and I turned to see Robert, Kenneth and Jack standing behind me. 'Bill, you son of a gun,' Robert said with a wide grin, swaying slightly on his feet.

'We're going into town,' Kenneth said. He was a burly Australian from Queensland who'd been about to take over the family cattle ranch before the war interrupted his plans. 'You coming?'

I drove my knuckles into my eyes. 'Nah… I'm gonna head back to base and turn in. Busy day tomorrow.'

'How busy?' He quirked an eyebrow, and Robert laughed raucously.

'Jealous, are ya, fellas?' I retorted.

Jack snorted. 'We oughta take bets on how many notches Bill's going to end up with on his bedpost before the end of the year.'

I pretended to look offended, pressing a fist to my chest as I grinned at them. 'I'll have you know I *always* have a lady's honour at heart.'

'You're a real heart*breaker* all right,' Robert drawled,

shaking his head. 'Just don't lose track of who you're seeing this time – you don't want another angry girl ruining your uniform.'

He was referring to an unfortunate incident a couple of months ago, when I'd agreed to go on a date with a local girl I'd seen once before, forgotten all about our arrangement and gone out with her best friend instead. It seemed the first girl had wrongly assumed things were serious between us, and when I and her friend bumped into her in a café, she poured my cup of tea over my head in a rage. Then the girls had stormed off together, leaving me there to gather the remaining sodden shreds of my dignity while the other patrons stared and laughed behind their hands.

'Well, if I do, I'll make sure I don't get caught this time. See ya!' I called as they headed for the door.

There was a truck heading back to Chedburgh; I managed to get a space in the back and dozed as it bumped along the lanes back to the aerodrome, my head lolling. For the first time since that awful flight over to Scandinavia, my mind was quiet. Maybe it was just the scotch, but it remained quiet as I returned to my billet and undressed, climbing wearily into my hard, narrow bed, and for once, I didn't look over at the corner of the hut that had been Des's. The last thing I saw before I drifted off to sleep properly wasn't his face, drained of blood, but Rose, smiling at me as she laughed at something I said.

The next day dawned sunny and warm. Amir, who didn't drink alcohol, had already got up, and while the others, who hadn't got back until almost four in the morning, slept off their hangovers, I whiled away the hours until it was time to call Rose by writing a letter to my parents. It had been a while since my last one, and I knew they'd be eager to hear from me, especially my mother.

At twelve-thirty, I headed over to the mess to use the telephone. 'Bill!' Rose said when she answered. She sounded genuinely delighted to hear from me. 'Can you get into Bury? There's a smashing film on at the cinema at half past three.'

'Sure,' I said.

'I'll meet you outside. Do you know where it is?'

'Yes,' I said. I'd been a few times since coming to Chedburgh, taking a different girl each time, although I thought it best not to tell Rose that. We chatted for a few more minutes before I went off in search of something to eat. Then I returned to my billet to get ready.

'Where are you off to?' Robert said groggily. He was sitting on the edge of his bed, still looking a little worse for wear, his chin grey with stubble and dark shadows under his eyes. The others were nowhere to be seen.

'Meeting a certain someone,' I said, peering into the mirror in the corner to check I hadn't missed any spots when I'd shaved, and straightening my collar.

He frowned. 'A certain—?' Then it dawned on him. '*Oh*.'

I grinned into the mirror at his reflection.

'Give her a kiss from me, eh?' he called after me as I left.

'In your dreams, Cauldwell!'

Thanks to heavy petrol rationing, the buses round here were hit and miss, but today, I was in luck: as I walked out of the base, there was one for Bury St Edmunds just pulling up. I found an empty seat at the back and spent the journey daydreaming about Rose. Although I reached the cinema almost half an hour early, she was already waiting for me, sitting on a bench near the cinema entrance with a novel in her hand. Even though she was in ordinary, everyday clothes – a tweed skirt in a muted shade of brown, and a cream-coloured blouse – she was even more beautiful than I remembered.

'Hello,' she said, smiling and tilting her face towards me so I could kiss her cheek. 'You're early.'

'So are you.'

'I was already in town and it's such a nice day, I thought I'd sit here in the sun for a while and read while I waited for you.'

'What are you reading?'

'*The Body in the Library*,' she said, showing me the cover. 'Agatha Christie. Have you read it?'

'Not that one. I like her books, though.'

'I won't tell you whodunnit, then.' She smiled, a dimple appearing in one cheek, as she tucked the book into her bag. 'Where do you fancy going? We're too early for the film.'

'I don't mind,' I said. 'How about a walk?'

'That sounds good to me.' She got up and tucked a hand into the crook of my elbow. 'One starts to feel dreadfully cooped up on these tours, going from hotel room to hotel room and air base to air base.'

We wandered through the town centre. Despite the damage from bombs, the tape over the shop windows and the government posters and signs about rationing and shortages everywhere, it had a busy, cheerful atmosphere. There were plenty of servicemen around – Bury was close to several air bases and a large army camp – but I couldn't help noticing the glances Rose and I drew from civilians. We made a good-looking couple.

Eventually, we found ourselves in the Abbey Gardens, a

park housing an impressive set of ruins. Despite the war, there were still flowers spilling from the flower beds, and the lawns were neatly manicured. 'I expect there'd be an outcry if they dug it all up for cabbages,' Rose said as we sat down in the shade of a large oak tree, away from the other couples promenading along the paths.

'No doubt.'

She leaned against me, and I breathed in the scent of her perfume. It was light, floral, and suited her perfectly.

'Tell me more about your life back in Canada,' she said. 'You said you worked at your father's factory—'

'One of his factories,' I said. 'He has three.'

'Goodness me! What do they do?'

'Clothes and shoes, originally. Now, they make munitions and aeroplane parts. He was struggling before the war, what with the Depression and all, but he's made a damn fortune since. He and my mother still live like paupers, though. I don't think they're used to having money yet.'

'Will you have to take on the factories one day?'

I laughed drily. 'I guess so, if I don't get myself killed.'

'Oh, don't say that.' Rose shuddered. 'You won't.'

I wish I could be so sure, I thought, and for a moment the thought of Des, suspended between life and death as he lay in his hospital bed, threatened to intrude, hovering like a dark cloud over the sunshine-drenched afternoon. 'Let's not talk about that, eh?' I said.

She gave me a wry smile. 'And you don't have anyone waiting for you back in Canada? No one to help you with your little empire once it passes into your hands?'

'Naw. I'm not the settling down kind,' I said. 'Not yet, anyway.'

Rose was still smiling, but didn't say anything. Her gaze searched mine.

Oh, hell, why not? I thought. *Make the most of it. She's bloody gorgeous, for God's sake, and you might never see her again after today.*

I leaned down and pressed my lips against hers.

We spent the rest of the afternoon lying there on the grass, doing more kissing than talking. The time for the film came and went, the sun moved round and the shadows grew a little longer, but I didn't want to move. It was always the same when I was with a girl: I could forget the stress and fear of flying; the bone-deep exhaustion that came from the hours-long missions; the way the cold bit into your bones no matter the time of year or how many layers you wore under your flying suit. I could almost forget there was a war on at all.

And right now, I could forget, just for a little while, about Des, too.

At last, just as I was fiddling with the top button of Rose's blouse, she sighed and sat up. 'I must get back,' she said, glancing at her watch and smoothing her hair. 'Dinner will be served soon, and after that we're giving a concert at one of the army camps.'

I felt an irrational stab of jealousy, imagining all those men eyeing her up as she stood on the stage, and tried to swallow it down. After all, it wasn't any of *my* business what she got up to after we went our separate ways, just like it wasn't any of hers what I did.

'Walk me back to my hotel?' she said as I stood and reached down to help her up.

'Sure.'

I looped an arm around her shoulders and we walked back through the town.

'I've had a lovely afternoon, Bill,' she said when we got to the hotel, which looked rather unprepossessing, with sandbags piled up outside and tape criss-crossed over the grimy windows. 'Thank you.'

'Me too,' I said, and I meant it.

'Perhaps I can call you next time I'm in the area?'

'Sure. I'd like that.'

I drew her in for one last kiss, and with a cheery, 'Bye!' she hurried up the steps into the hotel. I watched the double doors swing shut behind her and went to find a bus heading back in the direction of Chedburgh.

At the entrance to my billet, I was met by Robert. He looked even worse than he had this morning, his face pasty, a hunted expression in his eyes.

'You heard?' he said.

I shook my head. 'No, what's up?'

'It's Des. He's dead.'

All the good feeling from my afternoon with Rose drained out of me abruptly, like someone pulling out a bath plug.

'When?'

'Four o'clock this afternoon. The C.O. summoned us to his office to tell us.'

By *us* he meant the rest of our crew: him, Amir, Jonny, Jack and Kenneth. I swore, and sat down on my bed. I couldn't look over at Des's corner, which was still empty; each crew shared a billet, and we'd known that because of Des's injuries we'd be assigned a new mid-upper gunner before his next flight, but with our next flight not due until tomorrow night the guy hadn't moved in yet.

'They said he started bleeding again,' Robert said, his voice cracking slightly on the last word. He took a shaky breath. 'Nothing they could do to save him.'

I closed my eyes. I was thinking of Des's fiancée, Lily. We'd met her a few times, a sweet red-haired girl with a lilting Welsh accent and a wide smile. How must she be feeling right now, knowing she had to spend the rest of her life without the man she'd loved since they were kids?

I punched my pillow. 'This *bloody* war.'

The door opened, and Amir, Jack, Jonny and Kenneth came in. 'You told him?' Jonny asked Robert, glancing at me. Robert nodded.

'There's a lorry going into Mildenhall village again tonight,' Kenneth said. 'Heard there's a pub there giving out a free drink to anyone in uniform and thought we'd go and give it a look in.'

I nodded. I'd planned to have a quiet evening – perhaps go for a walk or sit in the mess for a while – but now, being alone with my thoughts was the last thing I wanted to do.

After dinner, we set out. The journey took almost an hour, the lorry jolting and chugging along the winding Suffolk lanes at an excruciatingly slow speed. The airmen around us were laughing and joking, but our crew sat in silence, gazing at our feet. The others, who had heard what had happened, left us alone.

The lorry dropped us off outside the pub, which was indeed giving out a free drink to anyone in uniform. As a result, it was already packed, and we and the other men from Chedburgh barely managed to squeeze inside. Our group eventually managed to commandeer a table in the corner and Kenneth went up to the bar to claim our pints, along with a soda water for Amir. After we'd drunk them it seemed rude not to stay, so I went up to get a second round, although this time I had to pay.

'So, Rose Legge, eh?' Robert said when I sat down again, elbowing me in the ribs hard enough to make me spill my drink.

'You're just jealous,' I told him. I looked round at the others and saw they were grinning. 'You're *all* jealous.' I raised my glass. 'Anyway, never mind her. Here's to Des, eh?'

The others joined the toast, their faces momentarily sombre again, and despite the comforting fog from the alcohol I'd consumed, I found myself remembering, unwillingly, the night of that disastrous mission.

The morning had dawned muggy, misty and damp, and with no sign of the weather shifting all day, we'd assumed we'd be stood down. Kenneth and I had planned an evening of cards and I was hoping to claw back some of the money I'd lost during our last game. But at 7 p.m. the mist suddenly began to burn away and we were called to the briefing room. We'd be taking G George, a Stirling we'd flown so many times we joked it felt more like home than our own quarters, for a spot of Gardening – the code name for laying mines – up in the Kattegat off the Swedish coast. Although it wasn't a bombing raid, it was still a dangerous mission, taking us over Denmark on our way there and back where we'd have to keep our eyes peeled for German night fighters.

G George's engines purred sweetly as the plane flew towards the coast. For all their shortcomings – there was talk of them being phased out soon – our crew was used to the Stirlings and we liked flying them. Awkward and lumbering on the ground, and with disproportionately short wings, for a machine of their size and weight they were surprisingly agile in the air. By the time we'd crossed the North Sea, the weather had cleared completely, everything illuminated by a bright three-quarter moon, and G George seemed to be alone in the skies. The mission went off without a hitch and with all our mines dropped, we turned for home.

But as I listened out for signals from ground beacons so Jonny could use the information to plot our course, a strange sense of foreboding crept up on me. I couldn't shake it. I tried to tell myself I was exhausted after hours of intense concentration, but we flew longer missions than this all the time and I'd never felt like this before, not even when we were trying to dodge searchlights and urban anti-aircraft fire. *Focus, damn it*, I told myself as we headed over Denmark again, everything still eerily still in the moonlight, the only sound the grumbling roar of G George's engines. *All we have to do is get back to Blighty.*

Moments later, I saw the first flash of tracer fire whip past us; a Messerschmitt Bf 110 had snuck up on us, seemingly out of nowhere. As more tracer fire flashed through the night sky, Amir threw G George into a sharp evasive dive while Jack and Des fired back at the German fighter.

Amir corkscrewed the Stirling from side to side, trying to shake off the Messerschmitt that clung to our starboard with the tenaciousness of a terrier hunting a rat. At last, with a burst of gunfire that made the whole of G George shudder, Jack fired a stream of shells that hit the Messerschmitt head-on, and it tumbled away from us in a ball of smoke and fire. I twisted in my seat to watch it go, my heart hammering. Jonny had taken off his mask and was watching it too, his skin sheened with sweat.

We'd just levelled out again and were breathing a collective sigh of relief when I heard Robert yell through my headset: 'Des is hit!'

I was up and out of my seat at once, grabbing the first aid kit as I went. All the crew were trained in first aid, but there was an unspoken agreement that it was my job to tend to the injured. When I got back there, Des was clutching his left thigh, his face a rictus of pain. I tried to ask him what had happened but the noise from the engines was too loud; I couldn't hear him. He pointed at his thigh and my stomach dropped as, in the moonlight, I saw a dark stain spreading across the seat below him. Swearing, I grabbed bandages and tried to tie his leg up as tightly as I could. In the kit was a syringe of morphine, and I injected him with it, watching as his eyes rolled back and his face relaxed. After that all I could do was try to keep pressure on his wound and pray no more German fighters would find us.

It wasn't until we landed that we found out exactly what had happened: a stray bullet from the Messerschmitt had ripped up through the floor of G George and slammed into Des's leg, severing the femoral artery. He was still alive when we landed, but only just, and after debriefing, what remained of our crew retreated to the airmen's mess. We were all exhausted, but we didn't want to return to our billet just yet. There, the military police would be emptying Des's locker in speedy, efficient silence – even if he survived his injury he wouldn't be flying with us any time soon. We'd sat in shell-shocked silence, drinking tea generously laced with Lamb's rum. It tasted terrible but I didn't care. My hands hadn't stopped shaking until I was halfway down my mug.

Now, I buried myself in my pint glass, trying desperately

to forget again. Before I knew it, another hour had slipped by effortlessly, oiled by alcohol and good-natured banter. At some point, Kenneth stood, stretching. 'I'm off,' he said. 'The lorry's heading back to the aerodrome. You coming?'

Jack, Jonny and Amir stood up too. 'Yeah, I better had,' Jack said. 'Need some kip.'

Hazily, I glanced at my pint – my fourth? Fifth? – which was still half full. Robert was only halfway down his, too.

'I'm gonna stay till they close,' I said.

'Me too.' Robert nodded enthusiastically.

'Bloody Canucks.' Kenneth shook his head, pretending to be disgusted, although his tone was good natured. 'You'll give us all a bad name.' He clapped me on the shoulder, and he and the others left.

'Better get us another before they call last orders,' Robert said, getting up. 'Same again?'

I made to get my wallet from my pocket but he waved me away. 'My turn, Billy-boy.'

When he returned, he was carrying a tray with two pint glasses and four shots of whisky balanced on it. 'Might as well make the most of it, eh?' he said as he slid back into his seat.

The night became a bit of a blur after that. Every time a memory of Des threatened to surface, I chased it away with another drink. Next thing I knew, I was outside, propping myself up against the wall as the pub doors closed behind us. Somehow we'd ended up being the last two men there.

'Need to get back to base,' Robert slurred, leaning close and squinting at me. 'Wanna walk?'

'Hell, no,' I said. 'Chedburgh's fifteen damn miles away.'

'Let's go to the station,' Robert announced confidently. 'Gotta... gotta be a train going back to Ch-Chedburgh, eh?'

We made our slow, staggering way through the town, heading in the direction Robert, who had been here before, recalled Mildenhall station being. It took us nearly an hour; there were no signs anywhere because they'd all been taken down in case the Germans invaded, and it was a cloudy night. In the blackout, the darkness folded thickly around us, and when we finally reached the station, it was deserted, and in darkness too.

'Damn. Last train must've already left,' Robert said, slumping down onto a low wall.

'So what now, genius?' I said.

'We could find somewhere to get a kip and catch the first train back.'

'Won't get us back in time for roll call,' I said, although at that moment the thought of lying down on the pavement was terribly tempting; my limbs felt sluggish and heavy, and my eyes kept trying to close.

'What about the bus?'

'Don't think there are any,' I said.

'Shit,' Robert said. I thought longingly of the lorry, long since gone.

'Need to find a taxi,' I said.

'Where?'

'Dunno.' I turned, squinting into the blackness as if I expected one to materialise right there and then, engine idling, ready to carry us back to the aerodrome and our beds. 'S'pose they've all packed in for the night.'

Slowly, it dawned on me that our only choice was indeed to make the long, long journey back to Chedburgh on foot. Robert was close enough to me that I could see his face, and I could tell he was thinking the same thing. I sighed. 'Come on.'

He swore again, groaning, heaving himself to his feet, and we began the arduous task of navigating Mildenhall's darkened streets, trying to find our way back to the road that led to Chedburgh.

We were near the edge of town when we saw a car sitting by the kerb outside a row of houses: a little Austin with its passenger door slightly open.

'Hey, look,' Robert said, pointing. 'Maybe we can get a lift.'

We went over to the car, but there was no one inside. Robert leaned in anyway, as if he expected the driver to be hiding in the back somewhere.

'What d'you reckon, Billy-boy?' he asked me, slurring his words worse than ever. 'Think there's enough petrol in it?'

I peered myopically at him. *Christ*, I was tired. What on earth did the Brits put in their beer? 'Whaddya mean?'

'If we borrowed this car, we could be back at base before midnight. Well, maybe just after.'

'Borrow it? You gonna knock on the door and ask?'

'Well… not exactly.'

'That's *stealing*, not *borrowing*.'

'It's *borrowing*, because I'll get some more petrol at the base and bring it back tomorrow afternoon. And—' He held up a finger, his face grave, as if he was about to make some vitally important announcement. 'I have *money*.' Brandishing his wallet, he pulled out some notes, which he placed on the wall outside the house, hunting round for a stone to weigh them down with. 'See? I'll leave these here as a down payment.'

Before I had time to think about what was happening, he'd yanked open the driver's side door and slid inside. 'C'mon,' he said, patting the seat beside him, then reaching under the dashboard to fiddle with something. I leaned into the car from my side, wondering blearily what he was doing, and jumped as the car's engine roared into life, the sound horribly loud in the quiet night. '*C'mon*,' Robert said, yanking my arm. The car lurched forward and I half slid, half fell into the passenger seat.

As Robert pressed his foot down on the accelerator, I scrambled to close my door. My head was spinning, and not just from the motion of the car as it wove rapidly along the road. 'Don't you think we'll get in trouble if—' I began.

'Who cares?' Robert said, his tone suddenly savage. 'You think anyone gave a shit about the trouble we were in when that fucking Kraut shot Des?'

His gaze met mine for a moment. The good humour had slipped from his face and he had a haunted look in his eyes, similar to the one we'd all worn as we sat in the mess and sipped our rum-laced tea that night. I stared at him, not knowing what to say, a fresh pain squeezing my insides as I imagined Des's fiancée again; the doctors telling her he'd finally passed away.

We turned a corner, Robert yanking the wheel round hard enough to throw me against the door. Mercifully, the road was empty, no other cars to be seen. The world outside rushed past the windows: flashes of the hedgerows either side of us and the occasional house looming out of the darkness. Soon, the sound of the engine began to lull me into a doze, and Rose's face drifted pleasantly into my mind. I wondered when I'd be able to see her again. Yawning, I shifted in my seat, pushing my knuckles into my eyes.

As I opened my eyes again I saw a shape pulling out of a side road twenty yards or so ahead of us. It quickly materialised into a truck. As it pulled forwards I realised Robert had forgotten to switch on the car's headlamps; in the blackout, the other driver hadn't seen us.

Suddenly, I was stone-cold sober, everything sharpening into a moment of chilling clarity. I saw the driver turn his head towards us; saw his mouth open in a horrified *O*. I opened my own mouth to yell, 'Robert look o—'

With a sickening crunch, we hit the truck side on.

There was a moment, as the car left the road, when I was reminded of flying: of the moment Amir eased back the stick and that sudden feeling of weightlessness as the lumbering Stirling lifted off the runway and there was nothing under its wheels but air. It lasted a second, maybe two. Then there was another crunch that jarred every bone in my body and sent me slamming against the dash. There was a smashing of glass, a squealing of metal as we tumbled and rolled. I could hear someone screaming. I didn't know if it was me or Robert.

We came to a halt with a final, shuddering impact. Pain, white-hot, sickening, jolted through my left leg and right shoulder and arm, and flared viciously inside my skull too.

As I struggled to work out what had happened, I became aware that the world seemed to have tilted upside down. A heavy weight was crushing me, something dripping onto my face, and I could smell oil and petrol and the coppery stink of blood. *Robert, are you OK?* I tried to say, but I couldn't get the words out. Couldn't even breathe. I tried to move, and that awful pain seared through my head again. I could feel myself losing consciousness. I battled against it but it rolled over me like a wave, unstoppable.

The pain faded, and everything went dark.

FIVE

HEDDA
Norway
September

'Mamma, I'm hungry,' Eirik sobbed as we trudged along the track through the forest.

'I know,' I said. 'I'm hungry too. But we must walk just a little further.'

I stopped, crouching to draw Ingunn's shawl closer around him for warmth. Panic stabbed inside my chest as I took in his face, which was thinner than ever, and the purple half-moon shadows beneath his eyes; the way his narrow chest heaved as he coughed and fought to draw breath. He'd fallen ill a week ago, and sometimes his cough was so bad it made him vomit. I had no medicine and neither of us were getting enough rest or food; my own clothes hung on me, my skirt loose on my hips.

We had spent the better part of a month now making our slow way south. Sometimes it was just me and Eirik, and sometimes we were with others, travelling in lorries, cars, farmers' carts or on foot. Each mile was a game of cat-and-mouse with the Germans and their sympathisers as we made our way between farms, villages and towns, moving along a sparse chain formed by pockets of *Milorg* – kind strangers who were prepared to help us in some way by giving us food, a roof over our heads for the night or arranging the next leg of our journey, and risking their own liberty and lives to do so.

There were times, though, I couldn't contact the person I was supposed to, or it was too dangerous to try. Then Eirik and I were forced to spend our nights wherever we could find shelter, huddling together for warmth with nothing to eat at all and listening to wolves howling mournfully in the hills and mountains around us. I had no idea how long our journey would take, and I was trying not to think about the way the days were growing steadily shorter or how the temperature was beginning to drop. Often, I found myself wondering if we would ever make it to Sweden at all. With every step, I could hear Anders jeering at me: *What do you think you're doing? Do you really think you're capable of this? You stupid woman!* His face loomed in my nightmares, and during the day it was as if he was right there with us, a ghost walking alongside and questioning everything I did. It was only the necessity of staying strong for Eirik that kept me from giving up completely. I had to keep going for his sake, no matter what the voice inside my head told me.

'Carry me, Mamma,' Eirik said, tears still streaming down his face.

'You're too heavy, my darling,' I told him, stroking his matted hair and moving to rub his back in circles as he began coughing again. 'But we can rest for a minute, if you want to.'

He nodded miserably.

We found a sheltered spot among a sparse stand of birches whose leaves were turning yellow. One tree had fallen, and after touching the moss-covered surface of its trunk to see how damp it was, I sat down, pulling Eirik into my lap. 'Don't fall asleep,' I said as he snuggled into me.

'I won't, Mamma.' Eirik's face was pressed against my arm, his voice muffled. Within minutes, his body had relaxed, his breathing growing steadier although it still rattled in his chest.

Sighing, I shifted him into a slightly more comfortable position, my own eyelids drooping. *Stay awake*, I told myself sharply. I tried to work out where we were and wondered how far we still had to go that day. We were walking along a valley I didn't know the name of, following a river as it wound its way through the fjords and mountains towards the coast. Last night, along with a young Jewish couple who were also fleeing to Sweden, we'd been given refuge with a husband and wife in their sixties who lived on a small farm at the edge of a little village. This morning they had directed us to another house some twenty miles away, the next link in the chain. 'Look for the red house with the white windows and the single pine tree behind it,' the farmer's wife had told me that morning as she repeated the directions to me and I carefully committed them to memory. When we arrived I had to ask for Harald Thoresen – those were the code words she'd told me to say so that the person she was sending us to would know we needed their help. Eirik and I had walked with the Jewish couple for a while, but they were fitter and stronger and eventually I told them to go on ahead. They'd promised to let our contact know there were others on the way.

I allowed Eirik to doze for fifteen minutes or so before gently shaking him awake again. 'We must keep going,' I told him as he shook his head and coughed.

'No, Mamma, no,' he whined.

'Yes.' Trying to sound firm, I stood and lowered him to the

ground. 'It's not far, I promise, and when we get there you will have something to eat.'

He looked at me with an expression that was utterly wretched, and I felt a pain twist through my heart. What had I been thinking, allowing Mette to talk me into taking those messages to the camp at Elvenes? I should have stayed out of it – should have put Eirik's safety first as I had tried to fool myself into thinking I was. Now we faced nothing but uncertainty – possibly even death.

Despite my promise to Eirik, it was early evening and almost dark by the time we reached the village the farmer's wife had described to me. I kept to the edge of the road like a nervous animal, watching and listening as I scanned the houses either side of us, searching the gathering gloom for the red house with the single pine tree behind it. Was that it? No – there were two pine trees, and the windows had been painted grey.

We trudged on. I began to wonder if we'd taken a wrong turn somewhere earlier in the day. I was so hungry my head was swimming and my stomach felt as if it was trying to turn itself inside out. Eirik was coughing steadily as he stumbled along beside me. But at last, I saw it up ahead, exactly as the farmer's wife had described: a red house with white windows, and a tall pine tree standing alone on the hillside behind it that seemed to lean down towards the building slightly.

'You see, *lille vennen*,' I told Eirik. 'I told you we would get here eventually. And if we are lucky the nice lady and gentleman we met last night will be here too.'

He clung to my hand, wide-eyed and silent, as we walked to the door and I knocked on it. It seemed an age before it opened to reveal a thin woman with a bony, hard-looking face, her hair lying in limp curls around it. She was holding a flickering oil lamp.

'*Ja?*' she said, in a voice as sharp as her features.

I cleared my throat. 'I've come to see Harald Thorensen,' I said, my stomach churning at her impatient tone – it reminded me of Anders. I couldn't meet her eyes.

The woman stared at me blankly.

'Harald Thorensen,' I repeated. 'Is he here?'

'I don't know who you mean,' she said. She looked me and Eirik up and down, taking in our travel-worn clothes, our thin, pinched appearance.

Something's not right, a warning voice said in the back of my head, sending prickles up and down my spine. I nodded. 'My mistake,' I said. 'I apologise. I must have the wrong house.'

Grasping Eirik's hand tightly, I pulled him back towards the road, and away from the woman's gimlet stare.

'But Mamma, you said there would be something to eat!' he cried.

'Be quiet.' I frowned at him, aware of the woman still gazing at us as we hurried away, no doubt listening to every word.

'But Mamma—'

'Eirik, *hush*!'

Tears welled up in his eyes and spilled down his cheeks; I was on the verge of tears too. I glanced back and saw the glow of the woman's lamp. She was still watching us from her doorway.

My heart was beating rapidly, a metallic taste in my mouth. One thing was very clear to me: that woman was not part of *Milorg*. Whoever the farmer's wife had thought would be here was not here now. This meant we had no food, save for the few dry crusts of bread remaining at the bottom of the bag I carried over one shoulder, only a few sips of water, and nowhere to sleep. The weather was clear, the stars were coming out, and the temperature was dropping fast. It was going to be a cold night. *Idiot*, Anders snarled inside my head. *Look what a mess you've got yourself and Eirik into now! You're not fit to be a mother!*

And what had happened to the Jewish couple? Had they managed to get away?

Then, to our left, in the last of the daylight, I saw an ancient-looking barn a short way along a gravelled track. It looked abandoned, one end of the roof sagging inward.

'Come, we will stay here. It will be an adventure!' I told Eirik, who was still crying. I tried to make myself sound cheerful, but I couldn't stop my voice from trembling.

Eirik hiccuped and sobbed. I led him to the barn and pushed open the door, which was hanging by one hinge. It was so dark inside I could hardly see anything, but I could smell old hay and thought I heard something squeaking: a rat, or a mouse. Suppressing a shudder, I told myself that it was better than sleeping out in the forest – at least in here, we'd have some protection from the autumn chill.

We went inside. Leaving the door open a crack so that I would hear if anyone came, I made us a bed in the musty hay nearby; there were heaps of the stuff everywhere. I gave Eirik the bread to eat and made him drink what remained of our water. Then I wrapped us both in Ingunn's shawl and we lay down. Sleep overtook me almost immediately, heavy as thick, black syrup. I was so worn out that for once I didn't even dream.

The following morning, I opened my eyes with a start. I had meant to wake early, but it was already light outside. Beside me, Eirik was still sleeping, his face grey, his breath rattling in his chest in a way that made anxiety twist inside me. My ever-present guilt built to a roar. He already had bronchitis, I was certain of it, and if we didn't get to Sweden soon I was scared it would worsen, perhaps even become pneumonia.

Anders is right, I thought. *He has always been right. I really am useless.*

I stroked a strand of hair back behind Eirik's ear, gently so I wouldn't wake him, and wondered what had woken me and what we were going to do.

Then I heard the voice outside. A woman.

The woman from last night.

'I think they're in here. That door was closed yesterday – my husband used to keep his tools in here and I came to check that they were still here.'

A man answered her. He spoke Norwegian, but not terribly well, and his accent was odd; I could tell it was not his native tongue. 'A woman and a child, you say?'

'Yes. They looked shabby, as if they had been on the road a long time. The woman kept asking for Harald Thorensen. I'm sure they are up to something. Perhaps they are Jews, or spies.'

'Thank you. I will take things from here.'

Realisation slammed into me. The man was German – Wehrmacht. The woman had led him straight to us.

I looked round wildly and saw a pitchfork hanging on the wall near where we had been sleeping. As I heard footsteps approaching outside, I crept over and lifted it down. The prongs were coated in rust but still wickedly sharp. I tried to imagine using it, swinging it frantically at the German to keep him back so we could escape. *You're crazy if you think it will work*, Anders sneered inside my head.

But what choice did I have?

'Mamma?' Eirik said, lifting his head.

'*Hush*,' I told him desperately, but the door was already opening. As daylight flooded into the barn I saw the unmistakable silhouette of a Wehrmacht officer. He stepped through the door, a tall solidly built man wearing the immaculate green cap and uniform I was all too familiar with from Kirkenes. It was impossible to tell his age; his face was stony and smooth, neat brownish hair showing at his temples beneath his cap. 'So, she was right. I have caught myself two rats,' he said in his careful Norwegian, a recognisable note of disgust colouring his tone.

He glanced at the pitchfork I was clutching and shook his head. 'Put that down, if you do not want to get shot.'

'Mamma,' Eirik said again, his voice thready with terror.

'Shh, *lille vennen*. It will be all right,' I told him, although I kept hold of the pitchfork, hoping he wouldn't see my hand trembling. I turned back to the officer, squaring my shoulders. 'We are just passing through on our way to visit family,' I said. 'The house we called at last night is the home of an old friend, but they must not live there any more. We were too tired to continue, so we stayed here.'

Please believe us, please, I begged inside my head.

His face remained impassive. 'In that case,' he said, 'you will have your papers. Show them to me.'

He held out his hand and I knew, then, that we were lost. We had no papers; I had not had them on me the day we left

Kirkenes and we had not been able to get any others yet, not even false ones.

The Wehrmacht officer shook his head. 'I thought so.' He unclipped his pistol from his belt and pointed it at me.

'*Mamma!*' Eirik screamed, leaping up out of the hay.

Startled, the officer swung the gun round, pointing it straight at Eirik. Seeing his finger tighten on the trigger, I cried out too and lunged forward reflexively, the pitchfork gripped in both hands. A noise halfway between a grunt and a scream escaped from between my clenched teeth as I thrust the prongs into the officer's lower abdomen. There was a second of resistance; then they punched through fabric and flesh. The gun went off with an ear-splitting bang as the officer cried out and staggered back, the bullet firing harmlessly into the air and leaving behind the sharp smell of cordite.

I thrust again, to make sure, and let go of the pitchfork. It fell noiselessly into the hay.

The officer clutched his stomach, his eyes wide. Blood was blooming rapidly across the front of his uniform, forming dark wet stains against the green as he staggered backwards. He murmured something in German I couldn't quite make out and let out a bubbling, gurgling noise; blood began to spill from his mouth. At the door to the barn, his legs went out from under him and he collapsed, still clutching his stomach, still making that awful gurgling sound. His legs kicked once, twice, his boot heels digging furrows in the dirt.

Then the noise stopped and he went still.

Oh God, oh God, oh God, I thought, pressing my hands to my mouth. *What have I done? What on earth have I done?*

Behind me, Eirik began to wail.

SIX

Searchlights slashed up through the darkness in front of our aircraft, G George, two questing fingers combing the night sky that moved together every now and then to form one giant cone of white light. For any aircrew pinned in its beam, all they could do was pray as the heavy guns on the ground below started firing at them; already, we had seen another Stirling ahead of us tumble to earth after it was coned and hit. Lips moving in a silent prayer behind my oxygen mask, my clothes under my flight suit stuck to my back with sweat, I crossed my fingers as Amir aimed G George for the black gulf between the searchlights. Then the Stirling began to shudder, vibrating so hard it felt as if it was trying to shake itself apart in mid-air. *Shit, what's wrong?* All of a sudden I was in the pilot's seat with no idea how I'd got there, and Amir was nowhere to be seen. I yanked at the stick, but it wouldn't move. I heard screams through my headset and when I turned Robert was beside me, blood streaming down the left-hand side of his face. 'What the hell are you doing here?' I yelled as I saw both searchlights swinging round towards us, moving as one in slow, perfect tandem like dancers and then coming together. We were heading straight and level towards that deadly cone of light. As I reached for G George's controls again, Robert grabbed me by the shoulder, pushing me back in my seat as the cockpit filled with the searchlights' glare and the world went white.

'Sergeant Gauthier. *Sergeant Gauthier.*'

I jolted awake with a gasp, sitting upright. The nurse who had woken me by grasping my shoulder – the one that wasn't broken – regarded me with a mix of sympathy and annoyance.

'You were having a bad dream, Sergeant,' she said quietly. 'We mustn't wake the rest of the ward, must we?'

Still half in the dream with Robert's screaming, bloody face dancing in front of my eyes, I looked round wildly and saw not the cramped cockpit of the Stirling, but the quiet hospital ward with a lamp burning low at the far end, and the huddled shapes of sleeping men in the beds around me. I lay back, throwing my arm across my face. 'Sorry,' I murmured.

'I shall fetch you a sleeping draught,' she said and bustled off, her starched uniform rustling. I lowered my arm, gazing up at the ceiling as my heart rate slowly returned to normal. I had been at the RAF General Hospital at Ely for five weeks now. My left leg and right arm, both badly broken in the crash, were in plaster, and I had stitches in my forehead where the glass from the car windows had sliced me up. Three days after I got here, Jonny Grant had visited me to break the news that Robert was dead. Not knowing what to say, I'd closed my eyes and pretended to drift off to sleep, feeling like the worst sort of coward. I hadn't seen Jonny or the rest of my crew since, but I was pretty sure they all held me responsible for what happened to Robert. And who could blame them?

The nurse returned with my sleeping draught, which I

swallowed dutifully. Whatever was in it plunged me into a black, dreamless sleep, and next time I opened my eyes it was morning, sunlight streaming into the ward through the big windows that lined the outside wall.

After breakfast, I dozed for a while, still under the lingering influence of the sleeping draught. Thankfully, again there were no dreams. I was woken again sometime later by another nurse. 'Sergeant Gauthier, you have a visitor,' she said. She was one of the younger ones, a brisk, cheerful, rosy-cheeked girl of about eighteen called Sister Morris.

I struggled to sit upright again, wondering, without much interest, who it was. One of the crew? My Wing Commander, come to dish out my punishment at last?

'It's such a nice day that she decided she'd wait for you outside on the lawn,' Sister Morris continued, before I could speak. *She?* 'Let's get you up, shall we?'

Despite her youth and slight build, Sister Morris seemed to feel no embarrassment about wrestling me into my hospital blues: the white shirt, red tie and ill-fitting jacket and trousers in itchy blue serge everyone here had to wear when they weren't in their pyjamas. They were rumoured to be left over from the last war; I could believe it, too. About the only thing going for them was that they were spotlessly clean. Once I was dressed, Sister Morris washed my face, shaved me, combed my hair and got me into a wheelchair, all with the same brisk efficiency.

As she pushed me through the ward, I wracked my brains, trying to work out who might be here to see me. The only person I could think of was my mother, but how would she have got here all the way from Canada? Why hadn't she written first? I'd sent her and my father a letter, letting them know I was in hospital but glossing over what had happened, and hadn't had a reply yet. It was likely stuck on a ship somewhere halfway across the Atlantic, or – if luck hadn't been on the crew's side – at the bottom of the sea.

Outside, the sun was too bright, and the air felt startlingly fresh after the stale atmosphere of the ward. This was the first time I'd been out of the hospital since I came here, despite the nurses' entreaties that some air would do me good. The light and space – the *reality* of it – was too much. I shrank into myself, wanting to tell Sister Morris to take me back inside, take me back to my bed, but I couldn't find my voice. Unaware of my distress, she pushed me around the side of the long, sprawling hospital building with its tower at one end, chattering away about the fellow she was seeing – some guy on ground crew at a nearby aerodrome – and the dance they'd been to the night before. I closed my eyes and tried to remember how to breathe normally. *In, out. In, out. For God's sake, Bill, get a hold of yourself.*

'Hello, Bill,' a familiar voice said. 'How are you?'

I opened my eyes to see Rose Legge standing in front of me.

'I hope you don't mind me coming to see you,' she said. 'I won't stay if you don't want me to.'

Aware of how I must look in my crumpled, ancient blues, I managed to force myself to speak, my voice sounding rusty and thin from disuse. 'No, it's fine. It's… it's good to see you. How did you know I was here?'

'I got a telephone call the day after we met in Bury,' she said. 'I thought it was you, again, but it was a doctor. He'd found the piece of paper with my number on it in your pocket and I suppose he must have thought I was your girl. I'm sorry it's taken me so long to visit – I've been so busy with ENSA!'

Sister Morris steered me over to a bench shaded by a tall

lime tree, and Rose sat down on it, folding her hands in her lap.

'I'll leave you here, then,' Sister Morris said. 'Toodle pip!'

'Gosh, she's rather bright-eyed and bushy-tailed, isn't she?' Rose said, watching the nurse march off. I grunted in assent, and Rose looked back at me, her face a mask of concern. 'I couldn't believe it when the doctor told me about the accident. It must have been dreadful. I'm so sorry, Bill.'

My heart jolted again unpleasantly. Did she know what had really happened? I felt as if I was in another dream; that at any moment I would find myself back in that eerily lit cockpit with Robert bleeding and screaming beside me. But the birds kept singing and the sun kept shining from the cloudless sky, the dappled shadows cast by the lime tree shifting across the ground in the slight breeze.

'Bill?' Rose said. 'Are you all right?'

I shook my head. 'Sorry. I wasn't...' I cleared my throat. 'I wasn't expecting to see you, is all.' Realising how that might sound, I added, 'I'm glad you came, though. Did you have to travel far?'

Rose shook her head. 'We're doing a series of concerts around Peterborough this week.' One corner of her mouth twisted up. 'But never mind me. How are you feeling?'

I tried to smile. 'I've been better,' I said thinly.

She touched my hand gently. If it had been anyone else – if it hadn't been for the misery and self-pity laying over me like a layer of cold soup – her action and tone would have irritated me. *Don't feel sorry for me, goddamnit. I don't deserve it.* But the sensation of Rose's fingers against mine ignited something inside me: a spark that, ever since I woke up and found out Robert was dead, I thought had been extinguished forever. She looked so vital, so alive, with her shining waves of hair and dancing eyes and mouth that seemed to curve permanently at the edges in a smile.

I *needed* this. I needed *her.*

We talked for a while about what Rose was doing with ENSA; she didn't press me for further details about the accident, which I was grateful for. Every so often, I'd remember that afternoon we'd lain on the grass in the Abbey Gardens at Bury and kissed. It gave me a strange sense of dislocation, as if it was something that had happened in a different lifetime, to a different person. I was starting to realise that that Bill – the one who flew, who went to parties and concerts, who could have a different girl on his arm every night if he wanted – was gone forever.

As for the Bill now, sitting here in this wheelchair... I had no idea who he was at all.

'What will happen to you when you're better?' Rose said at last. 'Will you return to the air base?'

'I don't know,' I said. 'The doctors aren't sure if I'll get the full range of movement back in my shoulder yet.' *And I still don't know exactly what sort of trouble I'm in*, I added inside my head.

I saw Sister Morris striding across the grass towards us. 'Visiting hours are over, I'm afraid!' she said, grinning at me and Rose.

Rose stood, picking up her handbag. 'Thank you, Sister,' she said.

As the nurse grasped the handles of my wheelchair, I touched Rose's arm. She turned, looking surprised, and I swallowed. 'Would you... would you come and see me again?'

At first, she still looked a little startled; then her face cleared. 'Yes, of course,' she said. 'If you'd like me to.'

'I would,' I said. 'I'd like that very much indeed.'

She smiled. 'Then I don't see why not.'

'Thank you.'

Rose bent down, clasping my good hand, and touched her lips to mine in a chaste, feather-light kiss. 'See you again soon, Bill,' she said.

As Sister Morris wheeled me back across the grass, I twisted my head to watch Rose go, her head high, her step confident and light; it was as if she was on the stage, all the world looking at her. 'You're a dark horse, you are, Sergeant,' Sister Morris giggled. 'Never mentioned you'd got a girl.'

'I – I didn't think I did,' I said.

Sister Morris giggled again. 'Could've fooled me.'

We went inside.

Before long, the doctors at Ely decided they'd done everything they could for me and I was moved to a convalescent home for injured servicemen nearby. It was some stately pile that had been requisitioned by the government at the start of the war, surrounded by fields and woodland with acres of landscaped lawns and rose beds. Despite our proximity to London, if it hadn't been for the Spitfires and Hurricanes buzzing overhead every now and then, and the air raids that saw all the patients who could leave their beds being hustled down to the cellars, you'd have been forgiven for thinking there wasn't a war on any more. I'd had the plaster on my shoulder removed and was doing exercises to help regain the strength I'd lost. 'You'll be as good as new before you know it!' the physiotherapist said cheerfully as I submitted to my daily dose of torture one Tuesday afternoon. 'That leg'll be out of plaster soon too!'

As he stretched and pulled at my arm, trying to coax my stiffened shoulder into moving properly again, I gritted my teeth against the pain and fixed my thoughts on Rose. She was in the area again and due to drop in later. We were going steady now and she came as often as she could; her letters and visits were the only thing I looked forward to. When she was here, I didn't think about what had happened to me and Robert; I could forget, briefly, the nightmares that still left me gasping for air as I woke, drowning in a snarl of memories and guilt.

Today, when she arrived, I was sitting on the veranda, a blanket across my knees against the slight chill in the air and re-reading a letter from home that had finally arrived that morning. Except for a guy at the other end of the veranda who appeared to be dozing, I was alone.

'Bad news?' Rose said as she kissed me and dropped lightly into the chair beside me. 'You look rather preoccupied, darling.'

I smiled wearily at her and shook my head, folding the letter up and jamming it in my jacket pocket. 'Just a letter from my mother. I didn't exactly go into detail about what happened, but she still worries – you know.'

'Gosh, tell me about it. I'm due to go to Edinburgh with the group next week and mine's terrified I'll get mugged or bombed.' Rose rolled her eyes. 'For someone who's lived in London all her life, she's got a dreadfully warped idea about what other cities are like.'

We fell, as always, into quick, easy conversation, chatting about Rose's latest concert and a party she'd attended with her mother where, apparently, she'd been subjected to a parade of suitable young men. I felt a lurch in my stomach at that, which I tried to ignore.

'Is there any other news?' Rose said at last. I knew immediately what she was referring to.

A week ago, I'd finally told her the full story of the accident, and that I was waiting to find out what was going to happen to me once I was well enough to leave the convalescent home. I'd thought she'd be horrified, but she hadn't really reacted at all, except to say, 'Oh, Bill, that must have been *dreadful.*'

I shook my head.

She worried her lower lip between her teeth. 'Do you think they'll send you back to Canada?'

'I don't know,' I said. The thought had crossed my mind too, although I knew it was unlikely, as Bomber Command needed every pair of hands it could get. Most likely, I'd be reassigned to ground crew somewhere.

'I'll miss you awfully if they do, you know.'

My heart gave a funny little lurch. 'Will you?'

A dimple appeared in her left cheek. 'Won't you miss me too?'

'Sure – I mean, of course I will.' My heart was beating faster now.

She slid her eyes away from mine. 'Or perhaps I've got the wrong idea – perhaps you only see me as a short-term fling...'

'No – no – that is, not unless that's how you see me...'

She looked up again, gazing at me through her eyelashes. 'Oh, Bill, you must know how I feel about you by now.'

I glanced round at the guy at the other end of the veranda. Still asleep. I lifted one corner of my mouth in a smile. 'So that's how it is, eh?' I said with a confidence I didn't altogether feel.

'Oh, *Bill,*' Rose said, a crease appearing between her eyebrows. 'Must you tease so?'

God, she was beautiful. I leaned over and kissed her, taking her hands in mine. 'That answer your question?' I said when we broke apart again.

She smiled at me, dabbing at her smudged lipstick, her cheeks flushed prettily.

I wanted to grab hold of her, kiss her again and never let her go.

'Marry me.' I hadn't known I was going to say it until I did: the words seemed to tumble out of their own accord. Even as I spoke, I knew it was crazy – what had happened to the guy who didn't want to get attached to anyone? And why the hell would someone like Rose want to marry someone like me? We'd only met a couple of months ago; I was good for nothing, with a smashed-up leg and shoulder. I braced myself, waiting for her expression to falter, and for her to paste on a kind smile to cover it up. *Oh, Bill, it's simply wonderful of you to ask me, but when I said I had feelings for you I didn't mean it like that…*

Instead, her smile deepened. 'Bill…'

A tiny spark of hope kindled inside me. 'I'll organise everything,' I rushed on. 'I have some savings. And if I get shipped out to another air base somewhere you'll be able to come with me – we can live in married quarters. You won't want for a thing.'

'Bill, *yes*. I'll marry you,' she said, still smiling. She placed one hand over mine. Slowly, a grin spread across my face too.

'Are you sure?'

'Of course.'

'I mean, we haven't known each other long – I know that…'

'But let's not rush,' Rose said seriously. 'If you were going to fly again then it would make sense, perhaps, but if you're likely to have a desk job you'll be safe enough. I want us to have a proper wedding, not some one-in, one-out job at a registry office.'

'Whatever you want, honey,' I said.

Nearby, someone cleared their throat. I jumped, looked round and saw a nurse standing at the door that led out to the veranda. I'd been so absorbed in asking Rose to marry me I hadn't heard her come out. 'Sergeant Gauthier, you have another visitor,' she said. I saw someone move in the deep shadows of the corridor behind her; caught a glimpse of uniform. 'They insist on seeing you immediately.'

'Forgive me,' Rose said, turning that brilliant smile on her. 'My fiancé and I were just discussing our wedding. I won't keep you any longer, Bill.' Gathering her handbag and cardigan, she stood, and leaned down to kiss me one more time. 'I'll come and see you again tomorrow, darling.'

The nurse stood to one side to let her pass. Then, nodding at my new visitor, she left too, and Wing Commander Gray, the commanding officer in charge of my squadron, stepped out onto the terrace.

I saluted him. 'Sir. Forgive me for not getting out of this chair,' I said, indicating my plastered leg stretched out in front of me.

'That's quite all right, Sergeant,' he said gravely. I wondered if he would sit, but he remained standing. 'I gather congratulations are in order?'

He meant Rose. How much had he overheard? 'Thank you, Sir.'

'I won't beat about the bush,' Wing Commander Gray said. 'We've had quite the time deciding what to do with you.'

I waited, silent. The atmosphere was so tense I could almost feel it buzzing. Had I really, less than ten minutes ago, asked Rose to marry me?

'However, the doctors tell me they expect to discharge you in a few weeks, and as your injuries will prevent you from flying again for the time being, we have decided you will complete your current tour early.'

Oh. I was expecting it, of course, but it still came as a blow.

'You'll face a court martial, of course – that goes without saying,' Wing Commander Gray went on.

'Yes, Sir,' I mumbled.

Wing Commander Gray cleared his throat. 'As for what happens after that… assuming they don't decide to make an example of you, a position has come up we feel you'd be suited to, working as an operator at one of our radar stations in Scotland. You'll receive the necessary training, of course – as soon as you're well enough we'll send you on a month's course at the radar school in Yatesbury.'

Scotland. I felt my stomach sink a little. The court martial was no surprise; I'd been expecting that, and all I could do was keep my fingers crossed that, as Commander Gray said, they didn't decide to make an example of me and send me to the glasshouse. But although I'd known deep down that I wouldn't be staying at Chedburgh, there'd been a small part of me that hoped that, if I couldn't fly, I might be transferred to ground crew at one of other the aerodromes around here or perhaps take up a role as an instructor.

I kept my expression neutral, reminding myself Scotland was better than prison.

'Thank you, Sir,' I said. 'Do you mind me asking whereabouts in Scotland?' I had visited Dundee a couple of years ago when I was still training, to see a distant, elderly relative of my mother. My overwhelming memory was of driving, sideways rain and a view from the sitting room window of the Tay estuary, steel-coloured and choppy, while I drank tea the colour of dishwater and made polite conversation.

'It's in Shetland,' Wing Commander Gray said. 'RAF Svarta Ness, on an island called Fiskersay. The full site went into commission in the spring. It's a Chain Home station, one of several in Shetland, a tiny place, but busy – the men there run a tight ship. They often get Canadians from the RCAF there too. We think you'd fit right in.'

I stared at him. Shetland? That was halfway to goddamn Norway. And he'd said *the men there*... didn't the Women's Auxiliary Air Force – the WAAFs – usually run the radar stations? Perhaps they thought it was too remote to send women there.

I must have remained silent for a moment too long, because Wing Commander Gray cleared his throat. 'You need to understand, Sergeant, that you're not being offered a choice here. While, of course, Cauldwell's death was a tragedy, this... *incident* has been a source of great embarrassment for the Royal Air Force. We must be seen to be giving the right message.'

I nodded, swallowing hard. 'Yes, Sir. Of course.'

'It's rotten timing, but I'm sure your young lady will understand. All being well with the court martial, you have a fortnight until you leave for Yatesbury.'

I swallowed again. 'Yes, Sir.'

'Very good.'

As soon as the door had closed behind the Wing Commander, I slumped in my chair, my hand across my face. *Shetland.*

What was I going to tell Rose?

SEVEN

HEDDA
Somewhere in north-west Norway
October

'Get up. There is a German patrol on the way. If you stay here, they will find you.'

I stared up at the fisherman. I was still half asleep and struggled to comprehend his words. He had found us when he'd lifted up his boat, which Eirik and I had hidden under the previous evening after reaching the little coastal village I didn't even know the name of.

'Up! You must hurry!' the man barked. At last, I understood. I scrambled out from underneath the boat, pulling Eirik with me, and we stumbled after the man towards the road.

After I killed the German officer, horror and panic had continued to flood through me, making it hard to breathe, to think, to even *move*. Eirik had continued to cry hysterically at the sight of the dead man, who had blood still leaking from his mouth, and it was the sound of his wails that finally spurred me into action; I'd scooped him up in my arms and run from the barn, leaving my basket behind, knowing that at any moment the woman from the house up the road could return, and we had to get away before she did.

But now, the chain of *Milorg* was broken. I no longer knew

who we could turn to for help getting to Sweden. All I was certain of was that the Germans would spare no effort in hunting down their officer's murderer, and I had to put as much distance between us and the town as possible. *That's right, run*, Anders had hissed inside my head as we hurried away. *Now you've really made a mess of things, you stupid fool.* Every night since then, Eirik had nightmares from which he awoke screaming and sobbing, and I knew he was dreaming about what had happened. Trying to soothe him, I would be overwhelmed by guilt, and find myself holding back sobs too. All I had ever wanted for my son was to give him a good life, and instead, I had married a man who turned out to be a monster, and then, through my own bad decisions – one on top of another, like a line of falling dominos – I had ended up a murderer, on the run from the Wehrmacht. Could things get any worse?

Finally, yesterday evening, we found ourselves in a small village on the shore of a fjord. The weather was windy and wet, so we sought shelter under one of the fishing boats that were resting, upside down, on the beach above the tideline. I'd planned for us to get away again before daylight, but once again, exhaustion claimed us; the next thing I knew it was morning, and the fisherman, a man in his sixties, was staring down at us, his eyes wide with surprise.

The fisherman took us to his home, a small house at the edge of the village. Inside, his wife was stirring a pot on the stove with a wooden spoon. She looked surprised to see us but not alarmed. 'Astrid, I found these two hiding under my boat,' the fisherman said. 'And a patrol is on the way.'

Terror speared through me, but before I could say anything the woman put down her spoon and came over to me, catching hold of my hand. 'Come,' she said. Picking up a lamp, she led us down to a basement with a packed earth floor. There, she handed me the lamp. In its dim, flickering glow, I watched as she bent to fiddle with something in the floor. 'Where is it?' she muttered as I wondered what she was doing. 'Ah!'

She lifted a trapdoor, so well-concealed it looked like part of the basement floor – it was invisible to the untrained eye. Beneath was another room, really no more than a compartment. When I climbed down inside, I discovered it was not even big enough for me to stand up in.

Eirik began to cry again, a thin, dreary sound as if he was almost too weary to force out any more tears. 'No, Mamma,' he said. 'No.' The woman picked him up and lifted him down to me. 'You must both stay here,' she said. 'And do not move or make a single sound until one of us returns. I cannot leave you the lamp, I'm afraid.'

I nodded, although dread squeezed my throat at the thought of being shut up down here in absolute darkness. God only knew how Eirik would react.

'Thank you,' I managed to say, my arms wrapped tight around my son, muffling his whimpers against my ragged skirt.

She nodded grimly. 'Do not thank me. Give thanks to God for Leif finding you in the nick of time.'

She stepped back and the trapdoor thudded closed, blackness closing in around us.

'Shh, *lille vennen*,' I said to Eirik, rocking him from side to side and feeling the alarming way his chest was heaving as he tried and failed to catch his breath. 'You must be quiet.'

'I'm so scared, Mamma,' he choked, and I knew he wasn't just talking about being shut up here. Fresh guilt see-sawed through me. Oh, if only I could go back to that night I decided to shelter in the barn. If only I had not killed that officer. We might be in Sweden by now – we might be safe.

I don't know how long we waited, crouched in that small, dark, damp earth-smelling space, but it felt like a lifetime. At some point, the patrol visited the house. I heard muffled shouts; heavy feet tramping across the floor; furniture being dragged around; voices talking in loud, harsh German right above where we were hiding. Eirik was trembling, his whole body wracked with shivers. *Don't cough, please don't cough*, I pleaded silently. I knew only too well what would happen if we were discovered, not only to us but to the fisherman and his wife and everyone else here too; the Germans would punish them all. In the spring, a village in the south of Norway called Telavåg had been destroyed by the Wehrmacht: it was discovered some of the inhabitants had been hiding two Norwegian resistance men, and two of the officers sent to arrest the men were shot. The whole village was burned to the ground, boats sunk and animals slaughtered. The Germans executed as many of the men in the village as they could, sending the rest to concentration camps along with the women and children. I had heard about it from Mette, and even though Kirkenes was over two thousand miles away it had the same impact on us as if it had happened in the next town. The thought that I could bring a similar tragedy down on the heads of people here made me want to vomit.

When the patrol left the house, Eirik and I continued to wait for what felt like hours. I was thirsty, and desperate to use the lavatory. Eirik was too; eventually he couldn't hold it any more and wet himself, weeping miserably. The sharp stink of urine filled my nostrils as I tried to comfort him. At last, the hatch above us opened and the fisherman and his wife peered down at us, their faces lit by the weak glow from the oil lamp once more.

'They have gone,' Astrid said. 'But they may return. They say they are looking for a woman, a spy, who murdered a German officer – they suspect she is in the area.'

They didn't ask if that was me. I supposed, from the emotions that must have wrestled across my face as I took in their words, that they didn't need to.

'Oh, God,' I said, my voice trembling and ragged with tears. 'What am I going to do?' I wasn't even sure why I was asking; I knew I'd reached the end of the road. My mind whirling, I wondered whether to beg the couple to take Eirik or to find someone who could – anything so that he would be safe once the Germans took me away.

Before I could speak again, Leif and Astrid exchanged glances.

'There is a boat about to leave for the Shetland Islands in Britain,' Leif said. 'It is taking four resistance men over there as part of an operation called the Shetland Bus, and they say you and your son can join them. It will be a difficult journey – there are storms forecast, it will take many days, and you will have to stay below deck the whole time, but if you make it, you will be safe.'

Inside me, hope fought with panic. Take a boat all the way over to Britain? It seemed impossible. But what other choice did Eirik and I have?

Nodding mutely, I allowed Leif and Astrid to help us out of the hidden compartment. There was no time to clean Eirik up, but Astrid gave us some bread and water. When we'd gulped it down they led us outside. I was startled to see it was getting dark again already; we had been in their basement all day.

'Good luck,' Astrid said, squeezing my hands. I was so grateful to her for her kindness I wanted to hug her, to weep on her shoulder, but there was no time. Lief took us back down to the little beach and in the twilight, I saw a single-masted fishing vessel moored out on the fjord. He hurried us into the boat we had hidden under that morning and, telling us to keep our heads down, rowed me and Eirik out across the water.

On board were four men in traditional fishing gear. They didn't say anything to us, but one of them hustled me and Eirik into a hidden room at the back of the boat's cabin, even more cramped than the room in Leif and Astrid's basement. Once we were inside, they quickly nailed boards across the entrance to hide us. The air was thick with oil and diesel fumes and I began to feel nauseated almost immediately, even though the surface of the fjord was calm. At least we had a small lamp hanging from a hook in the ceiling. There was also a bucket in the corner. Unable to hold on any longer, I used it to relieve myself, then huddled on the floor with my arms tight around Eirik, rocking him as he coughed and cried. A short while later the boat's engine chugged into life and with a *tonk tonk tonk*, it began to move through the water, out towards the mouth of the fjord and the open sea beyond.

The journey was uneventful at first. Eirik fell into a miserable, restless sleep, punctuated by more fits of coughing, and my nausea receded a little. I found, by focusing on my breathing and not allowing myself to think about anything else at all, I could keep the terror that kept threatening to rise inside me at bay. Eventually, worn out, I began to doze too.

I was woken by a low, ominous whistling sound and the boat beginning to pitch up and down.

'Mamma, what's happening?' Eirik said, sitting up too.

'It must be a storm,' I said, remembering what Leif had said before we left the hidden room in his basement. I wondered how far out to sea we were and if, should the weather get too bad, the men steering the boat would have to turn back.

Above us, on deck, I heard shouts. The lamp hanging from the ceiling flickered as it swung from side to side. 'Come here, *lille vennen*,' I said to Eirik, pulling him into my lap and pressing my back against the wall to steady myself as the boat continued to pitch and roll.

'Mamma, I feel sick,' he groaned.

'Try to take some deep breaths,' I said, but I was feeling nauseated again too. Slowly but steadily, the whistling of the wind rose to a scream, blotting out all other sounds. Eirik began retching between coughs; I reached for the bucket and rubbed his back as he hunched over it, trying vainly to soothe him even though I was almost overwhelmed by my own fear. Then a particularly large wave crashed into the boat, rocking it almost over onto its side, and the bucket tipped over, spilling the foul contents across the floor. I tried to scramble out of the way but there was nowhere to go.

'Mamma!' Eirik wailed, clinging to me as we were thrown against one wall and then the other. I could hear nothing except the roar of the storm, and we were being hurled around so violently now I was certain the boat would be smashed to matchsticks. Was the engine still running? Were those men still with us? Had we been forgotten – abandoned? Soundlessly, I began to pray, tears streaming down my face as I begged God to keep us safe for just a little longer. *I do not want to die. Please do not take my son from me like this. Please do not let us drown.*

As the boat lurched again I put a hand out to try and steady myself, and realised that I had put my hand down in an inch or so of water. My skirts were wet too, and I realised, with fresh horror, that the sea was coming into the boat. I tried to scramble to my feet but another jolt knocked me back down. Foul-tasting water splashed into my mouth. I coughed and spluttered. 'Mamma!' Eirik cried again in a tone I had never heard him use before.

We have to get out of here, I thought, pulling him into my arms. *We have to get up on deck.* As the seawater lapped around our feet. I turned towards the entrance to our hiding spot, wondering if I had the strength to pull the heavy boards that covered it aside.

Then the lamp flickered one last time and went out, plunging us into darkness.

EIGHT

BILL

RAF Svarta Ness, Fiskersay, Shetland
October

...Oh, Bill, I have found the most darling house out in the Surrey countryside! The next time you get leave you will have to come and see it with me. I think it will suit us perfectly. It has two acres of grounds, six bedrooms and a spectacular dining room, all just right for entertaining guests. And it's near Mummy and Daddy, but not too near, if you know what I mean... Of course we'll need a little place in London too for when we're there, but oh, I do hope you'll like the house as much as I do!

I sighed and dropped Rose's letter onto the table in front of me. For a moment, I tried to imagine it through her eyes: a house set in sunny acres of parkland, roses tumbling around the front door; flower beds and a fountain; a maid shepherding the kids up to the nursery for tea (we'd have a boy and a girl, Rose had already insisted on that); a dog running around. And a pony, of course.

It was idyllic – and utterly impossible. I had no chance of leave right now, not with Shetland being battered by one autumn storm after another, and although I had savings, and my RAF wages were nothing to be sniffed at, I knew they wouldn't stretch to two acres of grounds, six bedrooms *and* a place in London too. Rose's engagement ring, which I'd bought from Cartier in London before I left, had already cost me a small fortune. Anyway, it was highly likely when the war ended, I'd have to go back to Canada. I'd tried to talk to Rose about that little problem before I came to Shetland, but she'd silenced me with a bright, *Let's worry about it when it happens.* Not wanting to upset her – she was already on edge after a row with her father, which had been about *something terribly boring* she wouldn't tell me about – I'd changed the subject.

Sighing again, I glanced up at the men gathered around the tables nearby. They were laughing and joking over their mugs of tea, their newspapers and card games and their own letters they were writing to family and friends. They all looked so cheerful. That had been me once; now, for the life of me, I couldn't remember what it felt like. Although the NAAFI was busy, I was sitting alone, as I always did. I'd just come off the morning shift up at the operational site – the operators worked a four-watch system at Svarta Ness: 1–6 p.m., 8 a.m.–1 p.m., 11 p.m.–8 a.m. and 6–11 p.m., then two days off to recover – and had come here to get something to eat, with Rose's letter, which had arrived a few days ago, stuffed into my pocket.

I rubbed my eyes, which ached after the long shift spent staring at the round screen on my receiver console, watching for blips on the bright green line snaking left to right across it that might indicate an incoming raid. The Chain Home station at Svarta Ness was part of an early warning system, a literal chain of radar stations all around the British coast looking out for enemy aircraft. If any were detected, and there was no IFF – Identification Friend or Foe – signal to indicate it was one of ours, then it was action stations: I had to move a cursor to the position of the trace, automatically sending this information to the calculating machine. With my right hand, I'd measure the direction and height, and with my left, move a round lever called a goniometer that allowed me to work out the angle. All this meant we could calculate how far away the aircraft were, their speed and their altitude before telephoning everything through to the filter room at Lerwick, where the Plotters would work out a true picture of the aircrafts' movements before sending *that* on to Lerwick Fighter Sector HQ. Here, orders would be given and Fighter Command squadrons scrambled to intercept the raids. Because of the concentration required, and to avoid eye strain, each man on watch took turns to sit at the console for an hour before handing over to someone else, but it was still intense work, and I always came off duty feeling shattered.

I'd been in Shetland for around a month now, coming straight here after my court martial – where I'd been fined and demoted from Flight Sergeant to plain Sergeant – and completing my training course at Yatesbury. RAF Svarta Ness was, as Wing Commander Gray had said, a tiny but busy place, its buildings scattered across the north-eastern-most point of Fiskersay. But despite what he'd told me, I was the only Canadian here; the rest of the men were British, save for one fellow from New Zealand. Elsewhere on the island there were contingents from the Army and Navy, just like in the rest of Shetland. In mainland Shetland, airfields had been built at Scatsa and Sumburgh for the islands' air defence system, and there was an enormous base for flying boats at Sullom

Voe that had been built just before the war and added to as the conflict progressed. What Shetland's residents must have thought when the military descended upon them en masse I couldn't imagine, but here on Fiskersay they'd been nothing but welcoming to us so far.

Three miles north-west of Unst, Fiskersay was further away from the Scottish mainland than any other point in the British Isles. The operational buildings – the receiver and transmitter blocks and the power house – were out on the promontory that gave the station its name along with an anti-aircraft battery, all of it heavily camouflaged with banked-up earth and netting woven with strips of green and khaki sacking. At the southern edge of the operational site was the domestic site where I was now: four Nissen huts for the men's billets, a requisitioned house nicknamed the Manor that had been turned into the officers' accommodation, the medical hut and the NAAFI that, as well as housing the mess, doubled up as an entertainments hall and cinema. There was also the station office, an air raid shelter and a few sheds used for storage.

I stood, draining my tea and pocketing Rose's letter again, and made my way outside. It was just after four o'clock, and already the light was fading. Yet another storm was on its way, wind roaring through the camp as I made my way to the gates, huddled inside my greatcoat with my cap jammed down over my ears. Gales of up to a hundred miles an hour were forecast tonight; as a precaution the aerial had been lashed down to prevent it being damaged, and for now the station was off air.

Between the radar station and the island's main settlement, Talafirth – which everyone called *town* but was no bigger than a village – lay the Haug, a large, flat-topped hill that sloped steeply towards Talafirth on one side and plunged towards the sea and the jagged cliffs that made up the island's northern coastline on the other. It was the highest point on Fiskersay, and on its top stood the station's receiver and transmitter towers. Moving on autopilot, I headed along the muddy road that hugged its flank. My leg ached fiercely, making me limp, but I was used to that now. Breathing hard, I left the road – which had originally been little more than a narrow track; work to widen it so the station could be reached more easily had only been finished in the summer – and clambered up the hill. My boots slid on the wet grass, my ears filling with the thunder of the sea hurling itself against the cliffs somewhere below me. Finally, I reached my destination: a ruined crofter's cottage near the top of the hill, about two hundred yards from the towers. I found a sheltered spot among the tumbled stones and sat down. I'd discovered this place a week after my arrival on Fiskersay and often came here for some peace and quiet.

Now, I gazed out at the jagged rocks of Svarta Ness directly in front of me. To my right was the shallow, cliff-bound bay of Svarta Wick, and to my left, towards the west, a wider bay with a sandy beach called Odda's Bay. Another quarter of a mile out to sea was a tiny, uninhabited island, Holm of Odda, with a sharp stack the locals called Odda's Fang sticking up out of the sea just beyond. It was the sort of landscape that reminded you it had been here long before human beings had found it, and would still be here long after we'd gone.

The waves, whipped up by the wind, were enormous, white-capped and boiling; it wasn't raining yet, but from horizon to horizon, the sky was an ominous brownish-grey. Another hour or so and the storm would hit Fiskersay with full force. I thought about Rose and how far away she was, and was overtaken by a sudden longing to hear her voice; to hold her.

As I sat there, remembering the last time I'd seen her before I was sent to Fiskersay – we'd been shacked up at a hotel in London and had just made love for the first time in a hurried sort of way, aware that any moment there could be an air raid – a new sound reached my ears, blown towards me by the rushing gale. A boat engine.

I leaned forwards, narrowing my eyes as I scanned the surging waves. From time to time, small Norwegian fishing vessels were spotted passing the island, making their way to the mainland. Apparently, since the start of the war, there had been a steady stream of them, bringing refugees escaping German-occupied Norway. Sometimes boats were seen going the other way, too, usually at night, and there were rumours of an operation going on between Britain and Norway, all top secret, of course. No one on Fiskersay asked any questions, because we knew we wouldn't get any answers.

The note of the engine was unmistakable: the steady, distinctive *tonk tonk tonk* of a Norwegian fishing vessel. It rose and fell with the wind, faint at first but coming closer.

Suddenly I spotted the boat. With its wooden sides and small white-painted cabin, it looked like a toy in a giant's bathtub, plunging through the heaving water about half a mile away. The top of its main mast was broken, hanging down, and it was heading straight for the jumble of jagged rocks beyond the cliffs of Svarta Ness, its engine useless against the brutal power of the wind and the waves. My heart began to pound. There was nowhere safe to land a boat on the northern side of the island in weather like this. If it hit the rocks, everyone on board was doomed.

As I jumped up and started down the hill, the sound of the engine cut out. Then I heard the drone of an approaching aircraft. It was another sound I was all too familiar with: the snarl of a German plane, a Junkers Ju 88. Moments later it came into view, flying low and fast under the lid of dirty-coloured cloud, and I saw the muzzles of its guns flash as it began firing on the Norwegian vessel. Immediately, to my surprise, there were flashes of return fire from the boat.

I ran all the way back to the camp, my gait shambling and awkward, gritting my teeth against the pain in my leg and cursing myself for not being able to move faster.

'Another Norwegian boat off the Ness. Jerry's firing on her,' I gasped as I burst into the NAAFI. Everyone turned to stare at me. I grabbed onto a chair to steady myself; my leg was threatening to buckle underneath me.

Up on the point, the anti-aircraft guns began booming, their sound carried towards the dining hall by the wind. The Ju 88 – which, with no radar cover at Svarta Ness due to the storm, had managed to sneak in undetected – had finally been spotted, though too late for whoever was on board that boat, I reckoned.

The mess erupted into action.

'Are you OK, old man?' said Lewis Harper, noticing my grimace as I tried to straighten my leg out. Lewis was one of the other radar operations I shared a hut with who'd been on watch with me this morning. Too breathless to answer him, I nodded. No one here knew what had happened to Robert; I'd told them I'd been in an accident while I was on aircrew, and left it at that.

Lewis clapped me on the shoulder and followed the others outside. Ignoring the pain in my leg, I went after them.

At some point now lost to history a set of steep, rocky steps had been cut into the cliffs near the edge of the camp, leading down to the little bay at Svarta Wick. Most of the men were gathered near the top, looking out to sea. I joined them and, after a moment, spotted the boat. It was much nearer to shore now; the waves had pushed it around the point and it was drifting towards the rocks, listing dangerously as it was pummelled this way and that. I could see bullet holes in the deck. There were no signs of life on board at all.

'What're we gonna do?' I yelled to Lewis, trying to make myself heard over the roar of wind and water.

'Briggs has gone to alert the C.O.,' Lewis yelled back. 'Might have to try and get a boat out there.'

'In this?! No chance!'

'I know, but what else can we do? Can't get through to the Air Sea Rescue chaps – we've already tried – and it's not like they'd be able to do anything anyway, not in these conditions.'

In the end it was the sea itself that made the decision for us. A particularly large wave rolled in, hurling the boat, which by now was almost flat on its side, forward. I held my breath, sensing the others doing the same. Then the wave broke and the boat was thrown towards the base of the cliffs at the head of the bay where it finally capsized. At the same time, the storm broke and rain began lashing down.

The station's Commanding Officer, Flight Lieutenant Jackson, arrived at a run, a heavy length of rope looped over his shoulder, and threw it to us. I caught it. 'Tie yourselves together!' he shouted over the roar of the wind. 'No one's going down there unsecured – you'll get washed out to sea!' He also thrust a torch at me that I shoved into the inside pocket of my coat, and handed Lewis an axe. 'Use that to get into the boat,' he yelled at us. 'There's no chance of lifting it – it must weigh forty tons or more!'

My leg was still throbbing, but I barely noticed as I looped and knotted the rope around my waist. Lewis did the same, then handed it to the men behind him, Len Kane, the radar operator who had come all the way from New Zealand, and Alistair Briggs, a radar mechanic from Yorkshire. By the time the rope ran out we'd formed a human chain of eight men, fastened together as if we were about to climb a mountain. With me leading, we made our precarious way down the steps. Funnelled into the narrow, steep-sided bay, the power of the water was terrifying. The tide was almost in, and only a tiny strip of sand remained for me to stand on as, squinting against the spray and rain stinging my face and eyes, I tried to work out how on earth I was going to get to the boat, now caught on the rocks just metres away.

I have to do this, I thought. *If there's anyone in that ship left alive, I owe it to Robert to save them. And Des.*

'Hold on!' I yelled at Lewis. 'We'll have to try and climb over the rocks!'

It was a perilous scramble, made all the more awkward by the pain and stiffness in my injured leg; if it hadn't been for the rope around our waists and the other men at the back of the chain hanging on for grim life, I had no doubt whatsoever the four of us would have been dragged out to sea in an instant. As it was, every time a wave came in we had to crouch, gasping, all the air punched out of our lungs by the freezing water. The rocks were covered in barnacles that sliced my palms and knees and cut my trousers to ribbons.

At last, we reached the boat. Lewis began chopping at the side of the boat with the axe while Len, Al and I pulled at the planks, trying to work them loose. At last, the four of us had managed to make a hole big enough to crawl into. Taking a deep breath, I went first, reaching into my pocket for the torch Flight Lieutenant Jackson had given me and tearing off the paper masking the lens. It was horribly claustrophobic under the boat, the noise of the waves crashing against its other side almost deafening. I shone the torch straight in front of me and saw the men straight away: three of them dressed in fishermen's garb – trousers, boots, heavy knitted white jumpers – huddled and unmoving among the rocks and seaweed and splintered wood.

As I straightened up again something bumped against the top of my head. I shone the torch upwards, and saw another man hanging upside down behind me, trapped between two barrels that were still secured to the deck with heavy bolts. One of the barrels had fractured, and sticking out of it was a machine gun; the source of the return fire I'd seen coming from the boat. This poor bastard must have been the one who was manning it. I knew as soon as I pulled him down and dragged him out into the stormy half-daylight that there was nothing I could do for him. There were bloodstains across the front of his sweater; his eyes were staring, his mouth hanging open, his skin a dreadful shade of whitish-blue that brought memories of Des roaring back. Lewis, who had clambered through the hole after me, grabbed him under his arms and helped me pull him free before coming back for the others. All of them had been shot to death too. Laboriously, Lewis, Al, Lenand the other men passed the bodies back along the chain until all four were propped up at the bottom of the steps in the cliff. Who were they? I wondered. They might have been dressed as fishermen but with the boat armed to the teeth, it was clear they were anything but.

Then, in the gap between one wave hitting the boat and the next one thundering in, I heard a faint cough. I looked round, aiming the torch beam at the shadows, trying to work out where it had come from. I couldn't see anyone else.

Another cough. It sounded as if it was coming from behind somewhere, or inside somewhere.

Of course. The cabin.

'Hello?' I called.

No answer.

I shouted for Lewis, who was outside the boat again now, to come back. 'What is it?' he said when he reached me. 'Someone else here?'

'I don't know,' I said. 'I thought I heard something, but—'

I paused as it came again, muffled but distinct. '*There.*'

'But where's it coming from?'

'The cabin,' I said. 'Must be.'

Lewis tried to crawl nearer to where I was kneeling, but the rope around his waist stopped him. He cursed. 'Damn it.'

'Untie yourself,' I told him, fumbling with the knots around my waist with stiff, numbed fingers. 'It's no good being tied up like this under here. We need to be able to move freely. We'll be safe enough until we go back out.'

We freed ourselves from the rope, Lewis yelling to the others so that they knew what we were doing. Above us, a wave crashed over the rocks and against the bottom of the boat, making it sway and creak; Lewis glanced up, a brief flicker of anxiety passing across his face, but he did as I asked, and I tied the end of the rope to what remained of the boat's main mast, a jagged stump poking down from the middle of the deck, so it wouldn't get washed away.

Unhindered, I could now crawl across to the boat's cabin, although my path was blocked by a mass of splintered wood from the deck. I set the torch down and Lewis and I pulled the wood aside, working frantically. The cabin was smashed too, the walls buckling outwards and windows and portholes broken, but eventually we managed to get around the side to the door and between us, wrench it open.

'Hello?' I yelled into the darkness beyond. There was no reply; I could hardly see a thing. I climbed in, my hands out in front of me, and my fingers brushed against the back wall of the cabin, which was curiously shallow. I began feeling around until I found what felt like a seam in the wood.

'There's something here – another space at the back of the cabin,' I told Lewis, who was right behind me. 'Shine the torch in.'

He did and I saw, directly in front of me, a board nailed against the wall. When the top of the boat had landed on the rocks, the board had been pushed outwards and started to come away from the wood around it, revealing a space behind. Near the top was a gap my fingers could almost fit into; I managed to wriggle them into it and began to pull. With a crack and a groan and a screech of nails working free, the board came away and a white face stared at me out of the gloom.

'Bloody hell, what's a child doing in here?' Lewis said as I stared back, my heart pounding.

'Hello?' I said.

The kid coughed again. It sounded nasty, coming from deep inside his chest.

'You on your own in there?' I said. He shook his head, a movement so small I almost missed it.

'Who else is with you, buddy?'

He whispered something I didn't quite catch. Holding on to the edge of the doorway, I crouched down, ignoring the pain that zigzagged through my leg. 'What was that?'

He whispered it again, glancing over his shoulder. It sounded like *Mamma*.

'OK,' I said, my mind racing. 'We'll get you out first. Can you hold on to me?'

I reached out and hooked my hands under his arms so I could lift him. He was lighter than I expected, his clothes soaked and filthy.

'*Mamma*,' he croaked as I passed him up to Lewis.

'Got the torch?' I asked. Lewis handed it to me, and I shone it into the space, which was really no more than an alcove. Lying in the corner was what, at first, I thought was a bundle of rags. Then I realised it was another person, their arms thrown over their head as if to protect themselves.

I scrambled across. When I turned them over, I saw it was a woman, her face the same nasty shade of whitish-blue as the fishermen, or whoever they'd been. *Shit*. This must be the kid's mother – was she dead too?

Suddenly I realised that there was water lapping around my knees. It hadn't been there a few minutes ago. The tide was still rising; if Lewis and I stayed in here much longer we'd be carried back out to sea with what remained of the boat.

I hauled the woman out of the cabin, grunting with the effort; she was a dead weight in my arms. 'The other men have got the boy back onto dry land,' Lewis said. Then he saw the woman. 'Shit.'

'We've got to get out of here,' I said. 'I don't think this old tub'll last much longer.'

We tied ourselves together and to Len, Al and the others with the rope again and, carrying the woman awkwardly between us, wriggled back out through the hole in the side of the boat. Just as we did, another enormous wave broke over the top of it. With a horrible groaning sound the boat began to shift sideways as the sea began to drag it back out. I pressed myself flat, clinging to the woman for dear life with one hand and gripping onto the rough surface of the rocks with the other, gasping. A tug on the rope from Lewis got me moving again and somehow we made it back across the rocks and onto the beach that had now almost disappeared entirely, passing the woman to Al and Len.

They carried her up the steps. I barely had the energy to follow them, and Lewis had to hold on to my arm as we made our own way back up onto the clifftop. As the others laid the woman down a safe distance from the cliff edge, I collapsed onto the wet grass, gasping, my head against my knees. I was soaked to the skin and cold to my bones, shivering so hard my teeth clacked together. Somewhere nearby I could hear the boy crying.

A hand touched my shoulder. I looked up and saw Lewis. 'She's alive, just,' he said. He was shivering too. 'We're taking everyone back to the station. Can you manage?'

I nodded, although I didn't refuse when he reached down to help me to my feet. The rope was still round my waist; my fingers were so cold I could hardly manage to untie it. I looked over my shoulder and saw and saw a boiling mass of water where the rocks had been. Of the boat, there was no sign, save for a single plank of wood sticking straight up towards the sky. I shuddered.

'Where to?' I asked Lewis as we reached the camp.

'Medical bay?' he said, then shook his head. 'Blast, can't do that – it's full up with influenza cases at the moment.'

He was right; the 'flu had been tearing through Svarta Ness these last few weeks, taking out men like ninepins. I'd managed to avoid it so far and was hoping to keep it that way.

'How about we put 'em in our hut for now?' Turning, I saw Al Briggs behind me. 'We can bunk in the NAAFI tonight.'

Unable to see a better solution, I nodded.

'I'll see about some dry clothes for everyone,' Al said, and he was off again.

I followed Lewis into our billet. Hut 1 housed eight men altogether – along with me, Lewis and Al, there were Brian Jenkins and Pete Green, two more operators, and three other mechanics, Jamie, Colin and Wilf, who were currently on watch up at the ops site. Against the walls were four metal-framed beds with hard, sectional mattresses we called 'biscuits', one pillow and a khaki-coloured blanket; we had little cabinets next to them for our personal effects and each bed had clothes lines hung around it. There was a radio set on a little table at the far end of the hut, and photographs of Hollywood film stars and various drawings pinned to the walls. In the middle of the hut was a small stove with a flue going straight up out through the curving roof. The stove was still banked up from the previous night, giving out a few meagre rays of heat. As the other men dragged two of the beds together and laid the woman and the boy down on them, Lewis and I went over to it for a minute, rubbing our hands together and trying to get warm.

The woman, who was still unconscious, was around my age, early- to mid-twenties, and the boy, her son, looked about five. They had the same high cheekbones, the same nose, slightly turned up at the end. The boy stared at us without saying anything, wheezing as he struggled for breath. *What on earth were you doing out on that boat?* I thought as I stared back.

Al returned carrying towels, blankets and two sets of pyjamas. 'Damned if I could find owt that'd fit 'em,' he said in his broad accent. 'Better than nowt, though, I reckon.' Dumping everything on one of the other beds nearby, he added, 'The Corp got a call through to Doctor Gaudie at Talafirth – he's on his way.'

We didn't have our own doctor at Svarta Ness; the camp was too small. Instead, like everyone else here, we relied on the island's doctor, Archibald Gaudie, a gruff, no-nonsense man in his sixties, and Fiskersay's nurse Isabel Thomson.

I grabbed a towel. There was no room for embarrassment; working quickly, Lewis and I stripped the woman and the boy out of their sodden clothes and got them dried off. We dressed the woman in the pyjamas, but the boy was too small for anything but a shirt, which completely swamped him. As Al had said, though, it was better than nothing.

Al, meanwhile, had been building up the fire until it roared. As Lewis and I tucked the woman and the boy into our beds, wrapping blankets around them, Flight Lieutenant Jackson came in, water dripping steadily off the hem of his coat.

'Doctor's on his way. How are they?' he said.

'The woman's not come round yet, Sir,' I said.

Jackson shook his head. 'Christ, what filthy bloody weather,' he said as the wind hurled itself at the thin walls of the hut, making them shudder, and a squall of rain drummed against the roof like machine-gun fire. Then he remembered the boy, who was watching him with round eyes. 'I mean, what, ahem, filthy weather. These two are lucky to have survived...' He trailed off. An image of the four men, drowned and lifeless, swam into my mind, and suddenly I wanted a whisky, badly.

I was shivering harder than ever, Lewis too. Jackson noticed. 'Bloody hell, look at the state of you both,' he said, finally noticing my bloody knees and hands, and my shredded trousers. Lewis didn't look much better. 'Go and find something decent to wear and get yourselves a hot drink. Last thing I want is you coming down with pneumonia – this flu that's going round is bad enough. I'll wait with these two until Doctor Gaudie arrives. And Gauthier? Harper?' he added as we turned to follow Al and the others out of the hut. Lewis and I stopped and looked back at him. 'Thank you,' he said. 'You did a damn fine job out there.'

Gratefully, we murmured our own thanks, and went in search of dry clothes and tea.

NINE

HEDDA

I woke slowly, wondering why every muscle in my body hurt, and why, even though I had been asleep, I felt so deeply weary. I could barely open my eyes, and my throat and chest felt as if someone had attacked them with sandpaper. Was I sick?

It didn't matter. I had to get up. I had to prepare breakfast and lay out Anders' clothes for the day. If I didn't, he would be angry – and then there was Eirik to get ready for school…

'Mamma?' a scratchy voice said beside me.

When I turned my head and saw Eirik right beside me, I felt a stab of pure panic. What was he doing in our bed? He wasn't allowed. Anders wouldn't just be angry – he'd be *furious*.

I tried to struggle into a sitting position, alarmed at how much effort it took. 'Eirik!' I hissed. 'What are you doing in Anders' bed?!'

My voice, as croaky as Eirik's, faded as I took in my surroundings: not the bedroom I shared with Anders back in the little house in Kirkenes but a long hut with a curved roof and a row of beds on either side; the two we were lying in were nearest the door and had been pushed together. There were clothes hung on lines around each bed and pairs of boots – men's boots – pushed underneath them. It was completely quiet apart from the odd crackle from the stove in the middle of the hut, and the air smelled of woodsmoke and damp wool.

I stared around me, trying and failing to make sense of it all.

Then, all at once, everything came flooding back. Killing the Wehrmacht officer. Our mad flight from the barn. Arriving in the village by the fjord. The fisherman and his wife who had helped secure us passage on the fishing boat. The storm. The cabin filling up with water. The lantern going out.

Then nothing but fear, noise and pain, from which I couldn't sort out any distinct memories, no matter how hard I tried.

And now I was here. But where was *here?* What had happened to the boat and its crew?

I sat up in the bed and pulled Eirik towards me, allowing him to snuggle into my arms. Someone had put me into a pair of pyjamas – men's pyjamas in worn but clean blue flannel – while Eirik wore just a shirt that came down almost to his ankles. I leaned back against the pillows, looking around again at the other beds, the possessions everywhere, the pictures on the walls. I was so exhausted I felt as if I was in a dream. Perhaps I was. Perhaps, any moment, I'd wake up and be back in that pitch-black cabin with the storm battering the boat to pieces around us.

Then the door opened and a young woman came in. She was pretty, with light-brown hair and a good-humoured face, a leather bag looped over one arm. When she turned to pull the door closed behind her, I saw she was heavily pregnant.

'Oh, good, you're awake,' she said, slipping out of her

smart navy coat and draping it over the clothes line at the end of one of the empty beds. 'I can tell you, it's a lucky thing the soldiers saw you when they did. We'll be making you feel better in no time!'

Although she spoke English, her accent was nothing like the cut-glass accents of the BBC announcers Ingunn and I used to listen to in secret, on the little radio she kept hidden in her kitchen. Her dialect was almost Scandinavian in its crisp rises and falls, 'the soldiers' coming out as '*da sodjers*'; 'making' as '*makkin*''.

Moving energetically despite the size of her bump, she came over, smiling broadly. 'I'm the island's nurse, Isabel Thomson,' she said. 'What's your name? And what about da peerie bairn?'

'I'm Hedda Dahlström,' I said, hesitantly, in English. 'And this is Eirik. What – what do you mean, *peerie bairn*?' Surely she had not just said the Norwegian word *pirre*, which meant tickle?

Isabel laughed. 'Oh, I am sorry, I'm just spikkin' a bit o' Shaetlan. It means *little boy*.'

I still didn't quite understand. Eirik burrowed against me, hiding his face. 'It's all right,' I told him softly in Norwegian. Then I looked at Isabel again. 'Please – can you tell me where we are?'

'You're at the RAF radar station at Svarta Ness, on Fiskersay.'

RAF. The Royal Air Force.

'Where is Fiskersay?' I said. 'I am sorry – I don't know how we got here – I don't remember – we were trying to get to the Shetland Islands from Norway—'

'That's right! Fiskersay's in Shetland – about as far north as it's possible to get before you fall into the sea.'

It was then that I realised *Shaetlan* was *Shetland*. Of course. Oh, how slow my mind felt! I couldn't gather my thoughts at all.

I let Isabel take my temperature, and Eirik's. He began to cough, his thin shoulders shaking.

'Oh dear, oh dear, I don't like the sound of dat,' Isabel said. 'Now, where did Doctor Gaudie say he'd left that medicine?' She looked around. 'Ah!'

I watched as she marched to the little table at the far end of the hut, where, I noticed now, there was a large glass bottle on the table beside the radio set. Isabel could only have a few more weeks to go before her baby was born, but she glowed with good health. I thought ruefully back to my own pregnancy, where I'd become increasingly sick and exhausted as it progressed, my stomach growing while the rest of me shrank because I was unable to keep more than a few mouthfuls of food down at a time. It got so bad that Anders – usually reluctant to spend a single *øre* more than he had to – had summoned the doctor, who, much to his annoyance, had ordered me to stay in bed until Eirik was born. That was when the daily torrent of cruel words had begun, now that I thought about it; when he'd gone from being the distant, but mostly respectful man I married a month or so before – the man who knew Eirik was not his but had told me it didn't matter, that he'd raise my child as his own – to short-tempered and sharp-tongued, until, almost before I knew it, every interaction with him was like walking across a field littered with land mines. That was also when it had dawned on me that he had really married me because he wanted a dogsbody to replace his first wife who had passed away – someone to cook his meals, clean his house, wash his clothes

– and now he had to do all those things for himself again, he was furious with me. And after Eirik was born his resentment had continued, because Eirik was small and needy and it took me a long time to recover from his birth. I didn't even know how much of the money my aunt had bequeathed to him was left; he had always refused to let me access the bank account, saying the husband should control the household finances. What a fool I'd been to think he loved me!

Isabel came back over with the medicine, and between us, we coaxed Eirik into taking a dose.

'Those men that we came with,' I said when Eirik had settled down again, closing his eyes and appearing to drift off to sleep. 'Do you know what happened to them?'

Isabel's sanguine expression grew grave. 'I am afraid they were all drowned,' she said softly, glancing at Eirik. 'The sea was terrible, and a German plane shot at the boat – it drifted onto the rocks and was wrecked. Do you not remember?'

I tried, but my mind seemed to have blanked that out. I shook my head, filled with sudden grief for the men. I hadn't even exchanged two words with them, yet they had been prepared to risk their own lives to help us flee Norway along with them.

'Now.' All at once, Isabel was back to her former cheerful self, leaning over a little awkwardly to adjust my covers. 'Don't fret. Let's get you comfortable. If I go over to the dining hall to see what they've got, d'you think you can manage something to eat? The doctor will be calling in later, and it's a lovely day now dat storm has blown over. If you feel up to it, perhaps you can get wrapped up later and sit outside in the sunshine for a while.'

'When is your baby due?' I asked as she plumped my

pillows. Her smile grew even broader, and I smiled back. I couldn't help it; her cheerfulness was infectious.

'Oh, I've a month or so to go yet – at least, I hope so!' she said. 'There's far too much to do here at the moment, what with so many sodjers down with dat flu and half the island, too. Archie – that's my husband, he's a clerk here at the station and we live in a cottage just down the road – he's hoping for a boy, but I don't mind either way as long as it's healthy. Let's see about getting you some breakfast, eh, and perhaps a cup of tea!'

And off she went.

Later, after Eirik and I had eaten, slept again, and been visited by Doctor Gaudie – a gruff little man whose accent was even broader than Isabel Thomson's – we were allowed to get out of bed. A kind soul had donated some clothes that Isabel brought in to us: a jumper, skirt, blouse and coat for me, and a jumper, trousers and jacket for Eirik, along with a woollen cap and a scarf so long I had to wind it twice around his neck. There were underthings for both of us too, shabby but impeccably clean. I had no idea where our own clothes were; the only things of mine I appeared to have left were my shoes, which had been left under the stove to dry, and Eirik had nothing at all.

'Shall we get some fresh air, like the nurse suggested?' I said to Eirik once he was all wrapped up. Looking reluctant, he nodded slowly, and coughed.

'It will be all right, lille vennen,' I said, rubbing his back in slow circles until he'd caught his breath. 'It's safe here. No one is going to hurt us.'

He wound his fingers through mine, clinging on tightly. My heart ached as I thought about what he had been through. *This damn war – those damn Germans*, I thought bitterly as we made our way outside.

It was, as Isabel had said, a lovely day – chilly, with a stiff breeze, but nowhere near as cold as Kirkenes would have been at this time of year. The hut with the curved roof we had woken up in was one of four. Nearby was a jumble of other buildings, low and square, and a little further away, on top of a long, rounded hill just outside the camp, two tall structures made of criss-crossed metal struts – towers of some kind, which I guessed must be to do with the radar operations. The camp was up on the top of the cliffs and all around were breath-taking views of the hills and the sea, the water gleaming a soft silver in the watery winter sunlight.

The camp appeared all but deserted. Outside one of the buildings, in a sunny, sheltered spot, was a wooden bench. We sat down and I gazed out at the sea while Eirik leaned against me, swinging his legs. Which way was Norway? I had no idea. It seemed impossible to me that we could have come all that way, never mind that we'd made it in one piece, more or less. What would happen to us next? I'd talked, briefly, to Doctor Gaudie about it, and he'd told me that there'd been a few others who'd come to Fiskersay from Norway since the start of the war. From what he understood, as soon as we were well enough, we'd be taken to a place called Lerwick on the main island for something called *processing*, and from there, it was likely we'd be sent to London in England, as the other Norwegian refugees had been. Then, if all went well – he didn't elaborate on what *all* entailed, but I suspected they'd want to make sure I wasn't a spy – he supposed the authorities would find us somewhere in Britain to live.

I thought back over the conversation, replaying it inside my head. Where would we end up? Would we ever see Norway again? And what, I wondered reluctantly, was happening to Anders? Had the Germans arrested him too?

I hope so, a tiny, rebellious voice inside my head whispered, and I was immediately horrified at myself.

Lost in thought, and lulled by the soft boom of the sea breaking against the cliffs, I didn't notice the man walking towards us until Eirik whispered, 'Mamma, it's the man who rescued us from the boat.'

I looked round and a wave of adrenalin went through my entire body as I saw a man in a smart blue uniform coming our way, making my hands tingle. *Magnus? No, it can't be. That's impossible.*

As the man got closer I felt the adrenalin ebb away, leaving me feeling slightly shaky. Of course it wasn't Magnus. He was younger, for a start, around the same age as me. It was his hair, dark and curling slightly, and the slouching set of his shoulders, that reminded me of Magnus. But he didn't appear to have Magnus's confidence – the confidence that, as a naive eighteen-year-old, had drawn me in and held me under its spell until it was too late – or his arrogance. This man had lines in his forehead and around his mouth from anxiety, pain, or both; he walked with a pronounced limp, I noticed, perhaps from an old gunshot wound or a break.

'Hello,' I said, because I was sure that by now he must have realised I was staring at him.

He gave me a small smile. 'Hello. You're up and about, then?'

His accent wasn't British. Was he American?

'Bill Gauthier,' he said. He gave me another small smile and stuck out his hand. 'Pleased to meet you.'

I shook his hand. 'Hedda Dahlström. This is Eirik. We're very pleased to meet you too.' I swallowed. 'Eirik tells me you are the one who saved us.'

Bill gave a self-deprecating laugh. 'Oh, that wasn't just me. Practically the whole station was out there trying to get to you.'

'Well, I am very grateful,' I said, my face warming slightly. 'Please tell the others thank you, too.'

'Don't mention it. And I will.'

There was a moment of silence that stretched out for just a little too long. Eirik clung to me, looking sideways at Bill from beneath his eyelashes.

'Well,' Bill said at last. 'I'd better get going.'

I nodded. As he turned and limped away, I was again reminded overwhelmingly of Magnus, the man I'd given my heart to all those years ago and who had pulled it to pieces.

The man who had made me realise that love simply wasn't worth it.

TEN

BILL

'It's a terrible shame about those poor men,' said Bertha Sutherland, the postmistress and owner of Sutherland's Stores, as I paid for my things. She shook her head. 'They're burying them up at the kirkyard tomorrow. Things must be dreadful in Norway for them to take such a risk. Thank God the woman and child survived.'

I nodded, murmuring in agreement, and escaped outside. As I went through the door I could hear Bertha still talking in shocked tones to other people in the store about what had happened.

It was three days now since the Norwegian boat had been driven onto the rocks below Svarta Ness. The weather was dry again, rare for this time of year, although it was bitterly cold and the needle on the barometer that hung in the station dining hall had been dropping steadily since this morning. I'd got a few free hours so I walked into Talafirth to see if I could buy stamps, envelopes and tobacco. Usually I kept to myself when I came into the village, as I did up at the station, but from the moment I'd set foot in Talafirth this afternoon I'd been mobbed by locals wanting to know what had happened, and about the woman, Hedda, and her son. As one of those *sodjers up at da camp*, I was a prime source of information about the incident, and – understandably – the locals' appetite for it was insatiable. I'd tried my best to answer their questions, but now I felt exhausted. It wasn't as if I could say much, anyway; although most of the boat had been washed back out to sea by the storm, we had recovered the two barrels containing the hidden machine guns – the guns I'd seen firing in vain back at the Ju 88 – and been warned by Flight Lieutenant Jackson to keep their discovery to ourselves. It was clear those men had been no ordinary fishermen – they must have been Norwegian resistance men, which was why the Germans had fired on them. But what about Hedda? What had she been doing there? That question, more than any other, was the one constantly playing on my mind.

I rolled a cigarette, deciding to walk back to Svarta Ness via Talafirth harbour. My leg was aching, my shoulder too, but I gritted my teeth and tried to ignore the pain, hoping the slightly longer walk would do it some good. When I reached the harbour, it was unusually busy. I soon saw why: the *Zetland Princess* was docked at the slipway. She was the supply ship that did the rounds of the outlying islands three times a week, weather permitting, ferrying cargo and passengers between them and Lerwick in mainland Shetland. A small queue of people were waiting to board, mostly locals along with a few servicemen. Among them was a woman and a child, the woman gripping the child's hand as he struggled and tried to pull away. My heart jumped. I recognised them: Hedda and Eirik.

Tears were streaming down Eirik's face. He was shaking

his head and saying the same word over and over again. '*Nei. Nei. Nei.*' I didn't know any Norwegian, but I was pretty certain he meant *no, no, no.*

Hedda's face wore a mix of worry, exasperation and despair, while those around her looked on in sympathy and puzzlement. Hedda said something to Eirik in rapid Norwegian but he just began to cry harder.

Hedda looked round. Our eyes met and I felt my heart do the same odd little jump it had when I came across her and Eirik sitting outside the hut the other day. *Help me*, her expression said. The gangway had been lowered now and the queue was shuffling forwards, the captain checking papers as people went on board. I went over to Hedda and Eirik. 'Everything OK?' I asked.

Hedda shook her head. 'He doesn't want to go on the boat,' she said. 'He's scared – he thinks we will be shot at by a German aeroplane again.'

'You're leaving, then?'

She nodded, her expression strained. 'We are going to Lerwick, and after that we are being sent to London in England so they can check I am not a spy.'

The queue moved again. Hedda tried to move Eirik forwards and he wailed, '*Nei, nei!*' again, digging his heels into the cobbles. For such a small, scrawny kid he was surprisingly strong; Hedda couldn't move him.

'Hey, buddy,' I said. I considered crouching down, but I knew my leg wouldn't thank me for it, so instead I got down on one knee, ignoring the water that soaked into my trouser leg from the damp ground and the curious stares from the onlookers who had gathered, drawn by the scene Eirik was making. 'Eirik, hey. It's OK. No one's going to hurt you.'

I wasn't sure if he understood me or not. Anyway, it made no difference; he wouldn't even look at me. He was getting more and more hysterical.

'Can you move it along there, please?' called the ship's captain, a brisk English stiff-upper-lip type, looking exasperated. Everyone else had boarded the boat now.

Hedda said something to Eirik in a stern tone and tried to pick him up. He thrashed in her arms, screaming, his voice hoarse, and managed to wrench right out of her grip. Seeing he was going to run, I grabbed his arm to stop him and he began coughing, so hard that he started choking. He turned his head – away from me, thankfully – and vomited spectacularly all over himself and the cobbles at his feet.

'*Min Gud!* Eirik!' Hedda cried.

The ship's captain shook his head, his lip curling in disgust. 'I'm not taking him like that,' he said, and turned away. 'All aboard!' he called, and the *Zetland Princess's* gangplank began to go up, leaving me on the quay with Hedda and Eirik and a small knot of concerned onlookers.

'Eirik,' Hedda said in a pleading tone as Eirik began to sob. She looked up at me, her eyes clouded with panic.

Damn. 'We need to take him somewhere quiet,' I said, carefully lifting the wailing Eirik into my arms and trying to ignore the stench of vomit.

'Bring him to my house,' a woman said, stepping forwards. 'I live just up there.' She indicated a grey stone house standing on its own a little way back from the harbour. 'We'll get the poor bairn cleaned up in no time, and you look like you could do with a cup of tea,' she added, touching Hedda's arm gently.

Looking dazed, Hedda let the woman guide her towards the house. I followed with Eirik still sobbing in my arms.

Inside the woman's cottage, which was tiny, but spotlessly clean, I was instructed to lie him down on a sofa in the parlour, and she bustled off to fetch cloths and warm water. Hedda sank down beside Eirik, her face pale, while I hovered in the doorway, not knowing what to do with myself.

Hedda looked up at me. 'Thank you, Bill,' she said. 'And I am sorry – he has always been a sensitive child, but—'

'Don't worry about it,' I said quickly, shaking my head. 'Poor kid couldn't help it. If I was that age and I'd been through what he has, I'd be terrified out of my mind too.'

Hedda brought up a hand to the side of her face. 'I suppose we'll have to come back to the camp – will they be angry with us?'

'I don't think so,' I said diplomatically. 'I'm heading back there now. I'll tell someone so they can send a truck over the hill to pick you up.'

'Would you? I'd be so grateful.'

'It's no problem.'

Hedda seemed about to say something else when the woman came back with a bowl of hot water, soap, cloths and towels, and a small pile of neatly folded clean clothes. 'These were my son's,' she said, giving them to Hedda. 'He's all grown up now – away with the Navy – so he won't mind if your laddie wears them. Let's get him cleaned up, shall we?'

The two women busied themselves over Eirik, and I slipped away. As I walked back to the camp, finally lighting my cigarette, it started to spit with rain. I was replaying the scene on the quay in my head, seeing again the desperate look in Hedda's eyes as our gazes connected and remembering how my heart had given that strange little jolt inside my chest, as if some invisible force had leaped between us.

I gave myself a mental shake, turning my thoughts to the half-finished letter to Rose that was sitting on my bunk in the entertainment hall, where I and the other men from Hut 1 had been temporarily relocated. But even that brought my thoughts back round to Hedda. In the part of the letter I'd already written I'd told Rose what had happened the other day, albeit briefly so as not to attract the attention of the censor. I wondered what she'd make of it all.

As I stubbed out the end of my cigarette, I caught the unmistakable sour whiff of vomit rising from my coat sleeve. Raising it to my nose, I sniffed cautiously and made a face. *Damn it.* Looked like I'd have to get my coat laundered when I got back to the station, as well as breaking the news to Flight Lieutenant Jackson that Hedda and Eirik were still on the island.

Head down against the rain, which was getting heavier now, I walked the rest of the way back to the station, trying to figure out what I was going to tell him.

ELEVEN

HEDDA

As promised, Bill arranged for a truck to pick us up from the cottage and bring us back to the station. The woman – whose name, in my anxiety over Eirik, I hadn't even thought to ask – told me she'd hang onto his clothes, wash them and bring them up to the camp. I was so grateful I could have hugged her. I was grateful to Bill for sending the truck, too; by then it was raining hard and the wind was picking up again, and Eirik, although recovered, was quiet and listless. If we'd had to walk, it would have taken me hours to get him back to the camp.

Flight Lieutenant Jackson, the Commanding Officer in charge of the radar station, was waiting for us when we got back. He was in his early forties, around the same height as Bill, with a neat moustache and steady grey eyes. 'Weather's taking a turn for the worse now – doubt we'll be able to get you on another ship for weeks. The flying boats won't be able to get here either, and there's nowhere else on this island to land a smaller plane even when it isn't blowing a gale,' he said. 'I've already been on the phone to London – MI5 have asked us to interview you at the Manor, and then we'll have to decide what we're going to do with you. In the meantime, I'm afraid you and your son will have to stay in your hut. You will understand, I'm sure, that until we've checked your credentials and looked into your links with the Norwegian Resistance, that we have to be extremely cautious.'

What he meant, of course, was *We have to check you're not a spy.*

'I'm sorry,' I said, unable to look at him directly. I could tell from his tone he was annoyed, and it made anxiety churn inside me. I found myself flinching away from him, waiting for him to put his face close to mine and for the shouting to start, although of course he did nothing of the sort. All he said, as he went to hold the door open for me, was, 'And I must ask you to say nothing to anyone about those men being in the Resistance.'

'Of course not,' I said.

Not only did Eirik and I have to stay in the hut, but a guard was posted outside to make sure we didn't leave, even for meals. Although I understood the need for caution – until they had interviewed me and made sure I was not a spy, we could not be allowed to roam around the station – I couldn't help feeling a little humiliated. Every night, Eirik woke shouting from nightmares about the dying German officer and the voyage on the boat that had so nearly ended in disaster, and would cling to me, sobbing, 'Mamma, I don't want you to go to prison. Please don't leave me.' There was nothing I could say to reassure him. And now we were being treated like criminals!

They are only doing their job, I reminded myself. *There is a war on, and I have come from a country occupied by the enemy. They are quite right in thinking I could be a spy.*

★

The following day, Eirik and I were taken down to a house at the edge of the radar station called the Manor. Flight Lieutenant Jackson was waiting for us in what looked like a dining room but was now clearly some sort of office, sitting behind a table with a man my own age who he introduced as Sergeant Black. While Flight Lieutenant Jackson quizzed me on everything imaginable – my name, age, where I'd come from, my marital status, work and even my appearance – Sergeant Black jotted down my answers to his questions on a notepad.

'You say that *Milorg* were helping you get to Sweden after you were caught passing messages to the prisoners in Kirkenes,' Flight Lieutenant Jackson said at last. 'What changed? Why did you come to Shetland instead?'

I swallowed hard, my skin prickling as I relived those dreadful moments in the barn all over again: the Wehrmacht officer asking for our papers; Eirik crying out in panic; the man turning his gun on him; my lunge forwards with the pitchfork, not thinking about what I was doing until I had already done it and it was too late to take it back.

Murderer. I am a murderer.

But what choice had I had?

I drew in a shaky breath and glanced at Eirik, my heart pounding. 'May I have a piece of paper, please?' I asked. 'And a pen?'

'Whatever for?' Flight Lieutenant Jackson said.

'My son speaks enough English to understand what I'm saying,' I said quietly as Eirik looked at me with round eyes, 'and he's already badly traumatised.'

Eirik's hand wormed its way into mine; he gripped my fingers so tightly they started to go numb.

Flight Lieutenant Jackson frowned into his moustache. 'Black, would you pass Mrs Dahlström some paper and something to write with?'

'Yes, Sir.' Sergeant Black tore his notes off the pad, then slid it and his pen across the table to me.

'*Lille vennen*, let go of my hand,' I told Eirik gently.

'Perhaps you would like to take this young chap to look at the jigsaw puzzles in the other room, Black,' Flight Lieutenant Jackson said, but Eirik shook his head fiercely.

'I want to stay with Mamma!' he said, his voice trembling.

'It's OK,' I said to him in English. 'You can stay, but Mamma needs her hand to write with.'

Reluctantly, he let go of me, biting his lower lip.

I wrote fast, not reading back, my writing scrawling across the page because my hand was trembling so much. When I had finished, I pushed the notepad back across the table for the Flight Lieutenant to read. I felt sick.

Flight Lieutenant Jackson scanned the page, his frown deepening. 'I see,' he said at last. 'Of course, there's probably no way of corroborating this…'

'I promise you, Sir,' I said, drawing myself up and squaring my shoulders, and trying desperately to convey a confidence I did not feel. 'What I have written is the truth. I'm not here to spy for the Germans, and wherever we end up, all I ask is you do not separate me from my son. He has suffered enough.'

There was a moment of silence, the atmosphere in the room tense.

'Mamma, these men are very good at asking questions, aren't they?' Eirik said quietly in Norwegian, looking up at me.

'What was that?' Flight Lieutenant Jackson asked.

I gave him a small smile; I couldn't help it. 'He says you are very good at asking questions.'

To my relief, the two men permitted themselves a smile too, and all at once the tension in the room seemed to drain away. We'd passed their test, I realised.

'Well, he certainly seems to have got the measure of us,' Flight Lieutenant Jackson said, clearing his throat. He nodded at Sergeant Black. 'Will you write up the report and telephone it through to London when it's ready? Tell them I'm satisfied that Mrs Dahlström is who she says she is, and that we're prepared to offer her and her son sanctuary here in Shetland.'

'Yes, Sir,' Sergeant Black said. He got up and went over to another table in the corner, where there was a typewriter and a big black telephone.

'Right, Mrs Dahlström.' Flight Lieutenant Jackson cleared his throat. 'If you and Eirik are to remain in Fiskersay for the time being, we'd better see if we can find the two of you a more suitable place to stay. My men will be wanting their hut back – it's rather inconvenient having the entertainment hall out of action.'

'Thank you, Sir,' I said. 'I'm grateful for everything you and your men have done for us – very grateful indeed. And I am sorry we have caused so much trouble.'

He waved my apology away. 'Can't be helped. This whole war is a dreadful business.' He stood and held out a hand. 'Let me be the first to formally welcome you and your son to the island. If you'd like to return to the hut for the time being, I'll go and see what can be done.'

'Thank you,' I said again, standing too, and shaking his

hand as I fought back tears of relief. I was more grateful to him than he could ever know.

Two hours later, everything had been arranged. Eirik and I would leave the camp tomorrow morning, and we'd be staying – Flight Lieutenant Jackson called it *billeted* – at a croft half a mile away with a couple called the Sinclairs. I wondered what they would be like and if they'd mind us being there.

By late afternoon, another storm was lashing the radar station with full force, rain battering against the walls of the hut and the wind screaming like a siren. The stove went out, and when I went to light it again I realised there were no matches left.

'I'm going across to the office to ask Mr Thomson for some matches,' I told Eirik, who was lying on his bed, reading a copy of *The Beano* someone had brought to the camp for us. I wasn't sure how many of the words he understood, but he was looking at the pictures with a rapt expression. 'I will only be a few minutes.'

The anxious glance he shot me pierced my heart. 'I promise I'll be as quick as I can,' I added. 'You don't want to go out there – the weather's terrible.'

'Yes, Mamma,' he said, although he still looked unsure.

'When I come back you can read me some of your comic. How about that?'

He nodded, and I went over to kiss him on top of his head. 'You are so brave, *lille vennen*,' I told him, closing my eyes for a moment. 'I am so proud of you.'

I still didn't want to leave him, but the hut was growing colder by the minute. I wrapped my shawl – another donation

– around me and braced myself to open the door. Outside, the wind slammed into me like a giant fist; it was almost dark, the rain filled with shards of ice. Thankfully, the office was only a short distance from the hut, but I had to cling to the walls of the buildings as I walked so that I wasn't blown off my feet. It was a relief to get inside again.

The office door was closed, but Archie Thomson was still there; through the small window in the top of the door I could see the light from a lamp, burning low. I knocked and waited for him to say, *Come in*.

Instead, I heard a low groan.

I knocked again and pushed the door, which was slightly open, with my fingertips. It creaked. 'Mr Thomson?' I said.

My only answer was another groan. Heart thumping, I stepped into the office, wondering what I was going to see. Was Archie ill? Hurt? His desk was empty. There was a neat stack of papers in a wire tray on one side, a big black telephone like the one in the Manor on the other, and a typewriter with a dust cover over it. The lamp had been placed on top of a set of metal drawers in the corner, guttering slightly as if it was about to go out.

'Mr Thomson?' I said.

'Who's that?' a woman's voice said, thready and faint. I looked round and saw a slumped figure on the chair in the corner, just beyond the small circle of light thrown out by the lamp. Grabbing the lamp, I went over there. 'Isabel?' I said.

'The baby's coming,' she said, looking up at me with an expression like a hunted animal. Her face was pale, sweat standing out in beads on her forehead. 'I've been having pains all day and now my waters have broken. I tried to call Doctor Gaudie but the phone lines are down, so I came to fetch Archie instead but he's not here. I don't know if he—' She broke off, screwing up her face and gasping as another contraction hit her. 'Please help me,' she whimpered, and suddenly I was thrown back to that afternoon in the bomb shelter at Kirkenes, kneeling beside Anna Larsen. For several long seconds, I was frozen, overwhelmed by panic, remembering how Anders had shouted inside my head then, as he was shouting at me now: *You, help her? What a joke!*

No. Think, Hedda, think.

I whirled round and snatched up the telephone receiver but it was, as Isabel had said, quite dead.

'You can't have your baby here,' I said, looking round me. The room was no bigger than a cupboard, the atmosphere damp and cold. 'There's nowhere to lie down. Do you think you can stand up and lean on me?'

Isabel nodded, closing her eyes. I helped her to her feet and she slumped against me. My mind was racing as I tried to work out where to take her. I knew there was a medical hut here, but it would be full of men. Where, then?

'I am going to take you back to the hut I am staying in,' I told her. 'It is only a short distance away from here, and there is a bed for you to lie on.'

She nodded again.

We made our way outside into the screaming wind, pausing halfway to the hut as Isabel had another contraction. 'I can't do this,' she moaned when it had passed. 'It hurts.'

'You will be all right,' I said as we reached the hut, injecting a certainty into my voice I couldn't have been further from feeling. 'I will help you. I trained as a nurse too, back in Norway.'

Isabel looked round at me with a startled expression. 'Did you?'

I decided this was not the moment to tell her I had only officially worked at Oslo hospital for a few months, or that I had no experience delivering babies. I took her inside and she lay down on my bed.

'Eirik, come,' I said brightly, holding out a hand as Eirik looked round at Isabel in surprise, a question forming on his lips. 'Would you like to go to the dining hall?'

'But Mamma...' he said, holding out the comic.

'You can bring that with you,' I said. 'Come on!' I was keen to get him out of here before Isabel's next contraction came; he wouldn't understand why she was crying out and it would scare him.

'I'll be back in just a minute,' I told Isabel, who pressed her lips together. I hustled Eirik out of the hut and we hurried over to the dining hall.

'Mamma, you're walking too fast!' he complained.

'I don't want to be out in this rain and wind,' I told him, almost having to shout over the noise of the gale. 'And you don't want your comic to get wet! Come on, I'll race you!'

By the time we reached the dining hall, I was breathless and dishevelled. Inside, it was busy, and everyone turned to stare at me as I burst in. To my relief, I spotted Bill sitting by himself at a table in the corner, his hands cupped around a mug. When he saw me, he stood up.

'Hedda?' he said. 'Are you OK?'

TWELVE

BILL

Hedda swallowed, trying to compose herself, and glanced at Eirik. 'It's Isabel Thomson, Mr Thomson's wife. She's in the hut. She's going to have her baby,' she said in a low voice.

I gaped at her. 'What?'

Some of the others – Lewis Harper, Al Briggs and Len Kane – had got up and come over too.

'Do any of you know where Mr Thomson is?' Hedda asked. I could see she was trying to remain calm for Eirik's sake, but she couldn't quite hide the panic in her voice.

'Archie went over to Lerwick on the boat this morning,' Al said. 'I expect he's stuck there because of the storm. Has anyone tried calling the doc?'

'The phone lines aren't working,' Hedda said.

'Bloody hell. That's all we need.' Len ran a hand through his hair, then noticed Eirik. 'Sorry. Pretend you didn't hear that, eh, kid?'

Hedda swallowed again, her face flushing. 'I think I can help her – before I had Eirik I – I trained to be a nurse.'

'Really?' I said.

She nodded. 'Can one of you please fetch me some hot water,

soap and some towels and bring them to the hut? And some fuel and matches for the stove? Oh, and scissors, and some string.'

'I'll do it,' I said without thinking. 'I'm not on watch until eleven.'

'And how about you leave Eirik with us?' Lewis said. He smiled at Eirik who was gazing at the adults with a bewildered expression, a rather damp-looking comic hanging from his fingers. 'What's that you've got there, old chap? *The Beano?* Rather partial to that one myself. Been a while since I read it, though – why don't you come over here and tell me all about it? My name's Lewis, by the way, and these fellows here are Al and Len. I'm from Oxford, Al's from Yorkshire, and Len's come all the way from New Zealand, can you believe it?'

Lewis steered Eirik back to his table, keeping up a stream of cheerful chatter. Hedda watched them go, frowning, but the distraction seemed to work; soon Eirik and Lewis were sitting together at the table, their heads bent over the comic.

'He'll be fine,' I reassured her. 'Lewis has a couple of kid brothers, and after their mother died he helped look after them when he was home from school in the holidays.'

'I'll get the nipper a cup of cocoa,' Len said.

'And I'll see what I can do about that bloody phone,' Al said.

'Thank you,' Hedda said. 'Bill, I will meet you back at the hut.' I nodded and she hurried away.

Ten minutes later, I'd gathered everything I needed: wood and coal for the stove, which I loaded into a kitbag; a bucket of hot water over one arm; folded towels shoved under the other and the scissors, string and a bar of soap jammed in my pocket. I also had a rolled-up blanket looped over my shoulders. With the wind shoving me this way and that I staggered over to Hut 1; my arms were so full I had to go in backwards. 'Bill!'

Hedda said behind me, her voice full of relief as she came to my rescue.

I heard a groan and looked round. Isabel Thomson was lying on one of the beds – *my* bed – pressing her face sideways into the pillow. She gave a cry, arching her back and clutching the blankets in white-knuckled fists.

Oh, hell. It looked as if the baby was almost here already.

'You'll need to wash your hands,' Hedda said when I had got the stove going, and it dawned on me, with a faint sense of horror, that she was expecting me to stay. 'Then I need you to help me get this blanket underneath her.'

There was nothing for it but to do what she asked. As we tucked the blanket under Isabel I marvelled at how calm Hedda seemed, how in control; she must have been an excellent nurse back in Norway.

'It's all right,' she told Isabel when she opened her eyes and saw me. 'We haven't been able to reach Doctor Gaudie yet, but Bill is here to help.'

I would have felt embarrassed if I wasn't so scared, but none of that mattered; Hedda seemed to take it all in her stride, stripping Isabel down to her petticoat and giving me orders in competent, measured tones. I fetched more hot water, and handed her towels as she murmured words of encouragement and wiped the other woman's forehead with a cloth. Isabel moaned and sobbed. The stove was roaring now, the hut stiflingly warm and the air thick with the smell of blood and sweat. I thought again about Rose insisting she wanted a boy and a girl after we were married, and tried to imagine putting her through this. How could any woman stand it? What if something went wrong?

Suddenly, it was time. As the storm reached its zenith outside, the wind and rain battering against the hut, Hedda helped Isabel half sit up and moved swiftly to the end of the bed, saying 'All right, now you must push. *Push.*'

I kept my eyes averted, letting Isabel grip my hand, her fingers crushing mine until I had no sensation left in them at all. Isabel let out a dreadful sound, somewhere between a scream and a howl. 'Yes. Again,' Hedda said.

'I *can't*,' Isabel whimpered.

'Yes, you can. You are nearly there.'

Isabel gave another one of those awful animal howls. As it faded away, there was a moment of absolute silence, and then a small, reedy-sounding cry.

'Bill, is there another towel?' Hedda said as Isabel's hand slipped from mine. There was one left; flexing my numb fingers, I went to fetch it.

'It's a boy, and he is healthy, look,' Hedda said. Her voice trembled, and when I finally dared to look up – when I saw the tiny, red, wrinkled scrap she was holding, his face screwed up and mouth open in a toothless O as he bawled furiously – I realised she had been scared too; as scared as I was. She was better at hiding it, that was all.

Hedda wrapped the baby in the towel and placed him on Isabel's chest. 'All right,' she said to her, her voice steady again now. 'Now we must deliver the afterbirth, and then we can cut the cord.' She looked up at me, her face flushed, a loose curl of hair stuck to her forehead. 'Bill, will you fetch more hot water? And some tea?'

'Sure,' I said. It came out as a croak, and I had to clear my throat. 'I'll see what I can do.'

Weak with relief, I got out of there, barely noticing the storm as I headed back over to the dining hall in search of hot water, tea, and a bottle of brandy, too, if I could find one.

Thirteen

HEDDA
December

'Have you heard?' Elizabeth Sinclair said as she placed a loaf of bread on the kitchen table and I set out the plates. 'Archie and Isabel are calling the bairn William Eric.'

I looked at her, startled but pleased. 'Are they?' I still felt dazed when I recalled the events of that night. I had been so certain it would be a disaster – and if it had been a difficult birth or if Isabel hadn't been so young and healthy, it might have been – yet everything had gone smoothly. Was that really my doing? For the first time ever, a new, assertive voice spoke up inside my head, saying to the spectre of Anders who inhabited my mind: *You see? I am capable! I am!*

But it was thanks to Bill too, of course. Without him, I was sure I'd have gone to pieces that night.

Elizabeth's face crinkled in a smile. She was almost eighty, but as spry and energetic as a woman twenty years younger, and she reminded me, almost startlingly, of Ingunn, with her fluffy white hair and wiry frame. Eirik had noticed the similarity too; on our first night here, he'd turned to me after we had climbed into bed and said, in a whisper, 'Mamma, does *Tante* Ingunn have a sister in Shetland?'

The door to the cottage thumped open as Elizabeth's

husband, Donald, came in from feeding the sheep. He was Elizabeth's opposite physically in every way: tall with broad, sloping shoulders, and enormous hands that could wind a skein of wool into a ball for his wife as skilfully as they could mend a fence or lift stones to repair a wall, and although he was only a year younger than her his hair was still dark, with only a few threads of grey. The Sinclairs, Elizabeth had told me, had lived on this croft for generations. Donald had been a friend of her brother; she'd met him at a dance at Talafirth, and they'd married at eighteen. It was clear he still adored her, and she him; sometimes when I saw the way he touched the back of her hand or the way she'd look at him, her eyes soft and a half smile on her lips, I'd feel a small, tugging pain beneath my breastbone I couldn't quite explain.

'Ach, it's a day o' dirt oot there,' Donald said in his rumbling voice as he sat down heavily in the chair by the stove to remove his boots. His accent was the broadest I had heard yet, but, bar the odd word, I could understand the local dialect quite easily now.

'Now, where's da peerie bairn?' Donald said, turning with a smile to look for Eirik, who was sitting in the corner, absorbed in yet another copy of *The Beano* that one of Bill's friends, Lewis, had sent over from the station. Eirik looked round at Donald and grinned, jumping up to show him what he was reading. Although we'd only been here a week the two of them were already firm friends, and Donald didn't seem to mind Eirik following him around like a shadow as he got on with his work around the croft. Eirik's English wasn't quite as fluent as mine yet, but he had spoken it back in Kirkenes and was picking up more all the time, often mimicking Donald's broad Shetland accent and making him roar with laughter.

Watching them, I smiled too. The cottage was tiny, with only three rooms – the kitchen, a bedroom where Donald and Elizabeth slept and a parlour built as a later addition to the original house, where Eirik and I had a bed made up – but it was homely and cosy, and my son had colour in his face again for the first time in as long as I could remember, his cough almost gone. Only his nightmares seemed to linger. Most nights I still found myself surfacing from the clinging grip of my own bad dreams to hear him crying out in his sleep. I'd have to gently wake him so he didn't disturb Donald and Elizabeth and hold him until he was calm again.

The rich smell of mutton stew filled the air: dinner was ready. Just as we were sitting down to eat, there was a knock at the door.

'Now, who could dat be?' Donald grumbled, getting up again. He went to the door, opening it again just a crack against the cold wind and sleety rain that had been driving down outside all day. I heard a man's voice, and when Donald came back to the table he had an envelope in his hand. 'One of da sodjers from da camp,' he said. 'It's for you.' He handed me the envelope.

My name was written on the front in a neat, official-looking hand. With some trepidation, I slit the envelope carefully with my knife so that Elizabeth could reuse it. What did they want? Were they going to try and send me and Eirik to London again? Surely not in this weather. The island had been battered by storms again for the last six days and even the ship that usually brought supplies to Fiskersay hadn't been able to dock at Talafirth yet.

There was a note inside: a brief summons, written on a

typewriter and signed by Flight Lieutenant Jackson, asking me to attend the camp tomorrow afternoon. It didn't say why.

'What's wrong, Mamma?' Eirik asked me.

I tried to smooth away my frown. 'Nothing, *lille vennen*.' Then I added, in English for Elizabeth and Donald's benefit, 'I must go up to the camp tomorrow – would you be able to keep an eye on Eirik for me?'

'Of course,' Elizabeth said.

That night, I lay awake for a long time, wondering what the following afternoon would bring. The Sinclairs had made me and Eirik feel so welcome. It would be a wrench to leave them, especially so soon. But there was nothing I could do about it. Eirik and I were lucky even to have survived the journey to Shetland, and comfortable though the Sinclairs' cottage was, we were in limbo here, biding our time until the authorities finally decided what they wanted to do with us. In a way, it would be a relief to finally know. Wherever we ended up, at least Eirik might be able to return to school; perhaps I'd be even able to find work somewhere.

As for returning to Norway, and to Anders, I decided I wasn't going to think about that for now. I turned onto my side, being careful not to disturb Eirik, who for once was sleeping peacefully. As I closed my eyes, a face formed in the darkness behind my closed lids: Bill's.

After Isabel's baby was born, and I was sure it was safe to leave them both to sleep for a while, we'd returned to the dining hall and talked for a while over mugs of brandy-laced tea. There, I'd found out he wasn't from America, but Canada, and he used to be on a heavy bomber crew. When he'd said *used to*, his expression closed up; guessing it had something to do with his limp, and the sadness set fast into the lines of his face, I'd quickly changed the subject.

What had happened to him? I wondered now as sleep finally began to steal over me, my thoughts starting to fracture. I hadn't seen him since that night, yet he kept drifting into my mind. There was something about him that made me want to reach out, touch my fingertips to the grooves in his forehead and around his mouth and smooth them away, as if by doing so I could take away whatever it was that pained him.

Why are you thinking about him? I thought, my eyes opening again. *Stop. It's unlikely you will even see him again. And you're a married woman.*

I spent the rest of the night gazing up into the darkness, wide awake, my mind racing.

The next morning, heavy-eyed from lack of sleep, I walked up to the camp. The rain had stopped but the wind was still cold and cutting and the air smelled like snow. Flight Lieutenant Jackson was waiting for me in his office in the Manor. To my surprise, Doctor Gaudie was there too.

'Mrs Dahlström,' Flight Lieutenant Jackson said as I sat down. 'Thank you for coming. We won't keep you.' He glanced at Doctor Gaudie, cleared his throat, then continued, 'It's been decided, for the sake of the mother and baby, that Mr and Mrs Thomson are going to take young William over to Aberdeen and stay with relatives for the duration of the war. Which creates something of a problem, as it leaves Fiskersay without a nurse.'

In my foggy state, I nodded, trying to understand what all this had to do with me.

'Doctor Gaudie?' Flight Lieutenant Jackson said.

The doctor nodded. 'The Flight Lieutenant here tells me that you trained as a nurse in Norway,' he said in his gruff voice. 'Is that correct?'

'Yes,' I said. 'I got all my qualifications – I even worked in a hospital in Oslo for a short while. But I—' I swallowed. 'I became pregnant, and had to leave. Then, after I moved to Kirkenes and married, I began to work again in a – how do you say it—'

'An unofficial capacity?'

I nodded. 'At the time – this was before the war – the town was growing because of people coming in to work at the iron ore mine and bringing their families with them. Doctor Johannessen was struggling to manage.' I went on to tell him about the incident with the girl who had been kicked by the horse, and how, after that, Doctor Johannessen had asked if I would help him.

'And tell me, why did you want to become a nurse?' Doctor Gaudie said when I'd finished. I didn't get the feeling he was interrogating me, though; there was genuine interest in his eyes, as if he was talking to a colleague.

'It was because of my father,' I said. 'He was a doctor, and when I was growing up I used to spend time in his surgery, helping him organise his supplies and order medicines and bandages...' A wave of emotion suddenly rolled over me, making a lump rise in my throat as I remembered those precious hours I'd spend with him, hoping to get a *well done* or a *you've done a good job today, Hedda* as I showed him the shelves in his store cupboard with their neat rows of bottles, tins and jars, everything checked twice against the inventory. He was so busy that it was the only time I ever

spent with him; he rarely took holidays or time off, much
to the annoyance of my mother who would argue with him
about it late at night when they thought I was in bed, asleep.
I had never been close to my mother – even as a child, I was
tall and clumsy, the opposite of the dainty, pretty girl she had
dreamed of having – but when I was with my father I felt
wanted, purposeful. It made his wholesale rejection of me
when I discovered I was pregnant even harder to bear. I'd
expected it of my mother, but to have him turn away from me
too had been a knife through my heart.

I realised the doctor and Flight Lieutenant Jackson were
waiting for me to continue. 'So I decided that when I grew up
I'd be a nurse, so I could help people like he did,' I finished,
hoping that the feelings battling inside me just now had not
shown on my face.

Doctor Gaudie cleared his throat. 'Well, you did a grand
job delivering that baby – if it wasn't for you, young Isabel
could have been in a lot of trouble. Would you be interested
in stepping into her shoes while she's away?'

It took a few moments for his words to sink in; for me to
realise that not only was he offering me and Eirik a safe place
to stay and the opportunity to be useful again, but giving me
the chance to earn some money, too. I stared at him.

'We will make all the necessary arrangements for your pay
and so on,' Flight Lieutenant Jackson said. 'Your son will be
found a place at the school, and I will talk to the Sinclairs
myself and see if they're happy to continue accommodating
you both. If not, we will find an alternative.'

'I – I do not know what to say,' I said.

'Of course, if you'd rather not, I quite understand – we can try to get you to Lerwick again when the weather clears up, and from there to London—'

'No, no, it isn't that. I was just – not expecting *this*, that's all,' I said. 'I'm very grateful. Eirik would be so scared if they try to put him on a boat again, or a plane – it will be much better for him to be able to settle somewhere for a while. And if I can earn some money, I will be able to contribute towards the Sinclairs' household expenses and perhaps even save a little for when the day comes for us to return to Norway.'

'Wonderful.' Flight Lieutenant Jackson smiled suddenly, a beam that altered his stern countenance completely. He held out his hand and I realised that he meant for me to shake it. 'We're very glad to have you, Mrs Dahlström.'

Doctor Gaudie was smiling too, the corners of his eyes creased up. 'I'm sure the islanders will be happy to hear the news,' he said as we all stood up. 'There's been talk all round the place about how you both helped Isabel.'

Solemnly, I shook hands with them both. I waited until I was outside again to permit myself my own smile, hugging my arms around myself, the weariness from my sleepless night forgotten.

'Hedda?'

I turned and saw Bill behind me.

'Hello,' I said, trying to ignore the way my heartbeat sped up at the sight of him.

'Hello. What are you doing here?'

I told him, unable to prevent another smile from breaking across my face as I did so.

'That's great news,' he said. 'Hey – that means you and Eirik will be able to come to the Christmas party.'

'The Christmas party?'

'It's in the entertainment hall in a few weeks' time. The fellows from the station are putting it on. I was trying to keep out of it but I've been roped into making paper chains in my spare time. All the locals are invited and we've even got a band from town coming.'

I couldn't remember the last time I'd been to a party of any kind. Even before the Germans came to Kirkenes, when people did that sort of thing, Anders hadn't approved of them; he wouldn't even allow Eirik to go to children's parties.

But Anders isn't here, is he? I thought. *How will he ever know?* 'Yes,' I said. 'We'd love to.'

'I'll make sure you and Eirik get an invite. The folks you're staying with, too.'

'They'd like that. Thank you.'

We stood there a moment longer. 'Well, I'd better get going,' Bill said at last, looking at his watch.

'Bill,' I said as he turned to leave.

He looked back at me over his shoulder.

'Thank you. For helping me with Isabel, I mean. I couldn't have done that on my own.'

He ran a hand through his hair, his smile becoming wry. 'Hell, it was an experience, wasn't it? When I got posted here my fiancée said I'd die of boredom before Christmas, but it hasn't worked out that way so far. I've had almost as much excitement in the last few weeks as when I was on aircrew.'

My fiancée. Why did those words make my stomach sink? Of course he was engaged. Despite the lines etched permanently around his mouth and eyes, you couldn't deny he was a good-looking man. His appearance still reminded me of Magnus a little, but his personality, as I had suspected the first time we spoke, was completely different. Magnus's sense of humour had been sharp, sometimes to the point of cruelty, but Bill's seemed to be gentle and kind. And although we had only spoken a few times, I always felt as if he was really listening to me, whereas Magnus's attention used to wander; I'd often pour my heart out only for him to respond with a vague *Mm*, as if he hadn't heard a word I'd said.

No, they couldn't have been more different, and I was very relieved about that.

'Perhaps things will be calmer now,' I said, my words coming after a pause that, to my ears, lasted another beat too long. 'At least, I hope so.'

'It should do, unless Jerry gets any ideas,' he said, squinting up at the sky, and that made me remember something else he'd said just now.

'You mentioned you were on aircrew – were you a pilot?' I asked him.

He shook his head. 'Wireless operator. That's why they retrained me as a radar operator after—' He caught himself, as if he'd been about to say something he shouldn't. 'Why they retrained me as a radar operator.'

We parted ways then, and I walked slowly back to the Sinclairs, my mind full of everything that had happened to me since Eirik and I had come to Fiskersay, and of the conversation I'd had with Bill just now. I wished I didn't feel so awkward with him, but even though Anders was thousands of miles away, I always felt that familiar, cringing anxiety I got whenever one of the men in Kirkenes stopped to talk to me: the fear my husband would find out, or one of his friends would see me and tell him. Anders had always hated me talking to other men. *Do you want people to think you're a whore?* he'd snarl at me. *Never forget, you are MY wife, and you will behave appropriately.*

Back at the cottage, I told Elizabeth and Donald the news about stepping in as Fiskersay's nurse.

'Ach, that's marvellous!' Elizabeth said. 'And of course you and Eirik must stay on here – we won't hear of you going anywhere else, will we, Donald?'

Her husband shook his head. 'It brings da place back to life, having da bairn around,' he said.

'Does this mean I have to go back to school, Mamma?' Eirik said, a crease appearing between his eyebrows.

'Yes, but not yet,' I said. 'And when you do, I'm sure you'll make lots of friends.'

As I settled in front of the fire, picking up the socks I was knitting for Eirik with wool Elizabeth had spun from the Sinclairs' own sheep, I was thinking about Anders again. I wondered where he was and what he was doing, and just how angry he was with me for running away. Perhaps he would have gone to Sweden now, to the safety of his relative. I was sure he'd survive the war; he always seemed to come out on the right side of things. Would he try to find me? Or would he simply bide his time and wait for me to return? It was as if I was shackled to him by an invisible chain that stretched all the way across the sea back to Norway, its links locked tightly around my neck.

Thoughts of Anders led, inevitably, to thoughts of Kirkenes. What was life like for Ingunn and Marianne at the moment? I often looked through Donald's newspaper, both hoping and dreading that I might see the town's name mentioned, but so far, there had been nothing. And what about Mette? Had she managed to pass the radio on to Rolf? Had the Germans come back after I escaped to question her too? Panic gripped my throat as I imagined the dreadful things that could be happening to the people I loved. I wished I could write to them, but I knew my letters would be picked up by the censors; I had seen their work when I was back in Norway, whole paragraphs blacked out and that horrible swastika stamped on the envelopes. Even if I didn't put an address, the Germans might be able to work out where I was. Worse still, they might punish my friends for receiving a letter from me, thinking they knew where I had gone.

Some of this must have shown on my face, because Elizabeth, who was sitting nearby and working on her own knitting, said softly, 'Are you all right?'

I nodded. 'Just thinking of home.'

She gave me a sympathetic smile. 'This war is a terrible thing. So many people uprooted. But you've a home here as long as you need it – you and the peerie bairn both. I hope you know that.'

I had to swallow hard against a sudden lump in my throat. 'Thank you,' I said.

But despite her kind words it was hard to feel comforted when I had no idea what the future held. I knew it would be a long time before either I or Eirik forgot what had happened to us. Sometimes I wondered if we would ever be able to leave it behind.

FOURTEEN

BILL

'If I never have to make another paper chain in my life, it'll be too damn soon,' I said to Leonard Kane as I stepped back from the ladder to look at the results of our handiwork.

Len, still at the top of the ladder, pinned the last one to the ceiling and grinned down at me. 'Looks good, though.'

The station party was tonight; practically the whole island was coming and Flight Lieutenant Jackson had insisted we go all out with the decorations. The entertainment hall was festooned, not only with those damned paper chains, but anything remotely festive we could lay our hands on. There was even a Christmas tree in the corner; God knows where that had come from. There were tables laid out for food and the low stage at the front was set up for the group of musicians coming over from Talafirth.

Len climbed down from the ladder, jumping off the last few steps to the floor with an ease that sent a stab of envy through me. I was doing my physiotherapy exercises daily, but my leg still ached all the time, especially now the weather had turned cold, and I still couldn't raise my right arm more than ninety degrees. I didn't even turn twenty-five until March, yet some days I felt about ninety.

Len and I put the ladder away and he came back to Hut 1 with me as he wanted to talk to Al about something. I stretched out on my bunk and started writing to Rose. In my last letter, I'd told her about Hedda and Eirik and helping to deliver baby William; she'd replied with a fat missive telling me about the concerts she'd been singing in, a party she'd been to and an air raid on London that had flattened her early childhood home – *Mummy was devastated, even though we've not lived there for years and I can barely remember the place. Honestly, the way she's going on you'd think she was wandering the streets of the city, homeless, rather than safely tucked away with her sister in Sussex.* There were several paragraphs about the house in Surrey, too, which I hadn't had the heart to try and put her off yet. She hadn't even mentioned the baby or Hedda.

I'd read it with a sigh. The life Rose led felt so distant from mine here in Shetland that I could hardly connect the two. Sometimes reading about the things she got up to cheered me up, reminding me there was a world out there still, but more often, her letters left me feeling lonely in a way I couldn't really explain.

Dear Rose, I wrote.

I hope this finds you well. I'm afraid we will have to wait a while longer before I'm able to get leave. Winter has come to Shetland with a vengeance and even the supply ship can't get to Fiskersay at the moment, so there's no chance of me getting back to England any time soon!

Weather aside, things have been pretty quiet here. We are getting ready for a Christmas party tonight for the locals and everyone at the station...

I stopped, tapping the end of my pen against my chin as I wondered what Rose would make of the party. It would be nothing like the ones she was used to, that was for sure. I tried to imagine her here on Fiskersay, slogging through the rain and ever-present mud in her elegant clothes and expensive shoes, and couldn't help letting out a snort of laughter that made Len and Al glance round at me. I was pretty sure she'd hate it.

Hedda, on the other hand... As her face drifted into my mind, I felt a stab of guilt. Why was I thinking about her all of a sudden? I'd only seen her a couple more times since bumping into her outside the C.O.'s office that time: once when I was down in Talafirth, and once when I was walking past the croft where she was staying. It was a cold day, but sunny and still, and she'd happened to be outside. She'd hailed me and we'd made small talk for a few minutes, mostly about how Eirik would begin attending the local school in the new year. There seemed to be an awkwardness between us, but I couldn't quite put my finger on why. Talking to Eirik, who'd been there too, had been much easier; he'd been keen to show me some shells he'd found on the beach near the croft, chattering away enthusiastically in a mixture of Norwegian and English, and as I'd admired his collection, I couldn't help marvelling at the change in him. The kid I'd pulled from the hidden cabin in the boat, barely clinging to life, had become a smiling, talkative ball of energy with colour in his cheeks and a sparkle in his eyes. I was glad to see it.

I sighed, forcing my attention back to my letter to Rose, and managed to get it finished half an hour before the party was due to begin. By the time I got over to the entertainment hall, it was already filling up with locals, adults and children alike, and the band from Talafirth – three fellows with fiddles and a guitar – were setting up on the stage.

People greeted me, the women smiling, the men coming over to pat me on the back. It had been the same ever since little William Thomson was born; I couldn't even walk past one of the crofts now without being hailed and invited in for a cup of tea, and I'd often find myself being roped in to help with odd jobs, too. After so long keeping myself to myself, it had taken me a while to get used to it, but Lewis, Len and Al, who I was now starting to think of as friends rather than just colleagues, found it highly amusing. 'You know, Billy-boy, when you first came here I thought you were gonna be a bit of a cold fish,' Len had said to me a few days ago, just after we'd come off duty. 'Wasn't even sure you'd last if I'm honest. And now look at you – you deliver one baby and you're friends with the whole island. What a change, hey?'

I'd almost told him about the accident then – about Robert – but in the end, I'd just shrugged and laughed, and offered him one of the Sweet Caporal cigarettes that had just arrived in a much-delayed parcel from my parents. What a change, indeed.

As I wandered over to the stage, the band struck up a jaunty tune and Lewis and Len joined me. The three of us fell into pleasant conversation with old Bertie Sutherland, father of postmistress Bertha, about the fishing prospects in Talafirth harbour. Then I saw Charles Mackay, the island's headmaster, schoolteacher and captain of the Fiskersay Home Guard all rolled into one, pushing his way through the crowd towards us.

'Good evening, chaps,' he said as I groaned inwardly. 'Thought it went rather well yesterday, eh?' His accent was Scottish, but different to the locals'; he enunciated every word carefully and clearly. All those years as a teacher, I supposed. He was referring to an exercise that had taken place at the station the previous afternoon, intended to test the evacuation procedures on the domestic site and the manning up of the defensive positions. The Home Guard, pretending to be an attacking force, had stormed the camp, cutting the fence wire to sneak in. We'd 'won', but by a narrower margin than Flight Lieutenant Jackson would have liked; he'd gone about for the rest of the day with a face like a thundercloud.

I prayed Mackay wouldn't start going on about radio sets again. They were, as he'd told me yesterday, a passion of his, and after I'd foolishly let on I used to be a wireless operator, he'd gone on at me about them for almost an hour.

I gave myself a mental shake. Mackay was perfectly decent – a smart fellow in his early fifties with brown hair and a neat moustache. It wasn't his fault I found him dull.

Suddenly, over the music, I heard a shout. 'Mr Bill! Look!'

I saw Eirik pushing his way towards me, waving a toy Spitfire at me, with Hedda close behind. 'Hey, bud,' I said as he reached me. 'What's that you've got there?'

'I am sorry,' Hedda said, looking slightly flustered. 'I told him you were already talking to someone but he insisted on coming to say hello.'

'It's fine,' I reassured her, as Bertie said, at the same time, 'Ach, don't you worry about dat. We don't mind, do we?' and grinned at Eirik, showing two rows of large and startlingly white false teeth. Lewis, Len and Al greeted him too. Captain Mackay nodded politely and – to my relief – went off to talk to someone else.

'Right, show me that plane,' I said, making an effort to crouch down so I was on Eirik's level. 'Wow, that's fantastic – did you make that yourself?'

He nodded and gave the Spitfire to me. I turned it over

in my hand, making a show of examining it before giving it back to him. It had been carved from a piece of wood, painted green, with accurate if slightly wobbly RAF roundels on the wings, and a propellor fashioned from what looked like a piece of tin can held in place with a nail to allow it to spin.

'Now, Eirik, you had plenty of help from Donald, didn't you?' Hedda said. I glanced up and saw she was smiling wryly.

'Oh, yes, Uncle Donald made the shape out of the wood,' Eirik said quickly. 'He said his knife was very sharp and I might cut myself. But I did the painting and I helped attach the propellor!'

'Well, you did a wonderful job,' I said. 'I'm very impressed – you can hardly tell it apart from the real thing!'

Eirik beamed at me. 'Mamma said you used to fly planes!'

My heart gave a little jolt, remembering that conversation I'd had with Hedda a few weeks ago after she'd been asked to take up the position of Fiskersay's nurse – the conversation where I'd almost let it slip about the accident. 'I didn't fly them,' I said. 'I wasn't a pilot. But I flew *in* them, and helped the pilot work out where he needed to go.'

'In a Spitfire?'

'No, a Stirling. It's a very different kind of plane – bigger and heavier, and there are more people on board.'

'How many?'

'Seven of us altogether.'

He frowned. 'So why don't you fly in aeroplanes now?'

Damn, the kid was persistent. I took in a deep breath and was wondering how to answer him when one of the musicians on stage bellowed: 'Take your partners, ladies and gentlemen, for "Da Full Rigged Ship"!'

Relieved, I turned and saw everyone was lining up, the men

opposite the women and the boys opposite the girls. I ended up standing across from Bertha Sutherland.

'You'll have to tell me what to do,' I said, 'because I have no idea.'

Bertha laughed. 'Ach, don't you worry, I'll show you,' she said.

As the band began to play, I noticed Hedda was with Charles Mackay, and Eirik opposite a dark-haired girl his own age. The tune was fast and upbeat, everyone swapping partners as they wove in and out of one another and linked arms to spin each other in circles. Bertha and the other women led expertly, and didn't seem to mind that it took me a while to get the hang of the dance, bumping into people when I went in the wrong direction. Soon I was laughing breathlessly, the awkward end to my conversation with Eirik all but forgotten.

The song had almost finished when the air raid siren went off, its wail cutting the music off abruptly. A collective groan went around the hall, and I glanced across just in time to see Eirik's smile fade. He ran to Hedda and huddled against her, bunching her skirt in one fist, his eyes growing wide and fearful until he looked so much like he had that day I lifted him out of the boat cabin, I felt my chest ache.

Lewis got up onto the stage and commandeered the microphone. 'Ladies and gentlemen,' he said calmly. 'I'm afraid Jerry's trying to spoil our plans for this evening. If everyone could make their way to the air raid shelter in an orderly fashion, it would be much appreciated – our men will show you the way.'

I started directing people, wondering how the hell we were going to fit all these people into the station shelter. We managed it in the end, but it was so crowded there was barely room to move. I found myself standing shoulder to shoulder with Hedda and Eirik, who was trembling as we listened to the siren continue to wail. Then I heard the unmistakable drone of engines and the *crump, crump* of the station's anti-aircraft guns.

Eirik wasn't the only one frightened by the raid. Several other children began to cry, their mothers trying to comfort them in vain.

'Hey! Kids! Don't worry about those planes!' I didn't really know what I was going to say until the words left my mouth, but it did the trick: several pairs of eyes swivelled to look at me, including Eirik's.

'Did Eirik tell you I used to be on a bomber crew?' I said. 'We flew much, much bigger planes than those. The Germans don't have anything like that – *their* planes are weedy little things. You don't need to worry about them with our boys around!'

I knew it wouldn't fool the adults for a second – across the shelter, I saw Lewis grin at me and shake his head – but soon, I was surrounded by a small crowd of interested children as I regaled them with tales from my days as a wireless operator. Even Eirik forgot his terror, gazing up at me with a rapturous expression as I told them about the time when I was a trainee, and one of the fellows in my unit had 'borrowed' one of the bright yellow de Havilland DH.82 Tiger Moths we all practised in. He'd wanted to impress a girl who lived on a nearby farm but had taken a turn at too steep an angle and ended up having to ditch the plane in a river. It had been a long, wet walk back to the base for him. The kids all giggled as I described how he'd slunk into our hut to change, hoping our C.O. wouldn't see him, and found a tadpole in one of his boots.

By the time I'd finished that particular story, the all-clear was sounding. The raid had been a short one; less than forty minutes had passed by the time we got back to the hall.

'Did that really happen?' Hedda said as Eirik ran off to join the other children who'd been listening to me in the shelter, the little group accepting him into their midst with that ease only kids seem to have and clamouring to see the toy Spitfire. The band had already struck up another tune, the air raid a mere annoyance to be quickly brushed aside.

I grinned and shrugged. 'Ditching the Tiger Moth in the river? Sure. He got a hell of a roasting for it when the C.O. found out. I might have invented the tadpole, though.'

She laughed – the first time I'd seen her do that, I realised. 'Well, it certainly helped to distract them. Thank you.'

'Think there might be any more babies on the way tonight?' I quipped as we made our way over to the tables where the food and drink were laid out; I'd had enough of dancing for now.

'Oh, goodness, I hope not.' She pretended to look around the room, studying all the women present carefully as if she was making sure, and laughed again.

'Let me get you a drink,' I said.

'I would like that, thank you.'

Cups in hand, we found a quieter spot at the edge of the room where we watched people whirling around energetically to the band again, and spent the rest of the evening talking to each other about nothing in particular. Something was different, but it wasn't until much later that night, when I was lying in my bed and almost asleep, that I realised what it was: the awkwardness between me and Hedda had completely disappeared.

FIFTEEN

HEDDA

'Ach, you should have seen Fiskersay at Christmastime before the war,' Elizabeth sighed as I finished laying the table, and she lifted the chicken – one of the Sinclairs' own hens that they'd fattened up especially for Christmas Day – out of the oven in a cloud of fragrant steam, setting it down on the dresser to rest. 'The celebrations we'd have! And at the end of January there would be the Up Helly Aa festival where the island's young men would parade through the streets with burning torches. There would be a squad dressed in full Viking regalia with the Guizer Jarl – the man in charge – at their head, and all other guizers in different costumes. Every year Laurie Moar, the carpenter, would build an enormous Viking longboat out of wood, and on parade night it would be carried to the harbour where the squad would set it alight.' She shook her head, looking wistful. 'That's all had to stop now, though, thanks to Mr Hitler and all the men going off to fight. Donald, do you remember the year they asked you to be the Guizer Jarl?' she added, looking fondly at her husband, who was adding peats to the fire.

'Aye, I remember. Those were good times,' Donald said in his deep, rumbling baritone. 'Of course, I was a lad then – I couldnae run round like dat now. And I certainly couldn't carry dat big bloody ship!'

'It sounds wonderful,' I said.

'He had to dress up as Ullr that year,' Elizabeth said. 'I had to sew everything for him myself, and it was quite the job, I can tell you!'

'But Ullr is a Norse god,' Eirik piped up from the corner, where he had been prodding a promising-looking pile of gifts wrapped in brown paper stacked beside Donald's armchair. 'Mamma, he is, isn't he? He was in that storybook *Tante* Ingunn gave me for my birthday last year.'

'Well, Vikings were some of da first people to come to Shetland,' Donald said. 'Didn't you know dat?'

'Are *you* a Viking?' Eirik asked him.

He laughed. 'I might be, somewhere along da line.'

I laughed too. I could believe it; he was certainly built like one.

'Eirik, leave those parcels alone and come and help me,' I said sternly.

'But Mamma, there is one here with my name on it!'

'Yes, and it will still have your name on it after we have eaten. Come on!'

Reluctantly, he came over to the table. 'Would you like to light the candles?' I asked him, and his face brightened. 'Be careful!' I warned as he dashed over to the stove for the matches. I arranged the last of the six places laid around the table and stood back with my arms folded, looking at my handiwork with satisfaction. The cottage's main room was cosy and festive, with paper decorations hanging from the ceiling, candles on the windowsills and table, and a peg doll nativity arranged on the mantelpiece that had been made by

Elizabeth's mother when Elizabeth was a little girl. Seeing it all made me think about my friends back in Norway, especially Ingunn, Marianne and Mette. What were they doing today? Were they all right? Did they have enough to eat? I wished so much that they could be here; I missed them dreadfully, and I was scared for them too. I knew how hard life must be in Kirkenes now the Arctic winter had arrived, plunging the town into perpetual darkness. And I worried there might have been repercussions from the Germans for them because of what I'd done – after all, I'd run away while I was with Mette, and Ingunn had helped me escape. What if the Germans thought they had something to do with me killing the officer, too? It might sound ridiculous, but I knew the Germans only needed the smallest of pretexts to punish people. Mette and Ingunn could be imprisoned by now – or dead. I even found myself recalling my parents, who I hadn't seen or heard from since I was sent away to Kirkenes before Eirik was born and hardly ever thought about any more, remembering the Christmases we used to have when I was a child. Where were they now? How was the war affecting them?

Don't, I told myself sternly. *Not now. Not today.*

As Elizabeth put various dishes of vegetables on the table and went back over to the dresser for the chicken, there was a knock at the door. 'Ah, here they are,' Donald said, and my heartbeat sped up a little.

Eirik ran to open the door. 'Mr Bill!' he cried as Lewis Harper and Bill, both wearing their RAF uniforms, ducked into the cottage. Elizabeth and Donald had invited them to spend Christmas with us a few days after the party up at the station, when Bill and Lewis helped rescue the Sinclairs' cow from a bog.

'Merry Christmas, Elizabeth,' Bill said. 'Merry Christmas, Donald. Thank you for having us.'

As Lewis greeted the Sinclairs too, Bill turned to ruffle Eirik's hair. 'Merry Christmas, buddy! And Merry Christmas, Hedda,' he added, smiling at me.

I smiled back and dipped my head, wondering why I was blushing. '*God jul* – Merry Christmas. I am glad you could both come.'

'I'm glad Elizabeth invited us,' Bill said. 'Having lunch here makes the thought of being on watch all night bearable – almost.'

'We bear gifts,' Lewis said once the two men had hung up their coats and taken off their boots, lifting a bulging canvas bag for us all to see. 'This is for you, I believe, young man...' He handed Eirik a parcel wrapped in green and red paper.

'Put it with the others, please,' I said, shooting Eirik a stern look. He made a face at me, but did as he was told.

'And this is for you, Elizabeth...' Lewis gave her something large, soft and squashy, also wrapped in Christmas paper and tied with a ribbon.

'Ach, you shouldn't have,' Donald said as Lewis passed him what was clearly a bottle, but his eyes were sparkling.

'Hedda, here you are.'

Lewis gave my parcel to Bill, who passed it to me. As I took it, our fingertips brushed and I felt myself blush again. What on earth was wrong with me today? 'Thank you,' I said, trying to hide my embarrassment.

'And finally...' With a flourish, Lewis lifted out a small, round muslin bundle with string around the top. 'This was liberated from the camp kitchen by Sergeant Gauthier when our cook was otherwise occupied. You might like to open it now.'

He and Bill grinned at each other as Elizabeth untied the string. She gasped when she saw what was inside: a dark, rich-looking Christmas pudding, stuffed with dried fruit. 'Oh, my, will you look at that!'

'It even has sugar in it,' Bill said.

'We will have it after the chicken,' Elizabeth said, putting the pudding down in the middle of the table and beaming at him. 'Thank you.'

'Mamma,' Eirik said as I turned the little rectangular parcel over in my hand, wondering what it was. 'You must put your present over by the chair too!' He frowned at me, his hands on his hips. 'And you, *Tante* Elizabeth and *Onkel* Donald.'

Pressing my lips together to hide my amusement, I collected everyone's gifts and placed them with the rest of the presents. Then we sat down to eat. Lewis had one more surprise in his seemingly bottomless knapsack: a box of paper hats, which he handed out for all of us to wear. 'Did you liberate these as well?' I said, laughing at Bill whose hat was too big and kept slipping down over his eyes. He laughed too and pushed the hat to the back of his head.

'If I had, I'd've made sure I got some that fit,' he said.

'So, Hedda,' Lewis said when, at last, all the food had gone, and he and Bill had cleared the table and were washing and drying the dishes, shooing Elizabeth away whenever she attempted to help. 'How does this differ from Christmas in Norway?'

I leaned back in my chair, lacing my hands across my stomach. 'Well, when I was a child, my parents would always have a big party for all our family and friends on *Julaften* – Christmas Eve – with dishes such as *risengrynsgrøt*, a hot rice pudding with sugar, cinnamon and butter. Afterwards we'd dance around the Christmas tree and hold hands. It's a tradition of ours in Norway to have a tree – a real tree my father would cut from the forest near our home, which we'd decorate – and all the children would be terribly excited wondering what *Julenissen*, our version of Santa Claus, would bring us to put under it. We'd have a meal on Christmas day too, but it was always a much smaller affair, for family only, and we would go to church.'

I didn't tell him, of course, that my parents had disowned me, although I felt a pang as I remembered my father dragging the tree into the house, snow still clinging to its branches. And I didn't tell him that in Kirkenes, Christmas had just been another day for me. Anders loathed it, and forbade me or Eirik to go to any of the parties thrown by neighbours and friends. Instead, he would skulk around, muttering about how I was spoiling 'the child' by buying him presents. We did not put up any decorations or a tree, and there was no *Julaften* meal, only my husband getting progressively drunker and me and Eirik creeping around the house like scared mice.

Don't think about that, I told myself. *He is not here*. Looking around the room at the smiling faces of my newfound friends, I could not remember the last time I had felt so content and at peace. I was so glad that, at last, Eirik was able to have a proper Christmas, even if I had no idea what our futures held right now.

'Mamma, *please* can I open my presents?' Eirik begged me in Norwegian once the dishes were all put away.

'You may, if you hand the others out first,' I said. He nodded and raced over to the pile by Donald's chair.

We let Eirik open his parcels first. From the Sinclairs, he had a tin of colouring pencils, and from Bill and Lewis, a toy tank that Lewis had made from a piece of driftwood.

Elizabeth's gift from Bill and Lewis was a brand-new military-issue woollen blanket; Donald's, a bottle of rum.

For me, Elizabeth had knitted a beautiful pair of gloves in an elaborate pattern she called Fair Isle, and the parcel from Lewis's knapsack turned out to be an exquisite tooled leather writing case. 'Thank Bill,' Lewis said as I exclaimed over it. 'I had nothing to do with it.'

'I thought it might come in useful for your work,' Bill said, and when I looked up at him I noticed the tips of his ears had gone pink.

'Thank you,' I said. 'I love it! But wherever did you manage to find such a thing?'

'Ah, now that would be telling,' he said with a small, mysterious smile.

My own gifts – a new pincushion for Elizabeth that I'd found in Sutherland's Stores, a small bottle of whisky for Donald and cigarettes for Bill and Lewis – felt rather mean in comparison, but they all seemed thrilled with them. For Eirik I had managed to purchase the annual *Beano Book*, which had arrived from the mainland just in time. He curled up happily on the end of the couch with it and was soon absorbed.

'Will you have a drink?' Donald asked the adults, holding up the bottles of whisky and rum. Lewis accepted, but Bill and I both shook our heads. Elizabeth said she would make us a pot of tea instead.

'It must feel strange, being so far away from your family at Christmas,' I said to Bill as I sat down beside him on the thick woollen rug in front of the fire and tucked my legs underneath me; there weren't enough chairs for everyone.

He shrugged, stretching his bad leg out in front of him. 'I'm used to it by now. My parents have plenty of relatives they can spend time with, and my fiancée has a large family too. I doubt any of them are even missing me.'

'I am sure that's not true,' I said.

'How about you?' he asked. 'You're pretty far from home too.'

I glanced at Eirik, who was still absorbed in his book, wondering what to say. 'It is different,' I admitted at last. 'But we are much safer here than we were in Norway. It is a relief not to have to worry about German patrols every time we set foot out of the house, or about the Soviets dropping their bombs on us. Kirkenes felt like a prison sometimes.'

Even before the Germans came, I thought but didn't say out loud. Then Elizabeth brought us our tea, and I used the distraction as an opportunity to steer the conversation towards safer subjects.

At three o'clock, Donald turned on the wireless and we all stood, Lewis helping Bill to his feet, to listen to the King's speech. '*We still have tasks ahead of us*,' his voice crackling through the speaker said, '*perhaps harder even than those which we have already accomplished. We face these with confidence, for today we stand together, no longer alone, no longer ill armed, but just as resolute as in the darkest hours to do our duty whatever comes...*'

I glanced out of the corner of my eye at Bill and saw he was gazing at the floor, his expression pensive. I was thinking about Ingunn, Marianne and Mette again, and all my other friends in Kirkenes, and I knew Elizabeth and Donald would be thinking of their son, Willie, who was in the army and posted somewhere overseas. Who was Bill thinking of?

When the speech finished, they played the British National Anthem, and Donald, Bill and Lewis saluted. Then we sat down again and Bill and I resumed our conversation, although we were slightly more subdued than before.

At last, Lewis, sitting beside Eirik on the couch, glanced at his watch. 'I suppose we'd better get back, Bill, old chap,' he said. 'We're on watch in an hour.'

Bill groaned. I stood and reached down so he could hang on to my hand while he pulled himself to his feet again.

'Thank you,' he said, brushing off his uniform. Our eyes met and yet again, I felt that little jolt inside me.

For goodness' sake, Hedda! I thought. I looked quickly away, swallowing. 'You're welcome.'

He kissed my cheek, taking me by surprise. 'Well, I guess I'll see you at the next dance if we don't bump into each other before then.' Then he went to say goodbye to Elizabeth, kissing her on the cheek too. Lewis did the same with both of us, shook Donald's hand and pretended to pull a penny out of Eirik's ear, much to his amazement, and the two men left.

'Mamma?' Eirik said as we drifted off to sleep that night, drowsy and warm.

'What is it, *lille vennen*?' I asked, resting my chin on top of his head.

'I don't want to go back to Norway. Can we stay here in Shetland?'

I sighed. 'We'll have to wait and see.'

'I hope we can,' he said. 'I like it here.'

'So do I,' I murmured into his hair. My only answer was a soft snore; he had fallen asleep.

I lay awake for a while longer, replaying the day in my mind. I could still feel the place on my cheek where Bill had kissed me, and I remembered the way his gaze had met mine after I helped him up.

Don't be a fool, I told myself. *There is nothing between you. There can't be. Even if you were free to fall in love again, it is not worth the pain.*

I made myself think of other things and, eventually, managed to drift off to sleep too.

PART TWO

1943

PART TWO

Sixteen

HEDDA
January

'Now don't you worry about a thing, Mrs Dahlström,' Charles Mackay said as I ushered Eirik towards the schoolhouse. It was the new year, three months since Eirik and I had come to Shetland, and many more since Eirik had last attended school; deep down I felt almost as nervous as he did, but I was doing my utmost to hide it. 'Young Eric will be absolutely fine here.'

'Eirik,' I reminded him.

'Of course, of course, forgive me.' He smiled warmly at Eirik. 'We'll get used to each other in time, won't we, laddie? I expect obedience and diligence from all my pupils, but I'm sure we won't have any problems with you. A good, disciplined education provides an essential grounding for later life. Certainly didn't do me any harm!'

'Mamma, do I have to go?' Eirik said in Norwegian, turning to me.

Charles Mackay frowned a little. 'I will expect him to speak English while he is here, of course,' he said. 'It won't do for the other children not to be able to understand him.'

'No, of course not,' I said. 'He's still learning, that's all.' I turned to my son. 'Eirik, you must remember to speak English while you are at school. Don't forget.'

He nodded silently.

'Now, in you go. I will be here to collect you this afternoon.' I gave him a quick hug and gently pushed him away from me. Then Charles said sternly, 'David Couper! Late again?'

I glanced round and saw a small boy about Eirik's age hurrying through the snow, red-cheeked and breathless.

'Sorry, Mr Mackay!' he said breezily as he reached us. 'I had to help my father rescue our pony from a snowdrift!'

'That's no excuse,' Charles snapped at him. 'I told you last term I would not tolerate lateness from you, and I won't tolerate it now. You will stay in at lunchtime and write one hundred lines.'

David's face fell slightly. 'Yes, Mr Mackay,' he said, sounding subdued, while Eirik stared at Charles with wide, frightened eyes.

'Now, take young Er— *Eirik* here inside with you and show him where to sit,' Charles ordered.

David turned to Eirik, his glum expression vanishing again as a grin lit up his face. 'Hello!' he said. 'Are you new? You were at that Christmas party at the camp, weren't you?'

Smiling back tentatively, Eirik followed him inside, and I walked away from the schoolhouse, trying to ignore the anxiety still twisting in my stomach. *You feel guilty because he has been through so much, and this is the first time you have been apart since coming here, that is all*, I told myself as I trudged back to the Sinclairs' croft to collect my bag, pulling my shawl tight around me. Shetland was experiencing its heaviest snow in years, great drifts banked up beside the road. Every day, men from the station could be seen out and about with shovels, helping the locals dig paths through to the more isolated crofts and trying to keep the route into Talafirth open. The clouds were low and lead-coloured, promising more snow to come, and in the mornings the island was often blanketed in thick fog.

As I walked, my boots squeaking on the snow, I thought about the patients I would be calling on today. First on my list was Charles Mackay's mother Margaret. I hadn't visited her before; she had problems with her heart and Doctor Gaudie wanted me to check in on her and make sure she was correctly taking the new medicine he had prescribed for her.

'How did young Eirik get on?' Elizabeth asked me as I came into her kitchen, the warmth radiating from the stove welcome after the damp chill outside. She was standing at the kitchen table, kneading dough for bread. 'Ach,' she added, 'I'm sure they add sawdust to this flour to make it go further.'

'You should have seen the flour we had to use back in Norway,' I told her. 'I'm certain it was *all* sawdust.'

She gave me a wry smile.

'Eirik is fine,' I added. 'I am worried his teacher is a little strict, though.'

'Oh, don't you worry about Charlie Mackay,' Elizabeth said. 'He's a wee bit too serious for his own good sometimes, but he's an excellent teacher. Life's not been easy for him, what with getting hurt in the last war and having to come back here to look after his mother.'

'I'm going to see her now,' I said as I picked up my nurse's bag and checked through it one last time to make sure I had everything I needed. 'What is she like?'

'Ach, a sweeter woman you couldn't hope to meet. She grew up here and she and my younger sister Mary were great friends. But Magnus – Charles's father – died when he was three, and they had leave Fiskersay and stay with relatives in Edinburgh for a while. Charlie persuaded Margaret to come back here after he was invalided out of the army in 1917, and they've lived in their little house in town ever since.'

Magnus. Hearing that name made my heart lurch.

'It was terrible what happened to Charlie,' Elizabeth went on. 'He was the commander of a whole regiment of men – I forget the rank, I've never been any good with that sort of thing. But he was important, and a really good sodjer. One night the whole lot of them were shelled in their trench. Charlie was the only survivor, and he was terribly badly hurt. We thought for a while he was not going to pull through, but when he did recover and had to leave the army, he could not find work anywhere – no one wanted him, and the government would not help. Ach, it was a shame. A real shame.'

I felt a sudden pang of sympathy for the man. To look at him, you would never know any of this; he seemed perfectly ordinary – the sort of person who kept themselves to themselves. Elizabeth's story made me think of Bill, too. I still didn't know what had happened to *him* – why he had been taken off the heavy bomber crew he'd told the children about at the Christmas party, or why he'd been sent to Fiskersay, although I was sure his injured leg was something to do with it. I wondered if he would ever tell me.

Stop thinking about Bill. I shook my head, smiling wryly at myself, and headed out of the cottage again to begin the walk into Talafirth.

After meeting Charles Mackay that morning, resplendent in his smart tweed suit and leather shoes, I wasn't surprised to find that, although his house was a little shabby and old-fashioned, it was spotlessly neat and clean, a strong smell of disinfectant pervading the air. Margaret let me in with a smile, saying, 'You must be the new nurse Doctor Gaudie was talking about! Can I get you a cup of tea?'

She was pale and bony, her wispy grey hair pulled back in a knot, and had the same pale blue eyes as her son. Hobbling a little, she took me through into a tiny parlour dominated by a large table pushed up against the window. The table was the only thing in the room that looked out of place: its top was scattered with a jumble of wireless sets in various states of repair, and a few oily rags.

'Will you let me make it?' I said, rubbing my hands together. The small fire that burned in the grate seemed to give out no warmth; Margaret was bundled up in layers of jumpers and shawls against the chill.

'Are you sure you don't mind?' Even as she said it, Margaret was sinking wearily into a chair. 'There's tea in the pantry, in the blue tin, and the kettle is on the stove. Cups, the teapot and matches are on the dresser and the spoons are in the drawer underneath!' she called after me as I made my way through to the kitchen, just across the hall from the parlour.

The kitchen, too, was spotless, apart from the table where there were more bits of wireless sets in an untidy heap. While I waited for the kettle to boil, I gazed curiously at them. Did Charles take the radios apart or put them back together? It seemed an odd hobby to have. The kettle began to whistle and I fetched the tea tin from the pantry and found the teapot and a jug of milk. Mindful of the ration, although many in Fiskersay got round that by keeping their own cows, I carefully added a few drops to each cup.

'Now, you must tell me all about yourself,' Margaret said when I took the tea back to the parlour. 'You're the lassie who came over from Norway with her son, aren't you? On a fishing boat? You speak very good English, I must say. Oh, but wasn't it a shame about those poor men you were with…'

Margaret didn't seem to know that they had been resistance men; it seemed Flight Lieutenant Jackson had been successful in preventing that information from getting out. It was almost fifteen minutes before she stopped asking me questions and I was able to steer the conversation around to her heart medicine. She was clearly lonely, and desperate for someone to talk to, but thankfully she seemed to be taking her medicine as prescribed. As we were talking, however, I noticed she kept touching her shin and pressing her lips together as if she was trying not to wince.

'May I look at your leg, Mrs Mackay?' I asked her gently.

'Oh, it's nothing…'

'Please. It's no trouble. I might be able to help.'

Reluctantly, she rolled down her stocking, and I saw an angry-looking wound on her leg, purple-red and beginning to ulcerate. 'My goodness,' I said, trying to hide my shock. 'Does that not hurt you?'

'It is rather sore. I knocked my leg a few weeks ago and it doesn't seem to be healing as well as it should. I suppose it is because I am so old. We don't really have the money to be bothering the doctor all the time…'

I took ointment and bandages from my bag and dressed Margaret's leg carefully, wondering why Charles had not tried to convince her to do something about it. 'I'll need to return daily for a while to check on the wound,' I said. 'It's probably a good idea if Doctor Gaudie takes a look at it as well.' I had already made my mind up that if Margaret couldn't afford his visit, I would pay for it myself out of my wages.

'You are so kind,' Margaret said as I put my things away and stood to go and wash my hands. 'I really don't deserve it.'

Why don't you? I wanted to ask her, but I did not, because that feeling was all too familiar to me. Even now I could hear Anders inside my head: *You are nothing. You deserve nothing. I could take all this away from you – this house, these things – in an instant. If it wasn't for me, you'd be out on the street like the whore that you are.*

Had Magnus – Margaret's Magnus – ever said anything like that to her?

Stop, Hedda. It was no use thinking things like this. It was not my job to interfere in other people's business, especially when I was a newcomer to the island, mine and Eirik's future still a complete unknown.

'I must leave you now,' I said. 'But please, try to rest your leg as much as you can. I'll see myself out.'

I had three more patients to see; then I returned to the Sinclairs' croft where Elizabeth had a bowl of hot soup waiting for me. As I sat down to eat, I couldn't ignore the small but steady glow of satisfaction my work this morning had given me, knowing I'd been able to help and reassure people in their hour of need. It helped to quieten Anders inside my head. *I wonder what he would say*, I thought, *if he could see me now.*

No doubt he would still find something to sneer at – he always had. Nothing I ever did would be good enough for him. I tried to push Anders from my mind, not wanting thoughts of him to sour my good mood.

Later, I walked over to the school to meet Eirik. 'Mamma, I have a new storybook to read!' he said to me in Norwegian as he ran out, beaming.

'You must speak English, remember?' I admonished him,

seeing Charles Mackay emerge from the schoolhouse behind him.

'Sorry, Mamma,' he said.

'I hope he has been good?' I said to Charles.

'Oh, yes, a model pupil.' Charles smiled at me. 'We'll get him up to speed in no time!'

His smile was genuine and warm, but to me – perhaps because I was over-sensitive to others' moods after years of trying to predict Anders' emotional weather so I could avoid provoking a reaction from him – it seemed tinged with an underlying sadness; I remembered what Elizabeth had told me about him and felt another wave of sympathy for the man. I knew only too well what it felt like to feel useless and unwanted. It must have been a struggle for him, having to return here and begin again. Brave, too.

'Thank you,' I said, and smiled back. 'I'm relieved to hear it. It is so long since Eirik was last in school – I was worried he would have fallen too far behind to catch up.'

'Oh, no, not at all!' Charles said.

Thanking him again, I turned to Eirik, who was chattering away to David Couper and a few other boys. 'Come, Eirik. Let's hurry before we get too cold – it's beginning to snow again! You can tell me about your storybook on the way home.'

Eirik said goodbye to his friends, I bid Charles farewell, and with flakes falling softly like feathers around us, the afternoon already turning to dusk, we made our way back to the cheerful warmth of the croft.

It wasn't until we were almost there that I realised I'd called it *home* without even thinking.

Seventeen

HEDDA

The next few days were so busy I barely had a moment to myself. The evening of the third day found me standing by the croft's mantel with my fingers pressed to my temples to try and stave off a headache. Donald was dozing in his chair, his mouth hanging open, and I had just got Eirik off to sleep after reading a story to him for the third time. A pile of peats burned merrily in the grate, making the kitchen stuffy and smoky.

'Are you all right, my dear?' Elizabeth asked me, glancing up from where she sat with her knitting. I was so lost in thought that she made me jump, and my elbow caught a small china figurine of a milkmaid on the mantel, sending it crashing to the floor where it shattered on the tiles. 'Oh my goodness, I am so sorry!' I said, falling to my knees and trying to scoop up the pieces, knowing even as I did so that the figurine was beyond repair. Frightened tears threatened to spill over; my throat was tight. How could I have been so careless? Donald and Elizabeth would be so angry with me.

But to my surprise, as Donald snoozed on, Elizabeth laughed. 'Oh, my dear, there is no need to apologise. Donald's sister sent dat thing to us before the war, after a trip to London, and I've always thought it was awful ugly. Good riddance to it, I say. If she ever asks about it, I'll tell her it got smashed in an air raid.'

I sat back on my heels, taking a deep breath to calm my wildly leaping heart. My panic was an automatic reaction, I realised, coming from that watchful, cowering part of me that, even here, expected Anders to storm in, barking, *What was that? What have you broken now, you stupid woman?*

Elizabeth fetched a dustpan and brush. 'Let me do that,' I said. She tried to protest, but I insisted and quickly swept the figurine pieces up. 'Would you mind if I went out for some fresh air?' I asked as I got to my feet again.

'Ach, of course not,' Elizabeth said, settling comfortably back into her chair and taking up her knitting needles again. 'I will keep an ear out for the bairn. Mind you wrap up, though – it may have stopped snowing, but it's bitter out there.'

I did as she bid me, pulling on a jacket, shawl and gloves. When I stepped outside, I saw the heavy clouds that had blanketed Fiskersay for days had finally cleared. The sky was scattered with stars, the moon was a bright sliver, and the ground was covered in a thick layer of fresh snow that crunched beneath my boots. I breathed in deep lungfuls of the icy air, my breath forming clouds in front of me; my headache began to recede almost immediately.

The Sinclairs' croft was on the north-western side of Fiskersay, huddled at the foot of the Haug, the hill the road climbed over to the radar station at Svarta Ness. When I'd first found out the name I'd been struck by its similarity to *Haugen*, the hill where I'd lived in Kirkenes; many of the place names in Shetland had a Norwegian feel.

As I walked, I thought about how much my life had changed in the last three months; Eirik's, too. The Christmas just passed had truly been one of the happiest I had ever known, and the memory of that day with me, Eirik, Donald, Elizabeth, Lewis and Bill all crammed around the Sinclairs' table, Bill's hat falling over his eyes, still made me smile every time I thought about it. I kept the writing case he had given me in my nurse's bag, and used it every day.

My work as the island's nurse made me happier than I could remember feeling in a very long time too. In the short time I had been in Fiskersay, I'd got to know almost everyone dotted about this tiny island. The feeling that I was making a real difference to them, helping them to get well again, and providing them with comfort when that wasn't possible, was utterly rewarding. I still couldn't quite believe how kind and welcoming everyone had been. Would Eirik and I have found it as easy to settle if we'd gone to the mainland?

It must be very different here to Norway, my patients often said, and it was, but I hadn't found life here hard to adjust to. I could understand even the broadest of accents with ease now; the food was different, but despite rationing and the weather sometimes preventing the supply ship reaching the island, it was much more plentiful than it had been in Kirkenes, supplemented as it was with fresh eggs, milk and meat from the crofters' livestock. Not having the Germans breathing down my neck at every hand and turn made life easier, too. Although there were times when I still felt Anders crouched at my shoulder, whispering poison in my ear, there were also times when I'd catch myself and realise that, lost in my work and the daily routine of life here, I hadn't thought about him for hours.

I skirted around the bottom of the Haug to the path that led up its western side, heading for the remains of a tiny stone cottage near to where the radar towers stood. It had been another croft, Elizabeth told me, which was abandoned when she was a girl, and I hoped it would offer me a little shelter from the keen north-easterly wind blowing in from the sea. The cliffs were gentler on this side of the island than at Svarta Ness, which I still couldn't look at without a shudder, remembering how close Eirik and I had come to suffering the same fate as the brave men who'd steered the boat all the way over here from Norway. If it hadn't been for Bill...

As I approached the cottage, I heard someone clear their throat softly. Someone was already sitting on the low wall that had once surrounded the cottage, smoking a cigarette; I could smell the smoke and see the tip glowing orange in the darkness.

'I'm sorry,' I said, knowing they would have heard my footsteps in the snow. 'I did not realise anyone was here.'

'Hedda?' a man's voice said.

'Bill?'

'Cigarette?' he said as I went to join him. 'And where's Eirik?'

'No, I won't have a cigarette, thank you. Eirik is already tucked up in bed, fast asleep. What are you doing up here?'

'Felt kinda restless,' he said. 'Thought a walk would clear my head, and Doctor Gaudie's always nagging at me to exercise more because of my leg, so...'

I leaned back, tilting my head towards the sky. The night was very still, the only sound the waves breaking against the cliffs below us. As always, I wanted to ask him what had happened to him, and as always, I had to tell myself not to pry. Instead, I said, 'It is beautiful here, isn't it?'

'You know, it is,' he said. 'I didn't think so when I first came here. I was cursing the whole damn RAF for sending me here, and Rose wasn't happy either, but it's grown on me.'

'Is she in Canada?'

'No, England.'

'Of course – I think you told me, but I forgot. I'm sorry.'

'She's a singer with ENSA,' Bill went on. 'They go round and give concerts for the forces. That's how we met. How about you? You leave anyone behind in Norway?'

'Yes,' I said, carefully. 'My husband, Anders.'

'It must be a worry for you, him still being there, eh? And Eirik must miss his dad.'

A worry? No. Even though I knew it was only a temporary respite, being here without Anders was beginning to make me feel as if I could breathe again for the first time in years. And I doubted Eirik even thought about him at all.

I realised I had taken too long to answer. 'My husband… he is… a difficult man,' I said at last, hoping my voice was steady. I didn't dare tell him Anders was not Eirik's father; what would he think?

'I see,' Bill said in a tone that held more questions, but to my relief, he didn't press me. 'Hey, look,' he said, pointing with the hand that held the still-glowing end of his cigarette. Out to sea, just above the horizon, I saw a faint band of ghostly greenish-white light.

'The *Nordlys*,' I said, smiling. 'We get them in Norway, too.'

'We call 'em the Northern Lights in Canada, but I prefer what they call them here – the Mirrie Dancers.'

Mirrie Dancers. The lights did look like dancers, twisting and shimmering; ribbon-like and graceful. 'Yes, I think I do too.'

We watched them for a while, as Bill smoked another cigarette. 'When I was a girl,' I said at last, 'my father told me the lights were angels coming down from Heaven to look at us here on earth. He said they would protect us.' I gave a small, bitter laugh. 'He couldn't have known what was coming, I suppose.'

'I can't imagine what it must have been like,' Bill said. 'When Norway was invaded, I mean.'

'It was...' The English word momentarily evaded me. 'A shock,' I said at last, although the word felt utterly inadequate to describe how I had felt when the news came that Norway had fallen. 'It all happened so fast. We were so sure the British would stop the Germans, and then everything changed overnight – literally overnight. There was panic, people trying to buy food and supplies in the shops and stripping the shelves bare. I remember thinking, when the troops arrived in Kirkenes, that they were like a great wave, unstoppable, crushing everything in their path. And because we are so close to Russia there has hardly been a day without bombs since. I don't even know if there will be a town left to return to, if this war ever ends.'

'I'm sorry,' Bill said.

'I hate them for what they have done to our country. We were peaceful – we were hurting no one. They had no right to do what they did.'

'They've no damn right to do anything they're doing,' Bill said vehemently, and I murmured my agreement.

We sat for a while in companionable silence. Briefly, I

wondered what Anders would say if he knew what I was doing, and tried to push the thought away, desperate for the image of his angry, twisted face not to loom in my mind and spoil things. Bill was a friend, and I needed that. As for the way my heartbeat sped up a little whenever I remembered our conversations or the way he smiled... well, he was the first man to offer me kindness and companionship in as long as I could remember – for the first time, if I was honest. It was perhaps natural that sometimes, being around him made me feel like a giddy schoolgirl again. But that was all it was.

At last, Bill heaved himself to his feet. 'I'd better get back,' he said. 'I'm on watch in half an hour.'

'I should go back also,' I sighed, standing up. My headache was gone now, but even wrapped up in my jumper, jacket, shawl and gloves I was beginning to feel cold. I would be glad to get back to the Sinclairs' warm fire.

'Let me come with you,' he said. 'I need to ask Donald about a wall he wants repairing – Lewis and I thought we might come over and take a look at it next time we're off duty.'

We walked back down the hill to the croft together, the Mirrie Dancers still rippling in their silent waltz above the water behind us.

Eighteen

'Quiet for a change, fellas,' Len remarked, peering over my shoulder as I gazed at the circular screen of the cathode ray tube in the console in front of me, my eyes fixed on the uneven, flickering green line moving across it from left to right, and watching for larger downward spikes that might indicate a hostile contact. The small spikes I was seeing now were just the radar noise we called "grass". 'Think it'll last?'

'Don't tempt fate,' said Ray Marks, an operator from Hut 3, fixing Len with a stern look.

I passed a hand over my face, stifling a yawn. We were on the overnight watch; it was 2 a.m. and despite several cups of strong coffee in the NAAFI before my shift started, I was struggling with fatigue and my head ached although I'd only been in front of the screen for fifteen minutes. The room we were in was like a cave, low-ceilinged, dark and hot. The operational buildings at Svarta Ness were built from brick with a five-and-a-half-foot-thick layer of shingle in the roof and surrounded by sturdy revetted blast walls, all of which was – we'd been reassured – built to withstand a direct bomb blast. I hoped I'd never find out if that was true.

Suddenly, a large downward spike appeared on the far

right-hand side of my screen. As I watched, it moved across, growing and shrinking in size, the classic signature of two or more aircraft flying together. Another spike appeared, and another. I waited to see if any would develop that tell-tale pulse that indicated an IFF signal. None did.

'What were you saying?' I asked Len drily. This was a big one, by the looks of it. More contacts were appearing all the time, and coming closer; they were less than fifty miles away now. How many times had I seen similar scenes unfold on my screen in the last two weeks? Air attacks had intensified between Shetland and Scandinavia recently, especially at night, and so far, despite intense speculation – although, of course, there was no hope of us mere mortals ever being told what the higher-ups knew – no one could quite work out what was going on.

'Looks like they're coming this way,' I said.

'Not again.' Ray's face was grim.

'No chance of it being a flock of birds?' Len said lightly, referring to an incident back when I'd first arrived on the station, when what everyone had thought was a raft of German bombers had turned out to be a formation of migrating geese, causing equal parts annoyance and amusement.

'In February? Not likely,' Ray said, failing to register Len's attempt at a joke. 'Haven't they all gone south already?'

Once we'd passed the information to the filter room at Lerwick, there wasn't much more we could do except keep watching. First, our own aircraft showed up as another set of echoes, and then the spikes on the screen merged as a fierce dogfight unfolded somewhere over the North Sea; Fighter Command attempting to send Jerry packing or blast him out of the sky. I passed a weary hand over my eyes as memories of my own time on aircrew flashed in front of my eyes, and I remembered all those night flights on the Stirlings where we'd witnessed fighters battling with the Germans in the skies above and around us.

Despite being a whole continent away from home, it was easy, when I wasn't on duty, to pretend the war wasn't really happening. People in Fiskersay seemed to have the attitude that, despite the daily hardships – the rationing of food and clothes; the air raids – they weren't going to let that pesky Hitler dictate how they lived their lives. But here, crammed into the claustrophobic operations room with it playing out on the screen right in front of us, it was impossible to ignore. A glance at Len and Ray told me they were thinking the same thing; I knew we were all tired of the uncertainty. And the news that reached us here of the bombing raids on the British mainland was terrible – I couldn't imagine what it must be like in those places, living with the fear of being smashed to pieces night after night.

Focus, I told myself. I made myself turn my full attention back to my screen, waiting, with a mixture of dread and anticipation, for the next contact to appear.

The morning watch came to relieve us at 8 a.m. That afternoon, after I'd attempted to snatch a few hours' sleep – no easy feat with men clattering in and out of the hut – I ate lunch in the NAAFI and decided to go for a walk to clear my foggy head. We'd had yet more snow, and a week ago a particularly fierce storm had taken out the dipoles on Svarta Ness's transmitter tower, causing a major headache for everyone until they were repaired. Today, though, the sun was trying to shine, although it was bitterly cold and everywhere was still blanketed in a layer of white.

Bundled up in my greatcoat, scarf and hat, I found myself walking along the road that led past the Sinclairs' croft without even thinking about it; my feet seemed to take me there of their own accord. As I neared the cottage, I saw Hedda coming from the other direction with Eirik holding her hand. When he spotted me, he broke away from her and ran down the road, calling, 'Mr Bill! Mr Bill!'

As he reached me, I grinned at him, marvelling anew at the change in him. He was shooting up like a weed, his round-cheeked face now glowing with health. 'Hello, Eirik. Been making any more Spitfires recently?'

He began talking to me in his usual mixture of Norwegian and English, the words tumbling from his mouth. 'Woah, slow down,' I said, laughing, as Hedda caught up with us. She was carrying Eirik's school bag in one hand and a pail of water in the other.

'Here, let me,' I said, taking the pail.

'Thank you.' She smiled at me. She looked different as well, I realised: the deep lines around her mouth and eyes had all but vanished and the tense set of her shoulders had eased. 'I am sorry about Eirik. He is excited – the Sinclairs' son, Willie, heard we were staying here and sent an old camera for him. It arrived this morning. I promised him I would take him for a walk after he finished school so that he could try it out.'

We had reached the cottage; Eirik rushed inside. 'Eirik!' Hedda called after him, taking his school bag from her shoulder. He came back out and snatched it from her, and pelted back into the house. She shook her head, looking amused.

'He's looking well,' I said.

'Yes. It is good for him here.' She looked around and took a deep breath, smiling again. 'Me too. I know I said this to you before, but it is so nice not to live in constant fear of Soviet bombs or of saying the wrong thing and being arrested by the Germans.'

'I'll bet.'

Eirik pelted out of the house again, swinging the camera – a compact Kodak – by its strap. Hedda said something sharp to him in Norwegian, and he looped the strap around his neck, looking chastened.

'I am telling him to be careful as the camera does not belong to him,' she told me as the door opened again and Elizabeth Sinclair came out for the pail of water.

'Bill!' she greeted me effusively after thanking Hedda. 'How are you? Is dat leg of yours still troublin' you?'

'Sometimes,' I said. To be honest, I didn't pay much attention to the aches in my shin and shoulder any more. As for the nightmares – the ones where I was back in the plane, caught in that cone of light with Robert bleeding out in the pilot's seat, or of the truck pulling out of the side road and our car slamming into it, and Robert's screams – they'd become normal for me now, part of the background of my life. Most of the time I was able to lock what had happened away in a box in the back of my mind.

'Ach, I said to Donald, after we saw you at the dance in Talafirth last week, dat you're looking better every day,' Elizabeth said.

'It must be the air here,' I said, only half joking.

'Aye, and all that good food they're feeding you sodjers up at the camp.'

I chuckled to myself. What they served up in the NAAFI couldn't exactly be called *good food*, although it was better than the fare I'd had to force down at some of the aerodromes back in England. 'More likely it's your scones, Mrs Sinclair,' I said, and she blushed, looking pleased.

'*Mamma*,' Eirik whined, clearly impatient to get going.

'Shh, *lille vennen*,' Hedda said. 'I'm coming.'

'I'll walk with you,' I said.

We walked around the side of the Haug with Eirik skipping ahead. 'It's true,' Hedda said at last. 'You do look better. Like you are…' She stopped, and I could tell she was trying to find the right words. 'Less sad.'

'I suppose so,' I said. I still hadn't told Hedda what had happened and didn't know if I ever would. As thoughts of the accident and Robert threatened to loom in my mind, I slammed them back into that box and turned the key.

We reached the path that led down to Odda's Bay, facing towards the Holm of Odda and Odda's Fang. When we got to the beach, Eirik made us stop, standing next to each other, so he could take a photograph, laboriously winding the film on with his gloved hands before bringing the camera up to squint through the viewfinder.

'No, Mr Bill, you stand there,' he directed me. 'And look round at me. Mamma, you move closer to him. And both of you must smile!'

'He's a regular Cecil Beaton,' I joked, laughing, as we got into our positions. Hedda threw her head back, laughing too, and Eirik pressed the shutter.

'He will have missed our heads out of the picture, just you see,' she said as we sat down on a flat rock that was clear of snow and Eirik ran down to the water's edge. The bay was somewhat sheltered from the wind, and the sea glittered in the sun.

'You mark my words, he'll be shooting fashion plates for the magazines by the time he's ten.'

Hedda snorted and shook her head, but she was still smiling. 'I don't mind what he does, as long as he's happy,' she said.

Talking about magazines made me think of Rose, and that reminded me of something. 'There's going to be a concert up at the camp next week,' I said. 'ENSA are paying Shetland a visit.'

'ENSA?'

'The Entertainments National Service Association. They're different units who travel around putting on shows for the troops.'

'Oh, yes. You mentioned them before – your fiancée is in an ENSA unit, isn't she?'

I nodded. 'The locals are all invited. Will you come?'

'I'd love to.'

'I'll warn you, though – you never know what you're getting until the curtain goes up. This lot could be terrible. Probably will be. They're not going to send their brightest and best out here.'

'Will it be worse than Mr McLaggan and his accordion?'

I snorted. Old Hugo McLaggan and his accordion were a fixture at all the local dances. He didn't actually know how to play the thing, but he looked so damn happy as he wheezed away on it in the corner that no one ever had the heart to discourage him. 'I can't promise anything,' I warned her.

'But it will be fun, yes?'

'Oh, no doubt.'

'Then I'll be there.' She hugged her arms around herself, turning her head to gaze out at sea. Above us, gulls wheeled through the pale February sky, calling to one another. 'My goodness, if someone had told me a year ago that my life would be like this, I would not have believed them. It does not seem possible not only to have escaped the Nazis, but to be working as a nurse again. If my husband could see me now—'

She clamped her lips tightly together, and I remembered the night we'd watched the Mirrie Dancers, and her telling me her husband was a *difficult man*. She never talked about missing him, though, or about wanting to go back to Norway to see him. In fact, now I thought about it, she hardly ever mentioned him at all. What *was* he like? Was he only difficult, or was it worse than that? Had he been cruel to her? Was that why, when she'd first come here, she'd worn such a haunted expression? At the time, I'd put it down to the ordeal she'd been through, but what if there was more to it than that?

That's none of your damn business, Gauthier, and you know it, I told myself sternly.

'It goes to show, no matter what your plans are, life has a way of doing what it wants,' I said. 'We're just along for the ride, I guess.'

Hedda nodded. 'That is very true. But at times like this, I'm glad it is *this* ride, all things considered.'

For a moment, I could feel something buzzing in the air between us; not the awkwardness that had been there before the Christmas party and air raid, when we'd been unsure of one another, but the new tension I'd first felt at the Sinclairs' on Christmas Day. It was something I couldn't quite put my finger on, and I wasn't sure I should try to.

Then Eirik came running back to us, shouting something

to Hedda in Norwegian and pointing at the water's edge, and the spell was broken. Hedda stood, frowning.

'He says there is something in the water – part of a boat or a plane,' she said.

I stood too. 'Where, Eirik?' I asked him.

He led us to the other end of the beach. The tide had gone out, revealing a jumble of rockpools, and as I scrambled awkwardly after him I saw an enormous, twisted metal plate wedged in a fissure between two stones. I had a sudden flashback to the day I'd helped rescue Hedda and Eirik from the Norwegian fishing vessel, the sea pounding over the rocks, the capsized boat, Lewis and me.

'Be careful, it's slippery,' Hedda said, warily eyeing the lettuce-like weed blanketing the rocks where the sea had washed away the snow. I got as close as I could and squinted at the piece of metal. It was grey with letters and part of a number painted on it in black. One of ours. Then I noticed something else: at one edge, clearly visible, were two bullet holes, the metal that had been exposed where they'd punched through still bright. I thought back to the hostile contacts we'd seen on our screens last night – the swarm of green spikes. Was this the result?

'Do you know what it's from?' Hedda asked me quietly.

I shook my head. 'A ship, I'd say, but—'

'Oh!' Suddenly, she clutched my arm. Her voice dropped to a whisper. 'Bill – look – is that…?'

I followed her gaze. Just beyond where the metal plate was wedged was a huddled shape in a Naval uniform, bobbing face-down in the water.

A body.

'Eirik!' I said, trying to keep my tone light as I pointed

towards the top of the beach, desperately hoping I could distract him before he saw it too. 'How fast can you run back up there? I bet I can beat you!' Memories of the day Hedda and Eirik washed ashore were flooding into my mind yet again; I could see the bodies of the Norwegian crew laid out on the clifftop.

With a shout, Eirik took off, not waiting to see if we were following.

'Thank you,' Hedda said as we climbed back over the rocks after him. She was pale, and kept glancing behind her.

'I'll go straight back to the station,' I said. 'We'll come down and get him out.'

She nodded, worrying at her lower lip with her teeth.

'Mr Bill, you didn't even try to race me!' Eirik accused me when we reached him.

'Sorry, buddy, my leg was hurting me.' I tried to force a smile. 'We'll try again another time, eh?'

'Let us return to the cottage,' Hedda said, absently ruffling his hair. 'It is getting very cold. Perhaps Mrs Sinclair will have some warm milk for you if you ask her nicely.'

Eirik, thankfully none the wiser, kept up a stream of chatter, snapping photographs with his camera, as Hedda and I followed him in silence back to the Sinclairs' croft.

'Oh, I have finished the film,' he said sadly.

'Let me have it,' I said. 'One of the fellows up at the station has set up a little darkroom in one of the storage sheds – I bet he'd develop it if I asked him nicely.'

'Are you sure?' Hedda said. 'I don't want to put you to any more trouble.'

'It's no problem,' I said. Eirik gave me the camera and I quickly rewound the film and took it out, putting it in my pocket.

By the time I'd left them and was hurrying back to the station, clouds had begun to mass on the horizon: more snow on its way. I shivered, but not because of the cold. That guy in the water – had he been caught up in the attack last night, or had something else happened to him?

But I knew from experience that raking over things after the fact was useless. It wouldn't change anything. It certainly wouldn't save that sailor. The only thing we could do now was get the poor bastard out of the water and give him a dignified burial. I wondered if he had a family somewhere, waiting for him to come back to them and unaware – for now – that they were never going to see him again. That made me think of Des, and Robert, and all the other guys in my squadron who'd never made it home. My stomach twisted, the darkness inside my head yawning open like a crevasse.

Don't think about it, I told myself fiercely. I pushed myself to walk even faster, welcoming the pain that shot through my leg because it drove everything else from my mind.

NINETEEN

HEDDA

'Oh, it's terrible – those poor men. What must it have been like for them, knowing they were so far from home with no hope of rescue?' Margaret Mackay sighed, smoothing her newspaper out on her lap as I took ointment, a dressing and bandages from my nurse's bag.

Laying my things out on the little table beside her chair, I glanced at the headline of the article she was reading:

NIGHT ATTACK ON ALLIED SHIPPING CONVOY.

I couldn't read the rest from where I was standing, but immediately, I remembered the body Bill and I had found washed up on the rocks in the bay two days ago, and that piece of metal from a ship with bullet holes in it. I wasn't sure what had happened after Bill and I parted, as I'd taken Eirik straight back to the croft, but when the sailor was buried up at the church yesterday morning there had been a crowd of people there to pay their respects. I had gone along too, and spotted Bill, looking pale and tired, at the edge of the churchyard. Our gazes met briefly, and he nodded at me, but by the time the service was over he had gone. Had the sailor been one of the men who'd drowned in that attack?

Margaret had her bad leg propped up on a little footstool. I carefully unwrapped the bandage already wound around her calf, noting with some relief that at last the angry-looking wound was beginning to heal. I felt satisfaction, too – the satisfaction I'd felt as a young girl, knowing I'd been useful to my father; that I'd felt when I was training and my teacher smiled at me and said, *You've done well today, Hedda*; the satisfaction I'd felt upon walking into Oslo hospital on my first day as a qualified nurse, proud of my neat uniform and the hard work I'd put in to get here, sure that this was the start of a long career helping others.

That day I'd seen Magnus Tonning for the first time; I'd giggled about him with my friends, and we'd all agreed that he was a good-looking man. Little had I known, then, what would happen next: being singled out for praise; the requests to work late with him; then him asking me to accompany him to a conference in Bergen, where he kissed me for the first time. I'd been so young; so naive. I'd known he was married, and had been shocked at his actions at first, but when he'd told me that his marriage was an unhappy one – that both he and his wife had agreed, discreetly, to see other people – I'd believed him. Or rather, I'd convinced myself that I did, and that that made it OK. He had such a forceful personality that I didn't feel able to refuse him; I was scared he might make things difficult for me at the hospital if I did.

'How is it looking?' Margaret asked.

I smiled at her. 'Much better.'

'Oh, thank goodness for that.'

As I put ointment on the wound and re-dressed it, Margaret

went back to her newspaper, frowning and occasionally shaking her head and making small, sad tutting sounds. She often read while I was treating her. When I'd finished tying the new bandage, I sat back on my heels for a moment and looked around the room. It was as neat and sparse as always, the table under the window still cluttered with half-built radio sets, but one thing had changed: it was warmer now. The first thing I did when I got here for my daily visit was build up the fire until it roared. Margaret had protested at first, saying that Charles would be worried about wasting fuel, but when I'd relayed this to Doctor Gaudie he'd bellowed, 'Let him worry! If he's going to be that bloody stingy, I'll bring the woman some peats from my own supply.'

Although his outburst had taken me by surprise, he'd been as good as his word, telling me to keep an eye on the pile stacked up in the little wooden store beside the Mackays' outhouse and to let me know when Margaret needed more. I had still been worried that Charles might take offence, but a few days ago, when I'd gone to collect Eirik from school, he thanked me stiffly for taking such good care of his mother. 'I'm afraid I had no idea about her leg, or that she was letting the house get so cold,' he'd said. 'What with the school and my Home Guard duties, I am out for most of the day, and she tells me she's fine, of course.'

After that first visit to Margaret I'd been annoyed with Charles, thinking that he had been neglecting her, but it seemed I had got him wrong. 'Don't worry about it, please,' I had reassured him. 'She won't be allowed to get in such a state again.'

Charles had sighed. 'She's stubborn, that's the trouble. Still thinks she's a young woman and I'm a child!'

'I suppose none of us like to think we're getting older,' I said.

He sighed again. 'No, I suppose not.'

Truth be told, I still felt terribly sorry for the man. It couldn't be easy for him, having to care for his mother on top of all his other duties, especially when his own health was poor. Sometimes, when I was visiting Margaret on a Saturday or a Sunday and he did not have Home Guard duties, he would be there and we'd talk a little. He would ask me about Norway, saying that as a younger man, he'd wanted to go to Scandinavia; he'd once dreamed of being a painter or a writer and had planned to write a book about his travels. But then the Great War had come along, and that dream had been lost forever.

It was odd, because in some ways, I felt I knew more about Charles than I did about Bill. Certainly, if a stranger had asked me to tell them both men's life stories, it was details about Charles I could have furnished them with. But I felt much more at ease with Bill, and not just because we were close in age. With him, I could be carefree; I loved the stories he told me of his life back in Canada about his parents and friends there, and of his exploits when he was training to be in the RAF. The way he described the things that he'd done were so lively and vivid I could almost imagine I'd been there too. Charles, friendly though he was, always seemed to be always holding something of himself back, deliberately keeping me – and everyone else – at a distance.

But who could blame him? I knew all too well what horrors war could bring; the corners it forced you into and the terrible things it could drive you to do. Even now, the face of the German officer still lingered in my nightmares, and Eirik still suffered with bad dreams, too. What must it have been like for Charles in the trenches, surrounded on all sides by destruction and death? How could you ever leave something like that behind you?

I got up, putting my things back in my bag. Margaret folded up her newspaper and gave me a bright smile. 'Do you have time for a cup of tea before you go?' she said.

I smiled. It was our usual ritual, and when I looked at my watch I saw I had almost half an hour before I needed to see my next patient, a child who was recovering from pneumonia and lived only a few streets away. 'I will make it,' I said – also part of our ritual.

When I returned to the parlour with the tea things on a tray, Margaret said, 'I hear there's going to be a concert up at the camp.'

'Yes,' I said. 'I'm hoping to go. Will Charles bring you?'

'Oh, I hope so. It's years since I've been to a concert!' Margaret said. 'I can't manage the dances these days – not with my heart trouble, or my leg – but it would be grand to sit and listen. Will your young man be there?'

I frowned at her. 'My... young man?'

'Yes!' Her lined face wrinkled in another broad smile. 'That soldier. Bertha Sutherland came to bring me a parcel the other day and she told me that she saw you both at the dance at Talafirth Hall last week.'

Oh. She meant Bill. For some reason, I felt my face growing hot. 'He's not my young man, Mrs Mackay – I'm married, remember? My husband is back in Norway. And Bill is engaged.'

'Oh, silly me, of course.' Margaret flapped her hands, looking embarrassed. 'I'm sorry, what a dreadful gossip you must think me. I promise you Bertha and I were only making chit chat.'

'It doesn't matter,' I reassured her, although my stomach was tying itself in knots. Did other people think there was more between me and Bill than just friendship? Was I giving everyone the wrong impression? *What would Anders say?*

I caught myself again. Anders was not here. He was over a thousand miles away. How would he ever know? As always, the thought was a mere reflex, ingrained after years of enduring his temper and paranoia, and of having him inhabit my every waking moment, whether he was physically there with me or not.

Anyway, I was doing nothing wrong by being friends with Bill. Yes, I had danced with him that night. I'd danced with a lot of people, including fifteen-year-old Niall Sutherland, Bertha's son, and ninety-year-old Alan Robertson who was, as he liked to tell anyone who would listen, still as lively as he was in his days as a herring fisherman. Everyone danced together at these things. That was the whole point.

As if a man like him would be interested in an ugly thing like you anyway, I heard Anders jeer at me, and jumped; it was as if he'd spoken right in my ear.

I drank my tea. 'I must go, Mrs Mackay,' I said, forcing cheer into my voice and hoping she hadn't noticed anything.

She looked at me with mild surprise. 'Already, dearie? Oh, well, if you must. Will you leave the teapot? I think I'll have another cup.'

By the time my rounds were over, it was time to collect Eirik from school. I did not do this every day now as he often walked back to the cottage with his friends, but he did not seem to mind when I was there waiting for him. As we walked home, Eirik chattered to me – mostly in English now; his language skills were improving all the time – but I wasn't really paying attention. My mind was drifting as I wondered what it would be like to be married to someone like Bill – someone who was kind, who smiled at me and said, *oh, never mind about that*, instead of looking at me with loathing in his eyes because the bread hadn't risen enough or there was a missed cobweb in the corner.

Suddenly the new, rebellious voice inside my head spoke up. *What if you didn't return to Norway? What if you stayed here, on Fiskersay, or went to the mainland. After all, Anders has no idea where you are. You could even change your name – how would he find you then?*

My heart began to beat faster, even as I recognised it for the fantasy it was. I couldn't just leave Anders. I was his *wife*.

But the thought had ignited something that did not want to be extinguished. Since coming here, I could feel all the knots inside me – knots that were wound tight after years of tiptoeing around Anders, second-guessing everything I did – slowly but surely loosening. I rarely jumped now when someone came into a room I was in, or felt panic close around my throat like a hand as I dressed in the morning, wondering if what I had chosen to wear would be deemed acceptable. And Eirik had lost that permanently wary look he'd worn long before having to live under German occupation and constant bombardment from the Soviets.

What if, when the war ended, I didn't go back?

What if I took a different path instead?

But *how?*

TWENTY

BILL

'I'm sorry, chaps, but until we find out why these attacks on the shipping convoys keep happening, all leave is suspended,' Flight Lieutenant Jackson said, and a collective groan rippled around the NAAFI. There were about thirty of us jammed in here: everyone on the station except the men currently on watch over at the ops site. The previous watch, who'd been on overnight, hadn't even had time to go back to their huts and were slumped in their seats, grey-faced with fatigue. 'I had hoped it wouldn't come to this,' Flight Lieutenant Jackson continued, 'but we're beginning to suspect that not only is information about the convoys being leaked to the enemy somehow, but that it's someone here in Fiskersay who's doing it.'

The groans turned to exclamations. We all turned to look at each other. 'Are you saying we've got a spy lurking about somewhere?' Len Kane said, sounding incredulous.

'I'm afraid so, yes.' Flight Lieutenant Jackson took a sheet of paper from his breast pocket, unfolded it and crossed the NAAFI to pin it to the wall. 'Sergeant Black and I have been asked to interview each of you – a nasty business, and we feel as uncomfortable about it as you do, but those are the orders, I'm afraid. Everyone's names are on this list and when it's your time, you must come over to the Manor. We're starting straight away.'

'Well, when you find out who it is, let us know, and we'll all line up to help you wring his bloody neck,' Len said, scowling, as we made our way over to look at the list. As I searched for my name – it was near the top, and I was expected over at the Manor in an hour's time – I wondered if Jackson was right and there *was* a spy somewhere. It would certainly explain the sudden increase in raids. But surely it couldn't be anyone at the station. How would they be getting hold of the information in the first place? We weren't told about shipping movements near Shetland; like everything else to do with the war, information was given out on a strictly need-to-know basis; a whole fleet of submarines could have sneaked past Svarta Ness and we'd have been none the wiser.

Damn. What was I going to tell Rose? Leave from the station was hard enough to come by at the best of times, but I'd finally managed to secure fourteen days – which, what with having to take the ship to Lerwick, then another to the Scottish mainland where I'd wait at a rest camp for God knows how long before catching a train, and the train journey itself, then all that again in reverse, would be more like nine or ten – and I'd been planning to spend it in London with a quick visit to an old family friend near York en route.

As I headed back to Hut 1 to wait, I thought about the body Hedda and I had found nine days ago. The man had been identified as Ruben Clarke, a warrant officer with the Royal Navy, and he'd been part of a crew taking a convoy across to

Iceland from Scotland that was ambushed by the Germans. Clarke was the only man who'd been found; the rest of the crew were still missing, presumed dead.

When the time came for my interview, I made my way to the Manor, really just an ordinary, two-storey house in need of a new coat of whitewash and desperate for a lick of paint on the window frames and front door. The interviews were taking place in the dining room, which had been turned into an office. Flight Lieutenant Jackson looked more uncomfortable than ever as he and Sergeant Black, his deputy, questioned me about what I'd been doing and who I was with when I wasn't on duty.

'You've been spending time with that Norwegian woman, haven't you?' Flight Lieutenant Jackson said.

I frowned. 'Hedda? Yes – we see each other at dances sometimes, and we go for walks. That's all there is to it, though – we're just friends.' For some reason, as I said that, I felt my face warm up, remembering those moments where something – I still wasn't sure what the hell it had been – had passed between us.

'What she is to you is none of our business, Sergeant,' Flight Lieutenant Jackson said. 'We need to find out what's going on, that's all. And, well...' He cleared his throat. 'She has come from a country occupied by the Nazis.'

The truth of what he was saying suddenly dawned on me. 'But didn't you interview her when she first came here?' I said. 'Surely if she was a spy, you would have found out then?'

'I'm sure we would have,' Jackson said. 'All the same, I ask that you do not talk to her about any of this.'

I nodded. 'I understand, Sir.' I wouldn't have told Hedda anything anyway; we all knew the consequences of talking about the work we did here. I was certain, though, that the spy wasn't Hedda. It *couldn't* be.

After that, the questioning moved on. When he was satisfied that I knew nothing about how the shipping information might be reaching German ears, Flight Lieutenant Jackson let me go. 'And remember, none of this leaves the station,' he repeated in a warning tone as I went to the door.

'Of course not, Sir.'

'Very good, Sergeant. Dismissed.'

Outside, I passed a hand over my eyes. Christ, I needed a cup of tea. My head was a jumble as I thought about Hedda, the spy, and how I was going to break the news to Rose that I couldn't get to London after all.

I ended up getting permission to telephone Rose's flat in London later that morning from the clerk's office. A letter would've taken too long to reach her, if it even reached her at all. But Rose wasn't there. 'She's off travelling with that group of hers,' the woman who'd answered – her landlady – told me.

'Did she say where she was going? And how long she'd be?' I said, frowning. Rose hadn't said anything in her last letter about going away with her unit again before I came to London. Perhaps it had been a last-minute thing.

'Oh, no, she never tells me anything. Here one minute and gone the next, that's her, though I expect she'll be back in a few days – she usually is.' The landlady sounded sour. I remembered what Rose had told me about her in one of her letters a few months ago: *Mrs Cooke is an absolute dragon, you're not allowed to run taps or have the gramophone or*

*the radio on after 10 p.m., and if you go out for the evening
and she catches you on the stairs when you come back, she
looks at you as if you've been out walking the streets. My
goodness, I will be so glad when this awful war is over and
we're married and have a place to call our own!*

'Well, if you see her, could you please pass on a message
from Bill Gauthier?' I said.

Mrs Cooke sighed heavily; I'd never met her, and Rose
hadn't described her to me, but in my mind's eye I saw a thin,
middle-aged woman wearing a hairnet, thick stockings and
sturdy shoes, her mouth twisted in a perpetual scowl. 'Go on,
then,' she said, the *if I really must* unspoken but clear as a
bell.

'Can you tell her my leave next week has been cancelled,
please? And if you don't mind, perhaps I can give you the
number of my station so you can pass it on to her when she
comes back?'

Mrs Cooke let out another long breath. I added a cigarette,
permanently dangling from her lower lip, to my mental
picture of her.

'Right,' she said, and repeated the number back to me.
'That it?'

'It's a two at the end, not a three,' I said.

'Two not a three. Got it,' she said in a tone that left me
feeling rather unsure if she had. 'Anything else?'

'No, that's all. Thank you.' I hung up, feeling more deflated
than ever.

TWENTY-ONE

BILL

Rose didn't return my telephone call. I eventually went down to the Post Office and sent her a telegram, but she didn't reply to that either. By now, all the men in the camp and the small number of locals who worked here too – the clerk who'd replaced Archie Thomson after he, Isabel and their son had left for Edinburgh, and the two women who came up to the camp to do the laundry – had been interviewed, but no spy had been uncovered and no one was any closer to working out how the shipping information might be reaching the Germans. Despite that, all leave was still cancelled for the time being. Rumour had it the higher-ups wanted to start widening their net and interviewing locals with the help of the island's police officer. Meanwhile, almost every time I was on the night watch, I'd see the hostile contacts appear on my console screen in a pattern that now felt inevitable.

At last, my two rest days arrived. After spending the morning of the first one trying and mostly failing to catch up on some sleep, I decided to head over to the NAAFI.

'Looking forward to the show?' Lewis greeted me when I joined him and Len in the queue for the tea urn.

I looked at him blankly, still half asleep. 'Show?'

'ENSA. It's tonight.'

'Oh. Yeah. Sure.' I'd been so miserable about losing my leave that I'd forgotten all about it. I contemplated giving it a miss, then remembered I'd invited Hedda.

'We're taking bets on how bad it's gonna be,' Len said. 'Gotta be better than staring at the four walls of our huts all evening, though.'

Is it? I thought, a little drearily.

Behind us, I heard the doors to the NAAFI open, and whistles and cat calls. Len glanced round and raised his eyebrows, one side of his mouth quirking up in a smile. 'Huh, looks like the entertainment might have turned up early, fellas.'

I started to turn round too, but before I could see who everyone was whistling at, someone put their hands over my eyes and a familiar voice said, 'So *there* you are!'

I whirled round. Rose, looking very modern in smart slacks and a brown woollen jumper, was behind me, smiling.

I blinked, wondering if I was hallucinating. 'What – what are you doing here?' I said.

'Why, I'm here with ENSA, of course!' she said, and then I noticed the man standing behind her: her manager, Clive. He gave me a weak smile. He looked tired and a little green around the gills.

'It's your unit giving the concert? Why didn't you tell me? No wonder I couldn't get hold of you!'

She caught my hands in hers. 'We weren't sure it was even going to happen until a couple of days ago – the weather, you know. After that I decided it might as well be a surprise!'

'It sure is,' I stammered, still not quite able to believe that it was really her – that she was really here. Everyone in the NAAFI was looking at us.

'Well, are you going to kiss me or not?' Rose demanded, a dimple appearing in one cheek. I bent my head to press my lips to hers, and the whole NAAFI erupted into whistles and cheers again. I drew back self-consciously.

'We're staying in the hotel in Talafirth, if you can call it a hotel – there's hardly room to swing a cat! – but I convinced Clive we should come up and have a look at the camp before the show tonight.'

Clive gave me another of those weak smiles.

'Are you all right?' I asked him.

'Fine, fine. I was a little seasick on the way over here, that's all.'

'Oh, Clive, you should have told me you were still feeling ill!' Rose said, turning towards him with an oddly tender expression. 'I would never have dragged you all the way up here if I'd known!'

'It's fine,' he said. 'I'll be right as rain in an hour or two. I wouldn't mind a sit down, though.'

'You do that. I'll bring you a cup of tea,' Rose said.

I watched him walk across to a table in the far corner of the NAAFI.

'Well, aren't you going to introduce us?' Len said.

'Oh. Of course. Len, Lewis, this is Rose, my fiancée,' I said. 'Rose, this is Len Kane and Lewis Harper.'

'Very pleased to meet you both,' Rose said, that dimple appearing again as she shook their hands.

Len grinned, a devilish gleam in his eye.

'Hands off, Kane, she's Bill's,' Lewis said good-naturedly.

Rose made a face. 'Gosh, I'm not a pair of boots, you know.' But there was laughter in her eyes.

'Sorry. I'm only joking.'

She raised an eyebrow at Lewis, then turned back to me and pressed her lips to my cheek.

When we'd got our mugs of tea, Rose took one to Clive, and I watched them talk for a moment, Rose touching his arm, before she headed back over to me. We sat down with Len and Lewis. 'I can't stay long,' Rose told me. 'Your Commanding Officer – Flight Lieutenant Jackson, I think he said his name was – is driving us back to the hotel so we can all get ready.'

True to her word, once she'd drunk her tea, she pushed her chair back, saying to Len and Lewis, 'Thank you, boys. I'll see you tonight.' Then she looped her arm through mine – I'd stood up too – and said, 'Walk me out, Bill?' and held up a hand in Clive's direction. 'I won't be long!' she called to him.

He nodded; he still looked tired, but there was colour in his face again now.

Outside, Rose and I kissed again, properly this time, now no one was watching. As she pressed against me I felt all my old desire for her rushing back. 'Oh, Bill, I've missed you!' she said when we came up for air. 'I was worried you might forget me.'

'Forget you?' I said. 'How could I forget you? You were the only damn thing keeping me going when I was in that hospital, and as for when I was sent here…'

I trailed off. I didn't want to think about how I'd felt when I first arrived in Shetland; how completely alone I'd been, with only the terrible memories of what had happened to keep me company.

'Did you get my telegram?' I said instead.

She shook her head. 'I'm afraid I haven't been home for a few weeks – when I've not been travelling with the unit, I've been staying with Mummy. London was getting to be such a bore what with all the air raids, and there wasn't a decent afternoon tea to be found anywhere! Although I expect it's even worse here!' she added, looking round with a little shiver. 'It's terribly bleak, isn't it? Even worse than you described in your letters after you first arrived! It feels like the ends of the earth!'

I tried to remember exactly what I'd said to her back then, but I couldn't. All I remembered was the black, dragging misery that had now completely faded away. In its place was something that couldn't quite be called contentment – I still had those nightmares about Robert in the plane almost every night – but wasn't far off. I had friends here now, and most of the time, I felt OK. Just yesterday I'd gone for a walk, and even in the midst of my gloom over my cancelled leave, I'd been able to appreciate the vastness of the blue skies that stretched over the island from horizon to horizon; the way the sun glittered a dazzling silver on the sea. There'd even been a hint of spring in the air. It was nothing tangible – the daffodils that several locals had promised me would soon be blooming all over the island in spring proper were only just poking their heads above the ground – but even now, with clouds covering the sky once again, the air felt different, softer somehow, with the promise of warmer, longer days just around the corner. Bleak? No. Quiet, perhaps, but not bleak.

As for being able to get a decent afternoon tea, well, it was a pity there wouldn't be time to introduce Rose to Elizabeth Sinclair's scones. If there had been, she might have changed her mind about that too.

'Anyway, why did you wire me? Is something wrong?' Rose said, breaking into my thoughts; I'd become lost in them without even realising.

'I can't get leave next week – it's been cancelled.'

Her shoulders slumped. 'Oh, Bill, *really?*'

'Really. I'm sorry, sweetheart.'

'Why?'

'They need all hands on deck here at the station. That's all I can say, I'm afraid.'

She gazed at the ground, digging the toe of her shoe into the grass, her mouth twisted unhappily.

'I'll come as soon as I can,' I said gently.

She sighed. 'It doesn't matter. And it's probably all worked out for the best, really. You'd have to come and see me at Mummy and Daddy's, and Daddy's being an absolute beast at the moment.'

I was yet to meet her father, but she had opened up to me in her letters about him and I always remembered her telling me about him the first time we met. *He still treats me like a child*, she'd said. *It's infuriating!*

'He's putting pressure on you about the wedding again, eh?'

'Not half. He thinks I should have been married off *years* ago. As if being twenty-four makes me an ancient crone or something!'

I drew her close again and kissed the top of her head, breathing in the slightly herby scent of her shampoo and marvelling at the solid warmth of her slim body against mine, still not quite believing that she was here; that I was actually holding her in my arms after we'd been apart for so long.

'Forget him,' I said. 'He's there, and you're here. We'll just have to make the most of it.'

Briefly – just briefly – a memory of those moments with Hedda at Christmas and on the beach drifted into my mind.

I shoved them resolutely away.

Twenty-Two

HEDDA

'My goodness, I don't think I've been to a show like this since I was a girl,' Elizabeth Sinclair said to me as we got off the bus and followed everyone else through the camp gates. She was smiling, her face lit up with excitement. 'What do you think it'll be like?'

I decided not to share the warning Bill had given me about ENSA last week. 'I'm not sure,' I said. 'I've never been to anything like this either.'

Although I'd left Eirik back at the croft with Donald, who claimed he was too old for 'all dat concert nonsense' ('Ach, that's you wantin' an excuse to spend the evening dozin' by the fire!' Elizabeth had scolded him good-naturedly before we left), it looked as if almost everyone else on the island was here, all wearing their finest clothes under their heavy coats. Elizabeth was dressed in a lace-collared velvet frock that smelled slightly of mothballs, despite several days' airing, and a pair of worn but serviceable low-heeled leather shoes she said she had worn to her wedding fifty years before. I had on a smart fawn woollen skirt someone had given to me when I first came to the island, a cream blouse and the cardigan I had spent the long, dark evenings of Fiskersay's winter knitting, although I'd had to settle for a pair of sturdy everyday shoes as I had nothing else.

The NAAFI was crowded and noisy. 'Let me find you somewhere to sit down,' I told Elizabeth as we edged our way across the room. At the front, a stage had been set up with heavy red velvet curtains drawn across it. Elizabeth kept a hand on my arm as we made our way to the front of the room. I saw some empty chairs and guided her towards them.

'Ach, there's Bill,' Elizabeth said as we sat down. I followed her gaze and saw him standing near the stage, talking to a slender, glamorous-looking woman in a wine-coloured dress and matching cardigan, wearing lipstick in a brighter shade of red, her hair immaculately waved. Bill looked round and saw us. He grinned and said something to the woman – it was so noisy, I couldn't hear what – and they came over.

'Hedda, Elizabeth, this is my fiancée, Rose,' he said as I stood again and the woman's eyes travelled across me, taking in what I was wearing in one sweeping gaze. I suddenly felt very shabby and ordinary. After what felt like a long time, but in reality could only have been a second or two, Rose smiled, her whole face becoming animated; I could see why he wanted to marry her.

'Hedda – oh, yes! Bill told me about you! You're the girl from Norway, aren't you?' she said, clasping my hand. 'How terrifying it must have been for you, coming all the way over the sea in a little boat like that!'

Her tone irritated me; did she think I was a child? *Don't*, I told myself sternly. *She is being nice.* I forced myself to smile back and said, 'It is very good to meet you.'

But Rose had already turned away and was talking to

Elizabeth in that same gushing tone as she complimented her dress.

'It was quite the surprise when Rose turned up, I can tell you!' Bill said to me. There was no denying he and Rose made an attractive pair: he looked equally handsome in his dress uniform, each button polished to a shine and his hair slicked back. 'I had no idea it was her ENSA group who'd been booked in to play here.'

'What luck,' I said, keeping my tone light.

'I'll say. At least the show will be worth listening to.'

A thin, middle-aged man in a dark suit, holding a conductor's baton in one hand, appeared at Rose's elbow and said, 'It's time.'

'All right, Clive, just coming!' Rose turned her brilliant smile on the man, then leaned up to kiss Bill on the cheek. 'I'll see you later, darling,' she said.

'Break a leg,' he said, the fondness in his tone unmistakable, and I couldn't help the little twist of envy I felt inside me. If only I had someone who talked to me that way! Not even Magnus had done that. Even before meeting Anders, I'd been shy and had little self-confidence because of my mother's constant criticisms as I was growing up, and with hindsight, Magnus' nickname for me, *liten mus* – little mouse – felt more like an insult than a term of affection. *You're so quiet, little mouse!* he'd said to me one day near the end of our relationship (although I didn't know it was coming to an end, not then). We were lying in bed in his smart townhouse, the first time I'd been there. His wife was away, visiting a relative, and he'd let me in through the back door after dark so none of the neighbours would see me. *So meek! How do you expect anyone to take you seriously when you scuttle around and refuse to speak or look anyone in the eye? Your problem, Hedda, is that you don't believe in yourself.*

I'd waited for him to share some wisdom that might help my shy nineteen-year-old self find what she so obviously lacked, but it appeared the conversation was over; he'd turned out the light, and we'd made love. That was the night I became pregnant with Eirik. Two months later, by the time it had dawned on me why my menses had stopped – I had, at first, put it down to the stress of my new job – and I started to feel sick all day, I no longer existed as far as Magnus Tonning was concerned. A month after that, I'd been on my way to Kirkenes, deep inside the Arctic Circle, to stay with my father's aunt, as far away from the family as my father could manage to send me so that my pregnancy didn't cause a scandal in our little town. And it was shortly after *that* that that I met Anders. I was just starting to show by then, although my bump was still easily concealed at that stage; those who did know of my pregnancy were told I'd had a husband who was killed in a hunting accident. Anders had bumped into my great aunt and I in town one day and she had introduced us, grudgingly. I was captivated by his piercing gaze, its power rendering me barely able to speak, and afterwards Great Aunt Hanna had made a point of telling me about his role as the manager at Sydvaranger and how well respected he was by the townspeople. 'If you didn't have such loose morals,' she sniped, 'You could have got yourself a nice man like that!' She shook her head. 'Such a shame about his wife, Marit. She died last year. Cancer, it was – took her within a month. She just wasted away!'

So no one was more surprised than me when, the next day, Great Aunt Hanna invited Anders over for a cup of tea. I sat in an armchair while they chatted, too shy to join in the conversation except when Anders spoke directly to me.

At one point, I went to the kitchen to refresh the teapot. When I came back along the hall, I heard Anders say my name. 'She is a dear little thing,' he continued. 'If Marit was still here, I'm sure she would agree,' I frowned. Was he really talking about me?

But now, it seemed that it was me Anders had set his sights on. A whirlwind romance followed, Anders promising me that he would honour my 'husband's' memory by raising my child as his own, and saying that I'd be honouring his first wife's by marrying him and looking after him. It wasn't until after our wedding that I realised what he'd really been after – a maid who would clean, cook, mend and wash for him, clear up his empty *Akevitt* bottles and make sure the drink never ran out – and by then it was far too late. He'd targeted me because I was young and naive, and desperate to claw back some semblance of respectability and give Eirik a stable life.

Perhaps if I *had* believed in myself a little more, I wouldn't have fallen for Anders' charms, false as they were – or Magnus's before that.

'It really is lovely to meet you both,' Rose said to me and Elizabeth, wrenching me away from my memories. Then she was gone in a cloud of violet-scented perfume.

I watched Bill watch her go.

There was an empty seat beside me; I was hoping Bill would take it, but then I heard someone clear their throat. I looked round to see Charles Mackay standing there. 'Good evening, Hedda,' he said. 'May I sit here?'

'Of course,' I said, trying to smile at him as Bill gave me

an absent-minded nod before walking away to find a seat somewhere else.

'Before I forget, I want to say thank you,' Charles said as he sat down; he was careful about it, and I noticed him wince slightly, his hand going to his side. 'My mother's a changed woman since you started visiting her.'

I felt my cheeks warm slightly. 'Oh, I haven't done anything!'

'Yes, you have. As you've probably guessed, she's become increasingly isolated these last few years. Many of her friends have passed away and the ones who are still around live out on the crofts. Talafirth is too far for them to walk so she rarely sees them any more. I try my best of course, but, well, I'm just her son – it's not the same. Your visits make her feel like she has something to look forward to again.'

I felt a pang of empathy for Margaret, who – I saw now – was sitting a few chairs down from us beside Elizabeth, talking animatedly to her. They both saw me looking and grinned at me with childlike delight. I did know she was lonely, as Charles had said, but I hadn't realised she was *that* lonely – she had done a good job of hiding it from me.

'But what about you?' I said, noticing Charles wincing again as he shifted in his chair. 'Are you all right? Is something hurting you?'

'Oh, it's just an old injury. I was lifting something heavy the other day and aggravated it, that's all.'

'It looks painful.'

'Don't worry about me.' His voice was suddenly full of forced cheer. 'Fit for the scrap heap, that's all I am – the government didn't even think I was worth a decent pension after I was slung out of the army and left on the rubbish heap!'

Not for the first time, I remembered what Elizabeth had told me the day Eirik started school back at the beginning of January: *One night the whole lot of them were shelled in their trench. Charlie was the only survivor, and he was terribly badly hurt. We thought for a while he was not going to pull through. And when he did recover, and left the army, he could not find work anywhere – no one wanted him, and the government would not help.*

'I am sorry,' I said. 'That must have been hard.'

He gave me a smile that didn't quite reach his eyes, his gaze troubled and distant. It was the same look Bill got on the rare occasions he talked about his time on aircrew before coming to Fiskersay. 'Nothing to apologise for – it's not your fault. There were a lot of us in the same fix. I'm one of the lucky ones – at least I was able to bring Mother back here and start again.'

'Eirik certainly seems to be thriving at the school,' I said, and was gratified to see Charles's gaze soften.

'Thank you.'

The man with the conductor's baton who'd come to fetch Rose stepped onto the stage. 'Ladies and gentlemen!' he called, clapping his hands to get our attention, and a hush fell across the busy room. 'Thank you for welcoming us to Svarta Ness. My name is Clive Higgs, and I'm very pleased to present to you Rose Legge and the Reg Brown Orchestra!'

The lights dimmed and the curtains went back. Everyone applauded enthusiastically, the men whistling, as Rose, who'd shed her cardigan, stepped up to the microphone. Her shoulders were bare and her long dress clung to her elegant figure in all the right places. As she placed a hand on the microphone I saw the diamonds in her engagement ring winking in the beam from the spotlight that was shining on her.

Yes, Bill, I can see why you want to marry her, I thought as Clive raised his baton and the four men sitting behind Rose with their instruments began to play. Rose's voice soared up to the hut ceiling, clear and rich. She looked like a film star – like an angel. Again, I felt that twist of sadness inside me: grief for something I could never have.

But you have Eirik, I reminded myself. *And plenty of friends. And most importantly of all, you are both safe. So many people do not even have that.*

No, I might not have a man who loved me, but I had a lot to be grateful for; more than, at one point, I could ever have imagined. For now, that was enough.

I would worry about the future later, when I had to.

TWENTY-THREE

BILL

'Gosh, I don't like the sound of it out there,' Rose said, nestling against me as rain lashed against the sash windows and the wind, which had woken us up, rattled the wooden frames. 'Wild, isn't it?'

I picked up my watch off the bedside table, peering at it in the gloom to check the time: 8 a.m. It was the morning after the concert. When it had ended, I'd decided to return to the Royal Hotel in Talafirth with Rose and the rest of the orchestra, and we'd sat up late at the hotel bar, drinking and talking, until Rose and I were the only ones left. It felt almost like I'd gone back to my life before I'd had the accident and come to Svarta Ness, leaving me with a strange sense of dislocation that only intensified when, in the small hours, Rose and I had finally tumbled into bed. I had intended to go back to the camp, but she'd said, 'Oh, who cares what anyone thinks. We might not *actually* be married yet, but we're practically there. And who knows when we might see each other again?'

'You get used to it,' I told her now, lying down again with an arm flung over my head while she traced a finger across my chest. 'We have storms all the time here.'

Rose bit her lip. 'I hope it settles down by this afternoon, otherwise it'll be awfully rough trying to get back to the mainland. You should have seen how sick poor Clive was on the way here yesterday.'

'Thank goodness I didn't. I wish you didn't have to go so soon.'

'Me too.' Rose propped herself up on her elbow and looked at me sadly. 'But it isn't forever, darling. One day soon the war will be over, and then we won't have to do this any more – no more snatched moments together whenever we can get them, just married bliss!'

'We'll get sick of the sight of each other,' I joked.

She laughed. 'I'm sure we will. But once we have our house we'll be able to rattle about as we please and just see each other at mealtimes, so we shan't get *too* annoyed with one another.' The dimple in her cheek appeared. 'That place in Surrey is still for sale, you know. And as I've said in several of my letters, it's *so* convenient. It's a dreadful shame your leave was cancelled or could have gone to take a look at it.'

Damn. With everything that had been going on at the station – the attacks, the search for the spy – I had forgotten all about the house in Surrey, and forgotten to tell Rose it was beyond our means too.

'Honey,' I said, carefully, 'we need to talk about that.'

She looked up at me. 'You can't afford it,' she said flatly.

'Well – no. Not really. And even if I could, I'm not sure they'll let me stay in Britain after the war's over.'

One corner of her mouth twisted, and her eyebrows drew together.

'I wondered if you'd given any thought to Canada yet,' I said, heart thumping. 'I'll be able to get us a nice place over there, and I already have a job to go back to in my father's factory, you know...'

I waited anxiously for her to reply.

'Oh, let's not talk about this now,' she said at last. 'We've got plenty of time to sort things out, I suppose.'

I was a little disappointed at how dismissive she sounded, but I leaned up and kissed her. 'You're right. And I thought you wanted to make the most of your time here. Let's not fall out, eh?'

As she looked down at me, her hair falling across her face, there was a knock at the door. 'Rose?' I heard Clive say on the other side.

'Bugger,' she said under her breath; then, more loudly, 'Just a minute!'

She clambered out of bed and grabbed her robe, pulling it around her and tying the belt as she went to the door.

'Where's the fire?' she said as she opened the door a crack. 'I thought we weren't leaving until this afternoon?'

'We're not leaving at all,' Clive said. 'I've just been told there's storms forecast for the next four days, and the ship won't be able to go anywhere until they're over.'

'But what about the concert in Aberdeen?'

'I'm going to telephone in a bit – if I can get through – and try to postpone it. Sorry, nothing I can do. But perhaps we—'

'Well, I suppose it's good news, really,' Rose cut across him brightly. 'I'll be able to spend a bit more time with Bill! And you'll get a respite from your seasickness!'

'Yes.'

'Keep me posted,' Rose said, and closed the door on him. As she came back to bed, I was relieved to see she was smiling again. 'Now, where were we?' she said.

★

As forecast, the storm hung around for days, taking Svarta Ness off air for the duration as the aerial had to be lashed down. Back on watch, we whiled away the hours practising R/T procedures, using the telephones in the receiver and transmitter rooms.

For the first forty-eight hours, the weather was so bad I couldn't get off the station. Even walking between the technical site and domestic sites was a battle, with the wind trying to knock you off your feet and the sleet-filled rain soaking through to your underclothes in minutes if you'd been foolish enough to forget your mac. But by the third day, although it was still blowing a gale and the sea was heaving, the rain had passed. After I'd come off the overnight shift and snatched a few hours' broken sleep, I decided to walk down to the Royal Hotel. Being stuck there for three days solid while it rained sideways must have been driving Rose mad, and even if the weather had been good and her extended stay here had been planned, I couldn't exactly see her wanting to tramp around the hills and beaches.

As I walked along the muddy road, the sun was finally trying to break through the blanket of steel-coloured cloud sitting over the island like a lid. The calls of the gulls and the roar of the wind and the waves filled my ears, making me feel oddly content despite the fatigue that always came after a night shift. I remembered my realisation the day Rose had turned up – the day of the concert – that I didn't find the island bleak or uninviting any more. *Damn, Gauthier*, I thought. *This place really must be getting under your skin.*

When I got into the village I took a quick detour to

Sutherland's Stores, hoping I might be able to pick up a bunch of flowers, but the shelves were bare. 'I'm sorry, Sergeant,' Bertha said, 'but until the *Zetland Princess* can get to Lerwick again I've nothing in.'

'Don't worry about it,' I reassured her. 'Looks like the weather's on the turn anyhow.'

'I hope so. I'm ready for spring, I can tell you – we all are!'

Empty-handed but still cheerful, I made my way to the Royal Hotel and went up to Rose's room. As I reached the top of the stairs, I heard voices in the corridor beyond; a woman's and a man's, urgent but hushed, as if they were having an argument.

'But *when?*' the man's voice said, more clearly.

'Soon,' the woman's voice said, and I realised it was Rose. She and Clive were standing outside her room, Rose leaning against the wall with her arms folded and her head thrown back, almost defiantly. Clive wore an expression that was somewhere between annoyed and defeated.

I cleared my throat. They both jumped and looked round. 'Bill!' Rose said. 'You didn't tell me you were coming. Clive and I were just having a discussion about the upcoming concert programme, weren't we, Clive?'

'I must go,' Clive said. He pushed past me, hurrying down the stairs.

'What's got his goat?' I said.

'Heaven knows.' Rose caught my hand and leaned in for a kiss. 'I'm glad you're here – I was beginning to think I wouldn't see you again before we left!'

'No danger of that. I'm free for a few hours – do you want to go out and have a wander around? It's windy, but dry.'

She shook her head, her lip curling slightly. 'No, thanks. I can see everything of this place I need to from the window. I thought this was supposed to be a town? All that's out there is hills, sheep and the sea!'

She kept up a litany of complaints as we went into her room. As I'd suspected, she was going out of her mind with boredom. 'What do you *do* here?' she said as we undressed and got into bed. 'It's so… *provincial*. Everyone looks like they were born in the clothes they're wearing!'

'Hey, that's not fair,' I said. 'It's not like people can save up their coupons and nip down to Harrods like you can.'

She rolled her eyes. 'I know, I know. Look, I've just been a bit lonely here the last couple of days, that's all.' She relaxed into my arms. I began kissing her, sliding my hand around the curve of her breast, and after that, we didn't speak for a while.

'You should ask about getting a posting somewhere else,' Rose said afterwards, lighting a cigarette and blowing a stream of smoke up towards the ceiling. 'Oh, I don't mean flying again – that would be far too dangerous, I'd spend all my time worrying about you getting shot down or blown to bits – but surely there's a radar station somewhere near London you could ask to transfer to?'

I laughed. 'It doesn't quite work like that, I'm afraid.'

'Why not? Daddy has a cousin who's high up in the air force – perhaps I could write to him for you.'

'Please don't,' I said.

'But why *not*? You can't *like* it here! It's a wretched place – the absolute ends of the earth!'

'It's really not as bad as you think. Everyone's so kind – they do everything they can to make us feel welcome. And frankly, after the accident, and spending every night before that wondering if I'd make it back in one piece, being in Shetland's a tonic.'

Rose raised an eyebrow, taking another drag on her cigarette. 'I can't believe you really mean that!' she said. Her eyes narrowed. 'Is *that* why you aren't coming down to London next week?'

'No!' I exclaimed. 'I told you, our leave's been cancelled – there's nothing I can do about that! They probably *will* send me somewhere else at some point, but I don't get any say in it. They tell us where to go, and we go.'

Rose sighed heavily. 'I s'pose so.'

'C'mon,' I pleaded with her. 'Don't be like this. I don't even know when I'll see you again.'

She sighed again. 'It's not fair. This war is such a *nuisance*. If I could get to that horrid old Hitler, I'd shoot him myself.'

'You're at the back of a very long queue,' I told her, and quite unbidden, Hedda popped into my mind. Compared to Rose, she'd lost everything, yet I hadn't heard her complain about any of it – not once.

Jesus Christ, stop thinking about Hedda, I told myself. A wave of tiredness rolled over me; as usual, trying to catch forty winks in Hut 1 after being on watch all night had been like trying to sleep in a zoo. The hotel, by comparison, was quiet, save for the wind still making the window frames shudder.

'Wake me up at four, OK?' I told Rose, burrowing down into the pillows. If she answered me, I didn't hear her. I was asleep almost as soon as I'd closed my eyes.

TWENTY-FOUR

HEDDA

I stared at the columns of figures jotted down on the piece of paper in front of me, trying to work out if the money I was saving from my wages as Fiskersay's nurse – and after giving most of it to Elizabeth and Donald for mine and Eirik's keep, there wasn't a lot left – would eventually be enough to pay for passage to the Scottish mainland and find me and my son somewhere to live. Perhaps the authorities would let me stay here, on Fiskersay, but what would I do for work when Isabel Thomson and her family returned? My situation here was only temporary, and I was well aware that, if I wasn't going to return to Norway – *if you're going to run away*, my mind supplied unhelpfully – I needed to make sure I had some sort of plan in place so we could survive.

But how could I plan anything when so much depended on the outcome of the war? Everyone was sure, of course, that we'd beat the Germans in the end, but even the most optimistic of commentators couldn't say when that might happen. The uncertainty made me feel unsettled, like a boat that had lost its anchor.

Suddenly, the front door banged open and Eirik came charging in, his eyes red and his face streaked with tears.

'Mamma!' he said, rushing to me and flinging his arms around me.

'*Lille vennen*, what's wrong?' I said, my heart pounding inside my chest like that of a frightened, hunted animal. I had not seen him like this since we were fleeing the Germans back in Norway, and for one horrible moment I was back there, staring down at the officer's unmoving body with blind panic singing through my veins.

Eirik said something in Norwegian, his words coming out in a garbled rush. 'Shh, slow down and start again,' I said. Pushing him away slightly, I crouched down, taking him by the shoulders so I could see his face. 'Take a deep breath, *lille vennen*. Tell me what has upset you.'

Sniffling, Eirik held out his left hand and I saw three deep, angry-looking weals across his palm. 'Mr Mackay hit me,' he said.

I stared at the weals, horror, mingled with confusion, rising inside me. 'Why?'

He hiccuped. 'I was just telling David and Gordon how to say the days of the week in Norwegian.'

'In class?'

'No, in the playground. Mr Mackay heard us, and accused me of speaking German. When I tried to tell him it wasn't German, he got angry with me and hit me with his cane.'

I stared at Eirik, trying to match up what he was saying with the image of Charles I had formed in my head as I slowly got to know him: the quiet, well-spoken man who carried the pain of his past around with him like an invisible weight; who cared for his elderly, invalid mother without complaining;

who ran the school and headed the Fiskersay Home Guard, and was well-liked and respected by all the island's residents. I tried to remember if I had ever seen him show so much as a flash of temper, but I couldn't. Eirik occasionally complained that he was strict, and I had seen it for myself, of course, that first day he had gone to school and Charles had scolded David Couper for being late. But Charles did not strike me as an angry man, and God knows I had had enough practice at recognising *that*, being married to Anders.

I took a deep breath, trying to remain calm. 'Come, let me take a look at that hand,' I told Eirik, leading him gently to one of the chairs by the fireplace. 'Then you can go and help Elizabeth outside.'

Ten minutes later, with his hand bathed – it was, thankfully, not as bad as it looked, the marks already beginning to fade – Eirik joined Elizabeth in the garden, helping her to clear up her rain- and wind-battered plants, his tears almost forgotten.

'Elizabeth,' I said as I stepped outside too. 'I must call into town for something – is Eirik all right with you?'

She beamed at me. 'Ach, of course. He's da best peerie helper anyone could ask for!'

Drawing my shawl closer around me, I walked down to the schoolhouse. But when I got there it was dark and quiet, the door locked; Charles must have already gone home for the day. After a moment's hesitation, I walked the rest of the way into Talafirth, and rapped on the Mackays' front door.

'Hedda,' Margaret said when she answered it. 'I was not expecting you again today – is everything all right?'

'Everything is fine, Margaret,' I said, trying to keep my voice level. 'Is Charles here, please? I wanted to ask him about something.'

'He is at an emergency Home Guard meeting. He wouldn't tell me what it was about, just rushed off the moment he got back from school, but he should be home again in a little while.'

For a moment, I considered going up to the meeting hall in Talafirth where the Home Guard met for their drills; on a couple of occasions, I had been asked to take part in first aid demonstrations for them there. I imagined walking in, asking him, *why did you hit my child?*

Inwardly, I quailed, seeing the faces of the men staring at me. No, I could not do that. Charging up to the hall and accusing Charles in front of his men would be a terrible idea. For the first time in quite a while, I heard Anders mocking me inside my head: *How like you, Hedda, to get hysterical and lose your head. What a little fool you are! That child needs more discipline anyway – didn't I always say he was an ill-mannered brat?*

Shut up, shut UP, I snarled back, and, mercifully, he fell silent.

'You're welcome to wait for him,' Margaret said. 'Will you have a cup of tea? Oh, no, let me make it, you're not on duty now...' she added as I turned towards the kitchen.

'No, you sit down again,' I told her. Her leg was much better than it had been but still not completely healed, and she'd been worryingly breathless lately. 'She needs fresh air, sunshine and some good food,' Doctor Gaudie had said when I'd consulted him about it. His great, whiskery eyebrows had drawn together in a fierce scowl. 'If it wasn't for this damned war, I'd pack her off to the south coast of England for a holiday. Charles too.'

I went through to the kitchen. I'd never felt less like

drinking tea in my life – every muscle in my body was taut with tension, thrumming like the strings on a tightened violin bow – but it would give me something to occupy myself with while I was waiting. As I put the kettle on to boil and went into the pantry for the tea tin, angry thoughts were tumbling through my head It wasn't just me that Anders like to lash with his tongue. He'd always said cruel things to Eirik too, threatening to withhold food or make him stand out in the snow in his bare feet, although when it came down to it he never actually carried out these threats. Perhaps, if he actually *had* laid a hand on Eirik, I might have found the strength to leave him before the war started and the Germans came.

Even so, you should have protected Eirik – you should have stopped Anders saying those things, I thought, shame pouring hotly through me. That shame had driven me here, I realised. It was why I had to be brave, and confront Charles no matter what the consequences. He'd gone one step further than Anders – he had actually hit my son.

I was so deeply preoccupied with the guilt and sadness warring inside me that at first I didn't notice the object wrapped in a piece of sacking that was hidden behind the neat rows of tins and packets on the pantry shelf. It wasn't until I reached for the tea tin and caught a corner of the sacking with my sleeve, dislodging it and revealing part of what was underneath, that my mind caught up with my eyes.

I frowned. Why was Charles keeping radio parts in here? Why weren't they out with the other bits and pieces he had scattered around? And why were they wrapped up like this?

My curiosity piqued, I lifted the sacking to look at the radio properly. It didn't look like the rest of the wireless sets in the house, which were all in pieces; this set was complete, housed in a steel case. It reminded me of something, but I couldn't think what. Then, all at once, it came to me: the radio set Mette had shown me at the telegraph station the day the German officers came to arrest me; the set in the brown suitcase. I peered at it, my frown deepening. What was it doing in here, hidden away like this? Was it something for a Home Guard exercise?

The kettle began to whistle. Hastily, I pulled the sacking back over the radio set, making sure I left it as I'd found it, and grabbed the blue tea tin. What Charles Mackay did with his radio sets was none of my business. I was here to talk to him about Eirik.

He returned as Margaret and I were finishing our tea, Margaret chatting to me about a knitting pattern for a shawl she had been promised by a friend. I heard the front door open and even though it was only Charles, for some reason I immediately felt my whole body tense, the way it used to when I heard Anders come home after a day up at the iron ore mine.

He is not Anders, I reminded myself, squaring my shoulders as I listened to Charles's footsteps approaching up the hall. But as I placed my cup back on its saucer, it rattled; my hands were trembling slightly. I folded them in my lap, clenching fistfuls of my skirt.

'Hedda,' he said when he came into the parlour, giving me his usual friendly smile. 'I was not expecting to see you here. Is my mother all right?'

I stood. 'It's you I am here to see,' I said. 'I wanted to talk to you about Eirik.'

His smile faded. 'Ah. Yes.'

I glanced at Margaret, who, after greeting Charles, had

picked up her newspaper and was reading it. Charles glanced at her too. 'Shall we go through to the kitchen?' he said.

My heart was pounding as I followed him through there. 'He said you punished him for speaking Norwegian,' I said.

Charles's eyebrows drew together. 'I beg your pardon?'

'He said you accused him of speaking German, and then you caned him.'

'Oh dear, dear, dear.' Charles sank into one of the spindly chairs pulled up to the table covered in his dismantled radio sets; it creaked under his weight. He massaged his forehead. 'I'm sorry, Hedda, but that simply isn't true. I caught him and one of the other boys singing a rude song in the playground.'

I frowned at him. 'A rude song?'

'A *very* rude song.' He coughed into his moustache. 'It's about Hitler. I appreciate the sentiment, of course – who wouldn't – but the language in it is most unsuitable for boys their age, and they were setting a dreadful example for the others, especially the girls.'

I shook my head. 'I do not know any songs like that. I have no idea where he could have got it from.'

'It, er, refers to a certain part of the male anatomy,' Charles said, his cheeks colouring slightly. 'We'll say no more, eh?'

'Oh dear, I'm sorry,' I said, although I wasn't sure what I was apologising for. I felt as embarrassed as Charles looked, my resolve to challenge him for hitting Eirik wavering, then failing completely. *Coward*, Anders growled at me, illogically, because I knew he would have been delighted at what had happened to my son. *You can't even stand up for your own flesh and blood.* I felt more ashamed and foolish than ever; nonplussed, too, as if I'd been playing a game of chess and my opponent had tricked me into losing when I thought I was on a winning streak.

I swallowed and brushed my hands on my skirt. 'I must get back,' I said.

Charles stood up. 'I do hope this clears up any misunderstanding. I'd hate for you to think badly of me, Hedda.'

'I, er – no, of course I don't.'

He moved closer to me; too close. I took an involuntary step back, then another, but he followed until I found myself pressed up against the stove.

Charles didn't seem to notice anything was amiss. 'I must say, Hedda, the usual childish misbehaviour aside, having young Eirik at the school has been a breath of fresh air,' he said. 'Meeting you has been, too. Before the war it was so rare to see new faces in Fiskersay – we're too far away from anywhere for people to want to visit – and the locals can be, well, shall I say, a little inward looking...'

I frowned again, puzzled. He was still standing just a little bit too close to me. 'I... I haven't found them to be,' I said.

'Oh, but of course it's all new to you at the moment – if you stay here for a year or two you'll see what I mean. I am not saying they're not good people – of course they are. But when you've seen more of the world – when you've really *experienced* life – it broadens the mind in a way island life cannot.'

'I – I suppose so.'

Charles cleared his throat, his moustache twitching. 'I was wondering, Hedda, if, one Sunday, you might like to go for a walk across the island with me? I do enjoy talking to you – I'd like to get to know you better.'

He leaned towards me and for some reason I couldn't

quite identify, I felt a zigzag of panic go through me. Heart pounding, I ducked under his arm. 'I – I must go,' I said. 'Elizabeth will be wondering where I have got to.'

Was I imagining it, or did his face fall slightly? 'Let me walk you back to the croft,' he said.

'No – no, it's quite all right. I need to call in on someone else on the way – please don't trouble yourself,' I blurted.

I fled without even saying goodbye to Margaret, half walking, half running along the road until I was out of sight of the house. Only then did I slow down. My face was burning. What had happened just now? Had Charles meant to *kiss* me? Had he forgotten I was married?

I felt almost sick with embarrassment as I tried frantically to recall if I had ever given Charles a reason to think I was interested in him in that way. The only time I saw him outside of the schoolhouse or at his mother's was at the local dances. I didn't *think* I had led him on; I certainly hadn't intended to. We didn't even have all that much in common, and he was so much older than me.

You must go back and talk to him, set the record straight, I told myself. *Otherwise it will be awkward for you both.*

But again, my courage failed me. I couldn't face it. What if *I* was the one who'd misunderstood? What if I was so starved for affection, I was imagining men throwing themselves at me? After all, I wasn't exactly skilled at reading others' intentions. If I was, I wouldn't have ended up in that mess with Magnus, or married Anders. I longed for someone to talk to about it – someone who could help me make sense of what had just happened. But the only person I could think of was Bill, and he was busy with Rose. He wouldn't want to be bothered with me and my silly problems.

Oh, forget it, I told myself, suddenly angry at my own foolishness, and at the weight of my past that pulled like a heavy stone at my neck, no matter how hard I tried to distance myself from it.

When I got back, Eirik was with Elizabeth in the kitchen. I called him into the room we still used as a bedroom and closed the door. 'Eirik,' I said, careful to keep my tone neutral as I sat down with him on the bed. 'Did you tell me the truth about what happened at school today?'

He looked up at me, wide-eyed. 'Yes, Mamma.'

'You were not... being rude?'

He shook his head vehemently. 'No, Mamma. But—' Suddenly, he flushed. 'David had been singing a song which might have been a bit rude.'

'A song about Hitler?'

He nodded, biting his lower lip.

'And Mr Mackay heard you?'

He shook his head again. 'Mr Mackay wasn't outside then.'

'Are you sure?'

'Yes! Otherwise David wouldn't have started singing it.' He sighed. 'We're not *stupid*, Mamma.'

I gazed at him, more confused than ever. My son wasn't a liar, I was sure of that. At least, he wasn't a *good* liar. On the rare occasion he did try to pull the wool over my eyes, the tips of his ears would turn red, and there was no sign of that now.

But why on earth would Charles punish Eirik for doing something as innocuous as speaking his own language? And why on earth would he mix up Norwegian and German? They sounded nothing alike, and he was surely educated enough to be able to tell the difference, even if he did not understand what was being said. Hadn't he told me he longed to visit Scandinavia?

'Mamma,' Eirik whined. 'Please can I go? I am helping *Tante* Elizabeth make a cake.'

'Yes. Yes. But Eirik—'

Already halfway to the door, he turned.

'Perhaps it would be a good idea not to sing rude songs at school at all, just in case,' I told him.

'Yes, Mamma,' he said, sighing again, and for the first time, it struck me just how much he'd changed since we'd come to Shetland. The only remnant of our previous life seemed to be his nightmares. In the daytime he was a different child: taller, stronger, more confident than I had ever known him to be back in Kirkenes.

It is me who still needs to work out who I am, I thought as the door swung closed behind him and I sank down onto the bed.

TWENTY-FIVE

BILL

Despite her obvious frustration at being stuck on Fiskersay, Rose had cried when the weather finally settled enough for the *Zetland Princess* to leave the island and it was time for her to go. 'Who knows when we'll see each other again,' she'd sobbed, clinging to me as we stood on the quay, smearing my shirt with makeup and tears. 'I simply can't *stand* it, thinking of you in this awful, lonely place all by yourself – it's even worse than I imagined!'

'Hey, steady on. I've already told you, it's not awful *or* lonely,' I'd said, wishing she'd keep her voice down a bit; there were several locals standing nearby. 'I'm sure I'll get some leave soon.'

'But *when?*' she wailed. 'I wish you'd think about what I said about Daddy's cousin. I bet he could even get you a transfer back to aircrew if you wanted!'

'No,' I said firmly. 'I'm not flying again. Not unless they tell me to. I'm here, and that's that.'

'Oh, *Bill*.' Rose had dissolved into a fresh burst of sobs, her mouth turning down at the corners like a little kid's.

'Come on, now,' I'd murmured, patting her back. I felt

awkward as hell, sure everyone was looking at us. 'It'll be OK. I'll be in London before you know it.'

Truth be told, the last couple of days, which I'd spent with Rose whenever I wasn't on duty, had been a bit up and down. We'd had plenty of laughs but we'd fought a lot too; she still refused to talk to me about coming to Canada, swiftly changing the subject whenever I tried to bring it up. After she'd boarded the ship and I'd watched it chug out of the harbour, I felt a mixture of frustration and relief.

That had been a few hours ago. As it was my second rest day I'd gone to my hut to find a clean shirt, then grabbed the second-hand fishing rods I'd bought last week at Sutherland's Stores and walked out to Odda's Bay. The weather had become almost spring-like again now the storm had passed, and after almost constant company for the last four days the stuffy confines of Hut 1 or the NAAFI didn't appeal to me. I sat down on the rocks at the edge of the water, near to where Hedda and I had discovered the body of poor old Ruben Clarke, where I fished and smoked for a few hours, watching the sun glitter on the water and letting my mind go quiet. I didn't catch a thing, but it was just what I needed.

Eventually, it began to grow cold, and I started to feel hungry. I stood, stretching. As I packed my rods away, I suddenly remembered I had the envelope containing Eirik's photographs in my inside jacket pocket; Ray Marks, the operator who'd set up the darkroom, had finally gotten around to developing them and had given them to me last night. I'd stuck them in my jacket without looking at them. I decided to walk back to the station via the Sinclairs' croft and call in with them.

Eirik answered the door. 'Mr Bill!' he said, beaming, as I followed him into the kitchen, where Hedda and Elizabeth

Sinclair were cooking something savoury and delicious-smelling in a big pan on the stove, and old Donald was nodding by the fire.

'Hey, bud,' I said. I drew the envelope out of my pocket. 'Look, I've got your photographs.'

Eirik's whole face lit up. 'Are those really for me?'

'They sure are.'

'Thank you! Mamma, look!' Eirik spread the photographs out on the table.

'They're not half bad, eh?' I said, leaning over his shoulder to look at the black-and-white images scattered across the tabletop. And considering the kid was only, what – six? Seven? – they really weren't. Sure, there were some wonky horizons and a few cut-off heads as Hedda had predicted, but he seemed to have a natural eye for composition and light, and they were all in focus.

'I like this one,' Eirik said, pointing to the one of me and Hedda standing in the bay where he'd caught us mid-laugh, both of us looking utterly carefree. My heart gave a funny little jump; I'd forgotten all about it. 'Mamma looks happy,' he added, his finger hovering just above the photograph's shiny surface as he traced Hedda's outline. 'She didn't used to smile when we were in Norway, but she is always smiling when she is with you.'

I didn't look at Hedda; I didn't dare. I could feel my ears glowing.

'Bill, will you stay a while and have something to eat?' Elizabeth said from the stove. 'We have a rabbit stew, and there's a new loaf of bread.'

'I'd like that, thank you.' I took my jacket off and hung it on one of the hooks by the door.

The five of us had just sat down when, from outside, we heard the *boom… boom…* of the gun battery firing up at the station.

'What is that? An air raid?' Hedda said, looking alarmed.

'I don't know – I can't hear the sirens.' I went to the door and peered out, scanning the sky, but I couldn't see anything. Then, as if they'd heard me, the air raid sirens up at the camp and in Talafirth began to wail, almost simultaneously.

There was a terrific explosion, close and loud enough to make the ground beneath my feet vibrate. From the Sinclairs' cottage, you could see out towards the eastern edge of the island where the land dropped sharply away in the long chain of cliffs that curved all the way up to Svarta Ness, and beyond that, the sea. A cloud of black, oily smoke started billowing up into the air from somewhere below the horizon, and as the guns began firing again, I heard the drone of multiple aircraft engines. Moments later, they came into view: two Dornier Do 17 light bombers with distinctive bulbous noses and elongated bodies, the black and white crosses clearly visible on the sides and beneath the wings and swastikas painted on their tails. They were flying low and fast.

'What is it? What's happening?' Hedda said behind me, her voice threaded with panic.

'Germans,' I said. 'They're attacking something out at sea.'

Her hand flew to her throat. 'Oh *min Gud*.' Although I'd picked up a few words here and there, I didn't need to speak fluent Norwegian to understand what she'd just said. *Oh my God*.

'Go back inside,' I told her, wrestling my jacket on again. 'Take Eirik and Elizabeth and Donald down to the cellar. If those bastards come inland—'

I didn't voice the rest of what I was thinking: how the white-painted cottage stood out like a beacon against the fields around it. She was already frightened enough.

Hedda nodded tersely. 'Mamma, what's happening?' Eirik said, appearing in the doorway too, and she quickly shepherded him back inside, murmuring something in Norwegian.

I ran back in the direction of the station as fast as I could, keeping an eye on the Dorniers the whole time as they buzzed over the water like a pair of malignant hornets, dodging the flak from the anti-aircraft battery with apparent ease. When I was halfway over the Haug, there was another explosion, but it wasn't until I was over the top that I was high enough to see what was going on.

Behind me, about a quarter of a mile out to sea and just east of Talafirth harbour, a ship was listing on its side in the water. The black smoke I'd seen from the Sinclairs' croft was pouring from it in two great streams, orange flames leaping at their base.

The *Zetland Princess*, returning from Lerwick.

I stood, frozen to the spot, watching as the Dorniers circled back one last time and one released another bomb, aiming straight for the ship again. This one missed and splashed into the water nearby. Then I realised I was just standing there on the side of the hill, completely exposed; if either pilot saw me...

I made myself break into a run again, every now and then glancing back at the ship, which was beginning to sink. At last – *at last* – I saw two of our own planes, Hurricanes, speeding towards the Dorniers from the south. As soon as they realised they'd been spotted, the Dorniers turned tail and flew away, disappearing towards the horizon with the Hurricanes close behind. By the time I reached the station, all four aircraft were out of sight, and the air raid sirens were sounding the all-clear across the island.

The camp was in uproar, but it wasn't until I got back to Hut 1 that I found out from Lewis exactly what had happened. The Dorniers had apparently appeared out of nowhere, making a beeline for the *Zetland Princess* not long after she'd left the north-eastern tip of Unst. 'Air-sea rescue are on their way from Lerwick,' Lewis said, his face grim. 'And we've cleared the medical bay. I don't suppose there's going to be much they can do, though.'

If that had happened this morning, Rose would have been on board, I thought, and I had to sit down on my bed, my legs suddenly going shaky.

'Was it a random attack?' I asked, 'Or...'

'The Corp says there were a couple of radar mechanics on board, coming to replace the two fellows who've just been posted back to England. If you ask me, the Germans knew exactly what they were doing – they'd found out those men were on board and they were determined to make sure they didn't get here.'

I rubbed a hand across my face. 'Shit.'

'Indeed. I suppose we'd better go and see if there's anything we can do to help with the rescue efforts.'

I nodded and got up again, my legs still not quite steady.

Who's giving the Germans this information? I thought as I followed Lewis outside. *And why the hell haven't we caught them yet?*

I didn't know. No one did, it seemed. And until we did, these attacks were going to keep happening.

Twenty-Six

HEDDA

The moment I entered Sutherland's Stores, the whole shop went quiet. I could feel people's gazes on me as I joined the queue for the counter; a prickle of apprehension traced down my spine. 'Good morning,' I said to David Couper's mother, Hilda, who was standing in front of me.

Hilda, who until now I had counted as one of my many friends in Fiskersay, glanced at me and looked away again without returning my greeting.

I gripped my basket a little more tightly, my palms slippery with sweat as I gazed down at the floor. As the queue shuffled forwards, the silence in the shop was so heavy it could have been cut with a knife. When my turn came, Bertha Sutherland thumped mine and the Sinclairs' purchases down onto the counter with her mouth set in a grim line. Knowing full well she was only giving me these things because of Elizabeth and Donald, I handed over coupons and my money and left the shop as fast as I could, my throat tight and my eyes pricking with tears.

It was three days since the *Zetland Princess* had been bombed, taking everyone on board down with her, and two days since Fiskersay's police, the commanding officers from the station and Charles Mackay, in his role as Home Guard Captain, had begun an island-wide interrogation, interviewing people and searching houses. At first, no one had been sure what was going on, thinking the attack on the ship had been a random one, but before long word got round: there was a spy on the island who was passing shipping information on to the Germans, and the strike on the *Zetland Princess* had been a deliberate act of sabotage to kill two RAF men on board who were coming to work at the station.

I had begun to fear the worst when, yesterday, Eirik came home from school in tears, saying the other children were no longer speaking to him. Then, this morning, Doctor Gaudie had dropped by and told me, kindly but firmly, that he was very sorry, but until this business had been cleared up, my duties as the island's nurse were being suspended. As he said this, horror poured through my veins like icy water. My only source of income – of independence – was being taken away. How would I save money for mine and Eirik's future, whatever that might be?

'They suspect me because I'm a foreigner,' I'd said despairingly to Elizabeth after he left. 'And because I'm from a country that is occupied by the Germans. They think they have sent me here.'

'No, no,' Elizabeth had said, looking distressed. 'I am sure that's not what people think.' She and Donald were not treating me any differently yet, but as I made my way back to the croft from the store, I wondered how long it would be before they turned against me too, or decided that, if I wasn't able to contribute towards mine and Eirik's upkeep, they'd be better off without us. And what about Bill? Did *he* think I was the spy? I hadn't seen him since the evening of the attack, and I was starting to think he was avoiding me – or that he had been ordered to stay away.

Can things get any worse? I thought as I trudged along the road, head down. It was a beautiful day, the sky a soft blue and striped with high cloud, the new grass on the hillsides a vivid green, but I barely noticed any of it. Anders, silent for so long, spoke up in his familiar, jeering tones. *You know why this has happened, don't you, Hedda? It is because you thought you could be happy. It is because you dared to hope.*

Up ahead, the Sinclairs' cottage, with its whitewashed stone walls bright in the sun, came into view. But even the croft didn't feel like a safe haven any more. It was as if a pool of quicksand had opened up at my feet, threatening to drag me in. *What will happen to me?* I thought. *Will they make us leave the island? Will they split me and Eirik up? Will they send me to an internment camp?*

I had almost reached the front door when I heard an engine approaching. A military truck – one of the vehicles from the radar station – was driving along the road towards the croft from the other direction. It stopped outside just as I reached the front door; the doors opened and Flight Lieutenant Jackson, Charles Mackay and Hugh Leask, Fiskersay's police constable, got out.

'Mrs Dahlström,' Flight Lieutenant Jackson said, his voice cold, his demeanour formal. He looked nothing like the man who, only months earlier, had smiled, shaken my hand and welcomed me to Fiskersay. 'We need to come in and search the cottage, I'm afraid.'

I stared at them in silence. I'd known this would happen, yet now the time was here I was hardly able to believe it.

'If you please, Mrs Dahlström,' Flight Lieutenant Jackson said. Hugh Leask, his expression stony, didn't even look at me, but Charles, who was wearing his Home Guard uniform and cap, briefly met my gaze. Was I imagining it, or did he look slightly troubled? Since that awkward moment in the kitchen at his mother's house, I had deliberately stayed away from him, only seeing him when I went to collect Eirik from school where we'd make a few minutes of polite conversation. I still wondered if I'd imagined the whole thing. Before I could say anything to him, though, he'd looked away too.

Donald was out on the croft somewhere, but Elizabeth was in the kitchen and turned round, alarmed, as I came in with the three men. After Flight Lieutenant Jackson had explained to her why they were here, she sat down at the kitchen table, wringing her hands. I paced around the room, unable to settle. As the men went into Donald and Elizabeth's bedroom to begin their search, neither of us spoke.

The door to the other room had not quite closed – the wooden frame was swollen with damp from the long winter – and from behind it I heard Hugh Leask say, 'Remind me what we're looking for again, Sir.'

'Anything that looks like radio equipment,' Flight Lieutenant Jackson answered him. 'A lad in the village – an amateur radio enthusiast – came forward just this morning to say he's picked up several transmissions being made late at night that are coming from somewhere on the island.'

'And he waited until *now* to say something?' Hugh sounded amazed.

'He didn't realise what they were at first, and he didn't tell us right away because he was worried we'd think he was involved, the damned fool! He's in the clear, though – we've checked him and his radio set out thoroughly and there's nothing fishy going on.'

'We'd better check up the chimney and for any loose floorboards, then,' Hugh said. 'If there's anything here it'll be well hidden, I expect.'

Charles didn't say anything. I listened as they tore the room apart, shoving furniture across the floor and emptying drawers and cupboards.

'I am so sorry,' I said to Elizabeth.

She shook her head. 'It cannot be helped. They must do their job. The sooner they find that wicked traitor, the better. Those poor men on board the ship!'

Was I imagining it, or was there doubt in her eyes as she looked at me?

The men finished searching the bedroom and came out again. *Anything that looks like radio equipment...* I heard Flight Lieutenant Jackson's voice echo inside my head as they went into the parlour where Eirik and I slept and began searching there. Something was niggling at me, but I couldn't work out what it was. What with the attack on the ship and being suspended as Fiskersay's nurse, I was so weary that I was struggling to piece any coherent thoughts together beyond, *what will happen to Eirik if I'm sent away?*

Too exhausted to keep pacing, I sat down beside Elizabeth at the table. She placed a hand over mine. 'Ach, don't look so worried,' she said softly. 'They will catch whoever it is, you'll see.'

'It is not me, Elizabeth,' I said, a little desperately. 'I am not a spy.'

'Hush. I know. You're a good woman – anyone wi' an ounce of sense can see dat.' Her earnest expression made tears spring into my eyes, and I had to look down, biting the insides of my cheeks, to keep them at bay. I did not want to cry while the men were here.

At last, they finished their search.

'What's that?' Hugh Leask said, spying the packet containing the photographs Eirik had taken, which was propped up on the mantelpiece.

'Photographs. My son took them, and Sergeant Gauthier asked one of the men at the station to develop them for him – you are welcome to look at them.'

'Yes please,' Flight Lieutenant Jackson said.

I fetched them for him and watched as he looked through, passing them one by one to Hugh and Charles who studied them carefully too. Suddenly, I saw Charles's face convulse as if something had pained him. Then his expression smoothed out again; it all happened so fast I was left wondering if I had imagined it. Neither Elizabeth, Flight Lieutenant Jackson or Hugh seemed to have noticed anything.

'I will have to take the ones that show the radar towers in the background for further investigation,' Flight Lieutenant Jackson said at last, pushing several of the photographs into his jacket pocket before handing me the packet again. 'You may keep the rest. Is there any more film in the camera?'

I shook my head.

'Show me, please.'

I did, and they left, taking the camera with them as well. Elizabeth and I tidied up the cottage in silence, finishing just as Donald returned.

'Don't say anything to him, he will only be upset,' Elizabeth said as we listened to him knocking the mud from his boots on the iron scraper outside.

I nodded. 'I think I will go and lie down,' I said. 'I have a headache.'

It was not a lie; my head was pounding. I went into the parlour where I pulled the curtains, kicked off my shoes and lay down on my bed. I closed my eyes, but could not relax. My mind was racing. I sat up again and picked up the packet of photographs, shaking them out onto the counterpane. What had Charles seen there that caused him to make that strange expression? The only photograph that had anyone in it was the one of me and Bill, laughing together. The others were of seagulls, rocks, water and sky. Puzzled, I slid the pictures back into their envelope. Then I lay back down.

Something was still niggling at me. In my head, I heard the men talking as they searched the bedroom again.

Remind me what we're looking for again, Sir.

Anything that looks like radio equipment.

Radio equipment.

Transmissions.

My heart started pounding. I sat up again. The radio set I had found hidden in Charles's pantry the other day – the set that looked just like the spy set Mette had shown me at the telegraph station in Kirkenes – how could I have forgotten about it?

But Charles Mackay can't be a spy, I told myself. *He is the island's head teacher! The Captain of the Home Guard! And he is – well, he is Charles! It isn't possible!*

So what was he doing with that radio set? I remembered now how, at the time, I'd wondered if it was something for a Home Guard exercise. If that was the case, why would he conceal it like that? Why had it not been out with all the other pieces of radios he collected? It hadn't made sense at the time, and it didn't make sense now.

I should tell someone about it. But who? Flight Lieutenant Jackson? Hugh Leask?

No, not them. And not Elizabeth or Donald or Doctor Gaudie. They wouldn't believe me, I was certain of that – they'd known Charles since he was a boy. I could hardly believe it myself.

Bill, then. He would listen to me, wouldn't he?

I decided I'd go up to the camp later once Eirik was back from school, and if Bill was not around, or not allowed to come and talk to me, I would leave a message. I was probably wrong; Charles probably had a perfectly good explanation for having that radio set. God, I *hoped* I was wrong. But if I said nothing and there was another attack like the one on the *Zetland Princess*, or the one that killed that poor man who had washed up in the bay…

No; whatever the consequences, and whether Bill believed me or not, I couldn't let that happen. I lay back down, closed my eyes and pressed my fingers against my eyelids, trying in vain to clear my whirling mind and ease my thumping head, and quell the panic that threatened to overwhelm me as I wondered how I was going to do this.

TWENTY-SEVEN

BILL

'Christ, what a mess,' Lewis said as we sat down at a table in a corner of the NAAFI. We had just finished our 8 a.m.–1 p.m. watch, and we each had a plate of cottage pie in front of us, a grim-looking concoction made from greyish mince and lumpy-looking mashed potato with a spoonful of overcooked carrots on the side. It smelled about as appetising as it looked. As Lewis unfolded his newspaper to read while he was eating, I thought longingly of Elizabeth Sinclair's rabbit stew.

'The investigation?' I said, picking up my fork and steeling myself.

Len slid into the seat opposite me, his own plate in hand. 'Eileen was talking about it last night,' he said. 'Not that I've said anything to her about what's been happening, of course – the CO would have my guts for garters – but the whole island's in uproar about it, according to her.' Eileen was his girlfriend, a local girl he'd started seeing after the ENSA concert.

'What else are they supposed to do, though, eh?' I said. 'Whoever's behind this, they need to catch the bastard. I suppose they must know *something*, if they're searching people's houses.'

'Is it true people suspect Hedda?' Len continued, spearing a piece of carrot, pulling a face at it and taking a swig of tea instead. 'Eileen said people have been talking about her – they're saying she might be a double agent sent over by the Nazis.'

'I haven't seen her since the ship was bombed,' I said, trying to keep my voice even; Lewis looked up from his paper to shoot me a curious glance.

I looked away from them both and started ploughing my way through the cottage pie. What I'd just said wasn't actually quite true. The day after the attack, Flight Lieutenant Jackson had summoned me over to his office at the Manor, and as I'd stood in front of his desk, wondering why I was there, he'd cleared his throat, then said, 'I won't beat about the bush, Sergeant Gauthier. You and that Norwegian woman—'

'Hedda,' I'd said.

'Hedda, yes. You're good friends with her, aren't you?'

'We're friends, yes,' I'd said, wondering where this was leading. 'I believe I mentioned that to you before, Sir.'

'Has she said or done anything lately that struck you as unusual?'

'Unusual? No, of course not.'

'Has she ever talked to you about why she had to leave Norway?'

At that moment, I'd realised that she hadn't, not really. We'd only discussed it once, when she'd told me that she'd got into trouble, something to do with passing on messages to prisoners who were being held at a camp in her hometown. She'd said she and Eirik tried to flee to Sweden, but hadn't been able to get there, so they'd ended up coming to Shetland instead. I could tell from her tone and body language that even saying that much was painful for her, so I hadn't pushed her for details; after all, I still hadn't told her the full story of what had happened to me and Robert, only that I'd come to Svarta Ness after being involved in an accident while I was off duty. Even though I was no longer in the dark, desperate place I'd been in when I'd first arrived in Fiskersay, it was still too painful for me to think about what had happened, never mind talk about it – even to Hedda, who I suspected had similar feelings about whatever made her flee Norway with Eirik.

'I thought you interviewed her when she first came her, Sir,' I'd said. 'Didn't she tell you then?'

'She told us her story, yes. But I was wondering what she'd said to you.'

I'd repeated what I knew. Flight Lieutenant Jackson nodded, jotting something down.

'Thank you, Sergeant.' He'd cleared his throat again. 'I'm afraid that while our investigations into what happened are ongoing, I must ask you to cease any association with Mrs Dahlström and her son. Just as a precaution, you understand.'

'Sir, is that really—?'

'That's all, Sergeant. Good day.' Flight Lieutenant Jackson had reached for his blotter, and I realised I was being dismissed. There was nothing I could do; I either obeyed orders, or I got myself into all kinds of hot water, and after what had happened after the accident I'd had quite enough of that. I'd saluted, then left the Manor, a scowl appearing on my face as soon as the front door closed behind me.

They can't think Hedda's the spy, I thought now, chewing

a mouthful of gristle. *That's crazy. Just because she's from an occupied country...*

Lewis made a choking sound, tearing me away from my thoughts. 'Christ, this is bloody awful,' he spluttered, pushing his plate away. I went to thump him on the back but he waved me away.

'I heard they had to make it with minced-up seagull,' Len quipped. 'Apparently they can't get proper ingredients until there's a new supply ship.'

'Great.' I put my fork down and pushed my plate away too, my appetite completely gone. I picked up my mug of tea instead. 'You finished with that?' I asked Lewis, nodding at his newspaper.

'It's about three weeks out of date,' he said, handing it over.

'Only three weeks? That's practically straight off the press for this place.' I gave him a wry smile as I opened it and flicked through, looking for something to catch my interest that wasn't war, war, war.

A large picture at the top of the society pages made my breath catch in my throat. It showed a slim woman in a light-coloured dress – a dress that could quite easily have been silver – with a balding man in a dark suit. They were pressed close to one another, as close as lovers, the man's arm around the woman's waist with his hand on her hip and the woman's head resting on his shoulder.

ENSA SWEETHEART LEGGE SPOTTED WITH MYSTERY MAN, the headline said, and in smaller print underneath, *The show must go on as society's finest attend the annual King George Ball at Perivale House despite threat from air raids.*

I stared at the picture of Rose and Clive, trying to take it in. It was a mistake, surely. I skimmed the article, and quickly found what I was looking for, tucked away in the last paragraph.

...But who was the man spotted in the company of ENSA star Rose Legge? Legge, who last year announced her engagement to a Canadian airman, arrived at the ball with the man, who some sources say is her manager. They were seen dancing cheek-to-cheek for most of the evening, and she only had eyes for him.

My memory suddenly presented me with a picture of Rose and Clive standing at the top of the hotel stairs, mid-argument. *But when?*
Soon.
I remembered the way they'd jumped apart when they realised I was there.
No. NO.
'Everything all right?' Lewis said, and I realised I had clenched my hand into a fist on top of the page, smudging the ink.
'Oh. Sure. Fine.' I folded the paper up and gave it back to him. 'I'm gonna get some fresh air,' I said, making a show of patting my stomach. 'That seagull pie's given me indigestion.'
I walked out of the NAAFI and down to the gate, where there was a private I hadn't seen before huddled in the little wooden sentry hut. He must have just arrived. He was young, his cheeks sprinkled with acne, his uniform hanging off his skinny frame.

'Afternoon, Sir,' he said in a strong Cockney accent as I walked down there. 'Got your papers, please? I've been asked to check 'em for everyone on the way out as well as on the way in.' Sounding almost apologetic, he cleared his throat and added, 'Because of this business with the spy. The CO wants a record of all movement to and from the camp.'

'Sure.' Still preoccupied with thoughts of Rose, I dug my papers out of my pocket and handed them to him.

'Sergeant Bill Gauthier,' he said, pronouncing it *Gow-thye-ur*. He turned to make a note on a pad of paper on the shelf in front of him. 'Right-oh.'

'It's *Go-tee-ay*,' I told him, 'French-Canadian.'

'Oh, right, sorry, Sir,' he said, giving me my papers back. 'Gauthier, you say?'

'Yes. Is there a problem?'

'Oh, no, no problem, Sir. It's just there was a woman here yesterday evening, asking for you. Said she had a message.'

'A woman? What did she look like?'

'Tall. Blonde hair. Had a funny accent. I think she was called Helen or something.'

'Hedda?'

The boy snapped his fingers. 'Yes, that's it.' He narrowed his eyes. 'She a German or something, Sir?'

'Norwegian,' I said, trying, not very successfully, to disguise my impatience. 'What was the message?'

'I dunno. I telephoned for the C.O. to come down 'coz I wasn't sure if I was supposed to take the message or not, and he sent her away.'

'What?' I passed a hand over my eyes. 'Christ.'

'Something wrong, Sir?'

'It doesn't matter. Will you open the gate, please?'

'Of course, Sir.' The boy ducked out of the hut, saluting me as I went past him.

As I walked away from the camp, I wondered briefly what Hedda had wanted to tell me. Perhaps I should walk down to the Sinclairs' croft and see if she was there? No – Flight Lieutenant Jackson had ordered me to stay away. Whatever it was, it would have to wait.

Instead, I turned and trudged towards Odda's Bay, my mind once again filled with thoughts of Rose as I tried to work out what I was going to do about her and Clive.

Twenty-Eight

HEDDA

I took a deep breath, looking up and down the street to make sure no one was watching me before rapping on Margaret Mackay's door. *Come on… come on…* I thought, crossing my arms tightly over my chest as I waited for her to answer it.

'Hedda,' Margaret said when she opened the door. 'Doctor Gaudie said you would not be able to visit for the time being.'

'Oh, he must have been mistaken, Mrs Mackay,' I said brightly, picking up my bag from by my feet. 'I have been away for a few days because I was unwell, that's all.'

Please believe me. Please.

'Oh dear, I do hope you're all right?' she said and stepped aside to let me in. As she closed the door behind me, I felt my shoulders sag with relief.

'A sore throat, that's all. I'm – how do you say it – as right as the rain now,' I said with a cheerfulness I couldn't have been further away from feeling.

Margaret laughed. 'You mean right as rain, dear.'

'Oh dear, I thought I'd got it wrong,' I said. 'Shall we go to the parlour? And would you like me to make you some tea?'

'I'm awful glad you're back,' Margaret said as she settled into her usual armchair. 'I do miss our little chats.'

'I will go and put the kettle on,' I said with another smile; a smile that dropped off my face as soon as I was out of the room.

I went into the kitchen and straight into the pantry.

The radio set was not there.

Damn it, where has it gone? As I waited for the kettle to boil, I poked around the kitchen, taking care to leave everything as it had been, but there was no sign of the set anywhere.

Now the authorities have realised there is a spy, he'll be taking extra care, I thought. *He has hidden it somewhere else.*

But where? Was it possible that he was *not* the spy, and that the set was indeed just for a Home Guard exercise? But if that was the case, why would Charles have even hidden it in the first place? It didn't make sense. *Oh, I wish I could talk to Bill about this!* I had gone up to the camp yesterday to ask to speak to him, but I had been turned away at the gate by Flight Lieutenant Jackson, who hadn't looked pleased to see me at all.

I made Margaret a cup of tea – I was too nervous to drink one myself – and took it back through to the parlour where I went through the motions of checking Margaret's leg and listening to her heart.

'Do you mind if I use your outhouse, Mrs Mackay?' I said when I'd finished.

'Of course not.'

I took my bag with me; Eirik's camera, which Hugh Leask had returned yesterday, was concealed inside, with a fresh roll of film in it. If I found anything, I would take a photograph to use as proof.

The outhouse was a ramshackle, bad-smelling brick building in a corner of the tiny back yard behind the house. Breathing through my mouth, I scanned the dark little space, looking for anything that might resemble the radio set, but it wasn't there.

I slipped back into the house. Aside from the parlour and kitchen, there were only two other rooms: Margaret and Charles's bedrooms. I stood in the hall for a moment, paralysed by indecision. *Have courage, Hedda.*

I went into Margaret's room first. It was sparse and tidy, just like the rest of the house, with a narrow bed that had a faded coverlet over the top, a wardrobe, a dressing table and a wash-stand underneath the window. It only took me a few minutes to search in there; after that I moved across the hall to Charles's room.

The contrast to the rest of the house was stark. The room was cluttered and dark, the furniture piled with books, papers and yet more wireless sets. Everything was thick with dust; the air smelled of cigarette smoke and the walls and ceiling were stained yellow with nicotine. Mindful that I mustn't be gone too long, I began to look around carefully, lifting things and placing them back. *If I was Charles Mackay and wanted to hide a radio set, where would I put it?* I thought.

As I was about to open one of the desk drawers, I heard the front door open. I jumped. Surely Charles wasn't back already – there was at least an hour before school ended.

'You're home early, Charles,' I heard Margaret say from the parlour.

Damn. Damn!

'There's a water leak at the school. I've had to send all the children home,' Charles replied.

'Oh dear. Will you have some tea?' Margaret said. 'Hedda is here somewhere – she came to see me.'

'Hedda? Oh, no, Mother, I don't think so. She's been suspended.'

'Suspended? Oh dear. I thought she had been ill.'

'For goodness' sake, Mother, I know you're lonely, but if you start imagining people are visiting you Doctor Gaudie will think you've gone off your rocker,' Charles said. I was shocked at how cold he sounded. Was this, at last, a flash of the real man behind that bland, friendly persona?

'But I was not imagining...'

Margaret trailed off, and I heard Charles's heavy tread coming up the hall towards the room I was in.

Oddly, there was nothing beneath the bed. Thanking God I had brought my bag with me, I scrambled underneath, wriggling as far as I could towards the wall and lying with one cheek pressed against the stale-smelling carpet. My pulse was roaring in my ears as Charles came in and began shuffling through the papers on the desk. I had a clear view of his legs, clad in a pair of crisp fawn trousers, as he walked around the room. Then I saw him bend down and open the bottom drawer, lifting something out: a familiar small, square shape wrapped in a piece of sacking. There was no question of taking a photograph; all I could do was watch as he straightened up, closing the drawer with his foot, and left the room.

'I have to go out again and find someone to deal with this leak,' I heard him call to his mother. 'I'll be back for supper.'

As soon as I heard the front door close I grabbed my bag

and scrambled out from under the bed, brushing the dust from my clothes as I went back to the parlour.

'Was that Charles?' I said brightly. 'I thought he was still at the school?'

'He says there's been a water leak,' Margaret said. She peered at me, her expression clouded with confusion. 'He told me you'd been suspended – you haven't, have you, dear?'

'Suspended? Oh my goodness, no!' I said, with a laugh. 'He must have me mixed up with someone else. Anyway, I must go – I have another patient to see and I am already late.'

'Try some honey for that throat of yours if it's still troubling you,' Margaret said.

'I will.' I squeezed her hand, and left as fast as I could.

I could see Charles at the other end of Talafirth's long, straight main street. I kept my distance, ready to duck into a doorway if he looked round, but he seemed utterly focused, marching along purposefully with a canvas satchel over his shoulder I was certain contained the radio set. It wasn't until we were out of the village and he left the road that I realised where he was going: up the Haug, making for the ruined croft where Bill and I had watched the Mirrie Dancers all those weeks ago.

I couldn't follow him up there. There was nowhere to conceal myself; if he should glance behind him he'd see me straight away. I decided, instead, to make my way around the other side of the hill and approach the cottage from the back. If he was still there when I reached it, I could pretend I was merely out for a walk and carry on past.

But by the time I arrived, breathless, my shoes wet from splashing through a little stream, there was no one around. Charles was halfway down the hill again. He did not have the canvas satchel.

I waited until he had disappeared from sight, then went into the cottage.

Where has he put it? I thought, looking around. One end of the cottage had completely collapsed and was just a pile of rubble, about half as tall as a man, but the wall at the other end, where there was a chimney stack, was still intact, although the roof had caved in long ago. There was a rusted iron grate at the base of the chimney with grass growing out of it. I went over and reached inside, feeling around. There was nothing there. Perhaps Charles had just come up to make a transmission, and he *had* taken the set back with him.

Feeling slightly desperate, I wondered what I was going to do, gazing with unseeing eyes at the transmitter and receiver towers that stood at the top of the hill a few hundred yards away. I was absolutely sure Charles was up to something, but how was I going to prove it if it was just my word against his? He was the island's head teacher, and Captain of the Home Guard; I doubted even Elizabeth and Donald would believe me. The rest of the island had more or less made up their minds I was the spy, and I already knew it was no use trying to get a message to Bill.

Perhaps if he has left the set here somewhere, then he will be coming back to use it, I thought. But when?

Suddenly, I remembered what Mette had told me at the telegraph station when we were looking at the radio set in the suitcase. *They will mainly use it at night – the signal is stronger then and can travel further; something to do with the atmosphere.*

My heartbeat quickened. Was that what Charles was planning to do? It would certainly make sense, if he was transmitting information to the Germans. His radio signals would need to travel a very long way indeed.

You need proof, I thought again. *No one will believe you without it.*

I took a deep breath.

If I needed to get proof, then I knew what I had to do.

TWENTY-NINE

HEDDA

I returned to the Sinclairs' croft, ate supper, although I had no appetite whatsoever, and put Eirik to bed. 'One more story, Mamma,' he said as I tucked the covers around him and bent to kiss his forehead.

'Not tonight, *lille vennen*,' I soothed him. 'Mamma has to go out, just for a little while.'

'Where?'

'To visit Bertha Sutherland. She has some wool for me so I can knit you another jumper.' It was the story I'd been practising inside my head as I forced down my food, ready to casually mention it to Elizabeth before I left and hoping she hadn't found out Bertha was one of the people treating me like a pariah.

He pushed out his bottom lip. 'But I want another story!'

'If you're still awake when I come back, I'll read you *two* stories, how about that?'

'All right, Mamma.' He snuggled down under his covers, eyes already closing. I kissed him again and left the room, closing the door softly behind me.

'Will ye ask Bertha if her Arthur wants Donald to take

a look at dat calf o' theirs tomorrow?' Elizabeth asked me when I told her where I was going.

'Of course,' I said. 'I won't be long.'

'Ach, you'll be lucky to get away in under an hour – I've ne'er met a woman so in love wi' the sound of her own voice!' Elizabeth said, but there was a kindly twinkle in her eye. 'Don't you rush back. I'll keep an ear out for Eirik.'

'Thank you.' Suddenly, there was a lump in my throat, and I had an overwhelming urge to hug her. *Don't be ridiculous, Hedda*, I told myself. *You're behaving as if you will never see her again.*

'And dear me, I'll have to lend ye somethin' brighter to wear,' Elizabeth remarked, shaking her head at the dark-coloured clothes I was wearing. 'You look as if you're off to a funeral!'

I slipped out of the cottage. It was getting dark, although the evenings were drawing out now. I wondered what summer would be like here and if I'd still be here to see it. I felt more like a ship without an anchor than ever, directionless, with stormy waves rolling in from all directions.

As I left the road and began to climb the Haug, the towers at the top loomed like great metal skeletons in the gathering twilight. I approached the croft cautiously, but there was no sign of Charles, so I tucked myself behind the pile of rubble that had once been the end wall opposite the chimney stack. With my dark clothes and my hair covered with a headscarf, I was confident I was well hidden.

Now all I had to do was wait.

As I sat there, the absurdity of the situation struck me fully, and I had to stifle a laugh. All day, I had been skulking around: telling Margaret lies to get into the house; poking around the kitchen, the outhouse and the bedrooms; hiding under the bed; following Charles up the hill...

Perhaps I should have been in Milorg after all, I thought, realising the laughter bubbling up inside me was not because I found this situation funny, but because I was scared. I wondered what my life would be like if I *had* joined the resistance. Would I have stayed in Norway, working with people like Rolf Rasmussen and his men? If it had not been for Eirik, perhaps that is where I would be: in a snowy forest cabin somewhere, crouched over a radio set as I listened for messages with one ear, and for Germans and their collaborators with the other.

But instead, here you are in Shetland, hoping to catch a spy all by yourself. I felt another burst of hysterical laughter bubble up inside me and pressed my hands against my mouth to keep it in.

I had no watch, so I didn't know what time it was, but as I sat there night drew relentlessly in and the temperature dropped. Despite the jumper and shawl I was wearing, I shivered. Would Charles Mackay come? And what was I going to do if he did? I had no plan; I was just tired. Now the urge to laugh had faded away my whole body felt drained and heavy.

Then I heard someone clearing their throat. All at once, I was wide awake again, heart hammering. I peered around the heap of stones and saw the faint light from a torch or a lantern with a masked-off beam bobbing as someone approached the ruins.

I drew back, trying to breathe steadily and silently through my nose. Was it Charles, or someone else?

Whoever it was reached the cottage. They were breathing

hard after their climb up the hill. I heard them clear their throat again, and then a scraping sound, and what sounded like a fall of dirt or small pebbles.

I peered over the stones again. A figure was standing at the other end of the cottage in front of the chimney stack, pointing a torch at the chimney, about halfway up; the sound I'd heard was one of the square stones being removed. With their other hand the figure was taking something out of the hole.

So that is where he hid it, I thought, watching as Charles turned – for it was Charles; even in the near-complete darkness, I knew it – setting the radio down on another, smaller pile of stones nearby. Tucking the torch awkwardly under his arm, he began fiddling with it. Then, quite clearly, he said, in stilted German: '*Haben Sie mich verstanden?*'

Do you read me?

I remembered the body that had washed up on shore that day Bill, Eirik and I walked down to the bay, and the bodies being brought ashore after they were recovered from the *Zetland Princess*, and felt hot, prickling anger surge through me.

Think, Hedda, think. My only real option was to go to the station. If I was quick – if I ran – I could get there in less than ten minutes. Five minutes to summon help; ten minutes to get back; would that be long enough? Would Charles still be here?

I had no idea. What I *did* know was that I had to go now. Holding my breath, still watching Charles, who had his back to me, I got to my feet and crept forwards. It was so dark now that I didn't see the loose stone by my foot. My toe struck it, dislodging it with a clatter, and Charles whirled around.

'Who's there?' he said sharply.

I froze, holding my breath. He grabbed the torch and I ducked down just as he swung the beam towards me. 'Who's there?' he said again, his tone lower, more menacing.

I heard his footsteps as he walked over to the pile of stones where I was crouched like a frightened animal, fists clenched. I closed my eyes, curling myself into a ball, telling myself that if I stayed very, very still, he might not see me. I could hear the blood roaring in my ears; my lungs felt as if they would burst with the effort of not gasping for breath.

I smelled stale tobacco and damp wool – the same stale smell that had permeated his room in the little house on Talafirth's main street.

'Hedda?' Charles said. He sounded startled, and when I opened my eyes and looked up he was standing over me, shining the torch right into my face. 'What – what are you doing here?'

I got to my feet, brushing grit from my skirt. 'What are *you* doing here?' I challenged him, hoping my voice was not shaking.

He glanced behind him, towards where the radio was sitting on the pile of stones.

I took the deep breath my lungs were begging for. 'I heard you,' I said. 'You're the spy, aren't you?'

He didn't say anything.

'Charles?'

'You wouldn't understand,' he said at last, in a strange, cracked voice. He sounded so vulnerable that for a moment, all my pity for him came rushing back and I had to remind myself what he had been doing, all the lost lives he'd been responsible for so far. I had to get help – I had to get help *now* – but I did not dare move. Charles was bigger than me, and stronger. If I tried to run, who knew what he might do?

'Why would I not understand?' I said carefully. 'How do you know, if you don't at least try to tell me?'

'You really want to know?' He laughed, a harsh, humourless sound, and glanced up at the sky. 'Hmm. Perhaps she *does* care.'

'What do you mean?' I asked.

'Oh, don't play silly beggars with me, Hedda! You must know how I feel about you!'

A wave of horror went through me as, yet again, I remembered that moment in his mother's house when he'd loomed over me in the corner of the kitchen and leaned towards me. So I hadn't imagined it – he *had* been trying to kiss me.

'I am married, Charles,' I said, still fighting to keep my voice level. 'I have a son.'

'Married to a man all the way over in Norway, who could be dead by now!'

If only that were true, I couldn't help thinking. 'I do not know what has happened to him, but the fact remains that he is my husband.'

'Hmm. Yet you seem quite happy to throw yourself at that radar man of yours,' he spat.

For a moment, I couldn't work out what he meant. Then, quite suddenly, I remembered how his face had twisted with pain that day he, Flight Lieutenant Jackson and Hugh Leask had searched the Sinclairs' cottage, and I realised which photograph he had been looking at.

'Bill is just a friend,' I said. My legs were shaking; I sank onto the remains of the wall behind me. 'Charles, why don't you tell me why you are doing this? Perhaps I would understand,' I said carefully. 'Perhaps, if you told me, I could help you – I know you've been through a lot...'

I needed to buy myself some time to think; to work out how I was going to get out of this.

'Don't feel sorry for me, Hedda,' Charles said between gritted teeth. 'Don't you *dare*.'

'I don't feel sorry for you. I am just trying to—'

He cut me off. 'What is there to understand? I gave this country everything in the last war – my health, my happiness – and what did I get in return? Nothing! They threw me on the rubbish heap and left me to rot!'

'So you've gone over to the enemy? That makes no sense!'

'It makes perfect sense to *me*,' Charles growled. 'This government – this country – cares nothing for men like me, so why should I give a damn about *them*?'

The bitterness in his tone took my breath away. Charles' mind was broken, I realised – twisted beyond saving by what had happened to him after the last war – and he had lost his grip on reality. It was the only possible explanation.

He grabbed my arm. 'Help me, Hedda,' he said. 'Work with me.' In the torchlight, I could see the fanatical gleam in his eye, and for some reason that frightened me more than anything.

'No!' Perhaps I should have pretended to go along with him, but the words burst from my lips without me even thinking. 'Never! Let go of me!' I tried to shake free, but his grip was too strong.

'I'm giving you a chance,' he hissed between clenched teeth. 'You're an intelligent woman – you must know that if you turn down this opportunity for us to work together, then you leave me with no choice.'

'N-no choice about what?' I said, my mind racing. *You fool, Hedda*, I thought – it wasn't Anders' voice in my head but my own, filled with bitter self-awareness. *You should have gone to the camp first. You should have insisted on being allowed to pass that message on to Bill, or told Flight Lieutenant Jackson what you thought was going on.*

Charles reached under his coat and drew out a heavy revolver. 'I'm sorry,' he said, in a voice that didn't sound sorry at all. 'But if you won't agree to help me, I can't just let you walk away – you must understand that.'

And he pointed the gun straight at my heart.

Thirty

BILL

*D*amn *it, Rose, what are you up to?* I thought as I lit yet another cigarette. Those photographs of Rose and Clive were playing like a movie inside my head. It was dark now, and cloudy; night draped over the island like a heavy blanket. I'd been out for hours, sitting on a rock at the edge of Odda's Bay, and had about another hour to go until I was back on watch. I hadn't been able to face returning to the camp or my hut, where I knew Lewis, Len and the others would most likely be involved in a rowdy game of cards. I dragged on the cigarette, drawing the smoke deep into my lungs and blowing it back out of my nostrils in two angry streams.

The tide was coming in, water lapping at the toes of my boots. My head still whirling, I stood up. Almost automatically, I found myself making my way up the Haug, and to the ruined croft near the radar towers. *I have to get leave – I have to get to London,* I thought. Surely those pictures were a mistake.

Rose wouldn't be seeing Clive behind my back... would she?

As I drew near to the cottage, I realised I could see a faint light inside, shining off the end wall that was still standing, and hear voices – a woman's and a man's. Locals, perhaps, or one of the guys from the station up here for a rendezvous with his girl. *Damn it*. I'd have to find somewhere else to finish my cigarette and stew over the photographs of Rose and Clive.

I was about to turn away and walk down the hill when a sudden gust of wind carried the voices over to where I was standing, and I heard the woman say, quite clearly, 'No – please – my son—'

Hedda. I would have recognised her accent anywhere. She sounded terrified.

I ground my cigarette out beneath my boot and walked carefully, quietly towards the voices.

'Oh, stop going on,' the man said, 'I'm not going to *murder* you, for goodness' sake.' I realised I recognised his voice too. What the hell was Captain Mackay doing up here? And why did he sound so angry?

'No,' he continued. 'This is what's going to happen. I'll finish sending my messages, and then I'll take you and this set down to Hugh Leask and tell him I found you up here with it.'

'No – you can't do that!'

'Oh, I can, and I will.' Mackay's voice was suddenly mocking and cruel; he sounded as if he was enjoying himself. 'After all, who will Leask believe? The Captain of the Home Guard, or some foreigner who everyone already suspects of being the spy?'

'Please,' she said. 'Eirik—'

'Perhaps you should have thought about *Eirik* before you came creeping up here after me,' Mackay said, every word dripping with venom. 'And don't try any funny business. As I said, I don't intend to kill you, but I *can* wound you and say I did it in self-defence.'

Hedda gave a desperate-sounding sob. I yanked my pistol from my belt and marched into the cottage. 'What do you think you're playing at, Mackay?' I snapped as, in the semi-darkness, I saw two figures whirl towards me.

'Bill, look out!' Hedda cried. 'He's got a—'

There was a flash and a roar and something slammed into my right thigh, knocking me off my feet and my pistol from my hand. I groaned, putting my hand to my leg. My fingers came away wet with blood.

Shot me. He shot me, I thought incoherently.

'*Jævel!*' Hedda screamed. I had no idea what that meant, but she no longer sounded scared, just furious. I heard a scuffle happening somewhere above me – Mackay grunting for breath and feet scrabbling on the fallen stones. There was another bang, then a cry.

'Bill, help me!'

Somehow I got to my knees and back on my feet, ignoring the pain in my thigh. The torch had been knocked over and its masked lens shattered; it lay on its side, naked bulb illuminating the inside of the ruin with its weak yellow glow.

'No!' I heard Hedda cry. I saw Charles, his hair standing on end, his jacket torn at the elbow, staggering towards a heap of rubble in the middle of the cottage with a large stone in his hands. On top of the pile was what looked like some sort of radio set, wires hanging down.

'He's the spy!' Hedda said desperately to me. 'He's been using the radio to send information to the Germans!'

'Oh no you don't,' I snarled. As Charles tried to smash the stone down on the radio set I shoulder-barged into him, knocking him sideways. He fell over with a grunt, dropping the stone. I made a grab for him but he was already scrambling to his feet. I lunged at him again and he dodged around me, snatched up the radio set and ran, disappearing into the night.

I swore, then hissed and clutched at my leg as another bolt of pain shot through my thigh.

'Are you hurt?' Hedda asked me. We were both breathing hard.

'I'm fine,' I said. 'Go to the station and get help, now – we have to find him before he can leave the island. I'll start looking for the bastard.'

She ran from the cottage. I looked round for my gun, but couldn't see it. Then, a few feet away, I spotted Mackay's revolver. It was a Webley from the last war, immaculately maintained. I snatched it up, jamming it in my belt, grabbed the torch and hobbled out of the cottage. Christ, my leg hurt.

I stood on the side of the hill, swinging the light around me in a circle. *If I was Charles Mackay, where would I go?* I thought. Then I realised that wherever Mackay was heading, if I kept shining the torch around like this, he'd be able to see me a mile away. I switched it off and waited a few moments for my eyes to adjust to the darkness.

Odda's Bay, I thought. It was the nearest beach; Mackay could have a boat hidden there.

Moving as fast as I could, I hobbled back down the hill in the direction of the bay, torch in one hand, the Webley in the other. It was a still night, the moon covered by clouds. The only sound was the gentle thunder of the waves breaking on the shore. I turned on the torch again, but could see only shadows.

Then, as I peered into the darkness, the torch beam flickered and went out.

There was no option for me but to scramble back up to the road. By the time I got there, I could hear shouts and dogs barking above the thunder of the sea, and after five minutes of limping along, I caught sight of another torch up ahead. Flight Lieutenant Jackson's voice said sharply, 'Who's there?'

'It's me, Sir,' I gasped. 'Sergeant Gauthier. I've been down at Odda's Bay, hunting for Mackay, but I don't think he's there.'

Jackson reached me. 'Are you hurt, Sergeant?' he said.

'Bastard shot me. Is Hedda OK?'

'I am fine,' Hedda said, appearing behind Jackson. I was so relieved to see her, that Jackson had believed her and she hadn't been arrested or locked up, that I could have hugged them both.

'We're sending search parties out across the island,' he said. 'Although I have to say, I can't quite bloody believe it – *Mackay*, of all people…'

'I don't think any of us can believe it, but it's true,' I said. 'I saw it with my own eyes.'

'We have to find him,' Hedda said. 'If he manages to get away—'

'Gauthier, go with Mrs Dahlström back to the station and get patched up. I'll carry on this way. Do you know if the man's armed?'

'I've got his gun,' I said, showing him the Webley. 'He might have another, though. Wouldn't put anything past him.'

Flight Lieutenant Jackson nodded. 'Well, I've got my pistol. Hopefully I won't need to use it. Now, back to camp, please, Sergeant.'

I saluted him, and he strode off into the darkness.

'Do you want to lean on me?' Hedda said, offering me her arm.

'I'm *fine*, honestly. Come on.'

We made our way back up the road to the camp.

'We should go to the medical bay,' Hedda said as the gates came into view.

'Should we hell,' I said. 'I want to find that bastard.'

'Bill—'

The gentle pressure of Hedda's fingers on my arm made me glance round at her, and I saw the concern in her eyes. 'I'll be all right,' I said, feeling my face, already flushed from the evening's exertions, grow a little warmer. 'And when we've caught him I'll go straight to the medical bay, I promise.'

'All right,' Hedda said. 'But where might he have gone?'

'He wasn't at Odda's Bay, but I reckon he'll be on one of the beaches, looking for a boat to get out of here – it's a quiet night, good for sailing. If I was him I'd try and get across to one of the skerries off Unst, ditch the radio equipment and lay low for a while. I don't think he'll go to Talafirth harbour, though, or anywhere near town for that matter – not if he has half as many brains as people credit him with.'

'Where, then? Will he try to get over to the bottom of the island? Wouldn't that take him too long?'

I tried to think, scrubbing my hands through my hair. 'I don't know.'

What I did know was that the longer it took to find MacKay, the more chance he had of getting away. *Where was he?*

'Wait – what about the bay where you rescued me and Eirik?' Hedda exclaimed suddenly. 'That is not far from here, is it?'

'No – just up there.'

'Come on!' she said.

We made our way up to the cliffs at the edge of the camp, half walking, half running. I couldn't go any faster; the burning in my thigh had become a sharp throbbing now, as if I'd been kicked by a horse.

'Are you sure you are all right?' Hedda said.

'Yes. Come *on.*'

On the clifftop, I turned on the torch again, praying the battery would have revived somewhat. The last thing anyone needed was for me or Hedda to go plunging over the edge. To my relief, it flickered into life again.

'There,' she said, pointing, and I saw the gap where the steps had been cut into the rock.

I hadn't been back here since Lewis and I had pulled Hedda, Eirik and the four dead men from the capsized boat. As we began to descend the steps, which got slipperier the further down them we went, an involuntary shudder wrenched up my spine as I remembered the man hanging upside down from the deck and the others lying in a heap on the rocks.

Just like the day of the rescue, the tide was nearly in, but this time the sea had none of that brutal, devastating power. The only sound was the breaking waves again, and the blood pounding in my ears in time with the pain thumping through my leg.

I turned slowly, shining the torch around in a wide arc. 'Charles Mackay!' I shouted. 'If you're there, show yourself! It's over!'

Nothing, except for the soft drag and hiss of the waves.

Then Hedda clutched my arm. 'What was that?' she whispered.

'What was what?' I whispered back.

'I heard something over there.'

In the darkness, I could just see her pointing. I aimed the torch towards the rocks where the Norwegian boat had capsized, and saw a huddled shape. At first glance, it looked like more rocks.

Then it moved.

'Mackay!' I yelled, fumbling the Webley from my belt. 'Put your hands up!'

Crouched on the rocks, Mackay scowled at me. 'Piss off, Gauthier,' he said, spitting out my surname as if it were poison.

As I made my way towards him, Hedda right behind me, Mackay stood, looking around him wildly. Had he got a boat? I couldn't see one anywhere. 'Give it up, why don't you?' I said. 'What are you planning to do? Swim to the mainland? The water's freezing – you'll drown.'

Mackay scrambled away from us, using his hands as well as his feet to grip the rocks. 'You fool,' he hissed. 'Why did you have to go sticking your nose in?'

I realised he was talking to Hedda, not me. 'The only fool here is you, Charles,' she replied. 'Do what Sergeant Gauthier asks. It will be easier for you.'

He gave a harsh, manic-sounding bark of laughter. 'Why should I listen to you?'

He had reached the edge of the rocks and could go no further. I saw him glance behind at the water, and suddenly realised my hunch was right: either he was going to try and swim away from here, or drown himself.

'Stay right there, buddy,' I said. When I trained the torch beam on his face I realised had never seen a man look so hunted or so desperate; his lips were peeled back from his teeth, his hair plastered to his forehead with sweat, seawater or both. 'Don't come any closer!' he spat when I was only a foot or two away from him, picking up a loose stone the size of a grapefruit. 'I was captain of my cricket team at school – I'll knock that gun out of your hand before you've even had time to put your finger on the trigger.'

'Don't be a bloody idiot,' I told him, raising the Webley. 'I don't want to shoot you, Mackay, but I will if I have to.'

With a noise that was somewhere between a grunt and a scream, he hurled the rock at me. I'd been so certain he was bluffing that it took me by surprise, and I pulled the trigger a second too late; the rock collided with my hand and the gun fired harmlessly into the air as it skittered from my grip and landed with a splash in a rockpool.

Mackay and I both lunged for it. So did Hedda, and she got there first.

'Stay where you are,' she spat at Mackay, breathing hard as she shoved the muzzle of the gun into his temple. 'I killed a Nazi back in Norway – I am not scared of you.'

Clutching my fingers, which were throbbing almost as badly as my leg now – it felt as if Mackay had broken at least one of them – I stared at Hedda. She had *what*?

Mackay crumpled to his knees, covered his face with his hands and began to weep.

I closed my eyes, letting out the breath I hadn't even realised I was holding.

'Get up,' Hedda said to Mackay. Shakily, he stood and she moved the gun to the small of his back. '*Move*. And if you try anything, I *will* shoot you, do you understand?'

'Wait,' I said. 'Where's the radio set?'

Hedda jabbed the gun harder into Mackay's back. 'Answer him!'

'It's over there,' Mackay said, jerking his head sideways. I shone the torch in the same direction and saw a sodden, sacking-wrapped bundle near the base of the cliffs.

After I had retrieved it, we made Mackay climb back up the steps and onto the cliff. I kept hold of his arm as we frogmarched him towards the camp, but he seemed to know the game was up and showed no sign of trying to escape. In the sentry box, the soldier who'd been there earlier – the kid with the acne and the oversized uniform – was still on duty. When he saw us, his eyes widened.

'S-Sergeant Gow—' he stammered.

'It's Gauthier,' I reminded him wearily. 'Can you let us in? We've caught ourselves a spy.'

He all but ran out of his hut to unlock the gates.

'Thanks,' I said. I gave Mackay a little shove, suddenly overwhelmed by exhaustion and pain. 'Come on.'

Save for the kid at the gates, the camp appeared to be completely empty; everyone who wasn't on duty was still combing the island for Mackay. Hedda and I ended up shutting him up in one of the storage sheds, the only place we could think of that didn't have a window he might try and escape through. He didn't try to resist as we pushed him inside; all the fight had drained out of him and he was as meek as a kitten, slumping onto the shed floor and resting his head on his knees. I left him the torch, although its bulb was starting to dim again, and slammed the damp-swollen door on him, using a piece of wood to wedge it closed. Then I slumped to the ground myself, the radio on the ground beside me.

'I'd better stay here and keep an eye on him until the Corp gets back,' I told Hedda. 'Can you go and find someone, tell them we've got him?'

Hedda nodded, handing me the gun.

As the adrenalin ebbed from my body, exhaustion took over, and despite the pain in my leg and hand, by the time Hedda returned with Lewis, Al and Flight Lieutenant Jackson in tow, I was beginning to doze, my head lolling.

'He's in there?' Flight Lieutenant Jackson nodded at the shed behind me.

'Yes,' Hedda said.

While Jackson and Al dealt with Mackay, Lewis and Hedda helped me to my feet. 'You look all in, old chap,' Lewis said.

I waved him away irritably. 'I'm *fine*.' Then I put my weight down on my injured leg and hissed at the pain.

'I'll take him back to his hut,' Hedda told Lewis. 'I do not have my bag, but think there is a first aid kit in the office – will you bring it to me?'

Lewis dashed off, and Hedda and I made our way back to Hut 1, where she helped me take off my boots and lie down on my bed. A few minutes later, Lewis came in with the first aid kit, a cloth and a large enamel bowl filled with steaming water. 'Need any help?' he asked, frowning at me, and for the first time I realised just how dishevelled I must look, my clothes stained with earth, blood and seawater.

Hedda shook her head. 'No, I am all right. Thank you, though.'

'Okey dokey.' He left, pulling the door closed behind him.

Hedda examined my hand first. 'Can you move your fingers?' she said. I flexed them experimentally; they hurt, but not as badly as before.

'I don't think anything is broken,' she said, turning it over. 'Just bruised.'

'Hedda, what did you mean?' I said as she let my hand fall again. 'When you told Mackay you'd killed a Nazi?'

Her gaze became shuttered; she turned her face away. For a moment, I thought she wasn't going to answer me. Then she said, 'He was one of the Wehrmacht – the army who invaded our part of Norway.'

'Is *that* why you had to leave?' I said.

'Not the only reason – I have already told you about getting caught passing messages to prisoners at a camp near the town where I lived.'

'Yes,' I said. 'That's why you were trying to get to Sweden, isn't it?'

She pressed her lips together. 'Eirik and I had already been travelling for several weeks when we were directed to someone we thought was part of *Milorg* – the resistance – but she was a collaborator and she betrayed us. I had to kill the officer. I had no choice. He was going to arrest me, and they would have taken Eirik away.'

The colour had drained from her face as she spoke, and I saw her hands were trembling.

'But it's OK now,' I said. 'You're safe. Hedda. *Hey.*'

I reached out and placed a hand on her arm, watching as, bit by bit, she came back to herself.

She sighed. 'I am sorry. It is still hard to think about that time.'

'I know,' I said softly. 'Believe me, I know.'

She gave me a small smile. 'Will you let me look at your leg now?'

My face grew hot; as I wriggled out of my trousers, I couldn't look at her.

'How bad is it?' I said, clenching my teeth as she gently probed the wound on my thigh.

'The bleeding has stopped. You were lucky – I think it is just a graze. It does not look as if the bullet went in.'

She set to work, using the warm water to clean the wound. Although her movements were brisk, professional, her touch was strangely intimate, and I felt my face grow even warmer. Then I saw her gaze had travelled downwards and that she was looking at the scars from the accident. I was so used to them now I'd almost forgotten they were there. Although they had healed well they were still purple and angry-looking, snaking down towards my knee.

I took a deep breath. 'Car crash,' I said. 'I was with my buddy. I—' My voice cracked and I had to stop and swallow hard. 'One of our crew had just... he'd just died, and we went out and got drunk – we were trying to forget about it.' I took another shuddering breath. 'By the time we finished it was too late to get a lift back to our base at Chedburgh, and we had roll call first thing in the morning, so we – we staggered around for a bit, trying to figure something out. Then we came across a car someone had left outside their house, and Robert—'

For a moment I was unable to continue. I closed my eyes, pressing the heels of my hands against my eyelids.

'He decided we should borrow it to drive back to the aerodrome,' I went on at last. 'We were going too fast – he forgot the lights – and in the blackout we... we hit another vehicle side on.' Each sentence felt like vomiting up poison, forcing me to relive the dreadful memories I'd tried and tried to keep pushed down. I heard Robert's screams as he died in the driver's seat beside me and saw him in the nightmare that had plagued me ever since that awful night: his face bloody as he reached over to grab my shoulder; our plane getting caught in that blinding, deadly cone of light, moments before I woke up.

I took in a great, shuddering breath. 'So you see, you're not the only one who's killed someone. I didn't mean for Robert to die, but it was my fault. I knew he was too drunk to drive that car. I should have tried to stop him.'

'Bill?' Hedda touched my hand gently, and I realised I was trembling. She picked up my good hand and squeezed my fingers, her grip warm, steady and reassuring. '*Min kjærlighet,*' she murmured. 'It is all right. It is all right.'

We gazed at one another, and with her other hand she reached out and touched my face.

I felt my stomach drop, as if I'd been walking down a flight of stairs and missed a step.

Hedda's expression changed, her eyes widening slightly, and she snatched both hands away as if I had suddenly burst into flames.

'Hedda—' I croaked.

'I must go. It is so late – if Eirik wakes up he will be wondering where I am.' She turned and began packing things back into the first aid kit, fumbling them in her haste. Two spots of colour had appeared high up on her cheekbones.

'Hedda, wait—'

'You should rest,' she said, buttoning her coat.

I sagged back against my pillows, heart racing as I watched her walk to the door.

She didn't look back at me once.

THIRTY-ONE

HEDDA

'A terrible business, terrible.' Bertha Sutherland shook her head, clasping both of my hands in hers. 'To think it was Charlie Mackay all along. I'm so ashamed of the way I behaved, Hedda. Will you forgive me?'

I could tell that the postmistress meant every word. Her face was red, her eyes bright with unshed tears. For a moment, a small, mean part of me thought about telling her, *No, I do not forgive you. You suspected me of being the spy with no evidence whatsoever.*

But what would be the point? Now my name was cleared, I'd be staying in Fiskersay for the foreseeable future, and it would be a long, lonely time if I stopped speaking to Bertha and the rest of the islanders just to make a point. The other women in the shop were watching us, wearing similar apprehensive expressions to Bertha's.

'Thank you, Bertha,' I forced myself to say. 'I accept your apology.'

Bertha hugged me, sniffling. I patted her back, feeling a mixture of awkwardness and relief.

'I'm sorry too, Hedda,' someone else said, and soon they

were all gathered around me, voicing their regret at their behaviour and indignance at the actions of Charles Mackay.

After a day locked up in the police station, he had been taken off the island in handcuffs this morning, a great, jeering crowd gathering at the quay to see him off. I had been there too, although I had not joined in, and as I watched Flight Lieutenant Jackson march him on board the boat I knew I was finally seeing the real Charles Mackay: a twisted and bitter coward, shoulders slumped and eyes downcast as he shuffled up the gangplank, not looking at anyone. As I'd wondered briefly what would happen to him, I suddenly remembered the people the Germans had shot in the street in Kirkenes. Would Charles be executed for what he had done? A shudder rippled down my spine, and I'd turned and walked away, leaving the crowd behind.

Now, when I went to pay for my purchases, Bertha only took a few of my coupons, and added some extra flour. I felt more uncomfortable than ever about it all, but I thanked her and hurried out of the store, glad to be in the fresh air again.

As I walked back to the Sinclairs' croft, I paused to gaze at the vast, rounded shape of the Haug, with its two metal towers on top, and replayed the events of two nights ago in my mind. What had happened up at the ruined cottage was a blur of fear and adrenalin. After Charles fired the gun I'd thought, at first, that Bill was dead; I'd been so relieved when he got up again, I could have cried.

But it was that moment in Hut 1 that loomed large over everything else: the moment after we had finally revealed to each other the worst moments of our lives. I couldn't forget the way Bill had looked at me. I kept trying to tell myself that I had imagined it, but I knew I had not. I had not imagined the heat that flashed through me as our gazes connected, or that dizzy, swooping sensation I'd felt, as if the ground suddenly tipped away from underneath me. It was as if Bill had looked right into my soul and seen not the timid girl who'd let herself fall in love with Magnus and tried so hard to believe that he loved her back, or the scared woman who had married Anders because she had fallen for the person he'd pretended to be and then, when it was too late, couldn't see any other future for herself and her child, but the Hedda I wanted to be: a woman at peace with herself and her choices, who could let someone in and exist alongside them on an equal footing. I had never felt this sort of connection with anyone.

But I had called Bill *min kjærlighet* – my love – without even thinking. I had touched his face.

You fool. You have let yourself fall in love, I thought, clenching my hands into fists, despair bubbling up inside me. It was wonderful, and yet it was terrifying, too, because of what had happened the last time I let myself love someone. It didn't matter if Bill had looked at me like that. It didn't even matter that he felt the same way, although I was pretty certain he did. He was engaged to Rose – beautiful, glamorous Rose – and I was married to Anders. Even if I never returned to Norway and started a new life somewhere else, I would be shackled to him forever because of our wedding vows. In the eye of the law, I was his wife, his property. And that meant I would never wholly be able to give my heart to another person, no matter how much I longed to. I would never be able to remarry. After Magnus I had sworn I would never be a willing party to an affair ever again – and that included my own.

Unless you went back once the war is over, I thought suddenly, *and asked Anders for a divorce.*

I gazed at the radar station towers, turning this new idea over in my mind. When Charles had pointed the gun at me the other night, I had been convinced my luck had finally run out. I had felt the same during mine and Eirik's flight from Kirkenes; when we were caught by the Wehrmacht officer I'd had to kill, and during that terrifying journey to Shetland.

Yet the thought of facing my husband – of asking him to grant permission to dissolve our marriage – was more paralysing than any of that.

I've had enough of trying to be brave, I thought. *I just want peace.*

Then it is up to you to create that peace, a new voice in my head said. It sounded like me, but it was calm, rational, matter-of-fact. *You cannot be Anders' wife any more. He abuses you – he abuses your son. As long as you are married to him, he will have power over you no matter how far you try to run. You know there are no limits to that man's cruelty. If you want to be truly free, you must divorce him. Then you can start again properly.*

I dug my fingers into my temples as I remembered all the times when Anders had railed at me and said I was an unfit mother; that if I continued to cross him he would have Eirik taken away from me. I knew the voice was right. I could not – *would* not – do that to my son. Not when I had already sacrificed so much to keep him safe. I would not only be betraying the person I had become since arriving in Shetland. but I'd be betraying Eirik, too.

Of course, I had no idea how to go about getting a divorce

– how long it would take or what it would cost. But there had to be someone, somewhere who could help me.

And after that? I felt my fingers begin to quiver against my skull. I truly had no idea. But I had my nursing qualification and the work I was doing here – perhaps I could ask Doctor Gaudie for a reference to take back with me to Norway.

A sudden wave of calm rolled over me as I realised I had no choice. I had to do this. I had to go back to Norway. And if my husband had survived the war, I had to be brave one last time, and face him.

I owed it to Eirik, and to myself, to break free of that bastard forever.

THIRTY-TWO

BILL
London
April

As I stepped off the train onto the platform at King's Cross, my kit bag over my shoulder, I felt weary and apprehensive. I'd kept to myself on the long train journey down from Aberdeen, although the carriage had been packed with servicemen and women on leave, spending most of my time pretending to sleep, or smoking and reading the same page of my newspaper over and over without really taking any of it in.

It was almost a month since we caught Mackay at Svarta Wick. He had now been charged with high treason and sentenced to death under the Treachery Act. My leg had been painful for a couple of weeks as the bruising came out, but the wound healed quickly. I was more relieved than I cared to admit; the thought of facing another slow recovery had preyed on my mind for the first few days, when my leg had hurt so much I was barely able to walk. I'd lain in bed in the medical bay, staring up at the ceiling and cursing Mackay to hell and back for putting me here, and having unpleasant flashbacks to being stuck in the hospital in Ely.

As soon as I had recovered, Doctor Gaudie recommended I

finally go on leave for a couple of weeks. 'A change'll do you good,' he'd said in his gruff voice. 'A nasty business, all this.' He shook his head, looking pensive. 'It's Mackay's mother I feel sorry for, really. I'm not sure she'll ever recover from this.'

I'd been granted the leave the following day. To be honest, I was relieved; every time I thought about Hedda I remembered that moment when our gazes had connected, and felt that same sensation inside me, my stomach going hollow. The day I left to take the ship to the mainland, I bumped into her at the harbour; all the old awkwardness between us had returned and she would barely even look at me. It hurt more than I cared to admit. Had I imagined that look? I was sure I hadn't, so why wouldn't she speak to me? Even small talk – something to try to recapture a sense of the easy friendship we'd had before – would have been better than *that*. I felt as if I'd done something wrong, but I couldn't for the life of me work out what that might be. Her behaviour made me feel completely rejected.

I made my way out of the station, gazing at the bombed-out buildings. It wasn't a shock to see them, exactly – there'd been just as much damage when I'd visited London before leaving for Shetland six months ago, and I'd seen the photographs in the newspapers since. But insulated by Fiskersay's remoteness and relative peace, I'd forgotten just how bad it was here. How did people stand it, being pounded by bombs night after night? They were all going about their business as if nothing was happening, but it couldn't have been easy.

As I looked for a taxi, pushing my way through the crowds and breathing in the grimy air, I was suddenly overwhelmed by a wave of homesick longing for Fiskersay: for its wide-open spaces, rolling hills, its vast expanse of sea and sky.

Damn it, Gauthier, get a hold of yourself, I told myself as, at last, I spotted an empty taxi. I hailed it, told the driver Rose's address and settled myself in the back with my bag on the seat beside me, closing my eyes and pretending to sleep again so I wouldn't have to talk.

I hadn't told Rose I was coming. I hadn't even written to her. As we approached her street, my mouth was dry. What if she wasn't in? Or still staying with her parents? I hadn't really thought about that; hadn't thought about anything except getting to London and confronting her. If the formidable Mrs Cooke wouldn't let me in, I guessed I'd just have to sit on the front step and wait, until she got back, or I could find someone who knew where she was.

I paid the taxi driver and got out, taking a deep breath before pressing the doorbell for Rose's flat. A few moments later, I heard a window open above me and her voice call, 'Hang on a minute!'

I looked up, but she'd already gone. I drummed my fingers against my leg, unable to keep still.

The door opened. 'Bill!' Rose exclaimed. I saw a fleeting expression of shock pass over her face; then it was gone, replaced by a wide smile. 'Oh, how lovely! But I wasn't expecting you – why didn't you write, or send a telegram?'

'Thought I'd surprise you,' I said, as she leaned in to kiss me. At the last moment, I turned my head and her lips landed on my cheek. She didn't seem to notice.

As I followed her up the stairs, I heard a door open along the hallway somewhere and looked round to see a scrawny woman with her hair covered in a brown headscarf watching us through narrowed eyes.

'Mrs Cooke,' Rose hissed, and I marvelled for a moment

at just how close the picture in my head had come to the reality. 'For goodness' sake, don't let her see you looking at her whatever you do!'

Once in Rose's flat, I sat down heavily in an armchair.

'Tea?' Rose called from the little kitchen. 'I don't have anything stronger in I'm afraid, although we could go out somewhere if you like.'

'Tea's fine,' I said, listening to her opening cupboards and turning on the tap to fill the kettle.

'You're lucky you didn't turn up a few days ago!' she said. 'The water got cut off after a bomb hit the water main, and they've only just managed to restore it.'

A few minutes later, she brought out a tray, placing it on a little table by my chair. 'Shall I be mother?'

I watched her as she busied herself pouring the tea. She was wearing a light-blue frock and matching cardigan, her hair immaculately waved as always. The diamonds in her engagement ring – there were three – caught the light as she moved. I stared at them.

'You're awfully quiet,' Rose said with a little frown. 'Is something bothering you?'

I cleared my throat. *Come on. You have to do this.* 'What's going on with Clive?' I said.

I was not sure what I was hoping for, but it wasn't the shock and guilt that flashed across her face. She tried to rearrange her expression into something more nonchalant, but it was too late – I'd already seen it.

'I saw pictures in a newspaper,' I said, trying to keep my voice even. 'You two looked very… close.'

Rose pressed her lips together. *Deny it*, I pleaded with her inside my head. *Say it's not true – that it was just the camera angle.*

'How long?' I said, when she still hadn't answered me.

She put her teacup down with a hand that trembled just slightly.

'Rose.'

'It's just a – a *thing*,' she said at last.

'So it's still going on?'

'Yes – I mean, no – I – Oh, you've no idea what it's like, Bill! No idea at all!' She stood up and went over to the window, looking out, her back to me, her shoulders tensed and her arms folded around her middle.

'What do you mean?'

'I'm so lonely! You're all the way up there, in that – that *place*, and I'm here with no one! I mean, this is the first time you've even bothered to come and see me in London since you went there!'

'Hey, there's no *bothered* about it – I tried to get leave and I couldn't! I told you that when you came to the island with ENSA. Have you been seeing Clive the whole time I've been away?'

She didn't answer me.

'Were you seeing him while you were in Shetland?'

She still didn't answer. That told me everything I needed to know. Sadness wrenched through me; anger, too, but not at Rose. I was angry at myself: for being such an idiot, and for not seeing what was going on even when it had been happening right in front of my nose.

'Why?' I said.

'I told you why. I'm *lonely*, Bill.'

'I thought you loved me.'

She turned her head to look at me. There was a small frown line between her eyebrows. 'I do! Of course I do! But – oh, it's complicated!'

'Complicated *how?*'

She shook her head. 'You wouldn't understand!' she said, her voice trembling a little.

'Try me, for God's sake.'

She stayed where she was, staring out of the window again, and didn't answer me.

'Rose, *please*,' I said, hating the pleading note that had crept into my voice. 'Is it because we might have to go to Canada?'

'That's part of it, yes,' she said at last, sounding reluctant, as if it cost her a great effort to get the words out.

'You don't want to go.'

'No, I don't.'

'Well, what *do* you want to do, then? Because every time I've tried to talk about it, or written to you about it—'

At last, she whirled round to face me. 'I want that house in Surrey!'

'I can't afford that damn house in Surrey! And I thought you wanted to get away from your parents!'

'Not by going all the way to bloody Canada!'

I gazed at her, winded. I didn't know what to say.

Tears welled up in her eyes and began to spill down her cheeks. 'I was so lost after Derek was killed, Bill. You have no idea. I thought my life was over. And then you came along and—'

'And what?' I said. 'You heard I'd had my accident and thought, *here's a willing victim?*'

'No. *No!* It wasn't like that at all!'

'No – I've got it now – it's because I told you I'd inherit my father's factories one day, isn't it?'

'No!'

'You sure? You didn't think, *Well, his old pa'll shuffle off soon and then he'll be loaded. Better get hitched before that happens so I get written into the will?*'

'No! Oh, Bill, how can you say such a thing?!'

'Why, then? Tell me, Rose, because I'm struggling to understand here.'

'I thought…' she began, then covered her face with her hands.

'Yes?'

'I thought if I tried hard enough, I could make it work with someone else. That was one thing,' she said, her voice muffled. 'You were so easy to talk to, that first time we met, and so different from the sort of men Mummy and Daddy kept trying to introduce me to after Derek died—'

'So that was one thing. What's the other?' I asked. I could feel despair kindling inside me, mixed with a low, dull anger. I felt a bit sick, too. She'd picked me so her parents would stop trying to marry her off? Was that all?

At last, she looked up at me again. 'You were so charismatic, Bill. So good looking,' she said softly. 'I could tell as soon as I met you that you were the sort of man who only had to click his fingers for every girl in the vicinity to come running. It was sort of a thrill at first, knowing you were interested in *me* when you could have had your pick of any woman you wanted. After you got hurt and we continued to see each other, I began to think perhaps I was the one who could get you to settle down – that I was different to all the others. You helped me forget about Derek. You made me feel as if I had a future again.'

'So why throw it all away on an affair with Clive?'

'I told you, I was lonely! It doesn't *mean* anything – he's just been keeping me company while you're away. When you come back, we can forget all about him and start again. I'm sure you'd be able to get British citizenship – there must be a way.'

I closed my eyes. We'd been in love with the idea of each other, I realised. I'd needed hope; to feel whole again. She'd seen me as a means of escape, as someone she could mould into an ideal to make up for losing the man she'd *really* loved. Perhaps, under different circumstances – if we were different people, with different lives – we could have made it work.

But I didn't want that. I didn't want a marriage built on something that had never existed. I wanted something honest. Something *real*.

Once again, the memory of the moment my gaze met Hedda's rose in my mind, and I felt that dropping sensation in my stomach again.

But I couldn't have her, either, could I? She was married to someone else.

I got to my feet. 'Well, that's that, I guess.'

'Where are you going?' she said as I made for the door.

'Oh, come on,' I said. 'We both know it's over.' But there was no heat in my words.

'No! Bill, you can't leave me!' Rose began to cry again, but there was anger flashing in her eyes and she had a petulant set to her mouth, like a child.

'You've still got Clive, haven't you? Why don't you marry him?'

'I can't! He's already married!'

I shook my head. 'Jesus, Rose.'

I opened the door. I knew I had to get out of there before she reeled me back in; already, I was feeling guilty, as if *I* was the one in the wrong here. As I went out into the hall and closed the door behind me again, I heard Rose shriek, and something smashed against the wood on the other side: probably one of the teacups.

As I reached the bottom of the stairs, Mrs Cooke popped up again. 'What was all that noise?' she said sharply.

'She's exercising her lungs before her next concert,' I told her, leaving the sharp-faced landlady to stare after me as I let myself back out onto the street. As I walked away from the flats, I decided to go and find a bar.

I needed to get drunk, fast.

THIRTY-THREE

BILL

I returned to Fiskersay ten days later. I'd tried to make the most of my leave, but I'd been dogged by a persistent gloom I couldn't quite shake off, which deepened when I ran into a guy from my Heavy Conversion Unit training days and found out that what had remained of my old crew – Amir, Jonny, Jack and Kenneth – were all missing, presumed killed, after the Halifax they were flying had been hit and ditched in the North Sea on the way home from a raid two months ago. We'd always known that every time we went out, there was a high possibility we wouldn't make it back, but that didn't stop the wrenching stab of grief as he told me the news. I was sick of the war; sick of air raids; sick of blackouts and bombs and death. Yet it felt impossible, right now, to imagine things any other way. London had been crowded with American GIs, adding fuel to the rumours that, at some point soon, it wouldn't just be Bomber Command going over to Europe to try and beat the enemy back but troops on the ground, too. But *when?*

When I stepped off the boat onto the quay at Talafirth, weary after almost two days of travelling and waiting around, it was drizzling, the tops of the towers on the Haug's summit wreathed in mist. But despite the lowering skies and what had happened down in London, I felt a sense of peace returning. What was Hedda doing right now? I wondered idly. I'd been thinking about her a lot since I'd left Rose's flat for the last time.

'Bill!' Len Kane was leaning out of the driver's window of a station truck at the far end of the quay, waving at me. I went over, clambering gratefully into the cab.

'So, you see your girl?' Len said cheerfully as we bumped along the road out of the village. I'd told him and Lewis I was going to visit Rose, but hadn't said why. Then – had it only been a fortnight ago? How was that possible? It felt as if months had passed – I'd still been hanging on to a thread of hope that there was an innocent explanation for those photographs.

'Broke it off,' I said. 'She was having a fling with her manager.'

Len whistled. 'Jeez, that's rough. I'm sorry.'

I gazed out of the window. 'Don't be. At least I found out before the wedding.'

'Yeah, I s'pose. But her manager? That bloke who couldn't so much as look at the sea without spewing his guts up?'

I shrugged, and Len muttered something rude I didn't quite catch. We spent the rest of the journey in silence.

'You coming to the NAAFI?' Len asked as we got out of the truck.

'I'm gonna drop my bag off first,' I said, heaving it onto my shoulder.

'Okey dokey.'

Hut 1 was empty, but the stove was glowing, just warm

enough to chase away the damp chill in the air, and the hut's cluttered interior, with its pictures pinned to the walls, the radio sitting on its usual table and the clothes folded over the washing lines around the beds, felt familiar and snug.

As I put my kit bag down, I saw an envelope propped up on the little cabinet beside my bed, my name and rank typed on the front. Frowning, I picked it up and used my thumbnail to open it carefully so the envelope could be passed on to the station office to be reused; they were hard to come by here.

I scanned the single sheet of paper inside and felt my stomach lurch. It was a notification of a new posting. In theory, postings at radar stations were supposed to last six months before we were moved on to somewhere else, but the reality was that at remote stations like this most men ended up in the same place for much longer, and I'd accepted that would be my lot, too. Everyone grumbled about it, but there wasn't much we could do.

But it looked like the higher-ups had been listening to the complaints. In a week's time, I'd be leaving Fiskersay and heading back to England, to Stenigot Chain Home station in Lincolnshire.

Thirty-Four

HEDDA

'Well I never,' Elizabeth said, shaking her head as I came in out of the rain. 'You'll want to see this, Hedda.'

I'd just returned from Sutherland's Stores with some tobacco for Donald and knitting wool for me and Elizabeth. 'What is it?' I said, hanging up my damp coat. Elizabeth was poring over a newspaper spread out on the kitchen table. I went over to look.

SPY CONFESSES! the headline screamed. Underneath was a blurry photograph of Charles Mackay.

A Shetland man charged with high treason after being caught intercepting shipping information and passing it on to the Germans has made a shocking confession, the article said. When questioned about his motivations, Charles Mackay, 55, who was a head teacher and Home Guard Captain on the tiny island of Fiskersay in Shetland, claimed he had done it as revenge for mistreatment by the government after the last war, and because he believed in Hitler's vision for a post-war world.

Mackay said he was denied a decent pension after

being invalided out of the army in 1917, forcing him to rely on his mother in order to survive while he recovered from injuries sustained in the line of duty. It was during this time that Mackay developed his interest in radio transmissions and learned to build wireless sets, which led to him building the 'spy set' he was caught with,

But that is not the only interest Mackay developed during the inter-war years. A search of Mackay's property by local police uncovered a large collection of propaganda from the National Socialist League, the organisation founded by William Joyce, the traitor better known as 'Lord Haw-Haw' currently residing in Germany, from where he broadcasts Nazi propaganda on the radio. Correspondence between Mackay and other prominent figures in the British Fascism movement, mostly dating from around 1936 to 1938, was also discovered. Although no information has yet been found that could lead police to Mackay's German contacts, it is speculated that his anti-British sentiment can be traced back to the beginnings of his involvement with the NSL, which in itself was precipitated by the difficulties Mackay suffered after being discharged, for which he placed blame squarely on the British government.

The article went on in this vein for another two columns, although to my relief, I wasn't mentioned. By the time I'd finished reading, my head was spinning. Did Charles really think his actions were justified?

I shivered, remembering his face as he loomed over me in the ruined cottage, his features twisted and ghastly in the glow from his torch.

'I – I forgot something at the shop,' I told Elizabeth, rushing to the door again. 'I must go back – I won't be long.'

She watched me with a concerned expression as I pulled my coat back on, but didn't say anything.

Outside, with the wind whipping the fine rain that had been falling for the last two days against my face, I turned in the direction of Odda's Bay, wanting to drive the memories of that awful night up on the Haug out of my head.

'Hedda! Wait!'

I turned and saw Bill hurrying towards me.

My heart gave that funny little double thud it always did when I saw him lately. I'd been trying to avoid him, but now there was nowhere I could go. As I waited for him to catch up, I forced myself to breathe slowly and steadily, and tried not to think about the last time we'd been alone together.

'I didn't realise you were back,' I said when he reached me.

'Got here yesterday.' He was a little out of breath. I noticed how the rain had misted on his dark hair and in his eyelashes and wondered how I could ever have thought he reminded me of Magnus. He was far better looking.

'How was London?' I said. 'And Rose?'

'London was OK. Rose is history.'

'Oh?' I said, frowning.

'She was seeing that manager of hers behind my back.'

I stared at him in dismay. 'Oh, Bill! I'm so sorry. How awful for you!'

His mouth twisted as if he was struggling to keep his emotions in check. 'Don't be. It wouldn't have worked out anyway.'

'I was going down to the bay,' I said, and swallowed. 'Do you want to walk with me?'

'Sure. I wanted to talk to you anyway.'

'What about?' I tried to keep my voice light, my expression calm, but I wasn't quite sure I managed it.

'I've got a new posting,' he said as we began walking again.

'A new posting?' I wasn't sure what he meant.

'I'm leaving. I'm being sent to England – Lincolnshire – in six days' time.'

I stopped, completely unable to hide my disappointment this time. 'You're leaving?'

He stopped too. We were at the head of the bay now; the tide was in, leaving only a narrow strip of seaweed-strewn sand.

'That's why I wanted to talk to you,' Bill said. 'Hedda – I wasn't imagining it, was I? In the hut, I mean, after you'd cleaned the wound on my leg?'

'I – I'm not sure what you mean.' My heart was thudding wildly, the blood roaring in my ears.

'Yes, you are.' His gaze burned into me; I wanted to look away, but I couldn't.

I swallowed. 'Bill—'

'If I've learned anything since I joined the RAF, it's that life's too damned short to let the things you want pass you by,' he said hoarsely. 'I know you feel the same way about me as I do about you.'

'I'm married,' I said helplessly.

'Yes, to a man you don't love. It's as plain as the nose on your face. You never talk about him – the one time I asked you about him, you said he was difficult.'

I didn't answer him. I didn't know what to say. My heart was racing .Bill caught my hands in his. 'Hedda, I'll come back here for you after the war is over. It doesn't matter where they send me or how long for – I'll come back.'

I hesitated.

'That husband of yours is all the way over in Norway, and you're here,' Bill continued. 'You—' He paused, as if considering what he was going to say next carefully. 'You don't even have to go back to him if you don't want to.'

'No, I must. If he is still alive, I have to divorce him, or I will never be free of him.'

'But why do you need to go back for that? Couldn't you just write to him or something?'

'No! I must see him, tell him to his face.'

Bill's expression hardened. 'And what if he talks you into staying married?'

'He won't!' I cried fiercely. 'Bill – the only man I have ever loved is you! Anders is a monster! I ended up with him because I had a relationship with a married man and got pregnant with Eirik and I was lonely and vulnerable! He tricked me into marrying him – pretended he would care for us – but all he wanted was a – a maidservant. By the time I realised it was too late!'

The torrent of words burst out of me before I could stop them. I wished desperately that I could take them all back, especially the bit about Eirik being another man's child. I waited for Bill's expression to sour – for him to look at me with disgust and turn away – but I saw only sadness. It pierced through me like an arrow. Disgust would have been far easier to deal with; I was used to it. I knew what to do with it.

'Hedda…' he said. 'I don't care about any of that. Eirik's an amazing kid. If you'd let me, I'd love to be a father to him. I'd love us to be a family. I think we could all be happy.'

Despite my distress over having to tell Bill the truth about Eirik and Anders, joy leaped wildly through me. Did he really mean that? For a moment, I let myself imagine it – let myself picture waking up beside Bill every morning, and him holding me in his arms. I heard Eirik calling him *Papa* and Bill showing him how to fish and whittle sticks, and reading stories to him at night – all the things Anders had promised he would do for my son, and never had.

All too soon, reality came crashing back in. 'I still have to go back to Norway,' I said. 'I still have ask Anders for a divorce. If I don't, he could try to take Eirik from me. You must understand, there is nothing he wouldn't do if he thought he could use it to hurt me.'

Bill nodded. 'OK. I understand. But when you *have* got divorced—'

Sudden terror spiked through me. 'But Bill, the war – you are going away – what if something happens to you?'

He pulled me closer to him. 'It won't,' he said, his voice going hoarse again. 'All I'm good for is sitting in front of their machines – they'll stick me in another radar station somewhere in the back of beyond and forget about me. I'll be bored as hell, and safe as houses.'

'Do you promise me?' I said, searching his gaze with mine. 'I have already lost so much, Bill – I couldn't bear to lose you too.'

'You aren't going to lose me. I *promise*.'

We looked at each other for a moment longer. I could feel my heart leaping inside my chest. The rain was coming down harder now, plastering my hair to my head, but I barely noticed.

'May I kiss you?' Bill said.

I nodded.

He pressed his lips against mine. The kiss was gentle, soft

– nothing like the devouring kisses Magnus used to give me, intent only on his own pleasure, or the chaste, dry pecks I'd received from Anders at the beginning of our relationship which had petered out as fast as the pretence of his love for me. As I responded, desire rushed through me, every nerve-ending in my body tingling. It was so long since I'd felt like this that I'd almost forgotten what it was like, and I never wanted it to end.

Eventually, we broke apart. Bill let go of my hands and reached out to touch the side of my face. 'I have to get back,' he said. 'Will you let me walk you back to the croft?'

I nodded, and he smiled. I tried to smile too, but I was fighting back tears. I had finally fallen in love after all this time, and now Bill had to go away. It wasn't fair.

'Don't look so sad,' he said softly. 'While you're still in Shetland, we can write to each other.'

'Yes,' I managed to say, 'I would like that.'

'And this war will be over before you know it. You'll see.'

From out of nowhere, I got another sudden, odd sense of premonition, a stab of fear twisting through my gut. 'Bill – I know you said you'd be safe, but *please* be careful, won't you?' I said.

One side of his mouth quirked up in a smile. 'I meant what I said, you know – I reckon someone up there must be looking out for me, or it would have been curtains for me a long time ago.'

'Will you come and say goodbye to me and Eirik before you leave?' I said as we began, slowly, to walk in the direction of the Sinclairs' cottage.

'Of course I will – just try and stop me.'

We walked the rest of the way in silence, our fingers loosely entwined. The weather was so bad that there was no one around, and even if there had been I didn't care if they saw us or what they thought. Outside the cottage we kissed again. I closed my eyes, trying to make this moment last forever.

Then it was time for him to go back up to the station.

'Cheerio for now,' he said.

Reluctantly, I let go of his hand and stood there, watching, as he walked away. A sob tried to escape my lips and I clamped them together, biting down on the insides of my cheeks. But even though I knew I would see him again before he left, I couldn't help the tears that streamed down my cheeks. For some reason, it felt as if, when he went, I would be saying goodbye to him forever.

PART THREE

1944–1946

THIRTY-FIVE

BILL
Melsbroek Airport, Belgium
September 1944

My dearest Hedda,

I hope this finds you well. I am writing this to you from somewhere in Europe. My unit got here a few hours ago. There are sixteen of us, including me and three other radar operators. We flew over in a Dakota, all our kit strapped to the floor in the middle and us along the sides, with ten more planes carrying other units. It was quite an experience, I can tell you!

I paused, wondering what to write next, and – although I hadn't told Hedda exactly where I was – how much of my letter would make it past the censor.

It was sixteen long months since I'd left Fiskersay and Hedda. After my posting at Stenigot, I'd been sent to another station in Sussex, then to Renscombe Down near Swanage for battle training before going back to Yatesbury for a refresher course. Finally, at the beginning of June, D-Day – the subject of much rumour and speculation – had arrived. I'd been back at Stenigot by then, and was on watch when the invasion started; we'd all rushed outside to watch the Lancasters flying over in mass formation. When I got back to my billet no one had slept a wink, huddling by the wireless set for news, and after that, in the aftermath of Operation Overlord, things had really begun to move. Only a few days later, I'd found out I was joining Air Ministry Experimental Station (AMES) Unit 118 in preparation for an imminent posting to Europe, and now here I was with the rest of my unit, which included a laconic Welshman called Owen Prosser and another Canadian, Stan Barbeau, both of whom I'd quickly become friends with, sitting in a tent at the edge of one of the runways at Melsbroek airport, just east of Brussels. The airport had been used as a Luftwaffe bomber base and had been liberated from the Germans at the beginning of September. It was a vast sprawl of runways and structures with a collection of buildings at one edge that looked oddly out of place: shops and houses, and something that was like a cross between a hotel and a castle. Apparently, the Germans had built a fake village here, including the chateau-hotel, to try and disguise the airfield and protect it from air attacks.

It still felt as if I'd only left Fiskersay yesterday. The place and its people were always at the back of my mind, and in idle moments I returned to them like a loose tooth I couldn't stop worrying. I'd never felt homesick for a place before, but Fiskersay was different, somehow. I missed its wide-open spaces; the roar of the wind over the hills; the sea crashing against the cliffs below Svarta Ness and tumbling onto the beach at Odda's Bay.

And most of all, I missed Hedda and Eirik. I longed to see Hedda again – to hold her, to kiss her. I knew, now, that what I'd had with Rose was only a pale imitation of the real thing, and the man who'd gone out with a different girl every week before that felt like someone in another existence. There was only Hedda now, and I would wait for her for as long as it took.

Thank you for your last letter, I continued. *I read and re-read it every day, hearing your voice as if you were right here beside me.*

It's great to hear Eirik's doing so well at school with his new teacher, although I suppose she's not that new now, is she? And I'm glad Elizabeth and Donald are well. Remember me to them, won't you?

Right now, I am sitting in a tent. Looks like we're going to be roughing it for a while, but we'll be moving on soon and hopefully we'll have decent billets by the time winter arrives. What's the weather like in Fiskersay? Have the storms started yet? I remember them so well – trying to stay on my feet when I had to leave my hut at the station and the way the rain would blow at you sideways! That was really something! Anyway, I think we will be OK here. Our C.O., Barnes, whom everyone calls 'Barney', seems to be a decent sort of fellow and so are the other chaps in the unit. We're all determined to do our bit to send Jerry packing.

I must go, grub's up. I will write again very soon, my darling.

All my love,

Bill xxx

I folded the letter and put it in the inside pocket of my jacket for safe keeping until I could post it. Only then did it hit me that, because I could no longer tell Hedda where I was, she wouldn't be able to reply. I felt a sharp pang of disappointment and sadness. Her letters, with their bits of news about Fiskersay and the odd note from Eirik, had kept me going through the gruelling preparations for my posting to Europe. They'd made me feel as if she was still with me.

All you have to do is keep your head down and get through this war, I told myself. *The tide's turning – we've got Jerry on the run. Surely it can't go on for much longer.*

Right now, though, that day still felt as if it was a long way off.

THIRTY-SIX

HEDDA
Fiskersay
November 1944

I can't believe it, I thought as I stood at the top of the beach at Odda's Bay, the wind battering against me and sending the waves crashing against the shore. *It is more than two years since Eirik and I came to Fiskersay. How is that possible?*

Sometimes I tried to make myself remember that day in October 1942, but it was still a tangle in my memory, with many blank spaces between the storm hitting us somewhere in the Atlantic and waking up the next day in the little hut at the radar station with Eirik sleeping beside me. Perhaps I would never be able to recall it properly at all, except in the nightmares that still, occasionally, came in the darkest hours of the night. But even they were vague: the scream of the wind, the freezing water, the taste of salt and blood mingling in my mouth and my own and Eirik's cries filling my ears.

If it hadn't been for Bill...

I hugged my arms around myself, feeling an old, familiar sense of longing rising inside me. It was a month since I'd received his last letter, and because he couldn't tell me where he was, I couldn't write back to him. I remembered the dizzying mixture of emotions I'd felt that day in June as

Donald, Elizabeth and I sat around the wireless, listening to the news: joy that the Allied troops had finally returned to Europe; relief because, surely, this meant that now the tide of the war would begin to turn and the enemy would be beaten into submission; apprehension because I'd known Bill might be sent overseas soon, something he'd alluded to in one of his previous letters; and fear, for Bill and because this brought the day I'd have to return to Norway and ask Anders for a divorce ever closer.

As I shoved my cold hands in my pockets, my fingertips brushed Bill's last letter, which I had kept in my pocket ever since it arrived like a talisman, along with the photograph Eirik had taken of us on this very beach. I'd memorised every word of the letter. *I am writing this to you from...* The rest of the line had been censored, obliterated by a thick black line of ink, but I hadn't needed to read the words to know what they said. Bill was in Europe at last.

I turned my back on the sea and returned to the Sinclairs' croft. There, despite the stiff wind and icy rain, Eirik was helping Elizabeth feed the chickens, while Donald was chopping wood at the side of the house. I told Elizabeth I would start preparing the evening meal and went inside.

I filled the kettle and set it on the stove. While I waited for it to boil, I looked through Donald's newspaper, which he'd left lying on the table, neatly folded. A short article on the middle page, almost hidden among stories about the stock markets and rising fish prices and adverts for Jacobs Cream Crackers and Sylvan soap flakes, leaped out at me.

NORTHERN NORWAY GOES UP IN FLAMES,
the headline said.

The kettle forgotten, I carried on reading.

As the Germans retreat in the north of Norway, they are destroying everything in their path, in order to deny what is left of the country to the Soviet army. Norway's civilian population has been forcibly evacuated, with the Germans using dogs to track anyone trying to evade them; some people, trying to escape, have been shot in the street.

In the Finnmark region, the Germans were not able to evacuate the population, so on 21st October, they completely destroyed what remained of the town of Kirkenes by going house to house and setting fire to the buildings using drums of petrol. According to the latest reports, there are around twenty houses still standing, if their cellars being left intact can be called thus.

What now for the inhabitants of the town? Although they are liberated, as of 25th October, due to the destruction when Russian forces launched a comprehensive air attack on the town in July, many of them had been sheltering in Bjørnevatn, a waterlogged iron ore mine. Their future now looks uncertain, as does that of the population of the whole province of Finnmark.

I sank into a chair, my hand pressed against my mouth.

'Hedda? Are you all right?' Elizabeth said. I jumped; I hadn't even heard her come in. Behind me the kettle was whistling. Elizabeth took one look at my face and, turning to lift the kettle off the stove, said to Eirik, 'I expect Donald would like a hand to carry the wood to the woodshed.'

Eirik ran out again.

'What's happened?' Elizabeth said, rushing over to me. 'Have you had bad news? Is it...'

She didn't say *Bill*, but I knew that was what she meant. They still talked about him as if he was here; as if, at any moment, he'd stick his head around the door to see if Elizabeth had baked a new batch of scones or if Donald needed any help with repairs around the croft. I suspected they missed him almost as much as I did.

I shook my head, holding the newspaper out to her. 'Oh, my dear,' she said, her face falling as she scanned the article. 'This is your town?'

'It was,' I said woodenly. 'I don't suppose there is much of it left now – the Germans have seen to that.'

Then that little voice in my head spoke up: *Perhaps, if the town has been destroyed, Anders is dead. Perhaps you do not need to go back.*

I felt a momentary burst of relief. The decision had been made for me; I would not need to do the thing I had been dreading.

But the relief did not last. I knew that one way or the other, I would not be at peace unless I was certain. And I knew that if my husband *had* survived, then I still needed to face him. I'd had enough of running away.

I'd had enough of being scared.

The following day, when I'd finished my rounds, I went up to the radar station. Flight Lieutenant Jackson had recently returned for a second posting after being sent to England for a while, and I had bumped into him a few times at dances in

Talafirth. I'd been glad to see him, but his presence was also yet another painful reminder of Bill.

'Hedda, come in,' he said when I knocked on the door of the Manor.

He led me through to his office. It hadn't changed at all since the last time I was here, shortly after Eirik and I arrived in Shetland, but instead of facing each other across the table, we sat down in a pair of comfortable armchairs next to the fire, and Flight Lieutenant Jackson asked one of his sergeants to us bring some tea.

After some small talk, he said, 'So what can I do for you?'

Setting my cup down, I took the newspaper article, which I had cut out, from my pocket and showed it to him.

'Ah, yes, I've heard about the Germans doing this sort of thing,' he said. 'A nasty business. They're going to try and cause as much damage as they can now we've got them on the run.'

'I need to find out if my husband is still in Kirkenes – if he survived,' I said. 'My friends, too. Do you know how I could do that?'

Flight Lieutenant Jackson reached for his pen, inkwell and a piece of paper. 'The best place to start is probably the Red Cross – I know our lot have sister organisations in Norway and Sweden, and I expect they will be attempting to get into the areas the Germans have tried to destroy. There's someone I can write to who can find out who you should get in touch with. It may take a while, though.'

'That's not a problem. Thank you.'

'When I have an address I'll drop into the Sinclairs' with it,' he said. Our tea finished, we both got up, and he shook my hand. 'Is there anything else I can do for you while you're here?'

Not unless you can tell me where to find Bill, I thought, but I didn't say it out loud; I knew he wouldn't be able to help me with that.

I'm sure Bill will write to you again soon, I told myself as I left the Manor. *He said that he would. You just need to be patient, that's all.*

Please, God, let him be safe.

THIRTY-SEVEN

BILL
Roermond, Holland
March 1945

'I'm amazed those Yanks haven't blown themselves up yet,' Stan Barbeau commented as we leaned against a wall, watching a small group of American troops clearing mines along the road out of town. Taking a drag on my cigarette, I murmured in agreement. The way the GIs were joking around, throwing things to one another and cheering riotously whenever anyone dropped something, you'd think they were on a vacation, not one mile from the German border with buzz bombs flying overhead every half hour or so, and the risk of being blown to pieces if they took even one step in the wrong direction.

Suddenly, we heard a loud, clanging bell. With a grin, one of the GIs pulled a large alarm clock out of his battledress. 'Chow time!' he announced, and all the men downed tools and headed off.

I looked at Stan in amazement, and he shook his head, laughing. 'I guess that means it's *chow time* for us, too,' he said. 'Come on.'

We climbed back into our jeep to drive to the hotel we'd chosen as a temporary billet, with me driving. I still didn't like being a passenger, even though it was almost three years since the accident. As we bumped along the road, another buzz bomb went over, its engine making a sinister, burbling growl. We were so used to them by now, we didn't even glance up at it. Thankfully, it wasn't going in the direction of our hotel.

Our unit had arrived in Roermond in Holland three days ago, after being told, with twelve hours' notice, that we were moving north out of Belgium where we'd spent the entire winter in tents a few miles from Melsbroek. We were supposed to be living in tents in Roermond, too, but the site was slap-bang in the middle of the minefield the Americans were trying to clear, so for now AMES 118 had taken over the town's hotel. Now decidedly battle-scarred, it had once been a grand building, and although its water supply needed reconnecting and we didn't have any electricity yet, living there was sheer luxury compared to the tents. I even had a room to myself, although there was no glass left in the windows.

When we got back, Owen Prosser and one of the radar mechanics were waiting in the hotel lobby. 'Look at this, boys!' Owen said, grinning, and flicked a light switch by the door. The grand chandelier above our heads blazed into life.

'The Americans got us reconnected,' the mechanic said. 'And one of their chaps knows a bit about plumbing, too – he's working on the water supply as we speak.'

'Thank God for the Yanks,' Stan said, with feeling. 'I've had enough of being a damn boy scout.'

The rest of us nodded. Spending the coldest months of the year in a muddy, snowy Belgian field had been no fun at all, although we'd tried to make the best of it.

'Grubs up, chaps,' our C.O., Barney, said, putting his head around the door beside what had once been an elaborate reception desk, now covered in dust and rubble from all the bombings. Although he was considerably senior to the rest of us, he was as likely to be found in the kitchen peeling potatoes with our cook as he was in whatever passed for the officers' mess. Right now he was in shirtsleeves, his top button undone. The rest of us looked pretty dishevelled too. After all our months of rough living, none of us gave a damn what we looked like; all that mattered was that we did the job we'd been sent here to do.

I made my way to the hotel dining room. As the site wasn't operational yet no one could go on watch, so all sixteen of us were there. A veritable feast was spread out on the table: being so close to the American sector meant we got to share their rations, which they had more of than they could use, the smallest carton containing enough to feed twenty-five.

I had just reached for a dish of stew when we heard shouts in Dutch from the hotel lobby.

Owen Prosser swore, and I rolled my eyes. Roermond was mostly deserted save for AMES 118, the Americans and a handful of local resistance fighters, who, ever since we got here, had been wandering in and out of the hotel trying to bargain with us, mostly for petrol or boots. Generally they were pretty decent and accepted it if we said we hadn't anything to give them, but one fellow, Jan, was more persistent. An intense twenty-something with a rasping voice and a piercing gaze, he shifted constantly from one foot to the other as he spoke; there was something about him that reminded me of a hand grenade with the pin half-pulled out. Not long after we'd arrived, he'd cornered me and asked if I wanted to help him and his men round up local girls accused of fraternising with the Germans and have some fun with them. I'd already heard about what that 'fun' entailed – shaving their heads and subjecting them to countless other indignities – and he'd seemed taken aback when I'd told him I wanted no part of it.

I pushed my chair back and stood up. 'I'll go.'

Sure enough, Jan was out in the lobby, the rifle he always carried with him slung across his back. He was holding tightly onto the arm of another man – no, not a man, a kid. He couldn't have been more than sixteen, dressed in a tattered German uniform several sizes too big for him. He was scrawny, every inch of exposed skin filthy, and looked exhausted. He smelled pretty terrible, too. When he saw me he tried to take a step back and Jan snarled something at him, spitting on the floor at his feet.

Jan was twitchier than ever, his eyes wild; I wondered, not for the first time, if he'd got hold of a supply of wakey-wakey pills – Benzedrine sulfate – from somewhere. They used to give them to us in Bomber Command to keep us alert on long missions, although I'd only ever taken them a handful of times due to the way they made me feel afterwards, and their diuretic effect. Having to struggle out of the many layers of my flying suit to use the Stirling's Elsan in sub-zero temperatures was something I'd tried to avoid at all costs.

'I caught a rat,' Jan said in heavily accented English, shoving the kid towards me. The kid stumbled, falling to his knees on the tiled floor.

'Hey, that's enough,' I said to Jan, frowning as I stepped forwards to help the kid up. He wasn't the first German prisoner the resistance had brought us – there had been a fair few of them caught making their way through the town in the three days since we got here, trying to get over the border and home to their families after they realised staying to fight was a losing game. We'd feed them and hand them over to the Americans to transport them to the nearest POW camp.

Jan spat on the floor again and growled something else in Dutch. I resisted the urge to tell him to shut up, and took a carton of cigarettes from my pocket that I pressed into his hand as expected payment for the prisoner. 'Thanks,' I said. 'I'll take it from here, eh?'

Saying something that sounded rude, Jan stamped out of the lobby, letting the doors – which, like most of the windows in this place, had no glass in them – slam behind him.

'Come on,' I said to the kid. Wide-eyed, he shook his head. I wondered what the hell Jan had told him we were going to do to him. 'You're safe,' I told him. 'We have food.'

He stared at me uncomprehendingly. What the hell was the German for food? At last, I remembered. '*Mittagessen*,' I said, and mimed eating.

The boy's expression cleared a little. Fairly certain now he wasn't going to run off, I pointed in the direction of the dining room, letting him walk ahead of me. The others looked a little surprised when we came in, but to their credit, they said nothing. Barney got up and set a place for him at the far end of the table so we wouldn't have to smell him, and Owen passed him a plate heaped with stew, vegetables and bread. The kid ate like a starving dog, barely pausing to breathe as he tore into the food. I wondered when he'd last had a decent meal.

'What's your name?' Stan asked him when he'd finished, long before the rest of us. When the kid didn't answer, he repeated the question in German, which he was more or less fluent in.

'Erich Müller,' he said, and I stared at him. Erich. *Eirik*. Then Erich said something else. Stan gave a low whistle.

'What?' Barney asked.

'Sonofabitch says he's only fifteen,' Stan said.

We all stared at Erich. 'What the hell have you been playing at, boy? *Twpsyn!*' Owen said to him, but of course the kid didn't understand English, never mind the Welsh for *fool* – Owen's favourite interjection. He just looked at us, confused.

We ate the rest of our meal in silence, Erich taking a second helping of everything.

'Want me to take him over to the Yanks?' I said when we'd finished.

'Anything to get out of doing the washing up, eh?' Stan joked.

'I'll come with you,' Owen said. 'Could do with a change of scenery.'

We took Erich out to the jeep. He shuffled along with his head down and shoulders slumped, and although there was a little more colour in his cheeks now, he looked scared and miserable again. God only knows what Jan had told him we did to prisoners, but it was clear the kid had believed every word. He was *shaking*, for God's sake.

'It's all right, we're not going to hurt you,' I told him in a vain attempt to reassure him as we climbed into the jeep, Erich wedged into the middle seat with me and Owen either side. I patted him gently on the shoulder and he flinched away from me. I turned on the engine.

At the edge of town, the Americans were mine-clearing again. I glanced at Erich and saw he was staring at them, his whole body stiff, his eyes wide.

'Does he think they're going to shoot him on sight?' Owen said, shaking his head. He reached out to touch Erich on the arm to try and draw his attention away from them. 'It's all right. They don't bite.'

It was as if he'd pulled the trigger on a gun himself. Erich shot out of the seat and leaped out of the jeep, vaulting straight across the bonnet. I stamped on the brakes, bringing the vehicle to an abrupt halt, but it was too late. Erich was already running straight towards the yet-to-be-cleared patch of ground beside the road that bordered a patch of forest.

'Shit!' Owen was already climbing out of the jeep, me not far behind. 'Stop!' he roared at Erich. 'There's fucking *mines* there, boy! *STOP!*'

We both began to run after him. The American troops had turned to watch what was going on, puzzled at first, horror dawning as they saw Erich and realised what was going on. They began to shout too. I was closest to Erich; I tried to put on a burst of speed and my leg – the one that had been injured in the crash – gave way. I slammed to the ground with enough force to knock all the breath from my body. Gasping, I scrambled to my feet again, and as I did Erich stepped off the road into the weeds. There was a colossal explosion – so loud and so close that I sensed rather than heard it – and the boy disappeared, both of us engulfed by a black geyser of earth. The explosion made the air shudder around me and the ground beneath buck like an earthquake, throwing me off my feet again. Ears singing, I threw my arms over my head as stones, soil and shrapnel rained down around me.

Distantly, I heard another, smaller explosion. The ringing in my ears was growing louder, dark spots flocking across my vision. My head hurt, my back ached and there was a searing pain in my right hand. I found myself thinking about Hedda, who I'd posted my latest letter to yesterday, wondering if anyone would think to tell her I was dead; thinking how foolish I'd been to promise her nothing would happen to me, that I'd be safe. I almost wanted to laugh at the sheer absurdity of it all. I'd survived the car crash that had killed Robert; survived being shot at by Charles Mackay, yet now, with the war on the turn, I'd gone and got myself blown up.

I guess it's third time unlucky, I thought as I drifted away. *I'm so sorry, Hedda.*

THIRTY-EIGHT

HEDDA
Kirkenes, Norway
August 1945

'What happened, Mamma?' Eirik said, staring around
him with wide eyes and clutching my hand hard
enough to hurt.

I didn't answer him. I was staring too, trying to comprehend
the destruction that lay in front of us. I'd known it would
be bad, but nothing could have prepared me for *this*. It
seemed as if there was not a single building in Kirkenes left
standing – not even the church. All that remained were piles
of rubble stretching as far as the eye could see: the remains of
walls and cellars, scorched and sooty, and stubs of telegraph
poles and chimney stacks, the once-familiar roads that
stretched between the buildings pitted and scarred with bomb
craters. It was a fine day, with summer in full swing even this
near to the Arctic Circle, but somehow the sunshine and blue
sky made everything look worse.

I was struck by a sudden, visceral longing to be back in
Fiskersay. It was nearly three months since the war in Europe
had ended, a Tuesday in May that had begun like any other.
I had been up at the radar station, checking on one of the RAF
men who'd come down with a bad bout of tonsillitis, when

the door to the medical hut suddenly burst open and two of his friends came in. 'Have you heard? Jerry's just surrendered!' one of them cried. Despite my half-hearted protests, the man with tonsillitis had leaped out of bed and the three men had danced around the hut arm in arm, cheering. Before long, the whole island was buzzing with the news. That evening, there had been an impromptu dance at Talafirth Hall and everyone had come. I'd joined in, spinning around the floor to the merry sounds of the jigs and reels played by the band until I was dizzy and gasping for breath, a smile plastered across my face even though all I wanted to do was run from the hall, sobbing. I knew I should be happy, but all I could think about was Bill. I'd received his last letter a month earlier, and read it so many times I had all but memorised it. As with all his letters it had been heavily censored, but he'd told me he was living in a hotel. But since then, there had been nothing. *It's because he is busy*, I kept telling myself. *And it always takes a long time for letters to arrive, especially from overseas.*

A week or so after VE Day, when I still hadn't heard from him, I'd thought about getting in touch with the Red Cross again and asking about him, too, but I hadn't been able to make myself do it. It was easier to keep telling myself Bill's next letter had been delayed than let myself acknowledge something might have happened to him.

A few days later, Flight Lieutenant Jackson had called me up to the camp.

'I wanted to thank you, Hedda, for everything you have done since you came to Fiskersay – for us here at the station, and for the island's residents,' he'd said. 'And I wanted to ask you what you'd like to do now the war has come to an end and it is safe for the Thomsons to return. If you wish to, you and Eirik might be able to stay here on Fiskersay, or there is a Norwegian community on the Scottish mainland in a town called Buckie, near Aberdeen, where you would be made very welcome. We can help you to make the necessary arrangements.'

I had taken a few moments to consider what he had said. The offer was tempting; for the most part, I had been happy here, and Eirik was settled, with many friends. But shortly after Bill's last letter had arrived, I'd received one from the Red Cross after writing to the address Flight Lieutenant Jackson had found for me. Someone had been in contact with the Red Cross in Norway, and they had confirmed that many of Kirkenes' inhabitants were still living there in a temporary camp. As soon as I'd read that, I'd known I had to go back. The man who'd written the letter couldn't give me any names, but if there was even the slightest chance Anders was still there, I had to go and face him.

To my surprise, Flight Lieutenant Jackson leaped in straight away and helped me to organise everything, even our new passports. I was still astonished by the tremendous effort he made. He had also given me an address, insisting I contact him again if there was anything else he could do for us. Would I ever stop being amazed at how kind some people could be?

And now – after many sad goodbyes to Elizabeth, Donald and all the other friends we had made on Fiskersay, and promises to keep in touch, then weeks of travel, including a sea journey where both Eirik and I had been terribly sick and I had spent each day in terror that we would sink, still haunted by what had happened on our passage to Shetland – here we were, back in Kirkenes after almost three years away, with Bill's letters and the letter from the Norwegian Red Cross in my bag alongside our papers.

'Mamma?' Eirik said, his voice trembling.

'It was the Germans,' I said. 'But they have gone now. Come on. We must be brave, *lille vennen*.'

I took his hand and we began to pick our way through the rubble in the direction of the Haugen, where the house we'd shared with Anders used to stand. I couldn't think of it as *home* any more; truth be told, I never really had.

'Eirik!' The voice came from behind us. At first I thought I had misheard, but then it came again. 'Eirik!' And then, '*Tante* Hedda!'

We both turned around, and I saw a girl in a blue dress, her dark hair in two long plaits, running towards us.

'Marianne!' I gasped. She was taller, thinner, but it was unmistakably her.

'I knew it was you!' she said. 'I told Grandmother I had seen you!'

'Ingunn is here?'

'Yes! Come!' She caught hold of Eirik's other hand, tugging on it.

We followed her through the maze of ruined buildings and bomb-scarred roads. Up ahead, I saw a collection of Nissen huts that reminded me of the huts at the radar station in Fiskersay. They looked new, and strangely out of place among the ruins surrounding them; they'd clearly been erected to provide temporary shelter for the town's remaining residents. *How many are left?* I wondered. There didn't seem to be anyone around.

'Grandmother! Grandmother!' Marianne called, and as we

came around a corner I saw Ingunn, sitting on a wooden chair outside one of the huts, her face turned up to the sunshine. When she saw me, a broad smile spread across her wrinkled face.

I flew to her and we hugged, half laughing, half crying, with me trying to hide my worry at how tired and thin she looked. When she released me, I asked after the others – Mette, Doctor Johannessen, everyone else I had known and cared about before I had to leave.

'Mette went with her family to Sweden,' Ingunn said. 'She wrote to me a little while ago and they are alive and well. But Doctor Johannessen...' Her face clouded. 'He died in a bombing raid last year, I'm afraid.'

It was the same story for many others I knew – they had either fled, or had been killed. Those who stayed and managed to survive were beginning the long and arduous task of rebuilding the town.

'I've been so worried about you,' Ingunn said. 'I did not know if you were alive or dead!'

'I'm sorry,' I said. 'I thought about writing to you, but I was scared the letter would fall into the wrong hands. So much happened after Eirik and I left Kirkenes – I have so much to tell you!'

'Don't apologise,' Ingunn said, catching hold of my hands. 'I prayed to God every day to keep you safe, and he has.' She indicated another chair nearby. 'Come, tell me what happened to you both.'

Keeping half an eye on Eirik, who was playing on a nearby rubble pile with Marianne, I told Ingunn everything. When I reached the part about the German officer, her brows drew together and she said, 'Good riddance!' and when I told her about taking the fishing boat over to Shetland and how we had nearly drowned, she went pale.

'How on earth could they have thought *you* were the spy!' she said indignantly when I'd finished.

'It was only a misunderstanding,' I said. 'The people in Fiskersay were very good to us, as were the men at the radar station.'

A twinkle appeared in Ingunn's eye, and she smiled. 'Yes,' she said. 'This Bill – the one who saved you – you will have to tell me more about him.'

I did not return the smile. 'I haven't heard from Bill for months. It is quite possible he is dead,' I said. Before she could answer me, I took a deep breath. 'Ingunn, where is Anders?'

As soon as I mentioned his name, her face changed. She glanced at Eirik and Marianne, who were still out of earshot.

'You might as well know,' she said at last. She pointed a crooked finger. 'He is living in that hut over there with Solveig Aaberg.'

Solveig – Agnes Pedersen's sister. The woman who, before I left Kirkenes, had been seeing a German. 'He is?' I said. Suddenly, my heart was pounding – not with fear, but with anticipation.

'Please stay away from him, Hedda. He is worse than ever – he spends his days drinking and complaining about how hard his life is, as if it isn't hard for everyone else too. What Solveig sees in him, I don't know. Personally, I suspect she is with him to stop people attacking her for going out with that German officer a few years ago.'

'No. I want to talk to him.'

'But Hedda—'

'Oh, goodness, I'm not going back to him!' I cried, suddenly realising why she looked so worried. 'As far as I am concerned, Solveig is welcome to him. I want to ask him for a divorce. Hopefully, if he is happy with *her*, he will agree to it.'

'Ah, I see.' Ingunn's face cleared, but then she frowned again. 'But then what? Where will you go?'

'I don't know,' I said. 'I will do whatever's best for Eirik, I suppose.'

Ingunn glanced at Eirik and Marianne again. 'Did you not hear?' she said.

Now it was my turn to frown. 'Hear what?'

'In October, *Rädda Barnen* and the Swedish Red Cross have organised for all the children of Kirkenes to be taken to Sweden where they will live with foster parents while the town is rebuilt. It is for the best, I am sure, but they say it may be a year or more before they can return.'

'Even if their families are here?' I said.

Ingunn nodded. 'They say it's best for the children to go, even if it means being separated from their parents and grandparents. They can feed and educate them and help them grow strong again.'

I looked at my son with horror. I could see the sense in it – with the winters we got here, these huts would be no place for children – but after everything that had happened – after everything I had done to keep him with me, and safe – the thought of being apart from Eirik for a whole year was unthinkable.

I gave myself a mental shake. I needed to deal with Anders; I would worry about *Rädda Barnen* and the Swedish Red Cross later. 'Will you keep an eye on Eirik for a little while?' I said.

Ingunn nodded. 'Be careful, Hedda.'

'I will.' I patted her hand to reassure her, and made my way over to the hut she had pointed at.

I knocked on the door. I was not surprised when Solveig herself opened it and squinted out into the sunlight at me. What did startle me was her appearance. Before I'd left Kirkenes, she'd had long blonde curls and a voluptuous figure she'd been inordinately proud of. Now her head was brutally shorn, as if someone had attacked her with a razor, and she was thin and angular-looking. She stared at me as if she had seen a ghost. 'You!' she said.

Behind her, the interior of the hut was dim – too dim to see in properly – but I was hit by a pungent waft of cigarette smoke and unwashed clothes and bodies.

'I wish to speak to my husband,' I told Solveig. 'Is he here?'

After staring at me for a moment, she turned and called over her shoulder, 'Anders! Hedda is here!'

I heard a chair being pushed back with a clatter, I drew myself up, my hands down by my side, steeling myself to face my husband again for the first time in nearly three years.

Suddenly, he was there, pushing past Solveig. 'So you're back,' he said, one side of his upper lip curling in the sneer that would once have had me cowering away from him.

Now, I felt nothing but disdain. Why on earth had I been so scared of this man? He was nobody. Nothing.

'I am back,' I said coolly.

He pushed Solveig back inside and stepped out of the hut, closing the door behind him. 'I thought you were dead,' he said.

'You thought, or you hoped? I see you didn't waste any time finding another warm body to keep you company.'

His mouth dropped open.

'Anyway, I don't care. You can do what you want – be with whoever you like. The only reason I've come back here is to ask you to grant me a divorce.'

Slowly, he shook his head. 'You have changed. You have become... bold.'

I looked him right in the eyes and held his gaze. It was the first time I had ever been able to do that. He stared at me. 'Will you divorce me or not?' I said.

'What has happened to you?! Have you gone insane?!' His cheeks were turning a dull red. Almost instinctively, I felt myself begin to shrink away inside, but I made myself keep still and continue to hold his gaze. 'Believe me, I have never been more sure of my own sanity than I am now,' I said.

'Have you met someone else, wherever you've been? Is that what it is?' He sounded anxious, although I could not work out why.

'There's no one,' I lied. 'And even if there was, would you care?'

He glared at me for a few moments, puffing air through his nostrils. 'Fine, I will divorce you. But I am not paying a penny for that brat son of yours!'

'Believe me, even if we were starving, you're the last person I would *ever* ask for money. You can keep everything – I don't care, as long as I am free of you.'

His face relaxed, and I realised *that* was what he'd been worried about – that perhaps I'd try to claim what was left of the money my aunt had given him, or demand that he contribute to Eirik's care.

I began to laugh. 'Don't worry,' I said. 'If you like, I'll even tell the judge it's a mutual agreement – it will save you the embarrassment of everyone knowing how cruel you have been.'

'Get out of my sight!' Anders roared. 'Get out of Kirkenes, and don't come back!'

'With pleasure,' I told him. He went back into the hut, slamming the door in my face.

I returned to Ingunn, who looked relieved to see me. 'Are you all right?' she asked.

I smiled at her. 'I'm fine. I've told Anders I want a divorce. I am not sure how to go about it – there will be paperwork, of course, and I expect we will both need to sign lots of forms, so this may not be the last time I have to see him. But hopefully he will not change his mind. He seems as eager to be free of me as I am of him, so I think it will be all right.'

'Oh, Hedda, I am so glad. I prayed for years that you would come to your senses and walk away from that man. It was terrible listening to him shouting at you every night.'

'I am sorry,' I murmured.

Ingunn shook her head, and said in reassuring tones, her wrinkled face crinkling with empathy, 'Why should you be sorry? It was not your fault. I knew exactly what was going on. but I also knew I could not do anything about it – you needed to decide for yourself that you were going to leave. I will help you find out how to divorce him. Some of the men who were on the town council have returned. I will come with you to talk to them tomorrow.' She beamed at me. 'Oh, Hedda, I am so relieved you're free of that man!'

I crouched down beside her and wrapped my arms around her. 'Thank you for everything you've done for me, Ingunn,' I said. 'Not just helping me to get away, but for looking out for me all the time I was in Kirkenes, and for looking out for

Eirik, too. Without you, I'm not sure I would have been able to survive.'

'Oh, it's nothing,' Ingunn said, her cheeks flushing, but she looked pleased. 'I love you and Eirik as if you were my own family, you know that. And I always will, whatever you do next.'

'What do you mean?' I said.

'You don't intend to stay in Kirkenes without Eirik, do you?' she said. 'I can tell – you have that look in your eye.'

I shook my head and smiled. Nothing got past Ingunn – it never had.

From my bag, I took the leather writing case Bill had given me. Inside were his letters and a photograph: the one Eirik had taken that day at Odda's Bay of us standing together, laughing. It was creased now, and one edge was torn, but since we'd returned to Norway I had looked at it almost every day.

I handed it to Ingunn. 'This is Bill,' I said, my voice wobbling as I said his name.

She glanced down at the photograph, then looked back up at me. 'Sit down again,' she said gently. 'You said you think he might be dead, but do you know that for sure?'

I shook my head, not quite trusting myself to speak.

Ingunn gave me back the photograph. 'Then you must try to find out what's happened to him. And I will do everything I can to help you.'

THIRTY-NINE

HEDDA
Sweden
November 1945 – January 1946

Prästgårdsgatan 29
941 32 Piteå
Sweden

23rd November 1945

To whom it may concern,

I am trying to find out what has happened to a good friend of mine, Sergeant Bill (William) Gauthier, and have been told that you may be able to help.

Sergeant Gauthier is a Canadian national, but served with the RAF during the war. He was a wireless operator, then became a radar operator posted to RAF Svarta Ness in Fiskersay, Shetland. In 1943, he went back to England. He was sent to Europe in 1944 and although we were still in touch then, quite understandably he could not tell me where he was. I last heard from him in April of this year. I do not know if he is dead or alive.

If you have any information about him, please could you write to me at the above address. I now go by the

surname Gunnarsdotter, but he would have known me as
Hedda Dahlström.

Yours sincerely,

Hedda Gunnarsdotter (Miss)

I folded the letter, put it in an envelope and wrote the address
for the British Red Cross on the front. Then I picked up the
letter I had written the night before to Donald and Elizabeth,
who I'd promised to get in touch with once I was settled and
had a proper address. I pulled on my coat, hat, scarf and
boots, ready to go to the post office.

When I reached the ground floor, I knocked on Ingunn's
door; she was staying in the apartment below mine. 'I'm
going to the Post Office,' I told her. 'Do you need anything?'

'No, I'm fine, thank you,' she said, her face creasing into a
smile as she saw the letters in my hand. She touched my arm.
'Oh, Hedda, I am so glad you've decided not to give up.'

It was Ingunn who had begun encouraging me to write to
the British Red Cross when we were still in Kirkenes. 'You
say you think he is dead,' she'd said when, my courage finally
failing me, I'd tried to make excuses not to do it. 'But if you
don't write, how can you be sure? What if he is alive? Can
you live the rest of your life not knowing?'

But with the cold weather closing in fast, and officials
from the Swedish Red Cross and *Rädda Barnen* arriving
in Kirkenes to begin organising the exodus of the town's
remaining children to foster families in Sweden, I'd had
another, even more pressing matter on my mind: convincing
Ingunn that a metal Nissen hut was no more a suitable place
for an old woman in the middle of the Arctic winter than it

was for a child, and getting her to agree to go with Marianne. I was coming too. When I'd told the officials from *Rädda Barnen* I was a trained nurse, they said if I would like to come with them to look after the children, they would be glad to have me, meaning Eirik and I would not have to be separated. There was nothing for me in Kirkenes any more; I had been sent here as a punishment, and although I was no longer scared of Anders and proceedings for our divorce were under way, living in the temporary camp where I was likely to bump into him at any given moment still made me feel permanently on edge, a reflex from the time when I had lived my whole life in fear of him.

The journey to Sweden had been a long one. We'd travelled with the Swedish Red Cross, helping to look after the children, and all of us had to quarantine at a transit camp in northern Sweden for two weeks. After we were released, we'd travelled on to a town called Piteå, where many of the children were also being sent. Here, using some of the money I had saved from my job as a nurse in Fiskersay, I'd been able to rent an apartment for Eirik and myself, and Ingunn had enough money to take the apartment on the ground floor for her and Marianne. We'd now been here for almost two weeks, and next week I would start work as a nurse at the local hospital.

I left the apartment building with my head down against the whirling snow; winter had arrived with a vengeance. Eirik and Marianne were still at school, and the quiet, empty streets and the snow reminded me not of Kirkenes but of Fiskersay. I felt a sharp tug of longing as I remembered the gentle curve of its hills as they fell towards the sea on all sides, and the water stretching away in all directions. To some, the island might have seemed isolated and remote, and it was, but it was also a place that had saved my life in more ways than one.

I posted my letters, then walked back to the apartment, praying that someone, somewhere would be able to tell me what had happened to Bill, even if it was the news I most feared hearing.

Another month passed. Although Elizabeth replied to me, writing a long, chatty letter telling me how she and Donald were getting on at the croft, there was nothing from the British Red Cross. At Christmas, Eirik, Marianne, Ingunn and I were invited to spend the day with some of the other children from Kirkenes and their foster families. We had a pleasant time, but all I could think about was that Christmas after Eirik and I came to Fiskersay, at the Sinclairs' croft: the meal with Lewis and Bill; the Christmas pudding Bill had 'liberated', as Lewis put it, from the camp kitchens; the gifts we had all bought one another, and sitting beside Bill on the rug in front of the fire, talking as we drank our tea and the others sipped their whisky and rum.

It wasn't until the beginning of January that I received a brief missive, typed on a sheet of paper so thin you could almost see through it:

```
Dear Miss Gunnarsdotter, I am very sorry,
but we have not been able to find any records
for anyone called Bill Gauthier who served
with the RAF.
```

'It is not meant to be,' I said to Ingunn that evening,

helping her make bread in her kitchen while Marianne and Eirik sprawled on the rug in front of the fire in the other room, absorbed in the *Beanos* Eirik had brought with him all the way from Shetland. 'He must have been killed while he was in Europe – perhaps they were not able to bring him home.' There was a lump in my throat that ached as I tried to swallow; I couldn't prevent tears from springing into my eyes, although I had already cried for hours when the letter first arrived. 'Oh, Ingunn – why did I let myself fall in love with him?' I said as the tears spilled down my cheeks again. 'What a fool I've been!' I put my hands over my face, forgetting they were covered in flour, and sank into a chair.

Ingunn hurried to comfort me, abandoning the dough she was kneading to put an arm around my shoulders. 'No, no. Hedda, you must not give up,' she said in low, urgent tones. 'How about the Red Cross in Canada? Perhaps he went back there?'

I looked up at her. 'I don't know. How would I find out?'

She handed me a dishcloth so I could wipe the flour and tears from my face. 'Or what about the men he was with at the radar station? Might you be able to write to one of them and see if they know where he is?'

Flight Lieutenant Jackson, I thought immediately. But he'd already done so much for me. Could I really ask him for yet another favour?

'Of course you can!' Ingunn said when I voiced my doubts. 'Write to the Flight Lieutenant, Hedda. If anyone knows where Bill is, he will.'

'But what if something has happened to Flight Lieutenant Jackson too, or my letter doesn't reach him?'

'If you don't try, then how will you know?' Ingunn said

patiently, just as she had when I was debating whether to write to the British Red Cross.

I stared at the bread dough sitting in the middle of the table, remembering, again, those kisses we'd shared the day he told me he was leaving, and before that, all those other moments: the look that had passed between us that night in the hut; that wonderful Christmas at the Sinclairs', Bill in his crooked paper hat, laughing beside me as we sat by the fire; watching the Mirrie Dancers with him – moments that might seem trivial to someone else, but to me, had meant everything…

'Hedda,' Ingunn said, her tone so uncharacteristically sharp that I looked up at her again in surprise.

'What's wrong?' I asked.

'Tell me honestly, how do you feel about Bill?'

'I – I love him,' I said. 'You know I do.'

'And he loves you?'

I nodded. 'Yes. Of that, I am certain.'

'Then don't you owe it to yourself and to him to keep trying to find him?'

I looked down at the dough again. 'Yes,' I said quietly. 'I suppose I do.'

But what if I got an answer I did not want to hear?

FORTY

HEDDA

March 1946

January became February; February slipped into March. Officially, spring was approaching; the weather in Sweden was still cold, but not as cold as it would have been in Kirkenes, which would be firmly in winter's grip for many weeks yet. Whenever I was working at the hospital, all talk was of warmer weather. Everyone was longing for the sun, and for the days to lengthen again. It felt as if, as we waited for the spring of 1946 to begin, we were anticipating not only a new season, but a new start: after all, this would be the first peacetime spring in many years.

I was waiting too.

Waiting for my divorce from Anders to go through – an endless maze of forms and letters. Waiting to find out if Eirik and I would be allowed to settle permanently in Sweden when *Radda Bärnen* sent the others back. And waiting to hear from Flight Lieutenant Jackson.

One afternoon, when I arrived back at the apartment building after work, I found some mail waiting for me. I put it in my bag and went up to my apartment, where I added another log to the stove before removing my coat and scarf. Then I made myself a cup of coffee and sat down at the kitchen table with the letters.

The first one – more of a parcel, really – was from Elizabeth Sinclair; I recognised her handwriting on the front and turned it over with a smile, wondering what was inside. At Christmas she had sent me and Eirik two Fair Isle jumpers she had knitted, with exquisite colours and patterns, and we had both been very glad of them.

The second letter was from Britain too, and had an official stamp on the front.

Elizabeth's parcel momentarily forgotten, I tore it open, my hands beginning to tremble. Inside was a single sheet of paper. Flight Lieutenant Jackson's name was at the top, and an address in London.

I closed my eyes for a moment, then opened them again. *Whatever is in this letter, you have to face it*, I told myself. *Like Ingunn says, it is better to know.*

I took a sip of coffee to try and steady my nerves, and began to read.

Dear Hedda,

Thank you for getting in touch with me, and I am sorry it has taken me so long to reply. I was sent to the Far East for a while and am still moving around a lot, so it took a little while for your letter to find me.

I hope you and your son are well, and that you are both settled in Sweden now. It must have been a terribly worrying time for you, returning to Norway to find everything destroyed like that.

Anyway, forgive me – you asked if I would be able to find out what happened to Sergeant Gauthier, and I am delaying with small talk. I shan't beat about the bush any longer. It is not good news, I'm afraid...

FORTY-ONE

HEDDA
Fiskersay
September 1946

'Come, we do not want to still be on the boat when it sails back to Aberdeen!' I said to Eirik in Norwegian, my voice sharper than intended. I was trying to gather our bags and the small suitcase we were sharing, and looking around for Eirik's coat – where had he put it? *Ah!* There it was. 'Put this on, please,' I told him. 'Otherwise you will lose it.'

'It's too warm, Mamma,' Eirik grumbled. I gave him a stern look and he sighed and struggled into the coat. Really, it was too small for him – he seemed to be growing every day – but it was all I had been able to find before we left Sweden. We joined the throng making their way towards the gangplank of the *Zetland Princess II*, ready to disembark. I made Eirik hold on to the hem of my jacket, despite his protests – my hands were full with our luggage – and we walked down the gangplank and stepped down onto the cobbles, which were slippery from a recent fall of rain although the sun was shining now.

As I stood there, I was assaulted by memories. Although I had been away for over a year, Talafirth harbour looked exactly the same, with all the colourful fishing boats bobbing up and down in the water. The white-painted houses of the town were like old, familiar friends, and behind them I could see the rounded slopes of the Haug, looking strangely naked without its two metal towers at the top. On the other side would be Odda's Bay, where Bill and I had spent so many hours together; where we'd watched the Mirrie Dancers shimmer above the sea; where we had finally kissed for the first time. I closed my eyes for a moment, trying to calm my racing heart, and took in a deep breath of salty air.

'Mamma?' Eirik said, tugging on my sleeve. 'Where is he? I can't see him.'

'He will be here,' I said, as much to reassure myself as my son.

The harbour was as busy as ever, everyone waiting to greet the ship. There were plenty of people I recognised; they were delighted to see us and hailed me, clasping me by the hands and remarking on how much Eirik had grown.

Then Eirik spotted David Couper, one of his old friends from the island's school, and with an almighty shout, ran across to him. They greeted each other as if it was only a few days since they'd last seen one another. I watched them, smiling despite my nerves.

'What brings you back here, Hedda?' his mother, Hilda, asked me, coming over. Her broad Shetland accent was reassuringly familiar after so long away. 'We didn't think we'd be seeing you again! Are you here to stay? Look how tall Eirik is now! Oh, it's lovely to see you both – such a lot has happened since you left!'

As she chattered away I couldn't get a word in edgeways, but I didn't mind; although I was glad to see her, I was barely paying attention. What if I'd got the wrong time, or the wrong day?

No, no, I couldn't have. I had checked everything a hundred times – read the letter a hundred times more—

Then I saw him, sitting on the low wall at the edge of the harbour. I hadn't spotted him straight away because he was in ordinary clothes instead of the uniform he'd always worn before: dark slacks; a coat and a knitted jumper; woollen gloves that looked a lot like the ones Elizabeth had sent me in the parcel that arrived the same day as that fateful letter, and a cap pulled down over his dark curls that made him look for all the world like he belonged on one of the fishing boats anchored in the harbour. He saw me at the same time and waved. My heart gave a wild, joyous leap.

Eirik saw him too. 'Mr Bill!' he shouted, and before I could stop him he was running over to him. Bill grinned, getting to his feet, and swept Eirik up into a hug, lifting him off his feet. The noise and bustle around me seemed to fade as I started forwards too. Bill put Eirik down and came to meet me. Then I was in his arms, and he was kissing me.

'Hedda,' he said at last, holding me at arm's length and gazing at me. 'My God, you're really here. Both of you. I can't believe it.'

I gazed back, beaming despite the tears running down my cheeks. 'We are really here. And so are you.'

He pulled me close again and I pressed against him, his arms folded around me, my face against his shoulder, breathing him in. I wanted to cling to him forever. I had the unreal sensation that this was all a dream; that at any moment all this would shatter and I'd find myself back in the apartment in Piteå. Surely it was too good to be true?

'*Mamma*,' Eirik said impatiently.

We broke apart. 'Sorry, buddy,' Bill said, ruffling his hair. 'It's been a long time since I last saw your mother, you know?'

'It's been a long time since you saw me, too!' Eirik said, sounding so affronted that Bill and I both laughed. 'Where did you go?'

'Well, back to England for a while, then Belgium, then Holland,' he said. His gaze caught mine and I could see the question in his eyes: *Did you tell him what happened?*

Eirik answered before I could. 'Is that where you got hurt?' he said, frowning. 'Mamma said there was an accident.'

Bill nodded. 'Yeah. But I'm OK now. Hey, what have they been feeding you in Sweden? You're at least twice the size you used to be!'

Eirik puffed out his chest, beaming. 'I am the fastest in my school,' he told Bill. '*And* I am one of the strongest.'

With his left hand, Bill pretended to feel Eirik's upper arm. 'Hmm, impressive,' he said, his eyes dancing with laughter again. 'Have you thought of becoming a wrestler?'

'Don't encourage him!' I said.

Bill turned away; I could see his shoulders shaking.

I saw David Couper waving at us. 'Eirik, would you like to go and play with David for a while?' I said.

He ran over there without a backwards glance, and Bill finally let out the roar of laughter he'd been holding in, I swatted him on the arm. '*Stop* it.'

'I'm sorry, he's just too funny,' Bill said, wiping his eyes. 'God, it's good to see you both.'

We made our way back across the harbour and sat down on the wall again.

'When I got that letter from Flight Lieutenant Jackson, I

thought he was telling me you had died,' I said. 'I had to read the letter three times before it made sense.'

Bill shook his head. 'It was touch and go for a while,' he admitted. 'What with this, the car crash and getting shot by Charles Mackay, I guess I must have been a cat in a previous life. Nine lives and all that, eh?'

He slid off his gloves and I took his right hand, trying not to let any emotion show on my face as I took in the missing fourth and little fingers; the scarred, shiny flesh.

'I am so relieved you are all right,' I said. 'Does it still hurt?'

'Sometimes. My back's pretty messed up too – a piece of shrapnel from the blast just missed my kidneys, apparently. I'm getting better, though.'

Horror zig-zagged through me, even though I already knew all this; somehow it was different – worse – hearing him actually say it, and seeing his damaged hand. 'Oh, Bill!'

He put an arm around me. 'Don't look so worried. I'm OK, really.'

I leaned against him for a while and we sat there in silence, while I remembered that day in the Swedish apartment, and the words of Flight Lieutenant Jackson's letter, which were still etched into my brain: *It is not good news, I'm afraid*, he had said.

Sergeant Gauthier was caught in a mine blast in Holland, and nearly died from a secondary infection caused by shrapnel in his wounds. From what I understand it was also touch and go whether they would be able to save his hand, which was badly injured too. He did recover enough to eventually be demobbed and sent back to Canada, but

I am unable to trace his whereabouts further. Perhaps the Royal Canadian Air Force or the Canadian Red Cross will be able to help – I enclose their addresses.

I wish you the very best of luck, and do let me know if there is anything else I can do.

Yours Sincerely,

Frederick Jackson (Flt. Lt.)

Even though I was recovering from the shock of thinking Bill was dead, I'd still stared at the letter in despair. More letters to write. More waiting. And what if those people couldn't help me either?

Then I'd remembered the parcel from Elizabeth. Heavy-hearted now, and without much enthusiasm, I'd opened it, and a small bundle of envelopes with Bill's handwriting on the front, tied together with a length of rough string, had tumbled out onto the table, along with a note from Elizabeth that had the same date on it as Flight Lieutenant Jackson's letter.

Dear Hedda,

These arrived yesterday from your soldier. There must have been a delay somewhere as Bertha says they all came at the same time! I will write properly next week but I wanted to make sure you got these. I hope this finds you and Eirik well.

Love from us both.

It wasn't until I'd already torn the first of Bill's envelopes open that I'd seen the stamps on it were Canadian.

Dearest Hedda,

My darling, I am so sorry it's been so long since I last wrote. A lot has happened – so much that I don't even know where to begin. But here I am back in Canada at last, hoping that somehow this letter will reach you…

The letter had been dated December; at the top was an address in Edmonton. The other two letters were dated January and February. I'd read about his accident and his slow, painful recovery with a mixture of horror and profound relief, before bursting into tears.

'Thank goodness for Elizabeth,' I said now. 'If she hadn't sent me your letters, I might never have found you.'

I'd replied to Bill's letters immediately, telling him where I was, and after that we had written to each other every week, even if there was nothing much to say. It had been Bill's idea to come to Fiskersay again, and despite me telling him he didn't need to, he'd organised everything, even paying for our tickets. Finally, after waiting all summer, a date was set for me and Eirik to travel from Sweden to Shetland. Bill had already been here two days, and was staying at the Royal Hotel.

'Thank goodness for Elizabeth indeed,' Bill said, his voice slightly hoarse. His arm tightened around me and we sat in silence again for a while. I was certain he was thinking the same thing as me – imagining what would have happened if Elizabeth *hadn't* sent the letters and we were still searching in vain for one another. It didn't bear thinking about.

At last, he said, 'What time are she and Donald expecting us?'

'Later this afternoon – I wasn't sure when the ship would

be docking. It will be lovely staying with them again, like old times! What is your room like in the hotel?'

'Comfortable enough. Do we have time for a walk to Odda's Bay before we go over there?'

I smiled at him. 'I expect so,' I said. I got up, brushing down the back of my skirt. 'Let me find Eirik.'

Eirik was still talking to David, telling him in great detail about our journey here from Sweden. 'Mamma, Mrs Couper says I can come back to David's house with them for lunch. May I?' he said when I touched his arm gently to let him know I was there.

I glanced at Hilda, who smiled and said, 'It's no trouble, Hedda. I expect you'd like a bit of time with your soldier. And David's over the moon to see his friend again.'

'Are you sure?'

'Absolutely.'

I hugged her. 'Thank you. It's so good to be back.'

'Call for him in a little while,' she said with another smile, and then, like a mother hen gathering her chicks, she shepherded Eirik and David across the cobbles.

'Let's leave your things at the hotel reception for now so you don't have to carry them, and then we can go over to the bay,' Bill said.

'Are you sure you'll manage?' I said. He was limping again, and I could see the lingering effects of his illness in the shadows under his eyes. Another prickle of anxiety went through me; he'd said he was OK, but was he really? I couldn't help feeling that he'd only said that so I wouldn't worry.

You've had patients recover who were far worse, I reminded myself. *All that matters is that he's alive, and he's here.*

'I'll be fine if you hang on to me.' He stuck out an elbow, and I put my hand through it. His arm was strong and solid, and I felt reassured.

We went to the hotel, where the girl behind the reception desk said she'd be happy to hang on to mine and Eirik's luggage until I came to collect it later on. Then we made our way outside again. When we reached Odda's Bay, the tide was out, the sea flat and sparkling, and in the distance the jumbled rocks of Odda's Holm and the spike of Odda's Fang reared up out of the waves, white water foaming around their bases. Bill and I sat down and I turned my face up to the sun that was finally breaking through the clouds, enjoying its warmth. 'So,' Bill said. 'I hate to ask, but how is that divorce coming along?'

'Oh!' In all the excitement, I realised I'd quite forgotten to tell him. 'It came through two days ago. I received a telegram while we were on the ship.'

A grin broke across his face. 'That's fantastic news!'

'Yes,' I said. 'I am a free woman at last.'

This did not have the reaction I'd intended; the smile slowly faded from Bill's face. 'Does this mean you're giving up marriage as a bad lot?' he said, and I wondered if he thought I was rejecting him. I had a momentary flashback to watching him walk away from me that day we'd first kissed; remembering how I'd wanted to call him back, thinking – not so irrationally, as it turned out – that after he left Fiskersay I might never see him again.

'No, of course not!' I exclaimed. 'I don't want to give up on marriage. Not at all. Just *that* marriage.'

His smile returned; he looked relieved. 'Thank God for that. Because I was wondering...' With his good hand, he reached out for mine. His gaze was burning into me, and I felt my heart skip a beat as I saw him swallow, his throat bobbing. 'Look, I can't get down on one knee right now – I'd never get up again – but—'

'Yes?' I said. My heart was hammering now. I already knew what he was going to say and I felt dizzy with anticipation, and with gratitude for this wonderful, gentle man who was truly everything I could have ever asked for.

'Well, would you marry me?'

'Oh, Bill. Yes. *Yes!*'

As he drew me into his arms and kissed me again I felt as if I was soaring up into the sky to join the gulls gliding above our heads. Everything bad that had happened to me – Magnus, Anders, the war, the German officer, mine and Eirik's terrifying flight from Norway – fell away in an instant, and I knew that none of it would matter ever again.

'I mean, not immediately,' Bill rushed on when we broke apart again. 'There'll be a lot to organise – we'll have to decide where we're going to live – there's Eirik to think about too – and—'

I silenced him by pressing another kiss to his lips. 'We'll work all that out,' I said, gently taking his other hand. 'As long as I'm with you, I am home.'

Acknowledgements

The Girl from Norway is a romance in more ways than one. It's a love story about Hedda and Bill, but it's also a eulogy to wild places: to the way they can heal our bodies, minds and hearts, and help us discover who we truly are.

As this is, first and foremost, a work of fiction, I have taken some artistic and dramatic licence with my characters, settings and plot which I hope my readers will understand the necessity for. Fiskersay is not a real island, RAF Svarta Ness was not a real radar station, and it would have been unusual (although not impossible) for an airman to be redeployed as a radar operator. However, everything that forms the background to this story has its basis in historical fact. Although radar stations on mainland Britain generally had a largely female staff taken from the Women's Auxiliary Air Force (WAAF), the stations in Shetland were run by men. The 'Shetland Bus', a military operation between Norway and Britain, brought many Norwegian refugees to our shores, including women and children. And as I was looking for a way to tear Bill away from his world of (perceived) glamour and excitement as a member of a heavy bomber crew by sending him somewhere that at first he assumes is going to be a lonely wilderness, I came across a few lines in a memoir written by former Radar Mechanic Ray Barker, *Reflexions... On a Chain of Events* (Janus, 1992), mentioning a former airman who was redeployed to a radar station after suffering an injury in the line of duty. Here, I realised, was the 'spark' I needed to ignite Bill's story.

I am also grateful to Gordon Carle, a Fighter Controller in the RAF who was posted to RAF Saxa Vord in Unst, Shetland in the 1960s. During my research I discovered his blog, 'The History of Saxa Vord' (http://ahistoryofrafsaxavord.blogspot.com/), which contains every detail imaginable about the various radar stations operating in Shetland during the war and afterwards. It includes reproductions of *The Outpost*, a magazine produced by the men based at RAF Skaw on Unst who called themselves the 'Skawpians'. *The Outpost* gives a remarkable insight into what life at such a remote radar station must have been like, and informed many of the scenes and settings in this book, as well as providing inspiration for two major plot threads: Isabel Thomson's baby being born at the station, and the spy passing on radio transmissions to the Germans.

Willie's War and Other Stories by Willie Smith (Shetland Times, 2004) paints a vivid picture of what life in wartime Shetland was like for the people who lived there, and another excellent resource has been *Terror in the Arctic* by Bjarnhild Tulloch (Troubador, 2011), a first-hand account of life in German-occupied Kirkenes.

In addition, I'd like to say thank you to:

My RAF contacts, Senior Aircraftsman and Airframe Mechanic SAC Chris Callaghan (also a top children's author –

he didn't pay me to say that, I promise!) and Flight Sergeant Sam Ferrans, a Propulsion Engineer, who, with the help of an RAF historian friend of theirs, were instrumental in helping me work out not only what Bill's role at RAF Svarta Ness might have entailed but the reasons for him being sent there in the first place.

Dr Phil Judkins, chairman of the Defence Electronics Historical Society, for fact-checking some of the details in this story and for loaning me an enormous pile of books from his collection, and Graham Murchie, trustee at Bawdsey Radar Museum in Suffolk for letting me have a good nose around and try my hand at detecting enemy aircraft on a receiver console. Sadly, I don't think I'd have passed muster as a radar operator!

Daniel Aubrey for sharing his wonderful photographs of the forests and landscape in the Målselvdalen valley region of Norway and reminding me that here be wolves, and Jamie Russell for telling me the story of his great grandfather and the home-made radio equipment which landed him in hot water with the authorities in the late 1930s, another tale which partly inspired the spy plot thread.

Camilla Carlsen, curator at the *Grenselandmuseet* (Borderland Museum) in Kirkenes, Norway, for answering my questions about the town in wartime and providing me links to photographs and information about the bomb shelters there, and Hanne Marie Johansen, associate professor at the University of Bergen, for allowing me to access her article, 'The History of Divorce Politics in Norway' (*Scandinavian Journal of History*, 2018), and Ali Stubbins for help with the Welsh.

Any errors remaining are my own.

Finally, I'd like to thank my brilliant agent, Ella Kahn and my wonderful editors at Aria, Martina Arzu, Izzy Frost and Lottie Hayes-Clemens, for all their hard work and dedication in helping to bring Hedda and Bill's story to life, and Becky Glibbery and her team for the stunning cover.

Sheena Wilkinson for her expert beta read, and my wonderful community of writer friends in The Place – I feel so lucky to have you all to fall back on. An especially big thank you to Sheena and Rachel Ward for speed-reading my Christmas chapter!

My family, as always, for always having faith in me and my stories. It means so much! I hope you enjoy this one.

And last, but most definitely not least, Duncan and Auburn, for all the cups of tea, walks, reassurance and campervan adventures while I was writing this book. I couldn't do any of this without you!

About the Author

EMMA PASS grew up in Surrey and has been making up stories for as long as she can remember. She wrote her first novel – a sequel to Jurassic Park – when she was thirteen, in maths lessons with her notebook hidden under her work.

She previously worked as a library assistant and has published two novels for young adults and a non-fiction creative writing e-guide. In 2020 she was commissioned to create a poetry-film for the Derwent Valley Mills World Heritage Site. She is now a full-time writer, creative writing teacher, editor and mentor. She has ME and, at the age of 40, was diagnosed as being on the autistic spectrum.

Emma lives in Derbyshire with her artist husband and a very naughty retired racing greyhound called Auburn. When she's not writing she loves to read and knit (often at the same time).